The Scarecrow Rides

Black Curtain Press
PO Box 632
Floyd, VA 24091

ISBN 13: 978-1627554459

First Edition
10 9 8 7 6 5 4 3 2 1

The Scarecrow Rides
Russell Thorndyke

PREFACE

In Which the Visitor Puts back the Clock and Listens In Beneath the Rookery

Anyone visiting that thriving holiday resort of Dymchurch Sands to-day would be hard put to it to recognize the obscure village that it was in the days of Doctor Syn. However, if you will take the trouble, the mental trouble only, which will not disturb the peace, obliterate the bungalows which spring up like mushrooms in the fertile Romney Marsh, remove the obsolete wheel-less railway carriages which give camping shelter to so many happy families during the season, and pack up the enterprising little railroad whose express engines scream their way with such import across the Marsh, although one of them bears the name of Doctor Syn. Having done all this, you must then mentally demolish telegraph posts, loud speakers, electric lights and telephones, motor cars, aeroplanes, 'buses and the 'Bus Station. Then, down in your imagination with the teashops innumerable, leaving only those houses of call that are licensed to sell Beer, Wine, Spirits and Tobacco. Ruthlessly use a spiritual pickaxe upon every building that is not fashioned of mellow Queen Anne brick, Kentish rag and ship's timber. Rip off the concertina lines of corrugated iron and laboriously hang red tiles in its stead. Work your thoughts, and without asking permission from the Ecclesiastical Commissioners, knock down the modern rectory and restore the white-washed, rambling parsonage with its red-tiled roof, and in order not to tread upon the corns of sainted rectors dead and gone, re-christen it The Vicarage. Having done all this, sit down and rest upon the mounting-block at the road entrance of Sycamore Gardens, which you have now transformed into a rough meadow, a farmstead and barn behind your back, and let your eyes survey the old church and the Tudor building of New Hall, then as now, the Court House of Dymchurch and headquarters of the Lords of the Level. One thing more is left for this your thoughtful restoration. Since you have hypnotised yourself back into a period with Trafalgar yet unfought, and Pitt's Martello Towers not erected, you must replace the stately Memorial of the War in our time with a grim symbol of Justice which preceded it upon that very site—a gaunt and creaking gallows, and you may tell yourself that the skeleton which swings there in the sea breeze was in its living flesh a sheep-stealer; a crime unspeakable and unpardonable in the summing-up of Dymchurch magistrates.

Now listen to the swaying rookery above your head, for these black-feathered carrion have inherited their lofty homes from ancestors who actually picked the flesh from the bones upon the gibbet, saw the black-coated figure of Doctor Syn and heard his resonant voice exhorting the congregation from the top deck of the great pulpit in the little church beneath them. And you can hear his story also from the gulls, for every day he would walk along the sea-wall, having discarded his clasped Bible for a brass telescope, and as the salt tang filled his lungs he would change his tune from hymns to capstan songs, especially one old shanty that he was for ever singing when his mind floated off across the ocean wastes:

"Oh, here's to the feet that have walked the plank—
Yo ho! For the dead man's throttle;
And here's to the corpses afloat in the tank,
And the dead man's teeth in the bottle."

But never mind the screaming gulls as you sit beneath the rookery, for those birds are going to re-tell the story as their ancestors have cawed it down to them, repeating it caw for caw to their adventure-loving children and recapturing, like you, the 'good old days of smuggling'. They are beginning with the wreck of the good ship City of London that was driven ashore in Dymchurch Bay and, as you will hear, heralded, with thunder, lightning and mountainous waves, Doctor Syn's remarkable and uncanny return to Dymchurch-under-the-Wall.

"Caw, Caw, CAW"—which is, being interpreted—

CHAPTER I. Why Two Sour-Faced Men Braved the Storm

Never in the history of Dymchurch Rookery that sways above the church and court house had the black-robed inmates such cause to fear the snapping of their fighting tops as during the soul-shaking tempest that swept the English Channel on the night of November 13th, 1775. The giant elms creaked and groaned as the racing wind shrieked in their bent riggings. Far beneath on the flat grass of the low-lying churchyard the headstones of the graves were torn from their sockets and in some cases hurled and splintered against the church. The roof of the old Manor Farm house opposite through the weakening of a beam rained tiles upon the road, while all along the straggling village street chimney tops crashed down. It was braving death to pass the strongest buildings on that ghastly night. And yet two men were daring enough to attempt it, and that when the storm was at its height.

With their scarves drawn tightly round their jaws, the collars of their sea-coats up and their three-cornered hats pulled down to their eyes, they leaned their bodies forward at such an angle that if it had not been for the wind they must have fallen on their faces. Thus did they endeavor to keep their footage against the pressure, fighting their way step by step past the low churchyard wall towards the tall black looming sea-wall over whose top the surf was driving in sheets of foam water.

Two more opposite reasons for these two men thus braving the stinging spray could hardly have been found. In one, it was a dogged sense of duty—in the other a sordid greed.

They had been regaling their spirits in the company of Mr. And Mrs. Waggetts, the proprietors of the 'Ship Inn' and consuming a vast quantity of excellent French brandy which was cheap enough since no duty had been charged upon it. Then they had heard the gun. It echoed above the storm from the desolate pebble nose of Dungeness. A ship was in distress. Simultaneously both men had risen and buttoned their coats.

"You're never going out in this," protested Mrs. Waggetts.

"There's no call for Merry to, but I must," answered the shorter of the two. "If a ship's coming ashore, it's my duty to see what manner o' ship she be."

He was the Preventive Officer. A dogged, bitter man, and most unpopular in the village by reason of his trade. Unlike his companion he possessed at least one virtue. His duty was his god, and it was his dangerous boast that when he was called to discharge it, he had never run away or shirked the worst consequences, although he knew that no throat in Dymchurch was in such constant danger of being cut. He also knew that no one was more likely to cut it than his drinking companion who was, like him, buttoning up his coat.

This Merry belied his name. He was sullen, intractable and cross-grained. So much so that he was known in the village as 'miserable Merry'. But he had his use in the community, for he was a jack-of-all-trades. Tall and cadaverously thin, he was strong, and could pick up a living at most things that came his way. But he didn't say much, as the Preventive Officer found to his cost. He was never talkative in his cups. The Preventive Officer had never got any information out of him. An account of how he had been helping old So-and-so to patch up a boat, or mend a net, uninteresting adventures of fishing, or an opinion of the various harvests he had given a hand at bringing in, but never so much as a hint of the many landings of contraband that the Preventive man had found out about too late, and knew by instinct that miserable Merry had received good hush money.

"Why was he leaving the snugness of the 'Ship' parlour to court disaster outside?" the Preventive Officer asked himself.

A terrific crash near at hand.

"There goes our chimney stack," whined Mr. Waggetts, who sat propped up with pillows in a wheel-backed armchair by the fire. The blanket round his knees corroborated the fact which his pasty, melancholy face, sunken, the unnatural bright colour on his cheeks, and the large weakened eyes with hanging pouches proclaimed that Waggetts was a sick man.

His wife was the reverse. Large, ugly, vain, but capable. She it was who steered the 'Ship Inn' and made it the profitable concern it was. Her husband's terror lest the chimney would come toppling down upon him resulted in his trying to get out of the chair, but Mrs. Waggetts pushed him gently back as she thrust her head, regardless of the smoke, under the mantle-beam and up the chimney. When it reappeared, she nodded reassuringly to her husband. "Not ours, my love. Must have been one at Sycamore Farm."

There was another crash from the other side of the house.

"And that'll be something off of the old Manor," she said cheerfully.

"You won't be so happy when ours goes," whined her husband.

"Well, I says, it's one of them nights when one must take the crashes as they come and act according."

Such philosophy was beyond her husband's grasp. His answer was a violent fit of wheezing. Mrs. Waggetts pulled his head forward, pushed it down onto his lap with one hand and gave him several clumps on the back with the other.

Meanwhile the Preventive Officer continued to lash himself taut against the driving wind and spray outside, and as he watched the miserable Merry following his example he cudgelled his slow but sure brain to discover a motive. 'Why should Merry want to come with him?'

"But you ain't never going out, not really?" again protested the landlady.

"I've told Merry there's no reason he should, but if he will, he will," replied the officer.

"May as well go along and have a look as stay here," said Merry. A terrific gust of wind shook the old inn and blew the wood smoke into the room. "If the old place is coming down, I'd as lief be crushed under it outside as in here."

"The inn ain't going to come down," snapped Mrs. Waggetts. "Ain't it stood all these years? Well then. For shame, trying to scare a sick man."

"It ain't stood many storms like this one," argued the pessimist. "You weren't up on the sea-wall p'raps this evening? No. Well, I were. And I notices something that was queer. It's November, ain't it? And there ain't a weather prophet on the Marsh wot hasn't said we're in for a cold snap this winter. 'Severe', they all says. As I saw them copper-coloured clouds piling up beyond Dungeness to-night, I found I was sweatin' hot. And there was a hush all about one that by right you only get about midsummer. It ain't natural, not this heat in November. And there—"

A vivid flash of lightning lit up the dim room and with no more than a second's pause the thunder answered it in a sharp crackle that ended in a loud voluminous peal.

"What did I tell you?" asked Merry. "If that ain't unseasonable, wot is?"

"Thunder in November, eh?" was the comment of the Preventive Officer.

"Strange, eh?" wheezed the invalid. "What my grandfather would have called a 'Homen'. He saw lots. The last he saw was on the night he died, but I forgets what sort it was."

"Try and think, love," encouraged his spouse.

But the invalid's effort of thought was destroyed in a fit of coughing as the Preventive Officer opened the door and let the draught in.

Another gust of storm and another crash of destruction.

"Won't be much left of Dymchurch by the time this has done with it," pronounced Merry.

"I wonder," replied the Preventive officer. "That's right though, I'll be bound."

If Merry thought the Preventive man was answering him, he was mistaken. The Preventive Officer was answering his own thoughts, and was not aware that he had spoken aloud. His brain had been busy searching for a motive that would make Merry brave the storm, and his arguments to himself ran something on these lines: 'By my standard of judging men, this miserable Merry is without doubt the worst of the bad lots in Dymchurch. He can certainly put his hands to a job of work when it serves him, but beyond that he has not a redeeming quality. There's nothing he wouldn't or couldn't do, for he's capable enough. He'd cut a man's throat as soon as a pig's, and there's been human throat cutting on this Marsh in my time, and no murderer strung up. What more likely then that this dirty brute ain't the throat-cutter in chief for the smugglers. There's many a man who don't think twice about defrauding the Government who would shrink from violence. Such folk have only to mention to Merry that So-and-so is a menace, and Merry cuts So-and-so's throat, and when a hue and cry is raised, such folk keeps mum through fear of what this cutthroat might do or say. Now, suppose this 'ere ship in distress is nothing more than a laden lugger caught by the storm, full of contraband. She goes ashore here and in the name of the Government I make a seizure. That touches the pockets of most of 'em in Dymchurch, and might touch a neck or two with Jack Ketch hemp. A stab in the dark from this rogue would save 'em a lot of trouble. A cry wouldn't be heard on a night like this, nor no one notice a body sunk in the mud of the sluice-gate. Well, let Merry try such a prank and he's mine body and soul, and a very useful gentleman, too. I'd rather have him obeying me than a regiment of Dragoons. Let's see, left-handed, ain't he? Then his knife will be handy in his left pocket, or he wouldn't have done up his coat so tight.'

As he turned in the door and said 'good night', not even Merry noticed that a short-muzzle pistol had been transferred from the right to the left pocket of the officer's heavy coat. Merry did not suspect the reason why the officer fetched along beside him on his left side, and for support against the wind or comfort against the storm grasped his left arm tightly with his right. Indeed, the officer's hand dropped into Merry's pocket and gripped his wrist, almost as though he had put him under arrest. Meanwhile, the ugly knife lay at the bottom of the deep pocket, idle but safe. Even when these ill-assorted companions of Law and Disorder had to negotiate their way over the branches of a great tree that had been blown across the road from the Grove House, the comfortable residence of Dr. Sennacharib Pepper, the local physician and surgeon, even then did the officer keep Merry's wrist shackled in his strong fingers. Lights were burning in the Grove House. Evidently, Dr. Pepper expected the storm to give him a duty call, and was not yet abed.

At the corner of Grove House the road turns and forks into an upper path which runs up a bank and snuggles its way immediately below the sea-wall. Up this path the two struggled, making their way towards a snugly-gabled house known as 'the Sea-Wall Tavern'. The events of this night were, however, destined to change this name. The two adventurers looked up at the bedroom window, where in the light of a candle a good-looking young woman was peering through the diamond-shaped panes. Behind her loomed the figure of her husband.

Making a trumpet of his spare hand, the Preventive Officer shouted: "Ahoy, Abel Clouder."

In a vivid flash of lightning Abel looked down over his wife's shoulder and recognised the two men standing on the gravel path beneath the window. At the same time his wife pointed out to sea and uttered a frightened cry that was echoed by what seemed like the wailing of lost souls.

Abel made a sign to the men below and disappeared from the window. In a few seconds they heard the chains being taken down from the door, and it suddenly opened inwards. The two men dashed into the passage and turned to help the owner close the door. Against the fury of the wind, it took their combined force to do it.

"There's a ship in distress, ain't there?" asked the Preventive man. "Do you know her?"

"No," answered Abel. "Come upstairs and have a look. There'll be lightning again in a minute."

CHAPTER II. Meg Fears For Her Husband

Mrs. Clouder left the window as the men came in, and sat down on the side of the big bed.

Her husband dragged the Preventive man to the window, where they waited for the next flash. Merry stood just inside the door and turned his cadaverous eyes upon the girl. Like every other man in Dymchurch, Merry realised that Abel Clouder had secured the best looking young woman on the Marsh, when he made Meg Mrs. Clouder. But if the men, including Merry, were envious of Abel, the women were no less jealous of Meg, for Abel was the jolliest and the most handsome of the young fishermen, and there had been many a heart aching when Abel had led Meg to the altar. However, this envy and jealousy were only on the surface. Deep down there was no one who did not wish this ideal couple well. All save Merry. Meg's beauty disturbed him and made him realise his inferiority to Abel, who had won the only girl whose physical attractions filled him with a wild desire for her. Accordingly he hated Abel, and Abel's popularity only served to increase the hatred.

The shrieking destruction of the wild elements outside entered his wicked soul and filled it with a devilish glee as he watched Meg seated on the bed, her pretty face clouded with anxiety as she watched and listened to the storm. His hungry eyes feasted on her beauty. Her clear-cut, almost classic, features, her broad honest brow with the light brown hair that crowned it and fell in a provocative kiss curl upon her firm young breast. Her eyes had the green of the sea in them, and he was afraid of them, but the suspicion of freckles under them somehow stirred his blood. She was dressed in an orange-coloured frock of rough cloth, open at the neck, but the gay colour only made her look more puritanical in his eyes. He hated purity, and the only useful reason for it as far as he could see, was that it was a quality made for destruction. His eyes that had been devouring Meg's face and figure, shifted to her feet. They were bare, and he had a mad desire to crunch those beautiful little bones between his teeth.

As the lightning flashed he watched her, enjoying the look of fear that crept into her usually fearless eyes. 'Yes, to crunch those ankles with my teeth. To see the colour of her blood. To bruise that healthy flesh.' The thought made him involuntarily draw in his breath with a vicious hiss. She turned for the first time and looked at him.

"Are you cold, Mr. Merry?" she asked.

"No," he answered gruffly. "I've been wrapped up against the wet, but it's strangely hot for November."

As he spoke, he unbuttoned his coat, pulled it from him and dropped it on the floor. Then he unwound his scarf and kept it on his hand, for the sky was again lighted up with a succession of sheet lightning, while the fire forks cracked and hissed down into the sea. For the first time he saw what the others had been watching, a sturdy brig with broken masts and fallen sails, being hurled nearer and nearer to the sea-wall. He listened to the conversation of the two men in the window.

"She's no doubt striking the sand already as she dips," said Abel. "But she won't stick, not with that power of the sea. It'll lift her off every time. She'll be broke up within the groyne. Maybe she'll get hoisted on to the wall before she breaks her back. By gad. She's on fire, too. Look."

The sky had gone black as the thunder crashed, but a dull red spot suddenly leapt into a fierce tongue of orange flame, and once more arose the wail as of lost souls. And that their bodies were lost there was no doubt. That flame, venomous and spiteful, had the ship. It was as though one element were striving with the other for the victim. Fire and water fought for the doomed vessel.

"Oh, poor people," murmured Meg, trembling. "Can we do nothing but watch?"

"I fear that's what it will amount to, lass," replied her husband. "It's no use trying to launch a boat, because it couldn't be done. But, as we were saying just now, a line might help 'em."

The shrieking wind seemed to scoff at his words, for a sheet of water struck the lead-rimmed panes. Once more the lightning lit up sea and sky.

"She's nearer now," said Abel. "But every time the waves drop her she sticks. When she stops shifting, if she does, I'll risk it."

The forked spears of fire danced and darted in the sky as though daring him to make good his boast. Merry looked at the storm, not with the strength of pity that shone in Abel's eyes, but with the lust of destruction, and his black soul whispered secretly: 'If the storm will drag down the husband, then I will drag down the wife.' He looked at Meg, and overcame a wild impulse to seize her face and kiss her on the lips, but wisdom, or fear saved him from such folly as Meg stood up and said firmly: "You are not to go, Abel. It is madness."

Abel, however, had decided that he must go. He turned to his wife and laid both hands upon her firm young shoulders.

"I'd sooner you loved me as a dead brave man, than as a living coward. You ain't going to make me unworthy of your love?"

"Mrs. Clouder, that ain't a sea to swim in I allow," said the Preventive Officer. "There's but two men on Romney Marsh that might attempt it at a long hazard, and your man's the stronger swimmer of the two."

"And is the other one a married man?" asked Meg.

The Preventive Officer shook his head. "It's the young vicar, I mean. Parson Bolden."

"But look at that sea," protested Meg.

"Why, there is the parson," exclaimed Abel. "See him, crouching his way up by that boat-house wall. He's a dare-devil for all he's a parson."

"There's quite a crowd of the lads collected," said the Preventive man.

"Where?" asked Merry, going for the first time to the window. He had a purpose for doing it, too. He dropped his dark scarf upon the dark floor-boards. The light of the flickering candle did not betray this fact, as Merry leaned against the casement.

"On the lee side of the boat-house," was the reply to Merry's question.

"Then it's time we joined 'em," said Abel. "Have you got the key of the boat-house, in case them rescue ropes are needed, mate?"

"I've got it," answered the Preventive man, making for the staircase. "Come on, Merry."

Merry picked up his coat and began pulling it on as he followed down the stairs. But one look he shot as he went, and he saw Meg in her husband's arms, and he hugged his hatred to his soul.

"Give a look to the parlour fire below, lass," said Abel, "and keep a kettle going. We may get one or two of 'em ashore in spite of all, and they'll want reviving."

When Abel had his hand upon the bobbin of the front door, Merry put his hand up to his coat collar. "You go on. I'll join you," he said. "I've left my scarf up in the bedroom."

"You'd never pull this door to by yourself," laughed Abel. "Here, Meg. Mr. Merry's left his scarf up there. Heave her down, will you?"

But this didn't suit Merry. He had a word to say to Meg alone and he meant to say it. He was up the stairs before Abel realised he was going, and he entered the bedroom without a word.

Meg had evidently neither heard her husband call nor Merry's footsteps, for she was kneeling beside the bed with her face buried in her arms. Feeling a heavy hand upon her bowed head rumpling her hair, she imagined that her prayer was answered and that her husband had returned to tell her that the seas were too high to adventure.

Smiling through her tears, she looked up into the cadaverous face of the miserable Merry. Facing what he could not begin to understand, the man's face appeared stupidly wooden. Although he knew he would not hesitate t cut a man's throat if he was sure of his own skin, he was amazed at his own audacity in thus confronting Meg, and the nearness of her beauty paralysed him.

Meg found herself suddenly afraid. Not so much of the man as of the storm and his sudden appearance alone in her bedroom. Behind his tall hovering figure the lightning danced. He had drawn away his hand with an awkward gesture of fear. It was his left hand, and the twitching fingers seemed self-conscious of what they had done. These fingers, well-used to the stain of blood, recoiled from the silken touch of that light brown hair. To gain confidence, they dropped subconsciously into the left coat pocket and closed around the handle of the ugly knife. Then, without knowing what he did, he drew his hand out of the pocket, so that half the blade was exposed to her eyes. Strangely enough, her fear vanished. Thinking of it later, she knew that she feared those empty, groping fingers more than the clenched fist.

"What do you want here?" she asked.

He turned away, muttering, "My scarf." He hovered round the bed, pretending to search for it.

She rose from her knees, dashed the tears from her eyes with the back of her hand, and in a business-like way went to the window-sill and picked up the candle. Her quick eyes immediately saw the scarf where he had dropped it. With her other hand she pointed to it.

"There it is," she said, but made no attempt to stoop for it.

For a moment he watched her as she stood there in the candle-light, and a terrifying thought took hold of his brain. He knew that for this woman he could kill rashly, without taking pains for his own safety as he had always done before. The possible result of such foolishness frightened him. He somehow resented the power she had over him, and he vowed that though her spell might mean danger to him, he would utterly destroy her first.

The voice of Abel jerked him into action:

"Can't you find it, man? You're wasting time."

"Got it," answered Merry, as he shambled forward awkwardly and picked up the scarf. As he straightened himself up, he seemed surprised to find himself so close to her. There was only the candle which she held between them. Now, he decided, was the time to give her his message.

"Should anything happen to him," he whispered, jerking his head toward the stairs, "I shall be here to take charge of you, see?"

Meg looked bewildered, as indeed she was. "I don't understand you, Mr. Merry," she said.

"No?" he queried. "Well, you've made me understand something, you have. I see now why them damned fool moths gets caught up in the flame."

As he spoke he had dropped the knife down into his pocket, and his fingers had fluttered in tiny circles above the lighted candle which she held between them. Then suddenly they had dropped, extinguishing the flame and plunging the bedroom into darkness. Before she could cry out in her astonishment, her head was clenched in the crook of his arm and she was half suffocated against the wetness of his coat. As he held her there, she heard once more a wail of agonised terror from the ship outside.

"Come on," cried Abel, climbing the stairs.

She felt herself freed, and as the lightning flashed again she was alone.

"Have you got a light to rekindle the candle for Mrs. Clouder?" said Merry from the top of the stairs. "The draught blew the damned thing out."

Abel produced a 'flasher' from his pocket and passing Merry on the stairs went into the bedroom. 'Flashers' were small pistols without barrels, about four inches long in all, with flintlock and a pan to hold about a quarter thimble-full of powder. 'Flashers' were used by the Dymchurch men to signal night messages to one another across the Marsh, or perhaps to the crew of a lugger awaiting a 'run' on Dymchurch Bay. They could also answer the innocent purpose of a tinder box.

Presenting the flasher at his wife's head, Abel growled in mock sepulchral tones, "Stand and deliver," and then, as he flashed the powder and lit the candle, he added, laughing: "And how's that for your handsome Jimmie Bone?"

Jim Bone was the notorious highwayman who transacted a brisk business on the busy Dover Road and periodically went into hiding upon the Marsh when the chase became too hot. Though a hard man to cross, he was a good friend to his friends, amongst whom the Clouders were numbered.

"The seas are too high for you to attempt a rescue, Abel."

"That's for the other lads to decide," he answered. "If they think it's possible, I shall have to attempt something."

Meg, who was seething with anger against Merry's madness, turned her temper against the villagers who took her young husband's strength and daring so much for granted.

"But why should you risk so much for others, for strangers? You forget you are married, Abel."

"Not I," he contradicted. "Why, that's the reason I'm married to you, and it's because I love you that I have to do more than the rest. Don't you see that I must do things that others can't or won't do in order to be a little more deserving of my good fortune?"

Meg smiled. "You're a clever old flatterer, Abel, and as obstinate as you are good-looking. But for all that, I want you to do something for me."

"Why, anything, except to be a coward, and you wouldn't ask that I know."

"I want you to take care of that man Merry," she said solemnly.

"I reckon he can more than take care of himself, but why—"

"I mean avoid him," she corrected. "Keep clear of him. He hates you, Abel, and he carries a knife."

"Well, we all carry knives, but 'hates' me? Nonsense." Abel laughed. "Now why should anyone take the trouble to hate a good enough natured fool like me? I haven't an enemy in the world, please God."

"Perhaps there are some who are jealous of your good nature," she said.

"Jealous?" he repeated. "My faith, the only jealousy I shall meet in my life will be your fault. Everyone's jealous that I happened to win you, Meg, and quite right too. But you can take it from me that Merry ain't that way. He's altogether too sour and selfish to be taken up with a pretty girl."

"You may find you're wrong, husband, and later I'll tell you my reasons, but in the meanwhile don't give him a chance to use his knife behind your back."

"Trust me for that, but the fellow's a coward. There's no danger from miserable Merry so long as Jack Ketch don't run out of rope. I must go, lass. I wouldn't have 'em say that Abel Clouder hung back. I love you too well, Meg."

"Thank you, Abel," she answered with a smile. "And as I love you, watch Merry."

"Trust me," he nodded, and with her kiss on his cheek, he went down the stairs and gave the sour Merry a hearty clump on the back which made him look the sourer.

"Now, lads, open the door, and let's see if we can cheat the devil and snatch a few souls from his grip. Ready? Then out into the lightning and the waves."

A splash of spray in the passage, a gust of wind that set every beam and floor-board creaking, and then a silence, told Meg on her knees beside the bed that they had gone.

CHAPTER III. The Wreck Of The Brig On Dymchurch Wall

The three men reached the fast-gathering group under the shadow of the boat-house. They were joined by the parson with the news that the burning ship seemed to have stuck fast in the sand and that the waves breaking over the well deck, kept the fire in the after hold beneath the poop deck cabin, and prevented it from spreading amidship. He agreed with the fishermen that it would be impossible to launch a boat, but he did think that a strong swimmer might reach the wreck with a rope, and he stoutly maintained that he was quite willing to attempt it.

Accordingly, the necessary tackle was brought out from the boat-house. However, since both tide and wind were driving into the bay, it was doubtful whether a single swimmer would be able to make headway with the weight of the rope hampering him. Abel immediately suggested that if the middle of another line were fixed to the end of the rescue rope and each end attached to a cork jacket, that he would then adventure with the parson.

Both men accordingly stripped off their coats and boots and buckled on their life preservers to which the line's ends were fixed, and then with practically the whole male population of the village assembled to pay out the slack, the two heroes climbed the sea-wall, arm-in-arm, and waiting for a favorable backwash of a gigantic wave, they plunged in side by side and were swept out to meet the oncoming seas.

Meanwhile, the news of the wreck had spread through the village and reached the Court House, so that by the time the swimmers, fighting for every inch of progress, had cleared the end of the stone groyne which was about half-way to the ship, the helpers on the rope were augmented by the squire himself, four or five gentlemen who had been his dinner guests, and Dr. Sennacharib Pepper, whom they had collected on the way. With these extra strong and willing hands, it was simple for Merry to move away without being missed for while his colleagues were busy over the living, he decided that it might be more to his advantage to get busy with the dead, or nearly dead.

In his hatred of Abel Clouder—and of the parson too, for that matter—he could not help rejoicing that they had gone, through their own heroic conceit, to almost certain death. 'Yes—surely the devil would do his utmost to crush the man of God and the virtuous Abel? But if not? If they succeeded?—and the bare possibility made him curse the two heroes as 'damned flamboyant busybodies'—why, then a direct communication between the wreck and the land would be established that might at least save the strongest aboard. But with reasonable luck—not at all. The weaker bodies would be battered to pieces and be swirled under the upward curl of masonry that was the strong foundation of the sea-wall, and by calculating tide and wind in relation to the wreck, he imagined such bodies would come ashore near the flight of steps built into the sea-wall opposite Sycamore Farm. There, too, he would be able to crouch in shelter till a likely moment of action. If those busybodies, Abel and the Parson, failed, the heat of the ship's fire would assuredly drive passengers and crew overboard, or if they attempted to reach the fore-deck by way of the well, they would be washed over by the force of the breakers. Thus the bodies would be swept along to the steps just the same, and it seemed probable that he alone would be there to receive them. By the convulsive groping of his fingers for the knife, he knew what sort of a reception these victims of the storm would get, and looking at it from every point of view, he considered that such a barbarous welcome would be safe enough. The lure of the wreckage would keep the villagers opposite the breaking ship, when at low tide they could swoop aboard to get anything worth taking. They were not likely to think so cunningly as he. And yet it seemed obvious that any men of sense, travelling the world by sea where so many pirates were afloat, would secrete his valuables about his person, especially at the first danger of shipwreck. Well, the bodies that he found would not have the price of their own burial by the time he had shown them some attention.

Accompanied by these murderous thoughts, the miserable Merry scurried away under the shelter of the sea-wall till he reached his coign of vantage. Clambering up the rough tussocks of turf that faced the wall on the Marsh side, he gained the top, where he met the full violence of the wind and spray. As it was impossible to stand up, he crawled on his stomach across the flat summit to the cut steps, down which he slithered headfirst. Curling himself up against the masonry, he escaped the violence of the storm. And every cry that could be heard above the booming waves and lashing spindrift, whether the encouraging shouts of the party at the boat-house or the despairing shrieks of the people on the ship or the melancholy call of some buffeted sea-bird, this infamous man prayed to his master the devil to make it the death-cry of Abel Clouder. Once, a bright red reflection on some water held in a pool between the great boulders of the breakwater made him look round the edge of the wall towards the wreck, where he saw that flames were shooting up through a part of the poop deck, and he also perceived two men, their shadows silhouetted against the fire, climb over the bulwarks and jump into the sea. How would they reach him—dead or alive? However strong a man might be, surely the battering of those cruel waves would beat him on to the boulders more dead than alive? Besides, on reaching the shore after such peril, who would be prepared for a sudden knife attack? Not on the shores of Kent. Thus Merry comforted himself that on that score he had nothing to fear, for should the survivor thus prove himself a Hercules, he could have a good look at the fellow first by adopting the role of rescuer until, thinking himself at last to be free of peril, he might be taken off his guard, or should that be too risky, at worst there was the possibility of a handsome reward paid out in gratitude for his preservation.

So, crouched down in his strong recess like a wild beast scenting prey, he waited for what the devil would send him from the sea.

Crouched over the rope as they paid it out inch by inch from hand to hand, the villagers wondered what was happening at the other end, and whether both, or one, or neither of the men would effect a landing on the ship.

Crouched against the window, unable to pray more, Meg waited for each flash of lightning, trying to distinguish her husband's figure amongst the crowd, but the passing of the rope told its own tale, and she waited for the worst.

None of these watchers had long to wait, for catastrophe was at hand, terrifying in its sudden and surprising climax.

A particularly vivid lightning flash, which showed the valiant swimmers already beneath the broken bowsprit of the brig, was answered in the darkness that followed, by a roll of thunder, that grew louder and louder. All then that could be seen was the glow of the derelict's fire, which, confined to such a heat in the hold, had at last burst up through the flooring of the deck cabin, and up again through the ceiling which served as the planking of the poop deck.

While the rolling rotundity of the resounding thunder was drumming up to its last grandeur, a strong stench of sulphur swept down across the sea and hung in spreading fumes upon the sea-wall, until with a sharp crackle as percussive as a square of muskets, another fire, a ball of flaming gas enveloping a thunder-stone, darted across the sky and dashed with a hissing explosion into the sea.

Then up—and right above the sea-wall line arose the waters, lifting the ship into the sky and carrying it onwards, down the liquid hill that swept towards the wall. Rent sails held by the entangled cordage of the riotous rigging, streamed out their shreds of canvas, torn into strips like giant ribbons, while the ship's bell, swinging to the unnatural list, clanged out a dismal note of doom.

The sight of the brig racing helplessly in the jaws of the white-fanged breakers struck instant terror to the hearts of the men at the rope, and despite an encouraging shout from the squire to stand firm, many deserted their posts and fled for shelter of the boat-house.

Out went the sky as the thunder cracked, but not even that, nor the mighty roaring of the waters, could drown the great thud as the ship's bows cut into the masonry of Dymchurch Wall like a battering ram. The noise of rending wood splitting like a crashing forest, and the rush of water pouring over the sea-wall and sweeping them off their feet into the road below made them think that their valiant defence had been broken at last, and that the sea was flooding the Marsh. The dread of many generations had come true. The invincible wall was down. The skill and labour of centuries, paid for by hard-wrung Scots on acreage in order to keep the Marsh holdings in security, had at last been defeated by the elements. The slogan of the Marsh men, good and bad, "Serve God, honour the King; but first, maintain the Wall," was now of no account. Yet had these men but maintained their posts of danger on the rope, they would not have lost their faith in that dark hour, for as the squire and a few faithful ones braced themselves to keep their footing and their hold on the rope while the sea water swirled for a few ghastly seconds round their waists, they then knew the wall had not failed its children, whose lives and homes depended on its strength and holding power. Damaged, no doubt, it was; but at the first fall of the tide, the squire's foreman would once again organise the Marsh men into gangs for its repair.

CHAPTER IV. The Wooden Devil

Now although Meg, in a vain endeavour to catch sight of her husband, had braved the flashes of lightning, the terror of the fireball as it burst across the sky made her involuntarily clap her hands over her eyes, and during the destructive seconds of the storm's ferocity that followed, she felt the house shake violently, give a sickening tilt and then shiver, as joists and beams groaned and creaked in their shifting. Built as it was upon the lower level of the sea-wall, the foundations slid with the soil as the waves, bursting through the cellarage weakened it. The front door was torn from its hinges and blown bodily against the staircase, as the sea water gushed through the passage, silting up the floor with a loose deposit of gravel, sand and shell. At the same time the diamond-paned casement through which Meg had been looking, crashed inwards, its heavy leadwork striking her on the head and bearing her to the floor beneath its weight. This was the last wicked prank of the hurricane before departing. There followed what, in contrast to the noise, seemed almost a silence, broken only by the accustomed sound of waves against the Wall.

How long Meg lay there beneath that pile of twisted lead, glass panes and broken plaster, she could not tell, for the injury to her head had left her senseless, but when she recovered she still found herself looking through the casement, and for some time it puzzled her that she could only see the sky—a wild sky of fast-flying clouds lit with the full radiance of the moon. Then she realised that she was lying on the floor with the window resting upon her face. She remembered the storm. Its violence had gone, but in her heart it had left behind its terror, and it was not the thunder-bolt that had made her cover her eyes, nor the noise, nor the rocking house which made this terror so paralysing, but the thought of what it had brought, the thing which she had seen between her fingers, in that awful moment. It was the huge form of a giant, a devil of the storm, who with staring eyes had rushed towards her at the window. She had seen its face plainly, with its great eyes and black beard, for as it rushed, it waved a great lantern above its head, and this swaying light had revealed the horrid face. And its voice—for this thing had brought her a message—was the most terrible of all. The volume of its speech embraced the whole multitudinous din as vowels were formed by mighty waters rolling into hollow places with howling winds to govern them and consonants were framed by cracking timbers and the rasp of grinding stones.

"Clouder is dead. Your house is destroyed. This comes of serving God." How could she doubt the owner of such a sentiment to be other than the devil himself? He had made himself manifest in the shape of a wooden giant. He had surrounded himself with hellish elements and caused all this destruction because she, in her humble faith, served God. And God, the omnipotent, had given him free license. He had robbed her of husband and home, and God permitted it. She remembered that recently she and Abel had listened to a sermon on Job, preached by the parson, Master Bolden. On the way home from church, she had remarked to Abel that it was a strange story which was hard to believe. Now it was true. God had once more permitted just such an injustice.

Numbed in body and spirit, she gloried in her rebellion; and then she heard a simple, sacred sound which gave the lie to her terror, and which her simple faith was glad to welcome as a comforter. It was the tinkle of the three church bells, rung as on the Sundays to call the faithful to prayer. After all she had been through, she was in no frame of mind to put two and two together, and did not remember that the three bells were not only rung on Sundays to call the parish to 'serve God' but on days and nights of sea danger to summon the Marsh men to 'maintain the Wall'. However, forgetting this, she made a miracle of a mere coincidence.

As the inland farmers of the Marsh were being roused from their beds by the bell's slogan, so did Meg rouse herself from that old oak floor, which though never straight at the best of times was now canted at an alarming angle. With all this calamity, no wonder she had imagined even worse things. Of course, her husband was alive. If he were dead she would have been told by the men, and not by her nightmare of a wooden devil which was nothing more than a frightening dream. She could soon dispel that by looking out of the open space where the window had been. Comforting herself with these suggestions, she looked out.

Though her fears had been acute, they were as nothing to the overwhelming horror that now possessed her. Could she have mastered her physical attributes in order to let out one piercing scream, it might have given her brain a chance of a speedier recovery later on. But what she saw had paralysed her brain. All she knew was that in her attempt to give the devil the lie, the devil had given her the truth, for there, right opposite to her and leaning over the lip of the broken sea-wall, his lantern still alight, was the enormous head and shoulders of the wooden-looking giant. Its staring eyes regarded her with a fixed expression of contempt and hatred, and as she gazed, she listened too and heard a voice beneath her window saying: "Here's a shutter. Help me wrench it off." There followed a squeaking of iron and a bump of wood, and then the slow, regular tramping of men's feet.

The malignant face told her to come and look at what was going on beneath her window. He swung his lantern invitingly. She was powerless to move, but she knew that they were carrying her Abel away on the shutter, and she guessed he was dead, for she heard a voice which she recognised as the squire's say: "Wait, while I break the news to his wife." She heard him enter the passage and wondered why his footfalls sounded as though they trod on a beach. The she heard him say: "I'll want a hand here. The stairs are all but gone under this door." After much whispering and mumbling, and the noise of wood clearance, followed by the effort of someone climbing, she knew the squire was clinging to the crooked doorpost of the bedroom. She was unable to turn round, for the wooden man had her hypnotised, but she knew it was the squire before he spoke, which he did with difficulty.

"My dear Mrs. Clouder," he began, and then remembered that he had first seen her as the prettiest baby lying in a bassinet before the kitchen fire at the Long White Cottage where the Henley family lived. He recalled how one of the Henley men said: "Well, Master Tony, what do you think of our lobster catch?" He, as a little god fresh from Queen's College, Oxford, had replied: "It's true most babies are as red as boiled lobsters, but you wrong this one. She's pretty." "Oh, but I was meaning the cradle, Master Tony. Grandpa made it out of two old lobster pots when we heard that little Meg was thinking of living in Dymchurch."

The squire loved the Henleys, and perhaps Mrs. Clouder best of them all. So thinking of this, he paused and said with emotion: "My poor Meg, I'm afraid you've got to be very brave. Of course, all the village will help you, and you know that I'll always stand by you. You see, my dear child, I've got the worst possible news to break to you. You and I have lost our best friend. We'll have to comfort each other, Meg. You know I had the greatest affection and admiration for the man you loved. Look at me, please, Meg, won't you? It will help me to tell you."

"But I have been told, Sir Tony," she answered. "I've been told in a cruel way, not kind like you would do. He told me. Look. He's staring at me. He killed my husband and destroyed my home, and he's gloating on me there, leaning over the sea-wall. Do you see nothing, sir? Or does it only appear to me?"

"I see it very well, Meg," replied the squire. "But I see nothing malignant in it. You of all people should pity it, for it is a fellow-sufferer—a victim of the storm."

"It is the maker of the storm. It is the devil. He told me so. And he sent that other brute to warn me. He looked at me with fixed eyes, too. He stared at me like that, before he put out the light and seized me. Don't let him get me, Squire, oh."

The staring eyes, the monotonous, metallic tone of her voice frightened the squire. He had imagined that he would have to deal with a weeping, hysterical young woman whom he could have taken home to his wife to be mothered. But the deathly still horror which possessed Meg was a symptom altogether more alarming, and he feared that her reason might be affected permanently.

He answered her calmly: "Why, Meg, I really marvel that you, whose menfolk have been sailors since the days of Noah, should fall into such an error. This devil on the sea-wall, as you speak of it is no devil at all, but has, no doubt for years been the pride of every honest sailor behind it, for it is nothing but the wooden figure-head of the ill-fated broken brig, City of London. Your heroic husband and our no less valiant vicar had almost reached it with a life-line, when a great tidal sea wave lifted the ship above them. It is some comfort to know that their death was quick. It is a great comfort to know that their death was heroic. Now, Meg, I have come to take you to the Court House."

"And leave my home?" she asked, bewildered.

"It is unsafe to stay in it, Meg," replied the squire. "I will undertake to see that it is guarded by responsible men answerable to myself, and to-morrow we will repair the damage."

For the first time she cut the spell which the wooden figure held on her, and turning to the squire, asked in a matter-of-fact tone: "Where is—Abel?"

"They are carrying the—they are carrying him," he corrected, to a shelter for the night. It is customary to use the barn at Sycamore Farm in cases like this. Come, Meg, it is something to know that you bear the name of a man whom the whole of the Marsh will always be honouring. Let me take you to her ladyship."

Meg took two steps towards him and then turning suddenly looked once more at the figure-head. Then with a pathetic moan she collapsed into the squire's arms. He carried her through the door and lowered her unconscious body to willing hands beneath the broken staircase.

And so in solemn procession were the Clouders carried towards the rookery where the party divided, those bearing Abel's body turning into the Farm Lane, and the squire's party, who carried Meg, going on to the old Court House, where Lady Cobtree and her three daughters busied themselves in preparing a guest-chamber and making ready such remedies as Dr. Sennacharib Pepper prescribed for the unconscious young widow.

Meanwhile a messenger had followed from the sea-wall to say that although a strict watch was being kept upon the abating waves around the wreck, no sign of the vicar's body had appeared. The squire sent back word that the Preventive Officer was to take what steps he thought fit to guard not only the Clouder's tavern, but the wreck itself from pilferage. Neither plank nor beam belonging to the broken brig was to be touched till he invited on the morrow the Lords of the Level to view it. He also enjoined a strict watch to be kept all night and although he thought it likely that all the ship's company must have perished either by fire or water, should any survivor by the grace of God reach Dymchurch Wall in safety, such a person was to be carried to the Court House immediately and information lodged with the doctor, who could attend the said person in his presence. He also sent word to the sexton, who had been roused to ring the tocsin bells, to continue the practice till he received word that the foreman of the Wall was satisfied that sufficient posses of men had assembled to insure safe keeping of the Marsh.

Thanks to the skilful nursing of the ladies at the Court House and the strength of her own youth, it was not long before Meg opened her eyes and looked about her. She saw a beautifully proportioned room of white panelling edged with gold. She saw rich hangings, not only at the windows with their rigidly built-in seats, but also around the four-poster bed in which she lay. The feel of the bedclothes, softer than any material she had ever imagined, the glow of a fire in the grate beneath a carved mantelpiece, and the thickness of the carpet which enabled the pretty little satin shoes with sparkling buckles that were crossing it to make no noise. These shoes peeped out timidly from beneath a beautifully embroidered skirt. Meg's eyes slowly took in the rest of this dainty figure, a beautiful girl dressed as she imagined queens' ladies dressed at court.

As this exquisite being leaned over her and applied a cooling essence to her throbbing head, and the sweet perfume of lavender enveloped her, Meg told herself that she was dead; this was Heaven and that an angel was ministering to her. As she attempted to collect her impaired wits, she remembered a funeral procession in which she was carried to the village churchyard. Somehow, she did not mind this, for the gloom of that walk had resulted in a rest beyond her highest dreams; but, unfortunately, the brain recovering, turned traitor and showed her something which destroyed her heaven and made her shriek in terror. Immediately, three other ministering angels were around her, and one, whose hair was powdered white, asked her of what she was afraid.

"There by the fire. Oh, keep him away. He is all wet, and he'll be pressing my head against his coat."

The elder woman with the powdered hair, who was none other than Lady Cobtree, patted Meg's hand and asked: "Now, Meg dear, you know me?"

Meg shook her head. "I know him."

The youngest Miss Cobtree turned fearfully and looked in the direction indicated by Meg's wild eyes. Then, seizing her mother's arm, she whispered: "It is her husband she sees. 'All wet,' she said. Drowned people do appear, they say, to those they love."

"Is it your husband that you see?" asked Lady Cobtree.

"I am not afraid of Abel; I am only afraid of Mr. Merry," she said, as she stared and trembled.

"What, that 'wretched Merry' as they call him? You need not fear that he will come to the Court House, unless to be tried for some roguery at the Petty Sessions. The good-for-nothing has more reason to be afraid of the squire than you have to fear such a rogue."

CHAPTER V. The Death Of The Sea-Captain

Lady Cobtree's words were perfectly true. Merry had been responsible for many a crime which only needed evidence to hang him on the gallows beneath the rookery, and there were many men in Dymchurch who could have put him there, had they not feared to implicate themselves. Yet Merry knew that there was always a risk of one of his nefarious associates betraying him, for Sir Antony Cobtree had a devilish knack in using King's Evidence to clear up a mystery. Consequently, Merry held the squire in great dread, although while appearing to Meg in her imagination, he had been confronted by one whom he was doomed to fear more than any of his enemies, for his adventure on the sea-wall, all but accomplished with success beyond his highest hopes, had resulted in a situation which turned his blood to water. Merry was now in the power of a man against whom he had no counteracting blackmail. When Merry is spoken of as a coward, it should be noted that his cowardice was of the earth—earthy. That is, he shrank from physical discomfort. Moral cowardice he could he could hardly possess who had no morals. In plain words, he shrank from Jack Ketch who could hurt his neck, but did not give a brass button for God who could hurt his soul. As for the devil—well, he was so akin to him and all his works that the fireball which fell into Dymchurch Bay he welcomed as being likely to send God-fearing citizens scuttling to their homes, and so leaving him to gain what he could of such horrors. Merry recognised the fact that one thunderbolt in a million possesses the chance of striking a man dead, and the tidal wave that followed was taken by this gambler as a convenience that would probably lay a wealthy corpse at his feet. An iron mooring ring fixed into the wall secured his safety from drowning, just as sure as a hot brandy would secure him later against cold. Therefore, although soaked to the skin from salt water, it was a happy enough villain that adventured to peer out along the base of the sea-wall when the wave had receded.

The wicked elements favoured him, for the percussion of the thunderbolt had shifted the heavens and the black thunder clouds were rolling away across the Marsh to the distant heights of Lympne Hill, and their retreat from the sea uncovered the moon, which kept dodging in and out of fast-flying white vapours that were hard on the heels of the storm. The light of the moon showed Merry the dark huddled body of a man lying face downwards on the stones. The ghoulish wretch approached the body cautiously. He intended to find out first of all whether the man was dead. A knife wound would look suspicious if anyone discovered the body but he would run that risk if necessary. If, however, the man were dead, all the better, and no risk to run.

He perceived at once that the survivor was dressed as a sailor of rank, with long sea-boots, and his fingers were clasped around an oilskin package. Merry had some difficulty in wrenching it from him and when he had ripped open the waterproof case, found that it was no value to him, though of the greatest import to a conscientious captain, for it was the log book and bills of lading. The gallant captain of the brig had to the last preserved the good name of his ship.

A last wave of the full tide surged up and all but drew the body back with it, but Merry clung on, and when the water cleared, he dragged his find up the sloping stones beneath the shadow of the Wall. He then turned it over on its back, and in so doing heard the chink of gold. Of course, this would be the ship's money. With greedy fingers he unbuttoned the sea-coat and found, sure enough, a waist-belt fitted with many pouches. Fumbling for the buckle in order to transfer this to his own waist, the corpse of the captain, to his utter astonishment, opened his eyes and regarded him with an expression of wonder.

The captain was alive. What was more significant to Merry, the captain looked a man of iron, broad shouldered and with hands hard and hairy. It was no time to hesitate. His victim was recovering his senses, for with a protective gesture his hands moved to his belt. Better for him had he feigned death, for Merry flashed the knife out of his pocket and drove it into the captain's heart.

This cold-blooded murder did not upset Merry in the least, for what more likely than that the captain had been stabbed by a member of his crew. He drew out the knife and cleaned the blade upon the dead man's soaking clothes, and then, dragged the heavy belt from the corpse and fastened it securely beneath his own coat.

The tide having turned, it now occurred to the murderer to throw the corpse back into the sea, so that it would be carried out, and turning round to prepare for this new exertion, he saw to his delight that another body was lying a few yards away.

Leaving the captain for the moment in order to get busy with the other before being interrupted, he approached his second victim with every degree of caution. The body lay on its side with its face half-buried in the sleeve of an arm crooked under it.

Merry saw at once that this was a passenger, dressed in a suit of sober black. Despite the rough passage of the waves, this survivor had managed to keep on his shoes, which were fastened with handsome silver buckles. Beneath the heavy but well-cut top-coat, he saw long spindly legs in black hose and breeches. It seemed incredible to the murderer that this body had not only retained shoes but also a large imposing three-cornered hat, which fitting tightly to an intellectual forehead, had yet been tilted to a rakish angle during its journey across the stones.

With his left hand grasping his knife in case of accidents, Merry's right explored the corpse cautiously, raising its loose arm up and finding that it fell back into place, heavy, stiff and lifeless. To his great delight he found that this one had also a money belt, which by the size of its well-filled pouches promised a greater return than the one he had filched from the captain. He also noticed above the collar of the coat a lanyard, the ends of which disappeared beneath the white cravat, and wondering what valuable the man thus secured around his neck, he tugged it out and found a large, handsome silver key. That was no use to Merry, for it was no doubt the key of a sea-chest which would by now have been consumed in the hold fire. He then saw that a rope was fastened round one of the wrists. The other end was trailing in the water. The man had most likely been lashed to a spar which had broken loose.

On the whole, the belt interested Merry more than any other detail, but before transferring this to his own waist, a perverted sense of humour which this knowledgeable villain possessed, prompted him to a course of action which would save him the exertion of returning the bodies to the sea that brought them up. He resolved to stab this corpse as he had stabbed the other and then to lock them arm-to-arm upon the stones as though they had perished in a fatal fight.

He thereupon drew out his knife, and for greater caution glanced back over his shoulder to make sure that he was not being observed. That movement was his undoing, for as he turned his head he received such a violent crack over the skull that for some time he knew nothing.

CHAPTER VI. The Survivor Takes The Whip-Hand

The first thing he discovered on coming to himself was that the situation as he slowly remembered it, had been woefully reversed. In other words, he was now lying on his back while his intended victim was sitting upon his chest and grinning at his discomfort.

"So you've decided not to rid the world of yourself as well as of the captain, eh?" asked the survivor of the wreck. "Not that you would have journeyed together, for if ever a sea captain was sure of a berth in heaven, he was, and from the little I have observed of you, I should suggest that hell flames would not be hot enough. I say 'the little' I know of you advisedly, because here's to our longer acquaintance," and the speaker, producing a silver flask of large proportions, tilted a dram of good brandy down his throat. "No doubt you could do with a drop yourself?"

Merry could, and moved one hand, which in a mysterious way drew the other with it. He glanced at his hands and saw that his wrists were tied very efficiently with rope. He looked at the rope and saw that one end stretched away into the fast receding waves.

"What's the idea?" he grunted. "What did you want to hit me over the head for?"

His captor took another pull at the flask and sighed with satisfaction.

"You hit yourself over the head, my friend," he replied. "Your skull struck the stone on which you are lying. There's blood on it. Your blood, this time. And here's to our longer acquaintance."

Merry gazed at the queer figure above him and felt afraid. That repeated sentence of 'longer acquaintance' frightened him. There was something sinister about it. A man does not usually desire longer acquaintance with one who has tried to kill him.

"You asked me what was the idea?" continued the survivor. "I will tell you. Nothing less than a time-honoured objection held by many against being murdered in cold blood. In fact, I will go further and say that I would prefer to be the murderer than the murdered. Despite the morals of the case, make me Cain Rather than Abel. I will also confess that for some time I waited for you to recover in order to murder you. It would have been excusable, you must allow. Self-defence, in fact. It seemed a pity to miss such a unique opportunity. Believe it or not, but do you know I have never stabbed a man to death, and I was tempted to try the feel of it. In the ordinary way my instincts would be against it. There is no elegance in inflicting such a death. Now, to throw a knife at your man is elegant, because you are taking a gentlemanly chance and leaving yourself unarmed. To cross swords to the death is also gentlemanly so long as an elegance is preserved, but to stick a knife in a helpless man as you did to that unfortunate captain merely to steal a belt of money which is now round my waist—no, my friend, no elegance there. So ugly and brutal that you must not think for one moment that I would scruple to serve you the same with your own knife. And by God, I'd have done it and will do it, too, unless you comply with the terms of my toast: 'Here's to our longer acquaintance.'"

"And what are the terms?" growled Merry. "To say nothing about the money belt, I suppose."

"My terms are first of all obedience," replied the other. "Open your mouth wider."

Into his open jaws he poured a few drops of brandy on to the tongue, then took another generous pull of it himself, repeating: "Here's to our longer acquaintance."

"And now," he continued, "speak up smart and true. Your name?"

"Merry," replied the unfortunate.

"A lie to begin with," said the questioner.

"It's true. My name's Merry. Ask anyone."

"Your name belies you then. Occupation?"

"I do odd jobs."

"Very odd jobs, it seems. Where do you live?"

"Behind the old Ocean Inn."

"Which old Ocean Inn?"

"Here in Dymchurch. The inn by the great sluice gates. I've a room in the long white cottage that lies alongside, and what's more, I've lived there all my life."

"And what's more, you'll go on living there all your life," retorted the stranger, "until such time as it pleases me to send you to the gallows, for if you try to slip your cables without my leave, I'll have the constables on your heels for this night's murder, and get this clear in your head. Just as you have lived here all your life, so am I going to live here the rest of mine, and since I am all for peace and quiet and we are likely to be neighbors, you can take it that I shall keep a weather eye upon you, Mister Merry Murderer."

"But what are you going to do now?" asked Merry.

"About this murder do you mean? At present, nothing."

"Until you've got rid of that money belt, eh?" he sneered.

"I see that we must cultivate a mutual understanding, Mister Merry," returned the other with a smile. "And in order to do so, I would ask you to take a good look at me."

"I shall not forget you, though I never saw you again," growled Merry.

"Good," laughed the stranger, "but I must point out in my own defence that appearances are against me. You see a long-faced gentleman with something of a high forehead, and by this fitful light of the moon you may have noticed a certain rakishness in his appointments. His hat, as he himself can feel, has been cocked, by rough passage, into a disreputable angle. In one hand he fondles a brandy flask, and in the other, which as you see, he now removes from his pocket, is grasping a particularly ugly-looking knife—your knife. If this gentleman, in whom you are so interested, were to stand up, you would realise that he is more than commonly tall, that his arms are long in the reach and his legs, though thin, possessed of a stalking stride, perhaps ungainly, but yet able to cover the ground swiftly and silently. His general slimness is deceptive, so I am sure you will own, for his limbs are framed of living steel. Already he begins to sound an ugly customer, eh? And when we add to this description your knowledge that he is willing to compound with a murderer and keep secret a foul crime, your moral opinion may be further prejudiced against him. But that, Mister Merry, is where you make a grand mistake, for this gentleman, who has got you like the devil, stuck through the gizzard with a white-hot fork and about to toast you to his taste, has, in truth, stricter morals than the average. For example, the belt you mention. It contains seventy-nine gold guineas; I have not counted them, but I take the captain's word for it. I take it also that here in Dymchurch there will be poor widows who could put that money to better use than you. Therefore, I keep it and shall see that they use it. I shall also keep your knife, and woe betide you if I hear that you are possessed of another."

"Oh, stop talking," hissed Merry, "and answer yes or no to my question. Are you handing me over to the magistrates or are you not?"

The stranger smiled. "Hand you over to the magistrates? I think even you would not be so stupid as to make such a step necessary. You see, Mr. Merry, I am not without my selfishness and I fail to see why I should wantonly throw away such service as you must pay me. Whether your service will be hard or easy, I cannot tell, but it exists from now on, until you wish me to put a rope around your neck. And make no mistake that should such circumstance arise, I cannot safeguard myself. I assure you that I shall not be blamed when you appear at the Assizes."

While the stranger was speaking, he could not fail to notice the look of relief which had spread over the wretch's face beneath him, so that he was not surprised at the next question.

"I am a man of few words," said Merry, "and may be pardoned for not grasping the meaning of a gentleman with such a gift of the gab as yourself. But do I take it then that you force me to serve you and that you are not going to hand me over to the magistrates?"

"My good and murderous friend, it was not the magistrates you tried to murder, but me," replied the stranger. "I fail to see why I should not take advantage of my own misfortunes. It was to me a grave misfortune to witness the murder of my friend the captain, and it would have been a further mishap if my own quickness had not saved my own poor life. A dead man, swinging is only serviceable to the crows and rooks that nest above the gallows. To see you as a picked corpse is small compensation to me for the shocking reception I sustained at your hands, but as a strong living slave, as one who must willy-nilly do my bidding—why, there is every chance that I shall exact full compensation for your wrong-doing. And I take it that we now see eye to eye and that you agree? Very well. Now, tell me. Does a Cobtree still rule at the Court House here?"

"Aye, Sir Antony Cobtree. He's chief magistrate now."

"Then Sir Charles is dead, I take it, for he was never the man to retire."

"That was his trouble. He wouldn't retire even from hunting. Broke his neck after the fox he did."

"Well, there's a worse way of breaking your neck than that," replied the stranger with an ominous gesture. "And how long ago was this tragedy?"

"Ten or twelve years," explained Merry. "Twelve it was, as Doctor Pepper said he'd been here twelve the other day. He's the physician and when Sir Antony took over his father's place of New Hall and was sworn in at the Court House, he let Doctor Pepper come to live at Grove House, where he'll stay till Master Dennis wants a home of his own in Dymchurch."

"Master Dennis—the son?"

"Aye—there's three daughters growin' up and now at last a son born a month or two back."

"Well, with all respect to the late squire, I rejoice to learn that my old college friend Tony is now the King's Authority upon the Marsh, and the sooner the tide allows us to visit him the better shall I be pleased."

"But there's no need to wait for the tide," corrected Merry. "Here's steps up to the sea-wall."

The stranger pulled the rope attached to Merry's wrists. "But here's my baggage, on the end of this cord. The captain helped me to heave it overboard. It is waterproof, but I was not so sure of it being fireproof. The silver key which you ignored belongs to it. When the water goes out a little further you will wade in and lift it from the sand. You will also carry it to the Court House. It will be your first service.

"And now listen, Mr. Merry, I shall never ask you to do the impossible. Unless it is absolutely necessary, I shall never ask you to do even the difficult, and it may chance that I may never even ask you to do the easy, but whatever, whenever, and wherever I do ask, you will do it—or swing for Mister Ketch. So long as I am sure of your service, you will find me not only a good master but even a good friend, so for your own sake you'd best pocket your pride and make a show of liking me. Understand?"

"Well, I know when I'm beat," growled Merry. "You've got the best of me at the moment—"

"At the moment?" repeated the stranger savagely. "I've got the best of you for ever, and I'll keep the best of you for ever, for unless I have the best of you, the crows shall have the last of you. And now up on your feet and let us wind in this rope till it's taut. You're wet enough, and so am I, to bid defiance to further wading. But I'm hungry, thirsty and tired, and I dare swear you can say the same and add 'disappointed.' When my sea-chest is safe at New Hall of the Court House, I'll expend one of the captain's guineas on you, for after all, the widows know nothing of their windfall yet, and so can hardly miss it. A guinea will give you the price of a good hot supper, plenty of drink, and treatment for your head, payment against loss of a good knife and give you the means to be generous to your friends besides. Have you any friends? I hardly think so."

Merry got to his feet with some groaning occasioned by the wound to his head and the black hate in his heart. He followed his new master across the rough boulders to the level beach. He could do nothing else, for the stranger was pulling on the rope that had been so tightly fastened round his wrists, and each tug seemed to accentuate the pain in his head. At the water's edge the stranger stopped and gathered in the slack of the rope.

"The great wave was a help to you," said the stranger, as soon as the rope was taut. "It carried the chest further than one could have hoped, otherwise, you might have had a long vigil before reaching it. But we must wait even now until the water is only to your waist."

Merry, being sullen, sombre and suspicious and avoiding speech when possible, gave the impression to most that he was slow in movement and dull in the brain, but this was not so. He could shift when it suited him, and think quickly too. He was thinking quickly now. Never would he be safe while this mysterious stranger lived. And never would a safer opportunity arise than now for killing him. He was the only one in Dymchurch who knew of his safe landing. The beach was deserted, for between them and the villagers was the wreck, and they were waiting to board her from the further side. The stranger dead, Merry would win back the captain's guineas as well as the stranger's money belt, which promised to be the more valuable, and then there was the rope attached to the submerged sea-chest with the silver key around his victim's neck. Such a chance was a gift from the devil himself and he must take it. The thought of a hand to hand fight was dismissed. The stranger had taken his knife and he had experienced cruel proof of his physical strength, and what could he do with his hands tied.

The pain in the back of his skull gave him the likeliest notion. A similar crack on the stranger's head with a heavy stone would knock him out and then he could finish the business with the knife. But in casting about for a likely stone, the devil showed him a handier weapon. This was a broken billet torn by the waves from a wooden breakwater. In size it resembled a belaying pin, and its end was weighted with an iron plate from which protruded a heavily studded clamp bolt.

Covering his movement with a blasphemous oath against an uncomfortable sea-boot, Merry stooped, pretended to adjust the boot in question, and rose up again with the likely weapon in hand and hit it in the fold of his coat. The moment was ripe, for the stranger had not turned round, but was engrossed on the hidden sea-chest, flapping the rope upon the surface of the waves in an endeavor to locate its lie. Merry approached behind his back, slowly and stealthily.

Reasoning that the stranger had not got eyes at the back of his head and was therefore ignorant of his silent advance, he ignored the fact that he was following in his footsteps, and had he known the man he was about to attack a little better, he would have been sure that the 'likely weapon' had not escaped his eye. Indeed, the stranger had expected that Merry would stoop for it, and smiled grimly to himself at the string of oaths against the innocent sea-boot. Although he had not got eyes at the back of his head, his alert instincts told him just exactly when Merry was crossing the danger line, and then changing the rope to his left hand, he whipped Merry's knife from his pocket and balanced it in the palm of his hand, so that the moonlight shone on the blade.

"Nice knife, this of yours, Mister Merry," he said, without turning round. The glint on the blade and the suspicion of a threat beneath the words made Merry stand still. "Sharp and on the whole well-balanced, though a trifle heavy in the blade to my thinking. But not bad. Oh, no damme, not at all bad." And as he spoke he sent it spinning up into the air and caught it neatly by the handle. This he did not once, but many times, and at each toss the knife seemed to soar a trifle higher than the last and each time the knife was in the air Merry did some quick thinking and mental timing.

"The devil save us," laughed Merry, with what affability he could muster. "That's a pretty trick, mister. And where did you come by that?"

"A keen eye and a quick hand," replied the other pleasantly. "I find there's little one cannot do if you set your mind on it."

"I calls it wonderful," said Merry.

"Nonsense," laughed the stranger. "You must keep your mind on it, naturally. And for a high cast more than ever, for should the blade get you, it would get you with some force."

"And about how high can you toss it?" asked Merry, scarcely able to conceal the pleasure at his own cleverness.

"In the sunlight I have caught a knife falling from the height of a church steeple," boasted the stranger.

"I can hardly credit that," scoffed Merry. "It's easy to brag in the light of the moon about what you do in the sunlight."

"I'll not be accused of bragging without an attempt at proving my words," retorted the other, with some annoyance. "As you say, there's moonlight, and it's clear enough. I have been something of a thorn in your flesh so far, Mister Merry, that I feel it would be scurvy of me not to amuse you. I can't promise to judge exactly the height of a steeple, but I'll throw it as high as I can, and your eyes shall judge whether I catch or no."

The stranger took off his three-cornered hat, much to the satisfaction of Merry, who had not liked the look of it covering his target. The stranger dropped it on to the sand beside the rope and then looking up began to move the knife up and down.

"Keep your eyes skinned on it, Mister Merry," he enjoined.

"I will," laughed Merry, coming nearer as though in interest.

"One, two three and UP." The stranger had crouched and shot up, and away went the knife into the sky. Merry saw it go and then forgot it. He was watching the other's bent-back head. A perfect target.

Gripping the iron-loaded billet with all his strength, he swung it up when the stranger whipped around like lightning and the astonished Merry was driven back with a long blade pricking into his chest.

"Drop that, you dog, or I'll drive this knife out through your back."

Merry dropped the billet of wood and retreated gibbering with fear from the point of the knife.

"So you thought I was going to follow your knife up to heaven, did you? It never occurred to you that I had another of my own already to send you to hell. I seem destined to upset your plans, Mister Merry."

"All right," grunted Merry. "I'm beaten. Let me go and pick up your hat for you, sir."

The stranger shook his head. "Not yet, Mister Merry, for your knife is sticking in the sand but a yard away from it, and it might tempt you to be foolish again, and I am going to show you just how foolish. Since you interrupted one knife trick, I am about to show you another. You see the post behind you. It is about your height. Put your hat on the top of it."

Merry sullenly removed his hat and walked towards the breakwater, only too glad to escape from the pricking knife. He put the hat upon the six-foot post.

"Very life-like, upon my soul," laughed the stranger. "Let me introduce you, Mr. Merry that shall be, to Mister Merry that for the moment is. A man of your perception, Mister Merry that shall be, will realise that this Mister Merry that is has little to recommend him. He is at the best as stubborn as old oak and iron, but the oak is rotting and the iron eaten with rust. His brain beneath his hat is nothing but a seething mass of bravadoes. He is as wooden as an old Aunt Sally at the fair, and yet he has murder in his heart. Twice he has tried to murder me to-night, and he is thinking hard how best to try again. Let me show you how I deal with such a stumpy idiot. Ha!" The stranger made a quick movement.

The knife whistled past the live Merry and stuck deep and quivering in the centre of the post a foot beneath his hat.

"Right through the neck, Mr. Murderer. Right through the neck. Now pluck it out and give it back to me."

Once more Merry saw a chance, a faint chance, and leaping to take it, he worked the knife with difficulty out of the post. But when he turned he saw that the stranger had retreated and while settling on his hat, was also balancing the other knife which he had picked out of the sand.

"And now," said he, taking up the slack of the rope and giving it a spin on to Merry's wrist, "drop that knife in the sand in front of you and step in after my chest, for this little diversion has filled up time while the water dropped, and don't fear at being carried out by the tide, for I have the rope as a reins with you as one horse and the chest as the other."

Merry strode desperately towards the waves and then stopped.

"Is the chest a big one?" he asked.

"Very big, and very heavy," smiled the stranger.

"Then how do you think I can carry it with my wrists lashed together?" he demanded.

"I don't for one minute. If you will come here, I will free you."

"Then you'd best pick up your own knife," advised Merry. "It seems handier for cutting rope."

"I have been brought up to believe it a crime to cut rope wantonly. I'll untie it."

Merry watched the stranger's long, sensitive fingers working, and he realised that any man possessing such hands and such penetrating eyes must be someone above the average. In a few seconds his left wrist was free, but the rope's end still held his right firmly.

"I noticed that you are left-handed," remarked the stranger. "You killed the captain, at least, with your left. And in my own defence I should like you to realise that the first thing I remember after my buffeting on the stones, was the descent of your knife. Had I recovered sooner I should have saved your victim's life."

"Don't make another speech about it," growled Merry, striding off into the waves.

He picked up the other section of the rope and, lifting it from the water, waded along it.

CHAPTER VII. The Sea-Chest

The chest lay in deeper water than the stranger thought, for as Merry stooped to up-end it, a wave broke over his shoulders. This discomfort irritated the baffled Merry beyond all bearing, and he expended his rage upon the chest. Large it was, as the stranger had said, and had it been a bank chest it could not have been heavier. Merry decided that its owner must be a bank messenger bringing gold bar from America, and he cursed his ill-luck that he had not murdered him as well as the captain. His burning resentment against the stranger made him regard the chest as his own property out of which he had been cheated by gross injustice, and his only comfort was that, knowing the chest existed, the devil might yet give him another chance at it. He would anyway show the stranger that he was a man to be feared for his strength, and with a superhuman effort fed with rage and wounded pride, he somehow got the brass-bound breaking weight upon his back and staggered with it from the water.

"Splendid," cried the stranger, with a great show of admiration as Merry passed him.

'And when I have a knife in your shoulder-blades, I'll say "splendid" too,' said Merry to himself. Aloud he grunted: "To the Court House, you said?"

"I did," replied the stranger, "where I intend to spend this night unless Tony Cobtree be much changed from the gallant lad he was when I knew him."

As they climbed the steps cut in the sea-wall, Merry rested the chest upon the ledge of masonry, for the stranger, who had coiled the long slack of the cord over his arm, had given Merry's wrist a pull as he stopped and regarded the captain's body.

"Yes," ejaculated Merry, as though blaming the stranger for the dead man's plight. "What are you going to do about that? Best thing is to give him a sea-burial, eh?"

"No, we'll lay him to rest in the churchyard with full honours," said the stranger. "I happen to know his wishes on burial. We discussed it. I was for sea-burial, having witnessed one, and he, the sailor, said not for him. So we'll respect his wish and cheat Davy Jones. I'll take his papers and report his death."

"But the wound?" muttered Merry in interrogation. "They'll find that and wonder. Unless they think the fire aboard spread panic and it was a case of every man for himself. I've known cases where sailors run wild against authority. Now if you, being a survivor, could tell them some such panic took place—"

The stranger, who had stowed the oilskin packet in his pocket, silenced Merry with a gesture, then straightened out the dead man's limbs. A sea-gull screeching and hovering overhead, then caused him to lay his kerchief over the face. Having concluded the last service of respect, he removed his hat and with bowed head uttered a prayer. Then signing to Merry to proceed, he climbed the steps and fell in at his side, saying quickly:

"As to what they will think of the captain's death wound, I cannot say, but you can be sure of this. Cross me but once, and they shall know the truth, for just as surely as they will believe my word against yours, I shall denounce you for to-night's murder at the next Assizes."

They walked on silently save for Merry's heavy breathing. It was slow going, for the rough road was littered with branches of trees, and bricks and tiles. At the corner of the churchyard the stranger stopped and gave a little tug on the rope. Merry stopped too and eased the weight of the chest on the low churchyard wall.

"Yes, a moment's rest before we ring at the door, I think," said the stranger. "The old church, eh? Looking very beautiful in the moonlight. But I see that you are more interested in the gallows and the rags and bones that swing there. What was he? A smuggler?"

"No. Sheep-stealer," growled Merry.

"And to think that love of mutton should bring a poor fellow to that," philosophised the stranger.

"It was other people's mutton, you see," grunted Merry.

"Oh, I am not excusing him," replied the stranger. "The law of the Marsh must be kept, just as the Wall must be maintained."

"It seems then you're no stranger to these parts," said Merry. "Since we are to be further acquainted, it might be as well if I knew what your name and occupation might be."

"All in good time, Mister Merry. This is Friday? Very well then, on Sunday you will attend morning prayer inside there. Then you may learn something, if you keep awake."

"I don't attend church. I ain't a hypocrite," growled Merry.

"No one is a hypocrite who tries to turn over a new leaf, my friend, and next Sunday you will show the parish that you intend to turn one. You will be there early to insure yourself a seat."

"Me in church? That's good," scoffed Merry.

"Nevertheless, you will be there," continued the other. It is a command. Understand? And one thing more, before we part. To insure your good behaviour, your guilty secret will be made public at your first legal offense. In plain words, if Mister Merry appears for any misdemeanour at the Petty Sessions, he will appear also at the Assizes for the captain's murder and attempted murder on me. Now, up with the chest again and follow me."

As the church bells were pealing out their danger summons to the Marsh, the stranger and Merry had not heard the ringing of the Court House bell, but as they crunched their way across the gravel to the front door, they saw that they were forestalled, and that another man was being admitted into the hall. The footman was about to close the door again when the stranger called out to him.

"I wish to see Sir Tony," and then, without waiting for the footman's reply he turned to Merry and added: "You can bring my chest in here and put it down. Not on the rug but against the wall there on the flagstones, where the sand and wet won't harm."

New Hall, the residence which surrounded the Marsh Court House and legal offices, in those days kept up a great show of state, all the Cobtree serving men wearing scarlet liveries and powdered hair. Although taken back by the stranger's unexpected entrance and air of command, which assured him that he had to deal with a gentleman above the ordinary, the pompous young footman was not so impressed when he recognised the bearer of the chest was none other than the infamous Merry. Also, the stranger's clothes of solemn black were sadly deranged by sea water and sandy mud.

Before the footman could utter a word, the stranger continued: "I take it that the squire has not departed from the Cobtree habit of sitting up o' nights. However, if he should be abed, I fear that the occasion demands you to call him."

There was a something about the stranger which made the footman realise that if he tried any browbeating he would fare the worse. But the presence of Merry demanded that he should demonstrate his own dignity.

So, avoiding the stranger's gaze, which disconcerted him, he looked at Merry down his exalted nose and replied: "The High Lord of the Level is at present engaged in the company of several local gentlemen. One of the villagers who arrived just before you, and is the bearer of grave news, has been admitted, so that for a time the squire is fully occupied. No doubt, he would see you by appointment in the morning if your business is urgent."

"Urgent?" repeated the stranger. "It would seem so, I think, in that I have successfully negotiated fire, tempest and sudden death to transact it. When a man sets out from New England to Old in bad weather even those more exacting than yourself will admit the urgency, I think. As to the villager you mention, I rather gather that his bad news concerns myself, since I have but now swum from the brig, City of London, which lies with her back broken on Dymchurch Wall.

"Are you then a survivor of the wreck, sir?" asked the footman.

"Unless you can convince me that I am a ghost," smiled the stranger. "And I assure you I feel far from real. After so long a time to be picked up by a wave and deposited here into the Cobtree Hall, and 'fore heaven, how often, when I have seen false weights and measures in the New World, have I not thought of these."

He strode up the long hall, talking more to himself than to the footman and examined the solid brass measures that were arranged in sizes upon a great oak table. He picked up one of great weight with the King's crown in the centre, Romney Marsh Level writ round it, with the figures of weight, the orthodox weight by which all disputes must be settled.

The footman cleared his throat and followed the stranger. He was annoyed that anyone should handle the brass weights and measures, as he had the cleaning of them. "If you are a survivor of the wreck, sir—" he began, but the stranger cut him short with:

"If? Well, if not, how do you suggest I arrived here? Do you think I swam with my sea-chest from Boston?"

"I was about to say, sir, that if you are a survivor, Sir Antony will see you, and immediately, for such were his orders, though he had small hope that any could live."

"Then that bad news you spoke of," continued the stranger, "was no doubt a report that no survivor had reached land, eh?"

"It was somewhat worse than that, sir," replied the footman solemnly. "It was the report that the body of our vicar, who had attempted with another to swim out with a life-line, has been recovered. He is dead."

"The vicar of Dymchurch is dead?" repeated the stranger.

"Aye, sir. Parson Bolden. He went out with young Clouder. Both lost. The young widow Clouder has been brought here. Going on something shocking till Dr. Pepper give her something to quieten her. She's asleep now."

"Poor lass," said the stranger. "Crying out for her husband, I suppose?"

"Oh, she was sweet on Abel right enough," went on the footman. "For a married pair they were a regular brace of turtle doves. Which only seems to make it the more strange."

"Make what more strange?" asked the stranger.

"Why, that she didn't. Cry out for her husband, I mean. Instead, she gets the horrors. Keeps clutching her ladyship and pointing about the room. A nice room it is too. One of the best of our guest chambers. The squire's like that, sir. Always the best for Dymchurch folk in distress. Nothing the matter with the room except what she seemed to make of it. Kept screaming out that the devil was in the room, and what was very strange, and I had it from one of the chambermaids who was waiting in the passage, the devil she saw weren't like the one in church with a forked tail and pointed ears, but kept changing, first one and then t'other."

"One and t'other what—who?" asked the bewildered stranger.

"Well, now the devil would look like a wooden giant climbing over the sea-wall and then who do you think?"

The stranger shook his head. The footman looked back at Merry, who still stood beside the chest.

"Perhaps this man, with your permission sir, could tell you?"

"Was it—me?" demanded Merry fiercely.

"Aye, it was," returned the footman just as savagely. "'Keep him away from me. It's that Merry trying to get me,' and suchlike ravings. What's more, the quire heard it himself and so did Dr. Pepper, let alone her ladyship and the Miss Cobtrees. What you've been up to scaring the girl, I don't know, but my advice to you is to clear out before any of the household sees you here, or you'll find your name's mud because of it."

The stranger put down the weight and picked up a clothier's yard of brass, which he examined carefully. The dropping the point as though he were about to fence with it, he eyed the footman with displeasure.

"My young friend," he said quickly, "I have been absent from England for so long that belike the habits and manners of gentlemen's gentlemen have changed, but even in New England, where a democratic spirit is daily increasing, it is not yet the fashion for servants to argue, squabble or indeed expression opinions in the presence of superiors. As for you, Mister Merry, you have at least played my porter well, and for that must be rewarded."

He undid his coat with his left hand, for he still held the brass bar in his right, and his long sensitive fingers felt in one of the many pockets of the captain's belt. He took out a guinea piece and dropped it ringing on the table of weights and measures.

"And now, my very young friend of the scarlet livery, be good enough to carry that coin to the man Merry there."

"A guinea, sir?" ejaculated the astonished footman. "For a porter's fee? We can change this to-morrow at the bursar's office and he can call for a shilling."

"Give him the guinea, sir, and have done with it. The money is mine and the chest is heavy. I will give you the same if you can carry it up to my bedroom here later."

The footman eyed the stranger with a puzzled look, something between admiration and suspicion. Who was this man who came from Boston, referred to the squire as 'Tony', and boldly talked of his chest being carried to his room for a guinea? If he were a survivor of the wreck, then it was probable that the squire would offer him hospitality, and since he wore such a well-filled money belt and was obviously a gentleman of importance, it would be wise to show him attention in order to gain, perhaps, another guinea at his departure.

So he picked up the guinea and carrying it to Merry, handed it over with some disgust. Merry, however, showed no sign of moving.

"Well?" asked the footman. "Why don't you hop to it now that the gentleman's treated you handsome? You ain't wishing to stay the night, I suppose, for the only time you honour us is on a pallet bed in the cells. So get along with you."

"How can I get along when I'm lashed taut to the gentleman's chest?" asked Merry with a scowl.

"You have at least two free hands to unfasten the rope from the chest," suggested the stranger. "I shall not need the rope any more, I think, and I daresay you can find use for it, if only as a reminder that a knot at the wrist is better than a noose around the neck."

It took even the strong fingers of Merry some time to loosen the knot attached to one of the iron handles of the chest, for it had been tied by one who knew something of knots and cordage. But at last it was undone, and with a snort of disgust from the footman and quite a cheery "good night and keep Sunday in mind" from the stranger, Merry was shown the door and barred out.

He looked at the golden guinea. Under other circumstances he would have taken himself off to the 'Sea-Wall Tavern' and got drunk while feasting his eyes on Meg; but she was not there. But neither was Abel there. He had just heard that Abel Clouder was dead. That was news that compensated for a lot of disappointment. Of late, the puzzle of how to remove Abel without prejudice to himself had become an obsession. Well, his mind was free of that problem. Abel had most obligingly been heroic once too often. Meg was now a widow. What would she do? He cursed the fact that she had been taken to the Court House, and wondered how long she would remain under the direct protection of the Cobtrees, and an influence that boded no jot of good to his cause. The squire was no friend to him. At their last encounter he had told him plainly that if he (Merry) could not learn to behave himself, the Court would find means to rid the Marsh of such a rascal. Although born and bred in Dymchurch, Merry had no great love for it, for he hated his neighbours as cordially as they disliked him. But, on account of his strange passion for Meg, he had no intention of quitting it, and he knew that short of the gallows, even the squire would have a difficulty in shifting him, for he was a free-born Marsh-man. This fact could be got rid of by a vote of jurors, but Merry knew too much about them and he was confident that they would tolerate him rather than run the risk of his 'peaching' in public, which, of course, he was quite prepared to do.

As he clutched his guinea he was reminded again of what he had missed. The two money belts and the contents of that chest. With a little luck, he should by now have been a rich man, and then Meg would have been his for the taking. The exasperation at such a failure sent his blood racing in red rage, and he vowed that somehow or other he would find the means of settling scores with the mysterious stranger. Cudgelling his brain how best to accomplish this, a magnetic curiosity, common to criminals, compelled him to make his way towards the scene of the crime.

A glance showed him that so far the corpse had not been discovered, and it occurred to the murderer that it might be worth his while to go through the captain's pockets. No horror of what he had done assailed him. Only an increasing black hate that he had not accomplished more.

The white silk handkerchief placed there so reverently by the stranger had at least preserved the face from the greedy sea-gulls, who walked around it suspiciously, afraid of one of its flapping corners. As he appeared they flew off screaming.

Realising that he must not be discovered lest his story of discovering the corpse might not agree with whatever it pleased the stranger to tell the squire, he went through the pockets rapidly, becoming the richer by two crown pieces and three silver four-pennies, a brass whistle and a clasp knife, which he used to sever the rope around his wrist. It was then that he noticed particularly the flapping corner of the stranger's kerchief that had successfully kept the sea-birds at bay. It was worked. Now, although not claiming to be a scholar, Merry at least had this superiority over many—that he could write and read. A silk kerchief was, he knew, of sufficient value to safeguard, especially to a traveller who did not know his washer-woman. He ripped the kerchief quickly from the dead man's face and read by the light of the moon the owner's name. Yes—there it was. Beautifully worked in violet silk thread. A large 'D' and a small 'r'. That, he knew, stood short for 'doctor'. So, he thought, this arch-enemy is none but a bloody saw-bones. Then followed a capital 'S', a 'y' and an 'n'. 'Syn.' 'Doctor Syn.'...

And just as the murderer spelt out the name and committed it to his memory, the footman in the hall, turning back to the stranger, added: "Oh, and what name shall I say, sir?"

"Syn," replied the stranger.

They had been talking together for several minutes, the footman having pointed out that they should give the squire a little while to recover from what would be to him a great shock—the tragedy of the parson's death; and then the stranger remarking that the parson must have been a man of the highest courage, the footman delivered an appreciation of the dead man, which in spite of the pomposity of his office proved very moving in its simplicity. The stranger was impressed.

"He seems to have been the very man for this place," he remarked.

"Yes, sir," replied the footman, "and the more so as he followed one or two who, with all respect to their calling, were not what you might call entirely satisfactory. One was old and gouty and disliked the sea. Another was young and ambitious, so went to Canterbury Cathedral, and another was just nothing that none of us took to. He died of his own depressions. Then comes Parson Golden, young, strong and laughing glad to be here and hoping never to be called elsewhere, and naturally the squire felt settled like, having given the living to one everybody liked. That rascal Merry who carried your chest was the only one I ever heard with a bad opinion of our parson, but so he has of everyone, and the better the man, the worse opinion he holds of him. Well, let's hope we get a good man in his place—"

"Amen," answered the stranger.

"We're not likely to get a better. Now, why should he be taken? I call it strange."

"I agree with you," replied the stranger. "It is one of the most curious tricks of fate that I have encountered, and under these circumstances I think there is no one the squire would sooner see at this moment than myself. But before you announce me, I think we'll carry my chest into the inner hall, and then when I have spoken to the squire, you can help me up with it to my bed-chamber. For to tell you the truth, what you say of this fellow Merry, makes me anxious to move the chest from where he put it. There is a window there, shuttered, it is true, but such things have been opened before now. And having successfully preserved it through fire and water, not to mention wharf thieves and hostile Indians, it would be the height of folly to bring it to safety and lose it."

"Might be full of gold by the weight," exclaimed the footman.

"Well, yes, there is a little gold in it, I confess," replied the other, "but it is books mostly that give it such weight. Weighty volumes on the weightiest subjects. Valuable tomes, as you can imagine, since their weight makes them awkward travelling companions."

They carried the chest into the private hall which was built beyond the court room and legal offices, and set it down outside the squire's dining-room, and it was here that the footman had asked the stranger for his name.

His answer astonished him. At first he thought the gentleman was giving way to an oath, and resentfully he said, "Well, I must know the name in order to announce it, sir."

"Syn," repeated the other. "Not S-I-N but S-Y-N, and I rather imagine it will astonish the good squire more than it has you."

"I beg pardon, sir, but the name is unusual."

"I beg yours, but 'tis none of my fault," smiled the owner of the name. "All we can do for our names, whether those bequeathed by forefathers or given by godfathers, is to hold them in honour as well as we can, so that when we pass on the names we have done our best to make them the more honoured." He then repeated: "Doctor Syn."

CHAPTER VIII. Doctor Syn Returns

Around the great fireplace in the dining-room, the squire and three or four gentlemen of the Marsh were sitting, and had been gravely discussing the tragedy of the wreck. On a small table stood an enormous punch bowl full of steaming 'bishop', from which Sir Antony kept ladling generous allowances in order that his friends should recover from their exertions on the rope. The depression they had felt through dragging ashore the dead body of Abel Clouder was now increased at the news of the parson's death. They had hoped that since the parson's life-line had been cut by the plunging forward of the brig, that perhaps some miracle had saved him, and their hopes had been dashed by the news of the recovery of the body brought by the fisherman who stood respectfully drinking a glass of the warming punch, before being dismissed to the kitchens by a side door to get a bite of food.

When he had gone, the squire went on expatiating to his hearers concerning Parson Bolden on much the same lines as the footman had done already.

"So history repeats itself again," he said gloomily. "As you know, Sennacharib (for the doctor was of the party) my father was just as unfortunate in the bestowal of the living. Just as soon as he got a man he liked, he was preferred elsewhere, and it has been the same with me. I really did think that since poor Bolden liked the place that we were settled with him for life, and now his life has been sacrificed in this heroic, tragic fashion. If you are visiting patients Burmarsh way to-morrow, Sennacharib, you might ride to the vicar and ask him to conduct our service on Sunday morning, for there will be no time to get anyone else at such notice."

"I'll do that," replied the doctor. "You are quite right. We have been less fortunate than Burmarsh, certainly. Have you no one in mind that you would wish to appoint in poor Bolden's place?"

"I shall have to depend on the choice of the Archbishop, I suppose," said the squire. "There's only one man I can think of—and he is one I think of daily—to whom I would as gladly offer the living to, as I verily believe, he would gladly accept it, but whether he is alive or dead, God alone knows. Whoever I have could not satisfy me as he could. He had all the sterling qualities of Bolden that makes for popularity with the people here, and in addition a scholarship and a gentlemanly accomplishment that would be very acceptable to the gentry. He would now be my own age, but when I knew him he was even younger than Bolden. It was an understood thing that he should become vicar of Dymchurch, for he loved the place as we all loved him. He used to stay here during the Oxford vacations."

"I recollect the man surely," said Sennacharib Pepper. "He was an undergraduate with you at Queen's."

"That's the man," nodded the squire. "He was given a Fellowship, which he vowed he would hang on to till the living here was vacant."

"I talked with him often," said the doctor. "A brilliant young man."

"I should think he was," agreed the squire, turning to a glass-fronted bookcase at the side of the chimneypiece. "There's a book here somewhere—yes, here it is." He opened the glass door and drew out a leather-bound volume, which he opened at the title leaf. "A Solemn Discourse on Religious Assemblies and the Public Service of God, According to Apostolical Rule and Practice. What it all means, I can't explain. It's beyond me. But the book made such an impression upon Oxford that the University, despite his youth, conferred on him the title of Doctor of Divinity," added the squire.

"He was a fine horseman, too. He hunted here," added the doctor.

"And as magnificent with the sword as with the pistol," went on the squire. "He winged Bully Tappitt, the Squire of Iffley, in Magdalen Fields one morning. Fortunately, Tappitt was a notorious duellist, and we were able to prove that he had offered the affront, otherwise it would have gone hard with our friend. As it was, the affair made him the admiration of all, from the chancellor to the town's boys. What a supper we had at his acquittal. I remember so well that he was the only one who remained sober, though I swear he drank as much as any."

"What happened to him then?" asked another of the party.

"He went to America under distressing circumstances," said the squire. "But that was a few years later, after he had married the most beautiful girl you ever saw. Unfortunately, her beauty was but skin deep and she ran off with a blackguard, named Nicholas Tappitt, the nephew of the man he'd killed. I never heard what happened, for after telling me that he found life in England unendurable, he went abroad. I never heard from him again, but it is believed he was killed by Indians, for after much inquiry I learned that he went amongst them on a mission and has never been heard of since."

"What was his name?" asked Dr. Pepper.

The squire's eyes were filled with tears, and to hide his emotion he pointed to the fly-leaf of the volume and handed it to Dr. Pepper, who read the name of the author and nodded. "Of course, yes, I remember now. A good many years ago."

"What was his name?" asked one of the other gentlemen, as they both got up to look over the doctor's shoulders at the book.

The squire, after clearing his throat, said: "His name was—"

"Doctor Syn," announced the voice of the footman.

The squire spun around as though he had been shot, while the others looked up sharply from the name on the book, the name which they had just read, and which they had simultaneously heard announced.

In contrast to the bright livery of the footman who stood against the white panelling of the door which he held open, the sombre figure framed in the dark doorway seemed unreal. A shudder of superstition passed through the blood of everyone in the room as they gazed. No one moved, for concentration was riveted upon this tall, slim stranger. He had removed his heavy overcoat and thrown it over one shoulder, where it hung like a cloak. One long arm hung by his side and held a large, three-cornered hat, while the other was bent so that the white hand with its long, tapering and sensitive fingers rested lightly against his heart, as though he were about to bow in greeting. But he did not move, and until he did no one else had the power to. They looked at his face, pale and long, with fascinating lines cut into it, each one challenging the onlooker to respect his romance. A face carved by that master sculptor, Experience. The lofty brow, the queer but shapely head framed in a mass of raven hair. Eyes deep and piercing that seemed to each man in the room to be searching out the secrets of his soul. The nose was high with an aquiline droop. The cheeks hollow. Gaunt jaws that seemed to hold the whole decision of his destiny. A thin upper lip and fuller under one gave the mouth an expression of alert determination. The strong neck and full throat were shapely, exactly right to the carriage of such a living head. Though standing deathly still, every limb and feature conveyed quick and splendid movement momentarily arrested at the man's iron will. Showing no embarrassment at the silence, he showed no intent to break it, only allowing a gentle smile to twinkle in his eyes and gather at the corner of his mouth. It seemed almost as though he enjoyed their consternation and relished the thought that he was master of their sudden helplessness.

It was perhaps natural that the footman, being the only one not in a position to grasp the significance of the situation, should be the means of breaking the spell.

"The gentleman seems to be the only survivor of the wreck, sir."

"And consequently must ask your indulgence, gentlemen, for his appearance," added the stranger. "It has been a nasty night to swim in."

That he was still a stranger as far as the squire went was obvious, for all he did was to stare and mutter such phrases as: "No—no. Impossible. Asking too much. Incredible—"

"I hardly expected you to recognise me immediately," went on the stranger. "We have so many years to span, and a hard life alters most men. Although Time has dealt most generously with you, I have not yet quite captured from your features the gay and pleasant Tony that I knew. But I shall get him any moment, just as you will suddenly get me."

The jolly face of the squire was all puckered up into a vast frown, as he once more shook his head. He looked again and said: "Yes, it's more years than one imagines. But it would be too strange. Yet, wait, there is just something reminiscent. Of course, the room's confoundedly dark. Suppose we light another candle sconce."

"The room is light enough," protested the other gently, "at least to me who for many weeks have spent my nights reading the classics at a tallow dip, and if my poor features cannot convince you, I think the room can, for the last time I was here your father stood where you are standing, and with some nervousness I asked him to accept a book of mine. He stood there glancing at it, then sat me at that table and told me to inscribe it. Being my first inscription, I remember it. 'To Sir Charles Cobtree Baronet, of New Hall, Dymchurch, from his humble servant and admirer the Author.' He put it there, next to the Odyssey of Mr. Pope." He crossed to the bookcase. "Yes, there it is—the Odyssey—but where my book was—a space."

"We were but now admiring it, sir," said Sennacharib Pepper.

Mechanically the physician handed the volume to the squire, who passed it to the author. He, in his turn, looked at the title-page with a grim smile. "My faith, I must have been in a solemn mood when I penned this."

The squire could never decide afterwards whether it was the extra light supplied by one of the gentlemen carrying a candelabra from the further end of the room or some trick that the stranger had in handling a book, but it was certain that he suddenly brought his fist crashing down on the table.

"Gad," he thundered, "I see him now. Why, yes, I'd recognise him anywhere. The brow, the nose, the chin, the eyes. A little older. Those white streaks in the black locks are deceptive, but I can take my oath that this is my old friend, Christopher Syn, mercifully restored. Sennacharib, you are always boasting of your eyesight. Do you mean to say you cannot recognise him? You met him years ago."

"I think I recognised the gentleman before you, Sir Antony, but you gave me no chance of expressing my opinion," replied the physician.

"My dear friend," cried the squire, ignoring the physician and placing his hands upon Syn's shoulders. "My dear Doctor, welcome home." But feeling the wetness of his coat, he became immediately the bustling host. "My poor fellow, you're wet through. Positively soaked."

"I've been swimming, Tony," smiled Syn.

"Of course. Yes. And what's that? Your sea-chest? How the devil you managed to swim with that I don't know. And what are you standing there for, blockhead?" he asked the footman. "Run upstairs, tell them to light a fire in the best room available, to get busy with the warming pans, and ask her ladyship to step down here at once, and if the young ladies are in bed, tell her ladyship that they must be wakened immediately. Three daughters, my dear Doctor. Faith, to think you're not acquainted with my family, and you my best friend.

"Oh, and you (to the footman) come here. If my son is awake with the toothache or whatever it is that makes him cry at night, tell the nursemaid to bring him down. Yes, my dear Doctor, my dear friend, I have a son and heir, at last. Three strapping grown lasses, and a wee boy. It's true, ask Doctor Pepper about him, for he had the bringing of him into this world. Yes, that's right, Sennacharib, give the doctor some warm drink. Some smoking bishop for the Doctor of Divinity, eh? I suppose you're still a parson, eh, Doctor? Of course, once a parson always a parson unless you're unfrocked, which in your case is not likely. But you must be starved. I'll get food. Where's that blockhead gone? Here, where's anybody?" He tugged the long bell-rope vigorously. "And dry clothes you must have. A warm dressing-gown. Come to the fire and dry yourself."

Dr. Sennacharib Pepper, having shaken hands with his old acquaintance, suggested that he should relieve the ladies of their nursing and go up and visit the patient. "A poor girl who lost her husband in the rescue work of the wreck, Dr. Syn. I have administered a sleeping draught, but will go up and see that all is well. Someone must be with her."

On his leaving the other two gentlemen called for their horses, in order to leave the squire with his new-found old friend.

In a few minutes the whole house appeared to be alive with people hurrying this way and that on various errands, but on tiptoe out of respect for the invalid, and by the time Dr. Syn had been taken with his chest to a comfortable bedroom, had been arrayed in dry shirt and breeches of the squire's and wrapped in a red quilted dressing-gown, had been presented to the Cobtree family, especially to Charlotte, who was his godchild, and whom he remembered as a baby, and had insisted that the new baby should not be awakened, a magnificent cold supper was awaiting him in the dining-room, where he did full justice to a game pie and a bottle of claret.

Dr. Syn had told the squire that he had seen the body of the captain lying on the sea-wall, and as he was eating, news was brought that it had been carried with other bodies they had recovered to Sycamore Barn. Maintaining that his own story could wait, Dr. Syn wanted to know all the news of the village, merely satisfying their curiosity about his own doings by telling them he had been in the wildest parts of America preaching the gospel to the Indians.

"You must not expect the doctor to tell you all his adventures at one sitting," the squire said to his daughters. "I warrant that if he talks hard every evening, he will not be able to tell you half this side of Christmas."

Dr. Syn chuckled to himself and thought this more than likely, but aloud he said: "I have had adventures—yes, for I suppose to you it is an adventure to hear first-hand stories of the Indians. But you must not expect too much. You must remember that I was a preacher, not a gentleman adventurer."

"And none of your experiences could be stranger than the shipwreck," went on the squire. "A very strange thing. Here we were, talking of you, and in you walk. And there you were, wondering when the living of Dymchurch would be vacant, and the living vicar swimming out to rescue you is killed."

They all nodded gravely, and Dr. Syn said: "Yes, it seems like fate."

"Seems? It is," exclaimed the squire. "It seems as if poor Bolden had to go. Of course, we should have found some way out of the difficulty, but not easily. Bolden was popular. Anyone but you following him here would have been unfairly dealt by in comparison."

"He was obviously a very gallant fellow," said Dr. Syn. "Young?"

"Too young really; as least, I found him so," replied the squire. "These young ladies will probably not agree. He took his work seriously, but not with a long face. No, he was merry enough, laughed a good deal, but never drank. Now I'm of an age when I like a man to crack a bottle with me. Not that he was a prig. Far from it. He had no objection to others drinking, and he had something about him that made you respect even his crazy notions. A simple, good, jolly young man. He lived here, you know. Couldn't cope with the vicarage, though I furnished it for him. And you know it's when you live under the same roof with a man that you learn the worst about him. But there was nothing to find out about him. I'd have seen any other young parson a good deal further before letting him live here with these young girls about. They might have put ideas into his head, whereas with Bolden, good-looking as he was, why the three of them just mothered him, didn't you, young ladies?"

Charlotte nodded. She was the eldest, a beautiful blonde of nineteen. She wondered just how much she was going to miss the young parson, whom she had been content to mother because no other treatment had been possible, because it never entered the parson's head that it might be.

Maria, of seventeen, fair like her sister, and Cicely of fifteen, somewhat darker, had not quite realised the tragedy of the evening. It did not occur to them that the young parson had gone for ever. They knew something had happened, but her ladyship had told Charlotte not to tell them till the morning, and at present they were both thrilled with this strange man that had come up from the sea.

Charlotte, though experiencing a numbed feeling of bereavement which she hardly tried to understand, felt also a strange thrill in the presence of this newcomer. The pale, tragic face, the sad smile that was so ingratiating. "Yes," thought Charlotte, 'here is a man, a sad lonely man, who is unselfish enough to appear jolly, but a man of whom any woman in the world would feel proud."

Dr. Syn surprised the look that such thoughts wrote upon her guileless face, and he read an interest there, an admiration innocent enough, but yet a warning to him of something which this girl, the daughter of his friend and patron would never know, and it was this look that influenced him that very night to take a certain course. But this was after the household had settled down to quiet after the excitement of the storm. The physician had left his patient in Lady Cobtree's care, who had arranged to share the watches with Charlotte and the old housekeeper. After another bottle of port between the three of them, Pepper at length went home and the squire carried Dr. Syn's candles into his room.

"It's strange, too," said the squire, "that the servants got ready his room. I didn't mean to tell you, but I see you would have found it out."

The squire pointed to a wig and gown that hung behind the door. "He brought home the wig to have it dressed, I suppose, for he would only wear it in the church, and there only as a badge of his office. But why did he bring the Geneva gown? He always put that on just before preaching."

"He tore it on the chancel rail last Sunday, Papa. I noticed it and told him to bring it back for me to mend."

They turned and saw Charlotte standing in the doorway with a black coat over her arm.

"And what are you doing here, miss?" asked her father.

"I have been mending the sleeve of Dr. Syn's coat. I noticed it was badly torn when they were drying it, so I thought I had better do it at once. You will find the rest of your clothes hanging up. They are dry."

"That's very kind of you," said the doctor, taking the coat and examining the damage. "Now that is very beautifully done, Miss Charlotte. I have had to learn to work with a needle myself out of necessity, so I know when I see a thing done better."

"So you are starting in already to mother the doctor, are you, miss?" laughed the squire.

This had been a daily joke with the squire over the young parson, and it had never affected Charlotte. So that she was the more puzzled and perhaps annoyed that the same old joke with reference to Dr. Syn should make her blush. To hide this, she walked away to hang up the coat which Dr. Syn had put down on a chair.

"It seems that someone must mother the poor gentleman," she laughed, "for he very cleverly thinks of a way to save his sea-chest there, and then forgets to unpack it. I suppose you know, Doctor, that your clothes in there are most likely to be wringing wet."

The doctor shook his head. "I suppose my nice new young mother will be very disgusted to hear that my sea-chest is full of old books. My clothes, other than I swam ashore in, I am afraid were all destroyed in the fire, for they were hanging in my cabin. But I have a few guineas that will take me to the tailors."

"But your precious books?" she asked.

"All wrapped round in oilskin, my dear," he chuckled. Besides, I can assure you that this is a sea-chest worthy of the name. I have known it dropped into a river, and when rescued the contents were bone dry."

"What things you have seen," whispered Charlotte with awe.

"Well, yes, but there's not much to see in an old chest being fished out of the river. I'll perhaps tell you a real story one day. An exciting one."

"Do," she answered. "Were there crocodiles in the river?"

"And now off to bed," commanded the squire. "If you are not sitting with the invalid, you ought to be sleeping."

"Good night, Tony's daughter," said Dr. Syn, bowing over her hand. Then he straightened himself and laying both hands gently on her firm young shoulders, he smiled, and kissed her on the cheek, saying: "Good night, little mother."

Once more Charlotte found herself blushing, so with a hurried curtsey she left the room.

"You have nice children, Tony," remarked Dr. Syn.

"Wait till you see young Dennis in the morning," replied the squire, glowing with pride. "In the meanwhile, I think here is all you require save to be left alone to sleep. I ordered a cool jug of small beer for you. It is refreshing if one should wake, though I doubt not you'll sleep well enough." He opened a door in the oak panelling. "This is the powder closet. Why, the blockhead put the beer there. The worst spot for a beverage. Powder dust as a 'head'. Not that much powder has been scattered here since poor Bolden had this room. He thought it an affectation if he thought of it at all. Once he reproved my Charlotte—the only time, I think. He found her dressing his clerical wig. It's a good wig, she says, though you'd never notice it. Poor Bolden had no vanities, except perhaps in his swimming. See, I'll put the jug here beside the bed. Poor Bolden. It seems the text has been reversed, Doctor, 'The Lord as taken away, but the Lord gives'. Much as I regret the passing of poor Bolden, and a splendid passing it was, I thank God for your happy restoration, Doctor." And with a few more fervent good nights and God bless you's, the squire went to the door.

Before closing it, he pointed to another door. "That, by the way, leads into the next room, but it is locked and bolted. However, should the logs jump out of your fireplace and set fire to the room, you can get out through this door or through the powder chest. To-morrow we'll inspect the vicarage and you can see what you want before you settle in. I'll write to the Archbishop. Of course, you are welcome to live here if you would, but I think you should keep the vicarage up for your own dignity. Besides, as you say, you want your own library. Well, we'll talk of it more to-morrow—good night."

"God bless you," replied Dr. Syn, and after listening to the retreating footsteps he tiptoed across the room and very quietly locked and bolted the door.

The squire went off to his room and did not notice that the outer door of Syn's powder closet was wide open, and as for the doctor, he never gave it a thought, but it was the means of giving food for thought to Charlotte Cobtree for a long time to come.

CHAPTER IX. Doctor Syn takes Leave of Himself and Charlotte Sees
a Ghost

Charlotte had taken over her mother's watch at Meg's bedside, pleading that she felt strangely awake and could not sleep if she tried, so on the understanding that she would wake Mrs. Lovell, the housekeeper, in two hours' time, she had been allowed her wish.

Outwardly she busied herself with feeding the fire and creeping to the bedside whenever the poor girl stirred in her sleep, but all the time her inward thoughts were far busier, and it was the new guest that filled them. That his vivid personality thrilled her was not surprising, for as she told herself, this old friend of her father's was very different from gentlemen of the district. He was a romantic figure. He had lived a romantic life. But Charlotte had always prided herself upon her good sense, and she told herself it was folly to fall in love with a man so much older than herself at first sight. He was middle-aged, and from his conversation with her father, she knew that he had come to Dymchurch with a view of settling down. This indicated to her youthful mind that the man had wilfully put the best years of his life behind him. Dymchurch was a good living as livings went and her father, she knew, was a good patron, none better, but surely it was strange that this forceful stranger should be content to forego all ambition of making a stir in his profession. He was a Doctor of Oxford University. He had a fascinating voice, full of colour and distinction. When she had served him at supper, the red quilted dressing-gown, which she always thought looked rather ridiculous when the squire wore it, became an imposing costume. He lent it an elegance that was somehow royal. Such a man could get anywhere in any profession, and she had never seen a parson, even amongst the dignitaries of Canterbury, who could compare at all favourably with this dashing gentleman. Why, then, did he want to bury himself in Romney Marsh? Why did she think of him with such a swift beating of her heart? Why had she blushed when he had praised her needlework? And why had she blushed when he kissed her? Why did this extraordinary joy that she felt in his arrival override the sadness for the young parson's death and Meg Clouder's tragedy? Why could she think of no one else but this new inmate of the parson's room? Had he thought of her at all? If only he were thinking of her now.

And he was, but not quite in the way she wished.

He thought first of all about her advice concerning the contents of his chest. She was right. Everything should be taken out and dried. He was alone, and could not be disturbed till morning, and a splendid wood fire burned in the grate. He slipped the corded key over his head and fitted it into the lock. It turned easily and he blessed the locksmith whose work had not been damaged by salt water. He pulled the chest towards the fire and raised the iron lid. Inside was a second chest of teak reinforced with brass, and the inner one did not fit to the iron sides but was held in place by iron springs that gripped it tightly, and the small space between iron and wood was packed tightly with oakum, so that should any damp get through the outer iron case this caulking would absorb it before reaching the wood. A second lock on the top of this lid was unfastened by the same key and two doors could be lifted and opened out sideways. The interior of this second chest was packed tightly with various compartments, and in all, the packing was worthy of the chest. Carefully covered with a velvet pad and lying taut in a grooved tray was a pair of silver-hilted long swords with magnificent scabbards and carriages. In another corner, a case of pistols. Of the books he had spoken of so much there were but a few, and all bound round with oilskin to preserve their bindings. A Bible. The plays of Shakespeare. A volume on navigation. The works of Don Quevedo in Spanish. A book of Tillotson's sermons, and a Homer. All these he carefully spread out upon the hearth-rug to dry, though there appeared no sort of dampness on any. A brass telescope and a boxed sextant had their own departments, and when all these had been removed a tray for clothes, neatly strapped in place. This he propped against a chair close to the fire. The lowest department was tightly packed with bundles and bags. Dr. Syn's sensitive fingers tapped them one by one, as though recalling their contents to mind. Lifting out one of the bags in order to get the end of another package clear, a pleasant chink of coin came to his ears. The package was heavy and he weighed it lovingly in his hands, but he did not remove the piece of red flannel that was wrapped round it. In shape, it resembled a long brick, but was vastly heavier. He turned it over, patting the flannel and satisfied that it was bone-dry placed it back again.

Dr. Syn stood up and surveyed his property. It represented all his worldly goods, but having reminded himself of the contents, and being assured that nothing was missing, his face bore a look of infinite satisfaction. His next employment was to examine the Geneva gown of his predecessor. Slipping off the quilted dressing-gown he put the gown over his head. Although quite full in the body, it was too short in the arms and legs, but he thought that for a village pulpit this would not greatly matter. By the open door of the powder closet there stood a tall pier glass. Holding the lighted candle, he surveyed himself, and appeared dissatisfied. Not with himself—for Dr. Syn had his vanities, though in company taking pains to hide them—but in the general effect towards which he was working. There is no colour that can compare with black or white for a striking effect, especially contrasted with those of brilliance. Amid the garish court of King Claudius, the inky cloak and suit of solemn black rivets all eyes upon the solitary Hamlet. So thought Dr. Syn as he surveyed his pale face and raven locks that fell upon the shoulders of the Geneva gown. "My appearance like this in the Dymchurch pulpit will be too striking. People will be curious about me and talk, and if I preach as I know I can, the authorities will be preferring me to a pulpit of more importance. No, it won't do, my dear friend."

Thus he addressed himself to his reflection. True, a doctor of Oxford can reasonably be expected to cut a figure above the ordinary, but as he told himself in the glass: "In my case, it is dangerous!" The thought of his degree gave him an idea, and he went to the tray of clothes that had been warming by the fire. He unpacked his scarlet hood which had accompanied him on all his travels, put it on, surveyed it critically and shook his head. "It's the hair. It suits the face too well. It gives a romantic environment to the owner." He criticised his reflection as though it were a second party. "Tony's girl, Charlotte, gave me the warning of it, for the sweet girl had not the skill to disguise her thoughts, and it won't do. There must be no romance. Nothing of note beyond the ordinary. My degree will raise me dangerously enough above my fellow vicars, therefore I must tone myself down to keep the balance. If I am to lie low here, I must not be too conspicuous. I must be a leaf lying in a forest of leaves, a stone upon a stony beach. Above all, there must be no woman to play Delilah to my Samson in the time to come. My secrets are too dangerous."

He picked up the dead parson's wig and put it on his head. He looked once more in the mirror. The incongruity of the raven locks escaping from below the rigid white line of the formal wig, made him smile. He took a pull at the jug of small beer, and smiled again. From the chest he took his toilet case, and with a pair of scissors he cut away the rebellious hair that hung beneath the wig. He threw the cut hair into the fire, and as it fizzled, he found his dark-tinted spectacles that he had used in the tropics and pushed them on his nose. Once more he regarded himself in the mirror and was so elated by what he saw that he took a deep pull at his silver brandy flask. He then discarded the wig, the hood and the gown and began to dress himself in a fine suit of scarlet velvet trimmed with silver braid. The coat, which was full-skirted in the fashion that had already passed out in England, he bound round the waist with a silver sash into which he thrust his brace of pistols. Before fastening one of the swords to the carriage, he pulled on a long and elegant pair of thigh boots, and then attached the sword. Into his hat he clipped a fine ostrich feather, and then picking up the silver flask with one hand and fingering the hilt of his sword, he yet again approached the pier glass and favoured his magnificent reflection with a bow. Just then the stable clock struck three.

"Captain Clegg," he whispered, "I regret to inform you that we have reached in safety the parting of the ways. If I do not discontinue your company, it is as like as not that I should accompany you to Execution Dock, and I should be desolate to see you in such straits. I have to thank you for many thrilling years of companionship. Your long sword and your skill with it, your pistols and your skill with them, your quick wit and your gallantry have countless times saved not only my poor life but the lives of many a stout friend. Your successor, who will now take command, is in no ways comparable to yourself, though more suitable for the work at hand. I commit you with honour to lie in the chest which you have filled for me, and after your successor has turned me into a humdrum parson, I'll take my oath that there will come times when I shall itch for your gay life. By reason of the many services you have done for me, and for the fact that the name of Captain Clegg is known and trembled at over the seven seas, I rest your humble servant. Let me in parting present you to your successor, Dr. Syn—Christopher Syn, D.D., of Oxford University and vicar of Dymchurch-under-the-Wall, in the County of Kent."

Drawing his sword, he picked up the gown and wig upon the point and made it bob up and down before the mirror.

The same three strokes of the stable clock reminded Charlotte of her promise to her mother, so after seeing that Meg was still under the influence of Sennacharib Pepper's sleeping draught, she gently opened the door and crept along the gallery to awaken Mrs. Lovell, the housekeeper. There was no need for her to carry a light, as the moon, riding now in a clear sky, shone brightly through the landing window. Her mind, so running on the guest who had been cast up by the sea, it was only natural that she should look across to the door of the room she knew he was occupying. It was shut, of course, but she saw suddenly that the door of his powder closet was open. After his fearful experience of the wreck, she felt it would be too cruel if he were kept awake by a creaking door, so very quietly she crossed the landing to close it. Small as this service was, she found so much pleasure in doing it that her heart was beating so loud that she was afraid someone might hear it.

It was not until she reached the door that her heart-beats stopped in sheer terror. She had not even the power to speak or cry out, for there, standing in a most unearthly light, she saw a vision of her father's guest, the man who had so disturbed her heart. Overcoming her terror with all her strength, she forced herself to look at him more intently.

There he stood looking at her, yet not seeming to notice her. She had heard tales of ghostly visitants that looked through one and there was nothing real about this figure. It certainly resembled the man she so admired in feature, but the clothes were those of a swaggering gallant. True, she could not see too plainly, for in front of him there flickered a veil of light, a sheen that shimmered so that the face seemed to be hovering in airy darkness beyond the moving radiance. But why should a living man appear to her? It was then that she saw the dead one. A second form, vaguer than his, seemed to be dancing beside him, and she recognised the white wig and shiny-black silk preaching gown of the dead parson.

Then in sheer panic Charlotte fled along the gallery.

How she reached the housekeeper's room without falling she didn't know, but when she did she found to her infinite relief that Mrs. Lovell had her candle lighted and had just been getting ready to relieve her.

"But whatever ails you, Miss Charlotte? Did you fall asleep and dream? It was the stable clock that woke me. I wondered why you did not come at once."

"I've seen the dead parson," she whispered in terror. "He was in the powder closet of his old room."

"Nonsense, child," replied the old lady. "I never hold with ghosts and such things." But her terrified looks belied her, though she tried to show a brave face before her young mistress.

"I told her ladyship it was not right for you to sit up after such a night of tragedy," she whispered. "Come, I'll take you back to your room and you'll soon be asleep. We don't want another invalid to look after. Was it in the powder closet that you thought you saw him?"

"You don't think he's returned to harm father's guest, do you?" asked Charlotte.

"What, Parson Bolden do harm? Alive or dead, he could do nothing but good. It would cheer me to see him again alive, my dear." She did not add that she had no such desire to see his ghost.

Together they sallied out, clutching one another at every sound and encouraging one another with whispers. Mrs. Lovell held a candle high above her head and walked slowly, so that if they caught a glimpse of the distant ghost they could scuttle back to safety.

They reached the landing and paused, for they were now within sight of the door.

"The door was open, you said, dear?" whispered the old lady.

"I went to shut it, yes, and then I saw him." Somehow she could not bring herself to speak of the other that she had seen.

"Then you were dreaming, child," said Mrs. Lovell, mightily relieved. "For, look, the outer door of the powder closet is shut."

Charlotte could not believe her eyes till Mrs. Lovell tried the door softly and found that it would not yield.

"It's locked from the inside, my dear. You go and dream better dreams in bed, Miss Charlotte."

And when Mrs. Lovell left her in her room, Charlotte began to wonder whether she had seen anything or no.

As Dr. Syn drained his flask in a parting salute to his resplendent reflection, he heard a noise which he took to be the rustling of ivy against the window. He heard it again. It was very faint, but since his sea-chest was open, he had no wish to be surprised. Once more he heard it, but this time it seemed to be dying away into the distance. This time, however, he located it as coming from the powder closet. He could see the half-opened door in the pier glass, but beyond it was pitch dark. He felt a draught towards the door and remembered the squire had told him that there was a way through to the landing. Was it possible that someone had entered the powder closet? Was it possible that someone was still there? What he had thought to be the stirring of the ivy might well have been the rustling of a silk petticoat. He knew that the ladies were keeping vigil beside the bereaved young widow. For some purpose, one of them might have crept to his door.

As it would never do to be caught in his present finery, he quickly divested himself of hat, pistols, sash and coat. Then laying his sword upon the bed, he slipped into the quilted dressing robe, and picking up a candle tiptoed into the powder closet. The door leading to the landing was wide open. There was no one in the powder closet, and all was still and quiet on the landing and galleries when he looked out. But just as he was about to close the door, his eye caught something white upon the carpet near the wall. He saw it was a small lace handkerchief and picked it up. The faint odour of roses which it held, rolled back the years with that subtle swiftness that only scent possesses, and he felt young again, romantic and in love. All very ridiculous, as he knew, for between those far-off days which the perfumed piece of lace brought back, were all the properties of Tragedy—storm, tempest, villainy, death, destruction and a broken heart turned vindictive. No, those years rose up with the smell of powder, rum and blood forbidding romance with their stench.

Yet, being his first night in England since so long, Dr. Syn, with the same whimsicality that he had betrayed over his sea-chest, allowed himself not to do the sensible thing, which was to drop the little lace handkerchief where he found it. Instead, he held it to his lips, and when he heard footsteps and whisperings approaching round the gallery he took it with him, when he quietly shut the door and locked it.

He heard them approach the door. He was the other side of it when Mrs. Lovell tried it, and he wondered what dreams they had been when she said: "You go and dream better dreams in bed, Miss Charlotte."

He went back to the bedroom and began stowing all his property back into the chest. The throwing a towel around his shoulders, he sat in front of the dressing-table and cut his hair short. Having done this to the best of his ability in the candle-light, and promising himself to better it in the morning, he made up the fire, consigned a handful of black locks to the flames, put out the candle, and then after opening the casement wide, so that he could hear the sea grinding upon the beach, a soothing lullaby to one who had spent so much of his life upon it, he clad himself, by the light of the fire, in a nightcap and gown of the squire's providing, and took himself and the lace handkerchief to the sanctuary of the great four-poster bed, where, holding the kerchief close to his face in the hope that its gentle fragrance might breathe into his sleep sweet dreams of long-forgotten innocence, and thanking God for having preserved him through so many dangers and for bringing him home again, he heard the stable clock strike four and fell asleep.

CHAPTER X. Doctor Syn Makes Preparations

The next thing he knew was the same clock striking eight. Through the open casement he saw sea-gulls wheeling in a sky that, ashamed of its ill vapours the night before, was bright, clear and crisp.

Dr. Syn swung himself out of bed and crossed eagerly to the window. The first view of English countryside is always a joy to those who have been long abroad, and everything he saw was a joy to him. Regardless of his bobbing nightcap and white gown, he hung out over the sill to get a wider view. There across the red roofs of the farm and Little Manor rose the sharp grass bank of the sea-wall upon which a party of men were at work repairing the damages of the storm. Observing the eagerness with which they toiled, Dr. Syn repeated to himself the slogan of the Marsh, "Serve God, honour the King, but first maintain the Wall," and he added this comment: "Good men will serve God, loyal men will honour the King, but there's nothing that every man fights harder for than his own personal safety," and looking first this way and then that and delighting in all he saw, he told himself that so long as the Wall was maintained, a fairer spot than little Dymchurch-under-the-Wall could not be found on the coast of England.

A sharp, frightened scream immediately beneath him interrupted his meditations. A buxom dairy wench who had no doubt been tempted to look up from her task of pail-carrying in order to watch the screaming sea-gulls, circling the lofty rookery, who with their shrill sea voices seemed to be asking their sedater fellows, the rooks, how they had fared in the last night night's storm.

Expecting, therefore, to see sea-gulls and rooks arguing the point overhead, she was greatly alarmed to see the apparition of a strange, queer-looking man, dressed only in nightcap and shirt, looking round the corner of his window-sill like Mr. Punch awakened by the beadle in the puppet show. As their eyes met she dumped down the pails on the uneven ground with such a bump that rivers of pure milk ran here and there amongst the gravel. The yoke she threw from her shoulders backwards, tripped over it, saved herself with both hands and after crawling clear of the wreckage on all fours, picked herself up and fled in confusion back towards the farm.

Her exhibition was so entirely comical that Dr. Syn, feeling in the best of spirits, burst out laughing, when a door beneath him opened and the charming vision of Charlotte appeared, dressed in a green velvet riding habit trimmed with fur. It was her habit to go riding every morning with the squire. She had witnessed the disaster of the milk pails and had stepped out on the path to see the cause of it, when looking up at the sound of his laughter she saw the doctor in his very ludicrous costume.

Although she could not help laughing at the ridiculous situation, she pretended to be very stern with her father's guest.

"You'll catch your death of cold," she called. "After your wetting last night to be hanging out of an open window in nothing but a shirt. Why, you want looking after."

"Mothering, eh?" chuckled Dr. Syn.

"Quickly now," she went on. "Let me see you put on the dressing-gown we gave you, and then I'll have some hot chocolate sent up for you. I'm waiting."

Hastening to obey this order, he reappeared at the window in the added splendour of the quilted dressing-gown.

"That's better," she laughed. "Did you sleep well?"

"Very well. Did you?"

"Not very. I was anxious about our invalid, I suppose. She seems a little better this morning, but is still dazed."

"Poor girl," sighed Dr. Syn.

"Yes, it's dreadful for her, isn't it? Her husband was such a splendid young man. We were all devoted to him."

"By the way, Miss Charlotte," said the doctor, "I think it is my turn to be 'fatherly.' If you spent a poor night, why are you dressed and about so early?"

"I'm riding with my father at eleven, but I thought a gallop before breakfast would wake me up. Breakfast is ordered late to-day, and you are supposed to be sleeping still. Half-past nine breakfast; but it's a moveable feast, and you can come down when you like. Would you care for some hot chocolate now or later?"

"Now, please."

"I'll send Robert—he's the footman who opened the door to you last night. Oh, and if you would like him to shave you, you needn't worry. Father says he has not met a barber to equal him in London."

"Ah, then I will put my life into his hands and save myself the bother of cutting my own throat," he laughed.

She laughed too, but not at his facetious remark, but at her own exclamation of: "So you've got it all the time, and I've set all the servants looking for it. You see, it's not the value of the thing, though it is quite good, but it was given me with five others by my godmother, Lady Pembury; and as Lympne Castle is near enough for a surprise visit any day, I have to be careful, as she's one of those creatures who always wants to see how her presents are getting on. She asked to see my silver-backed hair-brushes the other day, and carried one away with her to have a dent removed. I suppose I dropped it in your room when I brought your coat."

"What?" asked Dr. Syn.

"Why, my lace handkerchief that you are holding so tightly," she answered, pointing up to his right hand.

Up to that moment Dr. Syn had been unaware that he had been doing any such thing. He now realised that he must have clutched it all night and risen with it still in his hand, but he had no intention of confessing this to the charming young lady below.

"If you drop it down, I'll catch it," she said.

"Always allowing that I am willing to part with it," he replied.

"Oh, but think of my godmother. She can be a positive dragoon when she's crossed. And think of me," she pleaded, holding out her hands.

"If I were twenty, nay, ten years younger, Miss Charlotte, I should think of nobody when it came to giving up this kerchief. But what should an old parson do with such vanities? I should have the parish crying 'shame.' Although, were I younger, as I say, I should find it hard to refuse you anything. Catch."

He dropped the kerchief and she caught it, giving him a curtesy of thanks, which he returned with a bob of his nightcapped head which, had the dairy-maid been witness of, would have heightened his resemblance to Mr. Punch.

The dairy-maid, who was spying round the wall that protected the cow-sheds, gained confidence when she saw that Miss Cobtree was joking with the strange gentleman, and since he was now robed more respectably than when she had first seen him, she advanced from her ambush into the garden in order to deal with the upset milk-pails.

Charlotte went in to send up the chocolate, and Dr. Syn, closing the window, went to unlock the door to admit Mrs. Lovell, who had taken it upon herself to bring material for the building of a jolly fire. Dr. Syn, with his bed-curtains half-drawn, sat upon the pillows with his knees drawn up and chattered to her, not forgetting to ask the latest news of the poor widow, knowing that the pleasant-looking old housekeeper was one of the voluntary nurses.

"But what amazes me, sir," she went on, after giving a lengthy mixed description concerning medicines, cordials, the popularity of Abel Clouder and Meg's love for him, "and it takes a deal to amaze an old body like me who, with all my faults, have learned at least a sympathetic understanding of most people, through being taught by the many who have lavished kindness on me, but now that poor Meg is recovered physically if not mentally, she does not distress herself so much over poor Abel, which one would have expected and respected. But no, sir, not a bit of it—she expends all her energy which she needs to build herself up with, on fear. It's what the doctor calls 'obsession." And her obsession is really very strange."

"How strange?" asked the doctor.

"Why, there's a worthless, God-cursed—and no wonder—drunken ne'er-do-well in this otherwise happy village called Merry. Instead of folk giving him the courtesy title of Mister, which a man of his years and strength might with reason expect, he's called 'Wretched' Merry, 'Savage' Merry, 'Cruel' Merry, 'that dirty dog' Merry, 'that double-faced' Merry, 'that fit of the miserables'—"

"In fact, everything opposite to what you and I would care to be called, eh?" interrupted Dr. Syn.

"Exactly, sir, and I thank you for stopping me, for when that man gets talked of, I can never stop giving my opinion of him."

"Which is not good, eh?"

"No more than yours would be, sir, if you knew the man," declared the housekeeper.

"He carried my sea-chest for me last night, and I had a long talk with him," explained the doctor. "He is certainly a forbidding man, but he has his qualities."

"I should like to learn one, sir," snorted the old lady.

"Well, he is strong-limbed for one thing. If you try the weight of my sea-chest, you will be convinced of that. I always prefer a strong bad man to a weak one."

"Oh, he's strong enough," allowed the housekeeper. "He could take a throat in each hand and throttle them with ease, and has done so before now, I'll be bound. There's ugly rumours about that man, sir, I can tell you."

"But what has he got to do with poor Meg Clouder?" he asked.

"Ah," exclaimed the housekeeper. "That's just it. What? For with a pretty, sweet-natured, respectably-married girl as she was, I say he should have had nothing to do with her. And yet, if he has not been near frightening her to death why, instead of crying out for her husband, which would be natural, does she only go on imploring us to keep Merry away from her. It must have been some black suggestion, and God forbid it's no more, that can so prey on the girl's mind in the midst of what should be collapse from natural grief."

"A merciful dispensation of Providence, perhaps, Mrs. Lovell," suggested Dr. Syn. "May it not be a case where one evil drives another out. The fear of one man overrides the love for another, and the latter will never be death-blow that the former might have been. We have that to be thankful for."

"You mean that if we can ease her of her fear that by then she will be reconciled to the loss which as yet she puts in a second place? Is that it, sir?"

To Dr. Syn's nodding nightcap she added: "But shall we ease her of it? If that vicious dog Merry knows the hold he has on her, he'll grip the tighter. Aye, sir, till his teeth meet in the poor girl's heart. I tell you he has only to be warned off Meg to make him torment her the worse."

The conversation was interrupted by the entry of Robert with the promised hot chocolate. Upon the tray was a single rose with pinky-white petals. Dr. Syn picked it up gently, or as it seemed to the others, gingerly, as though her were afraid of breaking it. He laid it on the palm of his hand, and slowly raising it to his face sniffed at it audibly. Meanwhile, Robert was balancing the tray securely upon the rich, if faded, damask covering of the bedclothes.

"Very kind of you, Robert," said Dr. Syn.

"The gift of the rose is not mine, sir," answered the stately young footman, who was honest enough not to accept thanks that were not his due.

"I meant for preparing this excellent chocolate," explained the doctor.

But yet again Robert insisted on being strictly honest. "I fear, sir, that I merely had the honour of carrying up the tray. The chocolate was prepared by Miss Charlotte herself, sir, and there is no better hand at making it, sir, believe me. The rose was also her idea, sir. Seeing that your reverence has been absent so long from England, she thought that you should be welcomed by what she was pleased to call 'the heraldic flower of the realm.' There was quite a altercation (Robert's tongue dwelt lovingly upon the word, which he felt could not fail to win the respect due to it from the housekeeper) a pleasant enough one, sir, and yet altercation it was, between the young ladies. Miss Maria and Miss Cicely brought forward very spirited objections when they saw to what use the pruning knife was to be put. You see, sir, there has been a good deal of innocent gambling in connection with that rose, not only below stairs, but amongst the family itself. You see, sir, it has for some time now been the last bloom in the arbour, and some were of the opinion that it would last the month out. It certainly survived last night's storm in a miraculous manner."

"My good Robert," put in the housekeeper, "if the arbour is not sheltered, what is?"

"And if that wasn't a big storm, what is?" retorted Robert, looking at the housekeeper as though surprised at her daring to venture an opinion in a gentleman's bedroom.

He turned again to the doctor, thoroughly satisfied that he had silenced Mrs. Lovell for good and all. "So you see, sir, there was every excuse for the younger young ladies' objection, though I must say that when Miss Charlotte said that since the frost had come after the storm it was better for the rose to die in the warm house than in the cold arbour, and added that she knew for a fact that there was nothing your reverence was so partial to as the perfume of roses, both younger and youngest young ladies give way to the eldest young lady."

"Very kind," said Dr. Syn. "I am sure Mrs. Lovell will bear me out that there is no more beautiful trait in a young lady being kind and considerate to the old. If it were possible to feel envy towards my dear friend the squire it would take the form of coveting such a daughter as Miss Charlotte. I can imagine no greater happiness than to be the proud father of such a beautiful young lady."

"Amen," said Mrs. Lovell, though it hardly applied in her case.

"Amen," repeated Robert, not to be behindhand, though he was far too young for such fatherly ambitions.

"And now that Mrs. Lovell has coaxed up such a cheerful fire, the sooner I am dressing by it the better. I hear, Robert, that you are an expert with the razor."

"Before taking service with the squire, your reverence, I was apprenticed to a barber in London, knowing that such accomplishments are necessary to gentlemen's gentlemen. I paid a good deal of attention to wig dressing too, for the same reason. I even cultivated acquaintance with a French perruquier, from whom, I am bound to admit, I learned a great deal."

"Then bring razors, scissors, soaps, powders and all the rest of the paraphernalia of barbering and prinking, and do your best to make an old gentleman look respectable."

Robert smiled as though this were a good joke and took his leave. Mrs. Lovell also got up to go.

"I have had a good deal of experience, Mrs. Lovell, one way and another with invalids of varying temperaments and suffering from all manners of injuries to mind as well as body," said Dr. Syn, "and have been fortunate enough to see success attend my poor efforts as a comforter. If I may be allowed to visit this poor young widow, I fancy I may be able to remove this obsession under which she is suffering. As to this questionable fellow, Mr. Merry—"

"Mister, indeed," snorted the housekeeper under her breath.

"Well, I have lived so long amongst the wildest people that I fancy I shall get this rogue under my thumb before long. In my ministry abroad, to which I have given the best years of my life, I have had to deal with men who made profession of committing even the seven deadly sins daily. White men, too, Mrs. Lovell, and professed Christians just as soon as they got scared and thought old Death was after them."

"And you've lived with such men, sir?" asked the astonished and horrified Mrs. Lovell.

"And that is not counting the Red Indians," he went on. "I have a great respect for the race on the whole, and count many a good friend among them, being sworn brother to several chiefs. But a bad Red Indian—well there—his ideas would be more blood-curdling than a Spanish Inquisitor. Not that the good ones stick at much when dealing with an enemy. But none stauncher to a friend. I'll give you an example. Suppose now I were to be the vicar of Dymchurch—"

"We should be very lucky, sir, what with your learning and being the squire's friend—" she said with a curtsey.

"We will suppose it then," he replied. "And suppose in this village I find I have a dangerous enemy—"

"Impossible, sir," declared the housekeeper. "Unless, of course, it was that pernicious Merry—"

"Well, let us have Merry then, by all means, as our supposition. Well now, being a man of peace, I find that I cannot soil my hands by punishing him—"

"Hand him over to the constables and see him hanged," suggested the housekeeper.

"Well, I hadn't thought of doing anything so drastic," smiled Dr. Syn. "In fact, I hadn't thought of punishing him, but just leaving his own conscience to prick him—"

"Which it wouldn't," put in the housekeeper.

"Perhaps not," he allowed. "But in order to relieve my feelings, I take up my pen and write to one, of at least five Redskins that I can think of straight away. I tell this good Redskin of the many wrongs done to me by the enemy. I tell it just in the matter of news, expecting nothing from it but his sympathy when reading it. What happens? My friend the Redskin goes to his people and begs absence. He goes to the length of settling his affairs in case he does not return. Then one day, some weeks later, maybe even some months later to account for delay, but certainly when I have forgotten the incident of writing, there walks into Dymchurch a Redskin in full chieftain's dress. Rich furs, leather and feathers. The village school children run to watch him. He asks them in slow, dignified English where he can find his friend, Dr. Syn. They tell him. They take the excuse to walk with him, though keeping their distance. We embrace like brothers. I prepare my best guest-chamber. My housekeeper thinks of dainties. The school children, finding he is my friend and kind, sit round him listening to his stories, Indian ghost stories, while he makes them bows and arrows. My housekeeper gives him a fire as you give me one here. He can have all we have, and for a sign of trust I give him the big key of the house door when I have locked up. He takes an interest in all I do. He asks me the names of such villagers that we see. 'That lady is Mrs. Lovell,' I tell him, 'and she is housekeeper to Squire and Lady Cobtree. That officer is the Preventive man.' And so on. Unknown to me, he leads me on talking and telling him of people until he finds out that Mr. Merry (I think we agreed on Mr. Merry, didn't we) that Mr. Merry is my enemy. He soon knows all about Mr. Merry's habits and tracks. At last my Redskin says it is time to return to his people. He will go the next day. He has booked a passage from Dover to Falmouth, and will then re-ship for New York or Jamestown. I fall asleep or lie awake on getting to bed. It makes no difference. I should not hear that silent footstep, that crawling down the stairs in the dark. But my friend has gone down with the key in his hand, a tomahawk in the other, and a knife in his teeth. He has left his feathers and finery in the room. He is naked and covered in oil to make him slippery. Also, he has put queer paint signs on his face to show the ghosts of his ancestors that he is on the war path and fighting to the death for his sworn brother. Perhaps I wake up and look out upon the churchyard and in the moonlight. Well, if I do, I see nothing. And yet there he is gliding from one tombstone to another and so over the wall and about his business. Next morning he is sad at leaving me but otherwise quite normal. I tell him he will soon see his squaw and children, and I have packed presents for them all, which I give him on the ship in Dover Roads. Just as I am about to leave the ship he gives me thanks for my hospitality and begs me to accept a package which is not to be opened till I am alone in my room with a locked door. He sails. I go home. I go to my room, lock the door and open my package. I will not shock you by telling you what I find, but I bury it deep in the garden beneath the heap of leaf mould. The next day, I am told by the gossips that Mr. Merry is missing. Indeed, he had mysteriously disappeared, leaving no word behind him. He is never found."

"And what did you bury, sir?" whispered Mrs. Lovell.

"His scalp, Mrs. Lovell. His scalp," he whispered more fearfully. "Mind you, this is only supposition. I am merely saying 'supposing I should write to that Indian.' I have told you the certain result of such a letter if I did. A Redskin sworn brother will go all the way to serve his friend. I therefore imagine that my experiences among such people during my long ministry abroad will enable me to deal with your Mr. Merry. Don't worry."

The reappearance of Robert forced Mrs. Lovell to retire.

"Excuse me, your reverence, but I didn't like to mention it before the housekeeper, and it may still seem a liberty, but have you tucked your hair up into your nightcap?"

"What's left of it, Robert. It's not much, and you must deal with it."

"But you had a very striking head of hair, sir. You've never cut it off?"

"I have indeed, Robert," replied Dr. Syn. "The ministry in America is not the same as it is here. I wore my own hair there for convenience. But in England it is meet and right that I wear the orthodox badge of my calling—a parson's wig, so if you'll shave and polish my skull, Robert, I'll be ready for breakfast at half-past nine. I am sure my predecessor will not grudge me the use of his wig."

"But sir, have you considered that a bald head is ageing?" pleaded Robert. "You will put on a great many years if you shave your head and wear a wig of this kind."

"My good Robert, that is just what I require," replied Dr. Syn quietly. "I am a Doctor of Divinity. I am about to accept the pulpit of Dymchurch. I have got a confounded sense of humour which must be hidden or my flock will not believe in me. I am here to do good, Robert, to be what I am expected to be, and to attempt to cut a romantic figure would not be in accordance with my calling. Shave my head, Robert."

CHAPTER XI. The New Doctor Syn Appears At Breakfast

At half-past nine Dr. Syn entered the old dining-room to find the three young ladies in possession. They were all kneeling on the hearth-rug, each armed with a brass toasting-fork on which were impaled rounds of bread.

"Good morning, young ladies," he said, bowing in the doorway.

They all turned and looked at him, and it was obvious that they were struck dumb with surprise.

To anyone less self-possessed than Dr. Syn, the focus of three pairs of beautiful eyes looking over three bread-loaded toasting-forks, might have proved disconcerting, but the dumbness of the young ladies gave him the assurance that he had altered his appearance sufficiently to surprise them.

"Why," cried the doctor, "you all look at me as though I were a stranger. Must I introduce myself all over again? I am Christopher Syn, Doctor of Divinity, late fellow of Queen's College, Oxford. I have just returned from a travelling ministry in America, and according to your father's positive assertion, I am to be installed as the new vicar of Dymchurch. Do you imagine that the happenings of last night were a dream?"

"But you're not a scrap what you were," stammered Miss Maria.

"You've changed in the night," echoed Miss Cicely.

"You look like the father of the ship-wrecked man," said Maria.

"Did you hear a witch in the night?" asked Cicely. "They ride on the Marsh, you know. There's one old woman we can show you who really is a witch."

"Have I changed then so much?" asked Dr. Syn.

"Utterly," exclaimed Cicely.

"And grown older?"

"Years and years," replied Maria.

"Dear, dear, how distressing," sighed Dr. Syn. "And what does Miss Charlotte think?"

"That my sisters are being very personal," she answered, smiling.

"But have you no criticism to add?" he asked. "I like to hear opinions. Please be personal too."

"Well then, I think you must give me your wig to dress."

"But surely," he argued, "one seldom sees a parson in a well-kept wig."

"One seldom sees a parson with a gay rose in his lapel," she answered mischievously.

Dr. Syn was saved from further attack by the arrival of the squire, who immediately became a new target for his daughters' criticism by reason of his being dressed in his bright red hunting coat, to which he was very partial.

"You mustn't be seen in that with the whole village mourning," said Maria.

"But I was going riding, and I have nothing so comfortable," pleaded the squire. "I thought Charlotte might stitch a black ribbon to the sleeve."

"I don't believe it entered your head, Father," said Charlotte reprovingly.

"On my honour it did, at least, I think it did," retorted the squire. "I confess that I don't feel so melancholy as I might have done had the wreck not brought us the doctor here. And my faith, he is dressed solemn enough to make up our deficiencies."

"As I have already been told by your daughters," laughed the doctor. "But surely, just because I have been in America you would not expect me to dress here like a Red Indian or a buccaneer?"

"I liked you best as you were last night, all wild and odd and wet," declared Cicely.

"But you surely wouldn't have me preach all 'wild and odd and wet'?" asked the doctor. "I'd catch my death of cold in the pulpit."

"Which we both shall, if you young rascals keep us from the fire much longer."

"Toast," cried the three young ladies, swinging their neglected rounds of bread toward the flames.

"Besides, there's plenty of room," added Maria.

"Thank you, but I don't give any little minx a chance to set fire to my coat-tails behind my back," laughed the squire. "I'll just cast my eyes over the sideboard and see what's what. Do you eat porridge, Doctor, because we ring for that? Personally, I'm going to."

"Who said he was going to give it up because it was fattening?" asked Cicely, looking at the toast.

"I'm not," retorted the squire. "I mean, I did, but I didn't mean it. If a squire can't grow fat, well who can? Besides, a good ride will slim me down again. Now then, plenty of butter on that toast, girls, and—" he was interrupted by Robert and an ancient butler bringing in a huge tureen of porridge, plates and milk.

Charlotte had been right in describing breakfast as a "moveable feast,' which it was not only in time but action. Lady Cobtree came in twenty minutes later with excuses that she had been inducing the invalid to eat, but apart from this, while the squire sat solidly sampling first one dish and then another and washing it down with brown ale, which he preferred to tea, one or the other of the young ladies was jumping up and carrying this or that from the sideboard, so that Dr. Syn began to wonder how soon he would become as portly as the squire.

"Why, this is jolly, upon my soul," cried the squire, attacking a large plate of home-smoked ham. "It's like old times. Seems only yesterday, Doctor, that you and I sat next to each other in college and ate as hearty as we're doing now."

"Yesterday?" repeated Dr. Syn. "It seems longer to me, my dear Tony. And during the time between, I have daily looked forward to the possibility of this home-coming. When I look round your table here and see you surrounded with so much goodness and beauty, not forgetting the son-and-heir upstairs in his cot, why, I can see that looking back is to you nothing but pleasure. But I prefer to look forward to the pleasant times coming amongst you all. The past has not been so pleasant that I wish to dwell in it. Rather do I thank God for this hour."

"Quite right, Doctor," cried the squire. "I applaud your sentiments. Let us help you to forget the past by making your present life as jolly as we can, eh? For my part, I never remember feeling jollier in my life." And he smiled at another round of toast which Charlotte had brought smoking from the fire to plaster it with rich home-made butter.

"I know you do, dear," said Lady Cobtree. "Hardly a day has gone by in our married life, Doctor, when my husband has not spoken of you, wondered what you were doing and wishing you were here. You know that we all welcome you as heartily as he does, Doctor, but I'm sure you'll support my urging the necessity for keeping our jollity under control till after the funeral. We must think of those poor bodies in the barn."

"Yes," nodded the squire, "and I hear their numbers have been doubled in the night. Three more found. That makes six, besides a heap of bits and pieces."

"Really, Tony, don't," cried her ladyship.

"Well, there, Doctor," sighed the squire. "Now what is a man to do? She asks me not to be jolly. She mentions bodies and funerals, and urges me to be miserable. But the moment I take a gloomy turn in the conversation, it's 'Really, Tony, don't'!"

"My dear, you may be as jolly as you like here amongst ourselves," went on Lady Cobtree. "But even then we must remember the servants, and the invalid. Now, dear, if you've finished breakfast, what's the order of the day?"

"Well, we'll dispense with family prayers for the first thing, as it's more than usually late," returned the squire. "There's lots to do. I thought some of us—you and I, eh, Doctor?—might stroll along and see what damage the storm has done. Then, my dear Charlotte, I'll be back for our ride at eleven o'clock. Now, Doctor, what about a horse for you? I suppose you have ridden a lot in America?"

The doctor said he would enjoy it.

"Very well, then," went on the squire. "Charlotte, will you see to it? We'll ride Burmarsh way and see how our neighbours have fared."

"And do see what can be done about the 'Sea-Wall Tavern,'" said Lady Cobtree. "From all I hear the place is uninhabitable. Poor Meg has got it into her head that it is left unprotected and that Merry, of all people, is rummaging about amongst her treasures."

"Tell her that I've put responsible people in charge," replied the squire. "You can also tell her that I shall make it my business to see that the house is restored. We'll all do what we can to make it a great deal better than it was before, and if she intends carrying on the business, why, we'll see it's well stocked with saleable liquor."

This idea of the squire's strongly recommended itself to the villagers, who one and all, and most readily, promised that as the squire was ready to bear all necessary expense, they would at least save him the cost of labour, and bind themselves voluntarily under the most fitting foreman, to be elected, under whom they would carry out all necessary labour.

In the same spirit the women of the village banded together to undertake, under the direction of the ladies at New Hall, all those necessary comforts that only women can supply, such as the making and fitting of new curtains, fresh furniture covers, and all the stitchings and sewings necessary for a well-regulated, comfortable house. Their labours did not end there, for Dr. Syn, inspired by this general generosity, opened a subscription list, heading it himself with the sum of seventy guineas, which he took for the purpose from the sea-captain's belt. Over this transaction his conscience was more or less clear, since the captain had told him during the voyage that having no relations or dependants, he was hard put to it as to whom he should leave his money, and supposing that the best remedy would be to have it divided amongst his crew, should death claim him. Keeping seven guineas back to pay for the captain's special burial, he entered one more guinea as coming from the savings of Mr. Merry, much to that rogue's disgust, since he would sooner have spent it on himself in the bar-parlour. This extra windfall enabled the committee of women to set about ordering new sets of household utensils, so that when Meg should start life afresh she would be equipped with the best copper, brass and pewter and china that a good housekeeper would delight in.

A suggestion made by one Josiah Wraight, who as master builder to the works of the Lords of the Level, carried full weight, was that since the same storm which had destroyed the tavern had also wrecked the brig and brought the two in such close proximity, the timber that was necessary to bind the house together should be taken from the brig, whose keel had originally been laid down in teak with ribs of solid oak, so strong, in fact, that they had withstood even the fire which destroyed the cargo. The idea appealed to the squire, who was thus saved the heavy expense of wood and cartage. So that very day the work of restoration was put in hand, everybody vying to do a little more than the next.

In the meantime, Dr. Syn made good his boast to the housekeeper, for having visited Meg and talked to her, she became more reconciled to her fate and actually began to take an interest in the new life ahead of her, which the kindness of the village was making possible. Her confidence in Dr. Syn even lessened her dread of Merry, and she somehow believed his assertion that she need have no fear of any further molestation in that quarter.

"I have always found," he told her kindly, "that in the worst sinner there is some hidden quality of goodness, and although this misguided man seems from all accounts to have little to recommend him, I am not despairing of finding some point of contact from which to work towards making him a better citizen."

This was very comforting to her, as she had no suspicion of Dr. Syn's real opinion, which did not tally with the above sentiment, for as he told himself: "The man's a blackguard and will always be a blackguard. He is also dangerous. I know the type. He will be like a wild beast at bay. He will comfort himself with thoughts of revenge, and the first chance he gets against me, he will take. For two ends he will strive. A knife in my back and this pretty widow in his arms. At present, I have got him on the raw, and mighty useful he may be, but I shall not underestimate the power of his hatred."

This self-advice the doctor kept to himself, so that all his well-wishers, from the squire down, began to warn him not to attempt any conversion with the rogue Merry, as he was beyond redemption.

The rogue in question was at the moment more than living up to Dr. Syn's private estimation of him. In a spirit of savage recklessness, he expended the whole of his guinea upon strong drink, laying in a stock of more brandy than he had ever hidden at one time in his room. He felt happier when the guinea was gone, for it only served to remind him of how fate had cheated him on the previous night. All the day he drank, and hoped that his tormentor would give him a call, for the command to appear at morning prayer the next day was a bitter thought which he would have been glad to avoid. He would sooner have spent a week in the Court House cells, and more than once he thought of ignoring the order. And yet, partly through fear of the devilish survivor whom he hated with all his soul, and partly through curiosity to find out who and what he was, he at last came to the conclusion that to go to church for at least this once was the only course to take. His vanity recoiled from the sneers that such an action would bring upon him. He knew very well that everyone's eyes would be upon him. It would be bad enough if they welcomed this gesture of turning over a new leaf, but it would be worse if they sneered. He could hear their tongues wagging as first one gossip then another gave out their ideas of his motive. Well, he would keep them guessing at all events. What was more, he would go unshaven and half drunk, and if any of the church officials interfered with him, it would be at their own peril.

CHAPTER XII. Doctor Syn Occupies The Pulpit

Sunday morning found Merry awakening early from a drunken sleep. The injury to his head where he had been dashed against the stone, and which he had but carelessly tended, added to the pains caused by alcohol. True to his resolve, he neither shaved, washed nor brushed his dirt-grimed and sea-watered clothes, and his only preparation for attending the church service was a further soaking of brandy. Realising that hymns, prayers, psalms, sermon and the Scripture reading, although bringing comfort to such fools as could swallow such 'jargon,' as he called it, could, would and should have no power whatever over him unless to depress him the worse, he took in the pocket of his great-coat a handy bottle of brandy.

The drink by this time had filled him with such concentrated hatred of the whole parish, that he began to hug the thought of making them disgusted. He knew that the church would be crammed to capacity, for the morbid curiosity of a funeral oration would attract those who seldom went, so he thought. That most of the parish did go to church he merely put down as 'toadying to the squire' and 'playing up for parochial relief in lean times.' No one did anything for nothing was his firm belief. He quite looked forward to hearing the preacher, whoever he might be, lamenting the death of the parson and Abel Clouder. Abel Clouder especially. He wondered whether the preacher would say: "Now why has God in His mysterious way, thought fit to take our brother Abel to His bosom?"

"Well if he does," said Merry to himself, "I'm damned if I don't give him the answer. 'Why, says you?' I'll say, standing up in my place and producing my brandy, 'why, so as I can marry his widow, of course, you old fat-head. And here's to Meg and me and damnation to the rest of you.'"

This speech gave him such a relief to his feelings, and caused him so much amusement in a grim fashion, that he really began to look forward to the service, so much so that a dread arose in his mind that the mere fact of his being drunk might prevent him gaining admittance. He resolved, therefore, to start immediately so that he would be on the spot to slip in quietly as soon as the sexton opened the doors. This would also do away with the unpleasant necessity of entering a filled church and being stared and frowned at while staggering to a seat.

So without more ado he made his unsteady way to the churchyard where, crouched behind a tombstone, he took sundry more nips at the bottle and kept one of his swimming eyes upon the church door.

At last, the sexton arrived with his keys to admit the three bell-ringers. As soon as the bells began to ring, he crept from his hiding place, for he knew that very soon the churchyard would be filling up with village gossips. The sexton was busy in the vestry, and the bell-ringers were hidden by a curtain, so that the rogue was able to take his bearings undisturbed. He avoided the family pews, and after experimenting one or two remote corners, his choice was in favour of a bench beneath a window where he could lean back against the angle of the wall which supported the great three-decker pulpit with its mighty sounding board. This position gave him the advantage of being more or less out of the general eye, and yet giving him a good view of the pulpit, and of the south door through which the congregation would enter. Therefore, he could watch for the man who had robbed him of the murdered captain's guineas. No doubt he would accompany the squire, and it was easy to see which was the squire's pew, as none others had those great red velvet cushions for the well-bound books. By the pile of ragged books that were heaped upon his bench, some of which had been defaced by crude and comical pencil sketches, he gathered that he was sitting in one of the school children's pews. Well, all the better. If they crowded too close to him, he'd pinch their legs.

In order to conceal himself the better, he wound his scarf about his face and turned up the high collar of his heavy coat. This was, after all, natural enough. In many of the seats which were too far removed from the squire's pew to enjoy the heat of the coal fire built inside it, those worshipers who were afraid of catching cold would tuck up their collars, or bundle their chilly chins into their cravats. But in his extreme desire to escape notice, Merry, in ignorance of church ritual, or rather custom, for 'ritual' still smacked of Popery, did the very thing to make himself the most conspicuous person in the congregation, in that he pulled his old three-cornered hat well down upon his brows. But as the congregation began to dribble in and then crowd in, no one took it upon himself to cross to Merry's corner and remove his hat, but each one stared at him and whispered to his neighbour: "He's got his hat on. Disgraceful."

And from beneath this hat which was such an offence to God and man, Merry watched for his arch-enemy, but in vain. There was no sign of that nameless one who could throw knives so cunningly. The awful thought occurred to him that he had left Dymchurch while he had been soaking in brandy: that the elegant and terrifying stranger had gone for ever, taking his sea-chest and the captain's guineas (his, Merry's, guineas) with him. The squire and his family were all in their places, and still no sign of the man he sought. Late comers came in timidly, looked this way and that, and then scuttled to the corner of the pews like frightened rabbits. Up and down the aisle went the Dymchurch beadle, resplendent in his brass-buttoned capes. Until the officiating parson took his place, it was the province of the beadle to thus walk up and down suppressing anything in the nature of whisperings from the adults and anything resembling giggles from the children. Upon this occasion the whisperings and sniggerings were more apparent than ever the worthy beadle could remember. Determined to find out the cause of it (for he had not yet noticed Merry's headgear) he looked around for a likely victim to use as the parish scapegoat. This 'looking around' was purely an affectation on the part of the beadle, assumed to lend more importance to his final decision, which was always the pew next the south door. This pew, although not one of those annually rented to a particular family, was however always occupied by the same tenants, three young men, the eldest twenty-two, the second twenty and the third eighteen, brothers by the name of Upton. These three young blades were acknowledged to be the bucks of the village and the very life and soul of it. The pew which they commandeered by the simple expedient of one getting there early to hold the fort against all comers, was most conveniently placed for smiling at the young ladies as they entered the south door. To these three had been bequeathed an 'odds and ends' depository in the village known as 'The Curiosity Museum. Everything for sale. Proprietors, Upton Brothers. Art Connoisseurs.' The last word they had captured from a French prisoner of war, who had given dancing classes to the ladies of the Marsh. Since all the merry mischief and innocent pranks of the village originated from one or another of these three swashbucklers, the beadle, when in doubt about any scandal, whether in church or out of it, approached the fountain head for information. In other words, he questioned the Uptons, who never failed to send him on a wild goose chase. Quick to observe the field of battle where the beadle was concerned, they, like experienced generals, could make up their minds quickly for the best advantage. The advantage as they now saw it, was that the unmitigated blackguard, Merry, alone on his bench, was isolated from the congregation by a crowd of school children who occupied the next pews, leaving Merry to himself for very fear of him, that he was not only far gone in liquor, but was defying the rule of Christianity by wearing his hat. When, therefore, they informed the beadle that the hat in question was offending the whole church, they wondered whether the beadle would have sufficient courage to order its removal.

　　Certainly, the beadle strode off like a Goliath of Gath intending to do battle, but perceiving a threatening look in Merry's eye and realising that in the midst of children he was in an enemy's camp, he contented himself with prodding a small boy in the back with his official staff and telling him to get up off his hassock and sit down. His inability to tackle Merry was naturally received as a great jest by the

Uptons, and many were the dumb-show signals that went from their pew to those of their friends.

Now it was a time-honoured custom in Dymchurch that whatever the hour, the moment the squire was seen to settle down in his pew, the bell-ringers should cease to pull. This was a polite way of deceiving the parish that the squire was nothing if not punctual. The silence after the jangle of bells had ceased, accentuated the intrusion of the smallest noise, and left the whole congregation in a somewhat nervous tension.

Therefore, all this whispering, and the consultation of the beadle with the Uptons, and his advance upon and inglorious retreat from the scowling Merry were all the more marked. And so much was the general attention focused on Merry's hat that no one seemed to mark the entrance of the parson officiating in the place of the drowned vicar. In fact, it was not until his rich voice resounded from the pulpit that they realised anyone was there, and then even Merry's hat was forgotten.

The first words of the sentence "When the wicked man" riveted the attention of everyone, and by the end of the Exhortation this strange parson, who it was now generally known had escaped from the wreck that had killed the vicar, and who was not only staying at the Hall but was rumoured to be the likely successor of poor Bolden, this arresting personality who wore the scarlet hood of his doctorship over the black silk gown, whose eyes seemed to burn with inward fire, had already compelled the congregation to attend and respect him.

Scowling at the beadle, and furious that the man who had tricked him of the guineas had also tricked him into attending church, Merry also heard those words, "When the wicked man," and they sounded in his ears like a threat. He had heard that voice before, and he hated its calm, superior aloofness, which gave it the right to command. Slowly his eyes turned to the parson and slowly it dawned upon him that there in the pulpit was his enemy. What was this insolent knife-throwing thief doing up there? Had he got those two belts of guineas round his waist under that black gown? As like as not. Aye and, the bit of string round his neck with the silver key of the sea-chest.

All through the Exhortation the congregation stood. Merry, no longer trying to escape since he knew that everyone whispered about him, yet remained seated as a protest against 'all the hypocrisy,' as he thought it. His rage against the parson was a thousand times more bitter than against that adventurer on the sea-shore. To think he had been worsted by a parson. And to think that this same parson was standing up to teach and to preach. Well, he'd find he wasn't going to have it all his own way. Into the fuddled brain came the idea of denouncing him there, before all the parish. Asking him to explain how he came by the belt of guineas? And before he could think of a fitting answer, to accuse him of having robbed and murdered the captain. "If he accuses me of the same thing, what reason could he give for having kept silent?" he asked himself. Yes, he would then say: "Do you suppose if I'd done such a thing, gentlemen, that he wouldn't have had me arrested? Of course." He couldn't look at him any more without doing it, and as the congregation meekly obeyed him and knelt down, Merry, uttering an oath, sprang up.

Dr. Syn turned on him sharply, just as though he had been waiting for this thing to happen, and in a quiet, kind voice he said: "Remove your hat, my friend, in the House of God."

"I will not," cried Merry.

"Oh yes, you will—or—" Dr. Syn put his hand up to his throat quite naturally, and smiled.

Merry saw inquisitive heads popping up here and there over the pews to see what the interruption was about. In the distance he saw the squire's face looking towards him, and he knew that whatever happened, he would get the worst of it from these people who hated him. Better to wait. He would get Meg first and then he would get the parson.

Hardly realising what he did, he pulled off his hat and dropped down, crouching on to the hassock as though in prayer.

Dr. Syn went on with the service. Merry, under cover of the pew, took a swig of brandy, then huddling himself into the corner, he shut his eyes against the whole hateful parish and fell asleep.

When he awoke, the sermon was nearly over, but the little he heard convinced him more than ever that his enemy was a powerful and clever man. The congregation was so profoundly moved by his eloquence that he found he was forgotten.

CHAPTER XIII. Doctor Syn Delivers An Ultimatum to Mr. Merry

The service over, everyone crowded out after the Cobtree ladies through the porch, for the squire had gone to the vestry. Merry sat huddled in his corner, intending to wait till the parishioners dispersed to their dinners.

The sexton avoided him and went to the vestry. The beadle had already avoided him and followed the Uptons into the churchyard to see what devilry they might not be up to.

But one man came along the aisle, and said: "Hallo."

It was the Preventive Officer.

Merry answered with a grunt.

"A popular man, this Dr. Syn. The whole village is waiting for him out in the churchyard. I wonder if he's going to be for me or against me?"

"How should I know?" growled Merry.

"If he's for me, he'll lose his popularity quick, I know that," said the Preventive man.

"Still of the opinion that smuggling's going on then," replied Merry.

"So much so that I could have walked round this blessed church this morning and clapped my hands on all that's in it," declared the officer.

"Then why didn't you do it?" demanded Merry. "I would, in your shoes. I'd give much to have your chance of getting my own back on 'em. Sneery lot of hypocrites. Oh, and make no mistake—they sneer at you just as they do at me."

"I know that," nodded the other.

"Then string 'em up and sneer back," retorted Merry. "Ain't you got the laws of England and the whole blessed Constitootion at the back of you?"

"I've no one at the back of me, I tell you. What's the good of knowing who they are unless I can prove it, and how am I to prove it in the Dymchurch Court House? There's only one man they'd let me hang, and that's you."

"Supposin' you had grounds, which you haven't," corrected Merry.

"But I'll get 'em one day," muttered the Preventive man.

"Aye, by God, and so will I," cried Merry. "Suppose now I was to give you the proof you wants."

"It would have to be 'proof absolute,' with you as witness, or you'd find yourself on the gallows before the lawyers had finished with you, aye, and I'd find myself dismissed the service for making the

Government look foolish. No, it ain't so easy, my friend. There's some cases where duty towards the Government is to is to keep the peace by leavin' hornets' nests alone."

"Bah," cried Merry with disgust. "A man of courage routs 'em out. I would."

"And so may I—one day," replied the officer.

"And so, by God, I will—one night," retorted Merry.

"Well, don't get caught up by no lawyers," enjoined the other. "Leastways, not on Romney Marsh."

Further conversation was interrupted by the arrival of the gentlemen from the vestry. Dr. Sennacharib Pepper, as people's warden and the squire as vicar's warden, had been counting the offertory with the help of the clerk of the Level. In lieu of any survivors from the wreck other than Dr. Syn, the offertory, which had been substantial, was to be devoted to Meg Clouder.

Dr. Pepper had expressed his doubts whether it was seemly to donate a church offertory towards funds for a tavern, but the squire had overruled him with: "Tavern be damned. It's to a poor young widow whose husband died in the service of his fellow-men. Besides, what's wrong with taverns? Nothing."

They were still arguing on this theme as they walked slowly from the chancel into the body of the church.

Dr. Syn, still in his robes, left the group and approached Merry.

"Ah, Mr. Merry," he said pleasantly, "I am glad to see you here. Another time, remember about that hat, won't you? And by the way, I have a little proposition to make to you which I fancy will be to your advantage."

Then he looked at the Preventive man and held out his hand. "And are you a parishioner?"

"I'm the Preventive Officer here, sir."

"Delighted to know you then," went on Dr. Syn. "You hold a position of great responsibility. Keeping us all up to the mark in our loyalty to His Majesty's Government, eh? But I am quite sure that from what I saw of the parish this morning that they do not give King George's officers any trouble."

"Appearances are sometimes on the deceiving side, sir," returned the other ambiguously.

"Oh, come now," argued Dr. Syn, "surely the men of Romney Marsh are loyal enough? I was delighted at the fervency of the amens when I prayed for the King's Majesty and the Royal family."

"There's many a man, sir, who serves God 'cos it pays him to—"

"And quite right," said Dr. Syn. "It should pay to be good and it always does."

But the Preventive man was not to be drawn into argument. He was only stating facts as he saw them, so he went on: "And there's many men, most men hereabouts, I'll say that for 'em, who are loyal enough to the King. In time of war they'll fight and none better, but when they say 'Honour the King' they adds—"

"But first maintain the Wall?" queried the doctor. "Well, that's natural."

"No, sir, they adds, 'and to Hell with the Revenue officers.'"

"I should be grieved to hear such a sentiment indeed," replied the doctor.

"You'll hear it if you listens. Good day, sir." And the officer strolled out of the church.

"Now, let me see, Mr. Merry," went on the parson, "what exactly is your work?"

"I told you last night—odd jobs."

"That's not very satisfactory, I'll be bound. Odd jobs mean odd payments, and surely it's better to have something regular. Now you'll work for me. As soon as certain documents come through from Canterbury, I shall be taking up my quarters at the vicarage. Once there, you will attend daily to the garden and carry messages; in fact, you will be my out-of-door lieutenant. Your pay shall be gone into, and fairly. In the meantime, whether I am vicar here or not, and for the moment I am legally but locum tenens, you will apply your elbow grease to the brass-work in the church. I am particular that brass should shine and good wood reflect a polish. You will start that to-morrow. In the meanwhile, I have put your name down on the list of subscribers for poor Mrs. Clouder. You have given a guinea, you understand. The rest of the captain's money has gone the same way, with the exception of what I have set aside for his grave and funeral, for which I feel responsible."

"Easy to feel responsible over money what don't belong to you, ain't it?" growled Merry.

"Perhaps so," replied the doctor pleasantly, "but in this case I happen to be responsible as executor for my good friend the captain, who on board the City of London, whether having a premonition of disaster or no who can say, asked me to act for him in the event of his death."

"And what of his relatives, eh? His dependants?" asked Merry.

"I think that had the captain's belt remained around your waist, they would not have benefited much. As it happens, he had no relations or dependents, and I was pledged to see that such money as he had should be divided amongst the last crew he might happen to command. So you see, there was I, thanks to your dirty work, an executor with no one living to attend. Knowing the captain, I guessed that he would approve of the way I have handled his property."

"I see," replied Merry sarcastically. "And I start doin' church work to-morrow, do I?"

"We'll put it like that when you are a little more worthy," replied Dr. Syn. "In the meanwhile, we will put it like this: From to-morrow you will give up odd jobs and work under my direction, and you will find yourself the richer. And while I think of it. The widow of poor Abel Clouder—"

"Aye, what of her?" demanded Merry.

"Like many other people in the village, she fails to understand you. I hope this lack of appreciation is merely due to the fact that your worth is not yet proved. But don't despair. We shall have you a pattern citizen yet—"

"I ain't goin' to be converted by no parson, so don't you think it."

"But I do think it," replied the doctor. "In fact, I'll lay my last guinea on it. However, in view of the fact that Mrs. Clouder is under a dreadful shock, I must forbid you to approach her. If you see her about in the village, you must turn another way. When you are in need of refreshment, you will go to the 'Ship Inn', or to the 'Ocean.' And talking of drink, you will in future, only drink in public. The habit of drinking brandy in your own room is not good for you. A publican is responsible for your sobriety, as you are not yet in a state to be responsible for yourself."

"Oh, and any more orders?" sneered Merry.

"Not at present. But remember what I have said about Mrs. Clouder. If you trouble her but once, I shall repent the fact that I have saved you from the gallows, and the moment I repent of that, Mr. Merry, why, as God's my Judge, you shall hang there. So remember and go easy with the brandy. Goodbye, my good man. God bless." And the parson hurried away to join the squire.

CHAPTER XIV. Mr. Merry Confronts Three Merry Blades

Merry, in his present mood, might have taken himself to task for not utterly and finally refusing to work for the new parson—'cleaning brass in the church, indeed! A job that for maiden ladies and old spinsters, with nothing better to do than toady round a parson.' But Merry did nothing of the kind, for into his brain had crept the idea that by working for this Dr. Syn, he would be near enough to spy upon him, and it would go hard if sooner or later he could not find the means of tripping him up.

So the results of the interview, although greatly increasing Merry's hatred, put him in a better temper with life, although it would not have been suspected by his face, which was as sour and hard as usual. Another thing evolving from the interview which caused him added satisfaction, was the knowledge that Meg Clouder feared him, and he resolved to circumvent the parson's orders by some cunning and see that this fear increased. For although Meg attracted him more strangely than anyone had ever done before, he preferred to win her through the power of fear than any stupid urge of affection. To have her at his mercy—to watch her fears growing and to see her realising slowly that she could not escape. These thoughts were his pleasurable companions as he slunk out of the church, much to the relief of the very old sexton, who had not the courage to tackle Merry single-handed inside the building.

Out in the porch, however, his courage rose, for sitting on the churchyard wall were the three Upton brothers who were amusing themselves with frightening the beadle, making imaginary passes in the air with their long canes, which were too close to his person for the beadle's peace of mind.

The courage that suddenly filled the old sexton's soul was not inspired by the beadle, but by the Upton boys, for whom he had a great liking. He knew very well that they would not sit idly by and see him ill-used by the unpopular Merry, so on the strength of this, he remarked that although some people drank and didn't eat, he was one who did both, and more than heartily upon a Sunday after morning prayer, and added that things were come to a fine pass indeed when irregular worshippers who didn't know what to do with their hats chose to lounge about the place after the officials had gone.

Merry regarded him with a brandy eye, but said nothing, so that the sexton was further emboldened to state that looking at Merry in a cold church might entertain some, but not him.

"Then," said Merry, "I fear you'll have to endure it the best you can, because you'll see a good deal of me in future. I'm an official, if you want to know. This new vicar ain't at all satisfied with the way the place is kept. He wants to see his own face in the brass, and since he's money to waste on such fancies, he's paying me to see 'em carried out. And to-morrow you'll find that what you calls bright brass, I don't. See?"

Satisfied that he had at least depressed the sexton's spirits, Merry went slowly out of the churchyard gate, deliberately brushing by the dangling legs of the Upton brothers as they sat on the wall, in the hope that they might be tempted to play tricks with their elegant canes on him, as they had already done to the beadle, when Merry would have the excuse to snatch hold of one of them and break it across his knee.

For the purpose of tempting them to an aggression which he was in the mood to welcome, he looked away from them as though they were for all their fine clothes, beneath his notice. As he turned his head towards the windows of the Hall beyond the Court House, however, he saw a sight which caused him to stop and stare.

Behind one of the large casements he saw Meg, supported by Charlotte and Lady Cobtree. She wore a rich dressing-gown, obviously lent her by one of the ladies, and her hair hanging loose about her shoulders caught the rays of the sun. Merry gazed, stupidly dazzled by her beauty, and began to congratulate himself upon his choice. "I'll even spend a bit of money on her," he told himself. "I'll make her dress up like that for me."

Although he was dazed, her appearance had the opposite effect upon the Upton boys. They sprang from the wall simultaneously and, displaying their fine clothes to the best advantage, advanced towards the Court House, using their handkerchiefs and walking canes with great effect. They then glanced up at the window, removed their hats with a fine flourish, and favoured the ladies with a bow in trio that had taken many rehearsals to perfect.

The Cobtree ladies whispered something to Meg, who smiled down sadly, but Miss Charlotte's eyes danced with a smile of real appreciation. As she was always saying to people: "Oh, but I adore those Upton boys," she saw no reason to conceal her pleasure and amusement.

However pleasing their extravagant homage was to the ladies, upon Merry it had the opposite effect. "Why," he asked himself, "should these three swaggerers presuming on the good cut of their clothes, be permitted to bow and scrape to the girl whom he was forbidden to approach—the girl that eventually was to belong to him body and soul—by the devil's grace?"

Since the three village gallants were not wearing swords (for they had not yet had the effrontery to carry them to church) and since they were disporting themselves in their London clothes (and it was rumoured that they patronised the same tailor as the Prince of Wales did), it was unlikely that they would risk disturbing such garments by a hand-to-hand rough and tumble with the dirtily-clad Merry, which supposition, prompted by wild hate against any that might now be eligible for Meg's hand, led Merry to make a sudden rush behind their backs and seize hold of the youngest Upton's cane, which he intended to break across his knee. The sudden tug which he gave it, however, did not jerk it out of young Tom Upton's hand, for the canes were all embellished with wrist-loops and tassels.

Tom had turned like lightning, so had the brothers, and had seized round Tom's waist so that Merry should not with his superior weight pull away the cane. And as this tug-o'-war continued, Monty, the eldest Upton, whispered in Tom's ear, who answered with a laugh. Merry, determined to get the cane, dug his heels into the gravel and leaned back, pulling with all his strength, and then suddenly Tom touched a secret spring in the handle. The cane came in half and as Merry fell on his back clutching the empty sheath, Tom sprang over him, pointing the fine blade of the sword-stick at his breast. By the same infernal juggling, Monty and Henry, the second brother, had likewise released the blades of their sword-sticks so that Merry saw nothing but their laughing faces above their shining rapiers. To add to his discomfiture, he thought he heard the silvery laughter of the girls behind the casement.

"If you break my sheath, I'll borrow your body instead," said Tom, looking so fierce that the beadle thought he was about experiment, and thinking it quite safe to interfere, he crept up behind Merry's head and plucked the empty cane away.

He then returned it politely to the owner, saying: "About time for me to interfere, I think, gentlemen." In fact, the beadle was quite satisfied that his prowess had encompassed Merry's defeat.

It might have been more diplomatic had the ladies retired from sight, but this Miss Charlotte had no intention of doing, since she had enjoyed the excitement to the full, while Lady Cobtree thought that seeing Merry worsted would go a long way towards dispelling the fear of him in Meg's mind, but their presence enraged Merry to the last point of brandy-flamed rage.

He stood up, and ignoring the grinning Uptons and the self-satisfied beadle, he pointed up at Meg, and growled out: "Oh, then that settles it."

With three blades so ready at hand and augmented by the sexton armed with the great key of the church, the beadle ventured to demand: "Settles what?"

"Never you mind," retorted Merry. "You'll se in good time—all of you. It'll come as a surprise when it does come. And very surprising it'll be round some of your necks, too. Yes. Your necks amongst others. For no respecter of persons it won't be neither. Whether's it's necks in the Court House there or humble necks like all of yourn, it'll have 'em just the same, you mind what I say."

And although Merry had not the faintest idea what he was saying, or what the 'it' was that was coming, he felt that the sentence expressed his hatred of the whole pack of them, and that if it really had meant anything more definite, it couldn't have sounded better.

It was, at any rate, a good enough speech to quit the field with, and so he stalked off chuckling aloud.

"Did you ever now?" ejaculated the sexton. "And all because I hauls him over the coals for keeping me waiting. What did he mean by all that talk? And what did he want to come to church for?"

"On purpose to keep his hat on," explained the beadle. "As to his talk, well, I must look up the Statutes. I seem to recollect that threatening an officer of law is a very grievous offence. What all his talk meant, I do not know. But there was threats in it. Distinct threats."

"And I think, brothers, it will be safer for the windows of our place of business," said Monty, "if we follow him up and see he intends no further harm."

"But don't go surprising him with them swords no more, or there'll be murder done," cautioned the beadle.

"Very neat canes, Mister Beadle, eh?" laughed Tom.

"We bought them in London last week, when we attended the sale of some bankrupt's goods," explained Henry.

"We're keeping them, of course," said Monty, "as they struck us as very elegant. But we bought a deal of other things. Some quite extraordinary things, which are for sale. You want to come and see."

"Now, if you'd got the same sort of thing as them canes," said the beadle, "only made to look like a beadle's staff with a blunderbuss inside, I'd buy it."

"Or a church key," suggested the sexton, "what was really a horse-pistol. Ah, I'd buy that."

"Nothing quite in that line, was there, brothers?" asked Monty. "But we could let you have a brass warming-pan very cheap. And they'll go up in price with the cold weather."

"I find a drop o' Hollands keeps the cold out better than them pans," said the sexton. "I can't take no warming-pan into a grave I'm digging, but Hollands, you see, I can."

"My missus don't hold with warming-pans," said the beadle. "Warm bricks we have used ever since the first day, or rather night, we slept in a Government House cottage. We'd be too scared of fire to use a pan. Suppose them coals jumped out and set light to our bed, why the bed'd set fire to the room and the room to the cottage and since the beadle's residence is joined to the Court House, as you can see for yourselves by looking at it over there, why, the Hall would be afire, and that would mean the First Lord of the Level of Romney Marsh would be afire and her ladyship would be afire, then she'd set the young ladies ablaze, and before they knew what they'd done, they'd have enveloped the precious baby in flames. No. It ain't good enough. Bricks for me."

"You wants to know your wife very well, though," suggested the sexton. "I mean, it ain't every wife you'd trust with a great brick to herself."

"Never had no difficulty," replied the beadle. "Every night just the same. 'Good night, dear.' 'Good night, love.' Both our feet go down upon our bricks and we're asleep."

"Ah," said the sexton, "you never had no children, did you?"

"Never," replied the beadle. "Nor never no warming-pans neither. Bricks is good enough for us."

"Ah, then, if we can't sell you a warming-pan, we'll go home to dinner," laughed Monty, and with a brother on each side of him, he swaggered off through the village.

This adventure of the Upton brothers, added to Dr. Syn's assurance that there would be no further trouble from Merry, went so far to dispel Meg's terror of the rogue that within a few days she was willing to venture out, escorted by Charlotte and the parson, to view the work of restoration being carried on under Josiah Wraight's direction in her old home, the 'Sea-Wall Tavern'.

CHAPTER XV. Meg's Tavern Becomes 'The City of London'

It was plain that everyone had worked with a will. The requests to help had been so overwhelming, not only from the adjacent parishes but from villages far removed across the Marsh, that in order to incorporate all these volunteers, night-shifts of labourers were enrolled, so that by the time Meg first viewed it from the sea-wall, it was obvious that as far as the house was concerned, the storm had been a blessing in disguise, for the old tavern, falling to pieces even before the disaster, was now strong, solid and straight, floors and ceilings interlaced with the fine old oak ribs of the brig, all cut even and fitted into place. Gone were the old familiar chinks and crevices through which the wind had used to whistle, and around the wainscot not a hole remained, for a mouse to air his whiskers. Lead-rimmed casements shut and opened easily, and not a draught could creep through the fresh-set diamond panes.

After careful estimation of what was required, it was Josiah Wraight's boast to the committee that every piece of wood left on the brig had been utilised for the tavern. Even the little hut erected as the office of works, and in which Josiah kept the plans, was knocked up out of the bulkhead of the fo'c'sle.

"There's more brig than tavern about her now, Master Foreman," laughed one of the workmen, and when Josiah went to meet Meg Clouder, and she exclaimed: "Oh, but it's so different, and so much more important. How Abel would have loved it like this," he paraphrased the workman's remark with: "Aye, Meg, and when you go aboard you'll say: 'There's more City of London than "Sea-Wall Tavern".' It's the brig what has rebuilt it so fine."

It was just as they were about to enter the front to 'go aboard', as Josiah put it, that a sign-painter from New Romney approached and asked if he were to get busy yet.

"Just a minute, son," said Josiah, and then looking at Dr. Syn, he gave the reverent gentleman a nod.

"Ah, yes," replied the doctor. "We will ask Mrs. Clouder what she thinks, and if her wishes are the same as the squire's this good fellow may paint the words. You see, Mrs. Clouder, since so many good folk have helped to rebuild the tavern, not only out of respect for your brave husband, but also for all those poor souls who perished in the brig which has now given its very ribs to build the house, the squire is of the opinion that the house should stand now, and in generations to come, as a memorial, and as he is giving you a new licence to run the tavern to more advantage, now would be the convenient time to change the title from 'Sea-Wall Tavern' to 'The City of London'."

"Aye, and I think Abel would like it," put in Josiah, "for in days to come, when strangers look at the sign and say 'What has London to do with Romney Marsh?' why, the story will be told of how Abel and Parson Bolden died, and how the wreck not only rebuilt your house but brought us our new vicar."

"If it is the squire's wish, and your wish, why then it is mine too," replied Meg.

"Then the sign-painter can measure out his letters," went on Josiah. "Between the two windows there, we thought, in large bold script, eh? And black paint, eh? It will show up against the white-wash, and is the fitting colour for a memorial. Then as to the sign itself—well, what better than this, Meg, eh? Will you step round to my little office for a minute?"

They entered the hut that had been set up on the grass patch before the inn door, and Josiah, waving his hand towards the far corner, said: "And what inn upon the whole of the Marsh has a finer sign than that. Just imagine him sticking out from an iron bracket between the two big bedroom windows, Meg, eh?"

Meg shuddered as she saw the honest Josiah patting the wooden face of the brig's figure-head. "Oh, no," she said, "just the words on the wall, but not that ghastly thing—please, Josiah."

"Ghastly?" repeated the astounded foreman. "I calls it handsome. Fierce, perhaps. Yes, it might have been carved jollier, if it's meant to be the City of London. I've been to London more than once, and though its smoky and gloomy with fog and river mist, there's a feeling of jollity in them City taverns and coffee houses. Now what might this gentleman be meant to be? A city sheriff or what, sir?" He thought that if Dr. Syn would only make the figure-head sound interesting, that Meg might be reconciled to it. Though why she didn't take to it immediately he was at a loss to understand.

"Why, yes," said Dr. Syn, "I can tell you all about this curious fellow, for during the voyage I enjoyed the full confidence of our ill-fated captain, whom I nicknamed 'The Lord Mayor' in that he ruled over us in the City of London. The owners of this brig formerly possessed two, built for the New England trade. One was called Gog and the other Magog, and they sailed from Boston to the Pool of London. This was the figure-head of Gog until her sister ship was sunk in fighting the notorious pirate, Clegg. Instead of building another ship, they re-christened this one City of London, though, as the captain pointed out, he had never heard of any good coming to a ship with an altered name. Fearing lest this vessel should also fall a victim to Clegg, they armed her with a brass cannon, and painted up poor Gog into a fighting uniform, so that the brig might seem to be a man-o'-war. Certainly, such merchant ships as we passed fought shy of us and steered clear. But for all that, we met Clegg's frigate, four days out of port, and it would have gone hard with us had not our captain run into a mist and made good our escape."

"Well, then," exclaimed Josiah, "if that don't make this 'ere Admiral Gog more valuable still. What a sign for a tavern. It'll draw the whole Marsh for years to come."

"I'd rather have it empty, Josiah," cried Meg, "than that I should see that ghastly face looking in at my bedroom window."

Now Dr. Syn, to whom she had confided the dreadful horror of first seeing the figure-head upon the sea-wall, began to argue on her side. "The ladies have likes and dislikes, Master Foreman," he said, "and it is well that they can generally tell us their wishes, and here is Miss Cobtree in full agreement with Mrs. Clouder that the figure-head is not a work of art that any woman would covet. Therefore, we must find some other use for it. We cannot set it up above the grave of the captain, though I dare say he would wish it, for as you know, a sailor takes a pride in his figure-head, but it would be unseemly in a churchyard. It would smack too much of a Popish idol, I'm thinking. Were I a sea captain, I should no doubt beg to be allowed to set it up in my garden, but imagine the fright it would cause the good parishioners who may care to visit me. Why, I believe it would scare me in the moonlight. No, since the master foreman is so struck with it, I propose that he sets it up in his building yard as a sign of his trade. You build boats, I hear, in your timber-shed, Mister Wraight. Well, what more fitting than to set it up high on the shed's prow?"

This suggestion quite made up for Josiah's disappointment at Meg's disapproval, and nobody objecting, he had the figure-head immediately removed to his timber yard and set up high on his great work barn, where to this day it is the honoured possession of Josiah's descendants. Indeed, Admiral Gog, in his resplendent uniform is still one of the popular sights of Dymchurch-under-the-Wall.

With the removal of the Admiral, everything was delightful in Meg's eyes, and even the hard aching void of separation from Abel was softened in a great measure by the glory of his death, and the kindness shown towards the young widow of such a hero by everybody upon the Marsh. So that after the bodies had been buried in honour, Meg felt not only ready but anxious to start in her new home, and that her tavern was patronised well went without saying. Even the buxom Mrs. Waggetts of the 'Ship Inn', who would have been quite justified in fearing this new rival, went out of her way to share her own prosperity with Meg, for she was often overheard to say to her own special customers: "Now, instead of having another round here, why not step along to 'The City' and try a glass of something at Mrs. Clouder's?"

So, even in her sorrow, Meg had a lot to be thankful for, and her youthful strength and winning beauty helped her to face her new life bravely.

As to Merry, it was the general opinion that he was making an effort, in his own morose way, to amend his ways. Certainly, he spoke to none, unless it was to whisper to his unpopular friend, the excise man. But he worked hard under the new vicar's direction. The brass shone bright in the old church and the vicarage garden took on new life. Dr. Syn had worked wonders with the man in some mysterious way, they all said, and agreed that the City of London brig had brought them a great blessing in their new vicar, for the squire, in his forceful, blustering heartiness, had lost no time in getting through the deeds of Installation from the Archbishop, who agreed with him that Dymchurch was fortunate indeed to find such an able divine willing to take charge of the parish.

On the day of his installation, Dr. Syn, who had till then remained at the Hall, took up his quarters in the vicarage, upon which the women of the parish, headed by the Cobtree ladies, had lavished as much care as they had already bestowed upon Meg's tavern.

"It's a wrench leaving you, my good Tony," he said, "although it is but for a matter of a few yards, but I know you agree with me that since this is the principal village of the Marsh it is meet and right for the vicarage to be maintained with that dignity it deserves."

"Well, I make it a condition that you dine every Sunday at the Hall, and that whenever I brew a particularly good bowl of punch that you shall be there for the ladling."

"Which means that I shall be with you every night," laughed Dr. Syn.

"And all the better, say I," cried the squire heartily. "In the meantime, my Charlotte has found you a jewel of a woman to housekeep for you. A quick tongue, which you'll no doubt cure, but one that can cook, and well. She's an ugly enough old widow too, so there'll be no scandal. She's a daughter to help her, plain as a cod-fish, so there you are. Name of Fowey. Hails from Cornwall or some such foreign place. But, as Charlotte says—she can cook. By the way, you seem to have done wonders with that rascal Merry, but I don't like to think of him around here."

"Oh, he's all right," said Dr. Syn. "I've got my eye on him, never fear. He seems to find quite a pleasure in obeying me."

Aye, and so he did, and he hugged himself when he did. And yet he did not obey him in all things. For one day he went all the way to Rye and purchased there a knife. A long, sharp, hefty knife. And every night when he returned to his own room at the end of the long white cottages over against the 'Ocean Inn', he would take out the knife from its hiding place to assure himself that it was sharp, both point and edge. And every morning when he went back to work he watched Dr. Syn out of the corner of his eye and thought, to cheer himself when he was being more than servile, of the knife's sharpness.

Meanwhile, the great pessimist would have said that at least Dymchurch-under-the-Wall in the County of Kent was a village ideally happy, but neither optimist nor pessimist could smell the black hate that smouldered in the heart of Dr. Syn's queer servant, Merry. But Merry bided his time and knew that it would come.

And Dr. Syn went in and out amongst the cottages daily, respected and loved by all, while Merry, shunning and shunned by all, thought of his knife, and nightly tried the edge and point of it.

CHAPTER XVI. Doctor Syn Sees Danger in Charlotte Cobtree

As the months went by, Sir Antony Cobtree realised with growing satisfaction that there was no fear of his ever regretting the bestowal of his vicarage upon Dr. Syn. His only fear in connection with his old college friend was that by virtue of his learning and popularity he would be tempted to accept some high preferment, and to counteract any such calamity, he used his influence and got his favourite the extra and honourable appointment of Dean of the Peculiars, which not only gave the doctor the status of a dignitary, but substantially increased his income, and merely putting him under the obligations to occupy the principal pulpits of the Marsh for the delivery of an annual sermon, which expeditions were undertaken with quite a show of pomp, as Sir Antony invariably accompanied him, and ordered out his state coach for purpose, so that it was not long before the fame of Cobtree's cleric was established near and far, which pleased the squire a great deal more than the doctor, who seemed perfectly content to remain an obscure village parson.

"It is a good thing I am behind you, Doctor," cried the squire, with great self-satisfaction, "for you are one of those easy-going fellows, who are content to hide their lights under a bushel. If I were King of England rather than the Ruler of the Marsh, I'd make you Primate of All England and take no refusal. As it is, I have given you all I can, and I verily believe more than you desire, so I trust you will not leave me in the lurch."

"I want nothing but to be vicar of Dymchurch, sir," replied Dr. Syn.

"And Dean of the Peculiars, I hope," added the squire largely. "You've been concealing your talents too long, wasting your career upon a lot of war-painted Red-skins. Oh, I know why you went out to America in the first place. I saw your point of view, though I did not agree with it. Your wife runs off with a scoundrel, and you follow. But when you heard your wife was dead and the rascal had disappeared, why didn't you come back to us? I don't mean to open an old wound, doctor. Forgive me."

"It's as well we have this talk, Tony, and then, if you please, we will forget it. You and your wife both knew why I went, and it is right you should know why I stayed. I think I was mad in those days. I know that I longed for revenge, which was not Christian of me."

"It was. It was manly," corrected the squire.

"Well, it struck me that I should atone in some way for my rage," went on the doctor, "and so I resolved to devote some years, perhaps the best, of my life to the dangers of the Indian territories so that I could preach and teach amongst them."

"Well, you've done it, and it does you credit," replied the squire. "But everything starts fresh now. As to your late wife, though I own she was the best looking girl I ever clapped my eyes upon, well—she treated you badly, and I for one never wish to think or speak of her again. Her seducer, that rogue Nick Tappitt, wrote to you that she was dead. Well, then why not marry again, Christopher my lad, and get happiness after all?"

"I can never marry, Tony," answered the doctor quickly. "Why, I could not take that scoundrel's word for anything. I never had proof positive of her death."

"Well, she's dead to you now, at all events."

"Oh, yes. She's dead to me."

"Well then. It's all so long ago, my dear fellow. You'll get the right wife yet."

The doctor frowned and shook his head. "I'll not marry again, Tony."

"Now be reasonable," persuaded the squire. "I'm talking for your own good. Do you realise that on the night of the wreck of the City of London, that when you appeared in my dining-room you cut quite a romantic figure. I tell you, my own daughters were all enthusiastic about you, and Charlotte for all her beauty, has got something in her head besides looks. She took to you immediately, when we can't get her to think seriously of any man, though she's been followed by all the young officers stationed at Dover Castle."

"But, my dear old friend—"

"Less of the 'old'," cried the squire. "I'm not old, so don't think it. Don't I ride to hounds with as much spirit as the youngest? And I am two years your senior. Besides, I aged quicker than you did. I was a reckless youngster, if you remember. I lived life to the full as a bachelor, and damme, it tells on a man. But I don'' go about as you do, trying to make myself older. Why the devil you cut your hair and popped on that sedate clerical wig beats me. Do you want to frighten the girls away? It looks like it."

"God forbid," replied the doctor, "but I would neither be misunderstood nor laughed at. Neither would I risk bringing unhappiness to any other woman as I did all unknowingly years ago. You mention your lovely daughter, for whom I have naturally a deep affection, but it is the affection of a father for a child. Why, good God, Tony, were I rascal enough to think of her in other terms, and you were not man enough to run me through the body for my presumption, I should be mistaken in my dear old friend. Your daughter is worthy of a younger man than I. When she marries, and God grant she marries happily, I confess I'll suffer a pang of jealousy, just as you will, Tony, and just as I should if I had a daughter of my own. And so you think I'm getting old, do you?" he added, by way of changing the immediate subject of the conversation.

"No," roared the squire, "I don't. I say you are trying to force yourself to look old."

"I must at least try to live up to my position as Dean of the Peculiars of Romney Marsh," smiled the doctor.

The squire, ignoring this, went on: "And rather than that, my old friend—"

"Old?" queried the doctor.

"My good friend then," corrected the squire. "Rather than my good friend in his humility, in his mistaken humility, should eat humble pie, I'll make his Blessed Majesty cook you a peacock pie in Canterbury Palace. I'd rather push you up the ladder at the risk of losing sight of you than have you imagining that you are old before your time. Damme, Doctor, life is too good, and for my own part, I refuse to grow old when I'm not, or pretend to be older than I am."

Dr. Syn laughed good-humouredly, but it was then that he made a resolution, for he had the soundest reasons for not wishing to eat peacocks in Canterbury or Lambeth. As time crept on, he kept his resolution faithfully, and yet so gradually were its ends achieved that nobody noticed the change.

In plain words, Dr. Syn realised that he must sacrifice a good deal of his brilliance if he wished to remain obscure, for whereas it was easy to lie low upon Romney Marsh, he had only to be asked to preach in Canterbury Cathedral to have his whole career searched out and diligently inquired into by some ambitious biographer, and once he allowed such an indefatigable Boswell to deal with him, he knew that he might as well make up his mind to the surety of his pulpit eventually turning into his scaffold, for certain chapters of his life, which would have afforded the compilers of Newgate Calendar a fair opportunity of moralising with high-flown adjectives, he had mentally locked in a clasped book, which like Prospero he had sunk fathoms deep into the bitter waters of his tragic past.

So two things he watched carefully. First, that his sermons should very gradually deteriorate into the usual long sleeping-draughts which parsons of this period were apt to administer to their spiritual patients. Secondly, that he kept a clear head whenever the squire was likely to demand a good true tale of adventure from America. On such evenings, with the Cobtrees all gathered around the fire, while the pungent fragrance arose from the fumes of burning logs, the smoke of Virginian tobacco and the steam of strongly-brewed punch, the doctor was never so popular as when recounting tales of the pirates, especially those of the notorious Captain Clegg. Often, after the recital of one of this arch-adventurer's exploits, the squire would demand if such a yarn had not grown with the telling, when the doctor would answer: "I have no reason to doubt the veracity since I was told that tale by a merchant of New England who, being a Quaker, I can depend on as a man of strict integrity." Or to another doubt raised by one or other of the thrilled circle, he would reply: "Now, that tale I can vouch for, since I had it first hand from an Indian who was there, a savage, certainly, but one whom I converted to the Gospel, and who would rather die than lie to me, since I am blood brother to his tribe by full ritual. Besides, these tales are all told of Clegg in family circles from Maine to the Carolinas."

And as the doctor watched the magic of his tales upon the faces of his listeners, and saw the squire nodding his appreciation, he would say to himself: "Aye, and wouldn't your eyes pop open the wider, my hearty squire, if you were to know that I who lean over your pulpit side with a clasped Bible in my hand have leaned to more immediate purpose over the bulwarks of my own frigate with cocked pistols? Aye, that I am the one of whom I speak, the calm bravado who paced the poop of the most successful pirate vessel that ever terrorised the seas? Would you credit the tales of Captain Clegg if you knew you were hearing them first-hand? I wonder. But that, please God, you shall never know, for what is the good of worrying an old friend and patron?"

So upon this argument, added to thoughts of his own safety. He talked about his own exploits as though performed by another, for since everyone coming from America spoke of Captain Clegg, it would have seemed strange if he was not full of his yarns too.

Being a magistrate, the squire was bound to hold Captain Clegg's exploits as very reprehensible, and Lady Cobtree, being the squire's wife, held perforce the same view; but the Misses Cobtree, not being so bound, and being romantic, looked upon the captain as a wonderful creature that they vowed they were all in love with. What adoration the doctor would have received from them had they known his real identity, but what is the worth of fame that leads one to the scaffold?

Although continuing to preach 'repentance' to his flock, he could never bring himself to repent the part he had played in his wild days, for he knew very well that he would do exactly the same if once more driven to it by cruel fate. Indeed, he could see no cause for repentance. He had lain aside the Bible for the sword in order to avenge himself upon the scoundrel who had stolen his young wife. He had given up his sacred calling in order to follow the guilty pair about America. The man he sought, in fear of the figure of retribution that was tracking him and keeping him and the woman ever on the move, finally wrote to him, telling him that she was dead and would he not now leave her poor soul in peace. This news, whether true or no, only made his want of revenge the greater, and when he heard that his enemy had taken refuge amongst the wild pirates of the Carribbean Seas, Syn had turned pirate himself in order to meet his enemy on his own ground. Blade to blade on some wild stretch of sand was all he asked.Calling himself Captain Clegg, with a well chosen crew of rascals who respected him, he became a success, preying particularly upon his rivals in the trade, in the hope of getting face to face with his enemy. No one ever thought of connecting the mysterious Clegg with the sad young parson who, against all advice, had gone out into the unknown in an attempt to save the savage Indians, for that same young saint had long ago been included by his American acquaintances as but another victim of the tomahawk and scalping knife. Unlike his contemporaries, Clegg took little pleasure in roaring debauches, although when it suited his purpose he would roar and sing with the wildest, in order that he might perhaps pick up in the drunken conversation some clue as to the whereabouts of his enemy. Setting little store upon the taking of treasure, except as a means to keep his crew together, his own share accumulated automatically where that of others was dissipated. And then at last he began to think that his enemy must be dead, and like all outlaws he began to hunger for home. Unlike other outlaws, however, he was provided with a handy alias. Although all his crew respected and feared him, there was one man, the ship's carpenter, who genuinely loved Captain Clegg, and to this man Syn unfolded his plan. To his crew he bequeathed not only the ship, but their own damnation, for not long after his leaving them, not a man of them was alive, for a mysterious explosion in the powder magazine sent the whole crew to their account.

In the meantime, the carpenter, to whom Syn had entrusted his precious sea-chest, made his way with it from Charleston to Boston, while Syn journeyed far inland, and claiming the services of a friendly Indian, brought him to Boston for the purpose of identifying him as the saintly parson named Christopher Syn who had not only converted him to Christianity but had lived as his brother for many years with the tribe. Thus it was that Dr. Syn was able to return to England with the good wishes, blessings and thanks of the American church.

A far enough cry from the Carribbees to Romney Marsh rendered him perfect safety. And how strangely it had all come about. The Boston captain had agreed to land at Dover, for it was inconvenient to anchor in the fairway outside Dymchurch Bay. From Dover the reverend gentleman had purposed to visit his old friends, the Cobtrees. Fate, however, not only saved him the trouble of the journey, but provided that the same tempest that carried him directly to his destination should also remove the man who stood in the way of the appointment he most coveted, so that he was able to pop his own head into Parson Bolden's wig that very night, to the great satisfaction of his patron, the squire.

Under such patronage most men would have felt secure against the past, but Dr. Syn always kept his watch against calamity, and his first care was to conquer his own restless spirit. When he went out with the fishermen to enjoy a little harmless sport, he made out that he was ignorant of sailing, and affected great delight in being instructed as to what to do. In the same frame of mind, he even went so far as to restrict his horsemanship, lest his daring and skill in the saddle should call too much attention to himself in the horse-loving community that dwelt upon the Marsh. So instead of riding neck to neck with the still reckless squire and showing him how a spirited hunter could be lifted across the widest dykes on magic wings like Pegasus, which he could well have done, he purchased a fat white pony and pretended to enjoy a meet from this comfortable armchair.

Perhaps his hardest task in the part he had set himself to play was forcing himself to an indifference where Charlotte Cobtree was concerned. Through his bitter experiences which had made him sceptical as regards human affection, he realised that from this young woman he could depend upon an unselfish loyalty and love that had always shown itself in his dealings with his dirty-looking little ship's carpenter. In fact, he went so far as to tell the squire one day that the amount of his affection for his eldest daughter was only comparable to that which he bore to two other people in the whole of his life.

"Your misguided wife being one?" suggested the squire, while hoping he was the other.

"Certainly not," retorted the doctor. "I find that my feeling towards my wife was nothing but a wild, young passion. Not what I should catalogue as affection at all. No, they are both men, and one at least is living, since I am talking to him now."

"And the other?" asked the gratified squire.

"A fellow of not much account as this world goes," replied the doctor, "since he was nothing but a species of sea-dog. The little rascal had a quick humour that appealed to me. I never met anyone of his class who would do me a service quicker than he."

"What was his name, I should remember him in my prayers for his service to you at least," said the squire.

"It proves that he must have a good hold on my affection," laughed the doctor, "since I cannot forget him, neither remember his name, nor do I know if he be alive or dead. Dead, I should think though."

"So Charlotte and I have a rival in your affections, eh?" replied the squire. "Well, we have no intention of letting you return to this sea-dog of yours, wherever he may be. I cannot be without you, as you're not only my oldest friend, but the very parson for the Marsh, and I'll answer for Charlotte that she feels the same. Do you know, I more than suspect that she's in love with you."

"Oh, nonsense," retorted the doctor. "In her great kindness she does much to cheer up an old bookworm who likes young people about him."

This was dangerous talk for Dr. Syn, who was conscious of how easy it would be to return that love which he knew she had given him at first sight. He had done his best to cure her, but even Bolden's wig had made little difference. Whether he acted rightly or wrongly in the matter is a debatable point, but as he saw it, an honourable union between him and his friend's daughter was not to be thought of, since he held it unfair to her and exceedingly unwise towards himself to lay a burden of secrecy upon her, and to marry her without giving her his full confidence was likewise not to be thought of, and as to how she would behave when she knew that his hands were guilty of bloodshed he had no means of telling. To such a loyal, loving nature, the knowledge of his wild days might be a dreadful shock, and would she understand that even amongst the pirates there was a strict code of honour in certain things? To add to his difficulty in this matter, the squire would always prove himself unsympathetic to the many young suitors who begged to be allowed to pay their addresses to his eldest daughter, especially since Charlotte invariably asserted that the young man in question was not for her. Then in a rage the squire would carry the story to his friend, beginning with, "Of all the pieces of impertinence"—and ending with: "I cannot understand Charlotte. She just laughed. It's my belief that she'll never marry anyone but you." And Dr. Syn would exclaim again: "Why, Miss Charlotte is far too young and too good to waste herself on an old widower like me. It's impossible."

And all the time, there was Charlotte running in and out of the vicarage on this errand and that in the most natural manner, and at each visit Dr. Syn suffered more and more from the longing that she would stay with him for good. But he cared for her too well to act unscrupulously where she was concerned, and so did his best not to succumb to such a temptation, but to do or say anything to hurt her, that he could not do, and so their friendship and affection increased daily.

Unlike Charlotte, the two younger sisters were surrounded with beaux, including many who had given up the eldest sister as unobtainable, and both Maria and Cicely flirted and frivolled to their hearts' content. Lady Cobtree devoted herself to her family, and the society in which they moved, and although interested in the parish, it was not the mother but Charlotte who carried out most of the work amongst the poorer class. This fact furthered her association with the vicar, who, like her, was loved and respected by all, giving not only a dignity to the little church but a jollity to the parish. Though his prayers were lengthy and his sermons long, he made up for any dullness, which he had purposely adopted, in the singing of the hymns, leading the congregation with a heartiness that compelled them to join in, and the fact that he could, according to the testimony of Robert, out-drink the squire at the squire's own table and yet remain sober, gave him a fine glamour with the Dymchurch men. Astride his fat white pony, he was a familiar figure all over the Marsh where he lived a pleasant, jovial life, doing good year in and year out to all who came his way.

And then Mipps came his way.

CHAPTER XVII. Mr. Mipps Appears

It was on a bright spring morning that Mr. Mipps came trundling along by the churchyard wall with his worldly possessions in a sea-chest which he pushed on a squeaky barrow that he had stolen in Hythe from the yard of the 'Red Lion'.

Although for many years a stranger to Dymchurch, anyone could have told that this quizzical little man was a mariner. He smelt of tar. He was covered in it. Not only had he given his sea-chest a generous daubing but he had screwed his scanty hair into a sharp tarred queue, which stuck out beyond his broken three-cornered hat for all the world like a jigger-gaff. He wore a faded blue cloth coat with tails which hung too low behind his short thin legs, and his dirty striped cotton bell trousers were furled up to show an ancient pair of thick shoes with brass buckles.

Although presenting a sorry appearance, his perky bearing gave the impression that Mr. Mipps was in excellent spirits. His clay pipe, with stem broken off too close to the blackened bowl, puffed a continual smoke-stream into the nostrils of the long thin nose that roofed it. An economical pipe-man, Mr. Mipps, for the smoke that escaped from the bowl was sucked up through his nose to join the rest of it in his lungs.

He set down his borrowed barrow by the low wall of the churchyard and looked around. Having the most admirable opinion of himself, he was never above taking himself into his own confidence by the simple expedient of talking to himself aloud, which he then proceeded to do.

"Well, Mippsy, I never did see an anchorage so snug and trim as this 'ere village, all kept taut and Bristol fashion by that old sea-wall, and I raises my Blog to the 'ole collection."

'Blog' was a word of his own orthography and referred no one quite knew why, to the black patch which covered his right eye, and which he now lifted in salutation to the place of his birth. It was significant to his character that the eye thus uncovered was perfectly sound; indeed, was more gimletty in its penetration that its fellow. He had a strange theory that an eye kept in the dark was readier for action when suddenly exposed to the light. He also found that its sudden lifting so surprised people that it took them at a disadvantage, and after much practice he found that he could finger his 'blog' with as much effect as any dandy who aided his affectation with a quizzing glass.

"There's the sluice-gates," he continued. "How are you, sluice-gates? Quite well, thank you? And them gulls are the very spit of their great-great-grandfathers I knew as a boy. Them rooks, too, ain't done nothing for their sore throats. The 'Ship Inn', the Court House and the church same as ever 'and not moved a blessed inch', as the prodigal says in the fifth Act, but the 'Sea-Wall Tavern' has—she's grown and painted up too. And, bury me like a lubber in a coffin, if it ain't—"

Mr. Mipps suddenly broke off his meditations, for he saw standing on the sea-wall, the black-garbed figure of Dr. Syn. "That's him," he muttered. "Trim and alert, peculiar and odd as when he faced the mutineers on the deck of the old Imogene off Anastasia, and spit the ringleader through the neck with his small-sword. He's a calm 'un, he is. Calm as hoil. And here he is, settled down to his old trade of preaching same as he told me he would."

Dr. Syn had been watching ships in the Fairway through his brass telescope. The sea-wall was his favourite walk, and up on it, behind Grove House, the squire had given him permission to re-erect Josiah Wraight's hut, that had been made from the bulkhead of the wreck's fo'c'sle. So upon the sea-wall behind Grove House it now stood, railed around to make it the more private, and one of the spars was erected as a flag-staff. Its windows faced the sea, so that the doctor's privacy was further assured. In this hut, fitted up inside as a cabin, the doctor would as often as not write his sermons, and after a time Charlotte went so far as to accuse him of liking it better than the vicarage. Certainly, it was a snug retreat. On the wildest day he could sit there with the little stove alight and laugh at the spray lashing against the window panes.

Dr. Syn thrust his telescope under his arm and climbed down the steep grass bank of the sea-wall, and as he watched him, Mr. Mipps, becoming strangely nervous of a sudden, vaulted into the churchyard and took cover behind a tombstone. He heard the footsteps of his master crunching briskly over the gravel. Then they stopped abruptly. Dr. Syn was eyeing the sea-chest.

"Mipps—his chest," he read quietly; then in sharp tones added: "Come out of that, and let's have a look at you."

"All aboard, sir," replied Mipps, jumping up and saluting.

"And what do you want with me?" The doctor's long, thin face was inscrutable.

"Well, sir," faltered Mipps, "knowing as 'ow you wished to settle down at your first profession, which you give up through no fault of your own, and hearing as 'ow a gentleman answering your description was beneficed 'ere, in my birthplace, I thought, sir, with all respects to your 'oly cloth, that you might be glad of a grateful old ship's carpenter what wants to settle down too."

"And what if I prefer to forget the past, eh?" A fierceness had flashed into Dr. Syn's eyes. "Suppose I deny ever having seen you before. What then?"

"What then, sir?" repeated Mipps, swallowing his disappointment with an effort. "Why, no offence took, sir, and I'll steer for an anchorage elsewhere. But I'd like you to 'ave this before I goes, sir, as it weighs a bit heavy in my coat-tail pocket."

After executing a difficult contortion with the coat-tail in question, Mr. Mipps drew from the pocket something wrapped in a bandana kerchief.

"What's that?" demanded the doctor.

"Your Virgil, sir, what was stolen by that cross-eyed nigger at Panama, who thought it was a book o' magic. Remember? Well, I fetched up with him a year ago, and he won't steal no more Virgils, sir, he won't."

Dr. Syn took the book and opened it. "My notes. I made them at Oxford. A long time ago, Mr. Mipps. A long time. I am glad to get this back."

"Glad you're glad. Good morning, sir." And vaulting into the road, he picked up the barrow-shafts, turned it round, and started back the way he had come.

As Dr. Syn watched the quaint back view of the little sea-dog thus setting off without a grumble, his eyes grew kind. "Come back, you rascal," he called.

Round came the barrow and back came Mipps.

"As I said, I am glad to get this volume once more. Steer your chest to the vicarage there, and wait for me. And take no heed if Mrs. Fowey, the housekeeper, should be short-tempered, as she usually is with sailor-men. She'll no doubt send you to the right-about, but I trust you to be sufficiently insistent to gain an interview with the reverend gentleman, eh? Then, if we can come to a very definite understanding, I'll find you the means of settling down."

"A job?" inquired Mipps hopefully.

Dr. Syn nodded. "Now off with you, for here comes the squire, and I want a word with him. But, remember this—I have never seen you before in my life. Got that?"

"Got it, sir." And Mr. Mipps squeaked his barrow towards the vicarage.

Had Mrs. Fowey seen Dr. Syn as he shut the front door behind him, after laughing so pleasantly with the squire, she would have marvelled at the sudden change in his expression, and would, no doubt, have guessed that there was something troubling his peace of mind, for no sooner had he hung his large three-cornered hat upon its peg than the divine benignity which ever shone from his saintly face and had gained for the kindly cleric the love of the country side faded utterly as the lines about his mouth and eyes set hard and grim. He pushed back the clerical wig from his classical high forehead which puckered into a deep frown, while into his large eyes crept a look as of one hunted.

His gaze travelled across the spacious hall which formed the main living-room of the vicarage, and he took in every detail. The door to his left, leading to the servants' quarters was shut. Directly opposite was his study door—also shut. To the right of this was the large open fireplace where crackled a wood fire, for although spring weather, the sea air was sharp. From the fireplace he glanced up the stairway which led to the bedrooms. The landing door at the top was open, but the bedroom doors were fast, and there was no sign of his housekeeper up there. No, she was in the wash-house at the back of the kitchen. The large casement window to his right was shut, and he could see no one outside on the lawn which sloped down to the dyke and the glebe field beyond, one which great Romney Marsh sheep were bleating to their young, for it was lambing time. In the dark corner to the right of the deep-set window was the large livery cupboard in which the glass was kept when not set out for company on the heavy refectory table which occupied the centre of the hall.

As he crossed to this cupboard and opened one of the top doors, his face set with a fierce determination. From a shelf he selected a bottle and without waiting to select a glass, removed the stopper. He looked towards the doors one by one as he put the bottle to his lips. Then he tilted it up, gulping the raw spirit down his throat. This he did with three separate jerks, and at each jerk much of the trouble cleared from his face, until with a sigh of great satisfaction, he held the bottle away at arm's length. He smiled and straightening his back nodded his head towards the bottle, as if to thank it for helping him to come to some momentous decision.

Now, had Mrs. Fowey seen all this she might have suspected that her master had been upset by the same individual who had been upsetting her for the past few minutes, for she had found it utterly impossible to get rid of the garrulous little sea-dog who had had the impertinence to set down his luggage on her nice clean doorstep. After much hard talk, during which she was unable to shut the door in the scamp's face by reason of one of his brass-buckled feet which he had firmly planted over the door-sill, she went to her master's study to complain.

Whenever she got flustered, Mrs. Fowey's vowels had a habit of slipping back to the wild part of England in which she had been bred. Nobody knew exactly its whereabouts upon the map, for she was not given to confidences, so that her past as well as her daughter's remained a riddle to the village.

"Moi dear vicar," she said, after curtseying to Dr. Syn, whom she found calmly doing parochial accounts at his table, "there's a filthoi, dirtoi scamp of a thing at the door who says he will see you willoi-nilloi."

The doctor looked over the top of his horn-rimmed reading spectacles and translated in a tone of kindly reproof: "Oh, so there's a filthee, dirtee scamp at the door who will see me willee-nillee. Is that it, Mrs. Fowey?"

"That's it, moi dear vicar," the housekeeper answered, ignoring the correction to her vowels. "And oi says, 'No,' oi says. 'The reverend gentleman is too busoi to meddle with the loikes of you, you dirtoi grub,' oi says. 'Look at thoi hands,' oi says. 'Tar,' oi says. 'Do you want our clean house to stink as a ship-yeard?' oi says."

"Tar, eh?" commented the vicar. "Then your scamp is a sailor, no doubt."

"Oh, he's a sailor o' sorts right enough, but what ship would let him on it, oi don't know, for the scarecrow in the field yonder cuts a better figure, and oi told him so. 'And oi'm busoi,' oi says, 'with moi washings-up.' And he looks at moi dirtoi china and says: 'Oi'll wash them for you, moi gal,' he says, and oi says: 'Wash yerself, if ever you do wash,' oi says, 'and don't you moi gal me,' oi says, 'you cheekoi old fellow,' oi says. 'You run and tell the reverend gentleman oi'm here,' he says. 'Oi won't,' says oi. 'You will,' says he, and he ups with his filthoi chest on to his shoulder and pushes in, wriggling his tarred fingers at me, and being afraid for moi clean apron, oi did what he wanted, 'cos here oi be."

"Well, Mrs. Fowey, rather than waste any more of your time, the best thing you can do is to show him in. After all, I don't think a clergyman should refuse to see anybody. Perhaps he has come to put the banns up." The idea made the doctor chuckle.

"When they have women scarecrows, oi don't doubt," she snapped.

"No, they don't have women scarecrows, do they?" said Dr. Syn gravely. "I never thought of that. I wonder why? Respect to the sex, no doubt. Does he know me? Did he say what his business might be?"

"He said something about having heard your reverence preach the Gospel in America, but that since the church was full, it is as like you won't remember him, but that he would like to thank you for a sermon which had helped him in his life. Oi must say, he don't look the kind to be helped by no sermon. Neither him nor his sea-chest. Oi told him not to bring the dirtoi thing in."

"I dare swear he's none so bad as you think, and remember a sailor's chest is his home. I warrant it's tidy enough inside. Mipps is his name?"

"He never told moi. Then you remember him?"

"I dare say I may when I see him, though his name means nothing. I saw a sea-chest on a barrow by the churchyard wall a while ago."

"That's it, sir. Sea-chest and all, as though he'd come to stay. I see letters on it, but being no scholar, it meant nothing."

"And what if he has come to stay, Mrs. Fowey? Who are we to turn away the poor wayfarer? We should not care to be turned away ourselves."

"No, sir, you are speaking the truth. Oi knows, because oi have been turned away, and oi try not remember." This was the nearest she ever got to speaking of her past. Tears came into the old lady's eyes as she continued: "We ain't all so good as you, sir, and that's the truth, but there is a limoit and oi veriloi believe that when you see this Mipps person you'll give him a small coin to move away, and oi doubt whether the good Samaritan himself would even give him a small coin, but you're too good to live, you are, sir. You'll be whisked up in a chariot one day."

"I hope not sincerely," interrupted Dr. Syn.

"Ah, but you will, and oi'll go and tell the person to woipe his filthoi shoes." Mrs. Fowey curtseyed to the vicar and backed out, closing the door, only to find that Mr. Mipps was already in the hall with his sea-chest, and having overheard her last remark, retorted promptly:

"They're as clean as if I was walkin' on the Admiral's planks, my old gal. I give 'em a thorough 'do' with one of your cloths. Polished the buckles, too. Now, do I wait here or march in there?"

"You'll leave that chest of yours outside," replied Mrs. Fowey. "It's filthoi."

But Mr. Mipps, with his sea-chest on his shoulder, grinned. "It ain't filthy, if that's what you mean by 'filthoi', and I ain't leavin' it outside neither, in case someone what won't mind her own business should muck about with it. There's jewels in 'ere. Jewels, my gal, what 'ud make the King's crown look silly, and wouldn't you just like to trickle 'em with your fingers, eh?"

"What sort of jewels?" asked the housekeeper, in spite of all impressed.

"Honyxes and rubies mostly," replied Mipps casually.

"Any garnets? I likes a garnet."

"Do you now? I don't," answered Mipps. "And what a pity, for I give away all my garnets. Pretty girl she was, too. Spanish. In Augustine."

"Still, I dare say onyxes is nice?" allowed Mrs. Fowey kindly.

"A very classy stone, ma'am," replied Mipps.

"Oi've read about 'em in the Boible, said the housekeeper reverently. "They has 'em, it says, in the New Jerusalem."

"Yes. They do go in for 'em there. It's the Jews," explained Mipps. They knows a good stone when they sees it."

"Is that gentleman waiting to see me?" cried Dr. Syn from the study. Then appearing at the door, he added: "Good morning, my good man. Now, let me see. Where have we met before? I seem to know your face."

"You was preachin' in the Seaman's Bethel on Johnny Cake Hill, New Bedford, Massachusetts, sir," said Mipps solemnly. "Your description of them Ten Virgins, sir, was very tellin'. We all seemed to feel as how we knew them young ladies personally by the time you'd done with 'em. If you remember, sir, you made them foolish ones keep giggling and simpering, and we all thought you did it very well."

Dr. Syn smiled. "Did I?" he remarked drily. "Well, I don't remember, but since you do, what's the odds? I recollect your face, however, very well. What can I do for you? Step inside. Thank you, Mrs. Fowey. I shall want your daughter to carry a letter to the squire presently. I'll call you."

CHAPTER XIX. Dr Syn and Mr. Mipps Come to an Understanding

Reluctantly the housekeeper withdrew, leaving, however, the door communicating with the kitchen open in case she could hear any further conversation connected with the jewels. But Dr. Syn had taken the precaution of closing his study door behind the visitor.

"And what have you got in the chest, my god Mipps, that you hug it so tightly. The gold bar?"

Mipps shook his head. "No, Captain."

"Don't call me 'captain'—'vicar'," said Dr. Syn sharply.

"Yes, Vicar. No, Vicar," replied Mipps, putting the chest down on to the floor. "The gold bar got turned into guineas, and the guineas got turned into different things what disappeared, such as drink, food and lodging. Then there come a sort of longing to be quit of travel, and I thought of home. I had no money for a passage, and merchantmen only employed men they knew, owing to fear of pirates, so I shanghaied a ship's carpenter in the Royal Navy and applied for his post for the voyage home. Had to get home, you see, Vicar, just as they had to have a carpenter. And what's more, Vicar, they got a better man than the one I detained, as the captain told me so."

"And how did you enjoy your time with the Royal Navy?" asked the doctor.

"A well-run ship it was, Vicar, and the discipline good. Put me in mind of your old Imogene. So long as everything was just so and spitted and polished, all was happy. I only had one unpleasantness the whole voyage, and that come of contradicting the captain before his lieutenant. They was arguing about Clegg, you see, and the captain said he'd seen him. Had him pointed out to him in a tavern in San Juan, and then, if you please, he starts describing him as tall, thin, handsome and elegant, till I come all over in a cold sweat and said: 'Well, that weren't Clegg, sir,' I says, 'and your informant didn't know what he was talking about.' Then I told 'ow I'd been captured by this Clegg, and got treated quite well till I was put ashore. I described him as a great barrel of a man, thick-set, rough and ready, with great brass rings in his ears, arms and chest covered with obscene tattooin's, and a vocabulary unbeaten even in the British Navy. A real savage, I made him out, but on the whole a jolly savage. In plain words, sir, I described your enemy."

Dr. Syn nodded. "That was good. That was clever. You were always the man for me, and I believe still will be if you care to play a very different game."

"I'm game for anything, Cap—Vicar," replied Mipps.

"Aye, but you may be game for too much," warned the doctor. "In other words, you may be too game to settle down."

"But it's just what I want," replied Mipps. "I never relished dying violent like most of 'em. A quiet settle down and a good long solitary chuckle about old days. That's me."

"Suppose then that I give you a snug berth here as parish sexton, can you keep your mouth shut? Can you forget that we two went adventuring together? Can you forget that you ever saluted me as your captain on the poop deck of the Imogene? Can you forget that I was anything other than Parson Syn, Doctor of Divinity by degree of Oxford University? Can you, above all, forget to talk about that great barrel of a man, thick-set, rough and ready, with brass rings and tattooings, eh?"

Mipps closed his eyes tight, and holding up his right hand, responded: "All them things I solemnly forgets."

Dr. Syn once more picked up his recovered copy of Virgil and began to turn the pages lovingly.

"Digging graves, now," he said casually, "I suppose you can manage that?"

"I've had to dig one or two in my time, sir, and quickly. Don't you remember that time when you and me—?"

Dr. Syn slammed the volume like the crack of a pistol. "No, Mr. Mipps, I do not remember," he said sharply. "I only remember to forget."

Mipps reproved himself by hitting his thigh with his clenched fist, and biting his lip.

Dr. Syn opened the volume once more and continued in a casual voice. "You can pull the bell for service?"

"Ain't I handled ropes and rung watches all my life?"

Dr. Syn frowned.

"In the Royal Navy, sir," added Mipps with a wink.

"And since our village carpenter, dear old Josiah Wraight, has more than he can do as foreman to the Lords of the Level, he has lately refused to make coffins, a work he has never stomached, as he says, and our dead have to be accommodated by an undertaker from New Romney, which is not right, since I take it that Dymchurch is the centre of the Marsh."

"And should have its own undertaker most certainly," nodded Mipps. "And in mentioning me with such a job, I think you show great wisdom. No one couldn't knock up a coffin quicker, solider nor more reliable. A ship's carpenter of the Royal Navy is, I 'ope, qualified to measure up any corpse at the double as they say. I'll make inquiries this very day from the local doctor as to the names and addresses of his most likely patients, and when he thinks he'll finish 'em off. I could make tactful suggestions to the poor sufferers and find out in the course of conversation whether they can run to oak, and if they has any fancies as regards handles."

"You will not be jocular on such a subject," reproved the vicar.

"Not when addressing my ruler to the corpse, sir. Oh, no. Solemn as an owl."

"And understand that in my parochial factotum there must be no strong language, and not much strong liquor. I shall expect you to set an example to the parish."

"And I'll set it," said Mipps, with assurance. "You'll hear mothers telling their babies to do as Mr. Mipps does, and be good children."

"And remember—we have not been colleagues in America."

"No, sir. But we'd better stick to that yarn of the Seaman's Bethel what I spun for the old girl."

"Very well," allowed Dr. Syn. "We'll let that stand. But you must refrain from 'old girling' Mrs. Fowey. She is a good soul, an excellent cook, and if not popular with the village she is at least respected."

"Leave her to me, Vicar. I'll butter her up."

"Yes, but don't overdo it. You have an infernal habit of exaggeration. Your clothes, for instance. They will never do. There is something comic about them."

"Comic? My clothes?" Mr. Mipps was very surprised.

"Certainly. I must get Mrs. Fowey to alter an old coat of mine. Black."

"A bit gloomy, ain't it, Vicar?"

"Sextons and undertakers generally are, and one must conform to type. Do you suppose it didn't hurt my vanity to cut off my hair? And you must discard that eye-shade. It is merely an affectation on your part."

"Not wear my blog, sir?" Mipps was amazed.

"Certainly. It makes you look too like a damned little pirate."

"Instead of a 'oly little sexton, eh? Any more discardations, sir?"

"Yes. If you want to talk about the sea, you will confine your reminiscences, true or otherwise, to adventures in the Navy."

"In plain words, not too much jaw about the Jolly Roger, eh?"

"No mention of it."

"Certainly, sir. Unless to drink damnation to it. Though, come to think of it, I've got one of the old flags in my sea-chest wrapped around your old harpoon head. Now, surely, Vicar, it's right and proper to run it up on top of the shed wherever I make my coffins. Skull and crossbones. Most appropriate. And where do I knock up my coffins and sling my hammock?"

"I'll bespeak a cottage for you. There's one available called 'Old Tree' at the other end of the village, and next door there is a small barn that will do for your workshop. The ground will want clearing. It has been used for a dump."

"Dead cats and kettles? I knows. I'll soon clear it ship-shape."

"Your position as sexton and verger will entitle you to sit at the lowest desk of the pulpit, and since you can both read and write, you can not only lead the Responses and Amens during service, but will earn a little more helping me to keep the parochial books and registers."

"That makes me sexton, undertaker, verger, bell-pull and clerk."

"A great responsibility, Mr. Mipps. You see then that your conduct must be exemplary."

"The blessed Archbishop himself won't look no 'olier than me, I gives you my word, sir. I'll be sober, diligent and take a pride in my work, whether it be births, marriages or deaths."

"And one thing more," said Dr. Syn, "and perhaps the most important."

"Something else for me to do?"

"No. Something else you must never do. Wait here a minute and I'll tell you."

Dr. Syn went into the hall and once more opened the livery cupboard in the far corner. He returned with two glasses and a bottle.

"French brandy, Mr. Mipps. I drink to our better acquaintance and to our settling down."

"And I drinks my respecks, sir."

"Thank you. And talking of French brandy, Mr. Sexton—I hope you find it to your taste?"

"Very nice and mellow, thankee, sir," said Mipps, passing his glass for more.

"The Frenchmen are up to other tricks than fighting," went on Dr. Syn, "and I warn you, Mr. Sexton, not to traffic in any way with their brandy-runners, for that smuggling goes on, I have no doubt. This part of the country being independent and lying so handy to the French coast, there is a good deal of illegal money to be made with comparative safety. But it will not be so for long. Romney Marsh holds its independence only on its good behaviour. She is pledged against smuggling. She has promised and vowed to maintain the excise laws of England, and periodically suspicious Government officers show themselves inquisitive. That is the danger always. That is why I am ever exhorting my flock, for whom I feel responsible, not to traffic in any way with those devils across the water."

"But surely, Vicar, no Frenchman dares to venture over the Channel these days?"

"I have every reason to believe that they do occasionally," replied Dr. Syn. "Though most of the venturing is done from this side to theirs. I think also our fishing boats do not meet their French rivals in mid-Channel with the antagonism that one looks for in patriots."

"Well, what I says it, 'maintain the laws and the discipline," said Mipps stoutly. "For even though the Government makes you curse, there's always the King, God bless him."

"Yes, there is always the King, as you say," agreed the vicar.

"Though, come to think of it," went on Mipps, "I don't see no harm in robbin' the French of good brandy when you can."

"No, no. That won't do, Mr. Sexton. It is a dangerous sentiment, and one that I will not tolerate. There must be no such talk, if you please, and no dealings with the brandy-runners, and you will kindly oblige me by drinking to the sentiment."

Dr. Syn passed Mipps the bottle. Mipps stroked it lovingly.

"Then I take it that this 'ere bottle's ship-shape? We can stomach this, I hope, with a good conscience?"

"A present from the squire," replied the vicar reassuringly.

"And I hope he knows where it come from," said Mipps piously. "Never do for the magistrate himself to go trafficking. And talking of the liquor trade, is it true that Mrs. Waggetts still runs the 'Ship Inn'? And does old man Waggetts live?"

"He is sinking rapidly," explained the vicar.

"Funny if he was to be the first I knock up solid. I'd better measure him up, eh?"

"That would frighten the poor fellow to death and leave Mrs. Waggetts a widow," replied the vicar. "She was an old sweetheart of yours, I think you told me once?"

"I give her up to Waggetts after we left school here. She was such a fat girl that I was cautious. I warned Waggetts that she'd get fatter and fatter, but he had no imagination, poor fellow. Good thing I didn't marry her. I'd have to go round now and tell her all about that Spanish woman what took such a fancy to me."

"As it is, she'll no doubt make a rare fuss of you," said the vicar. "But my advice is to keep free of the women, Mr. Mipps. Women get men talking, you know. You remember how Delilah cut Samson's hair?"

"I'd like to see any woman cut mine," cried Mipps indignantly.

"Be careful then," cautioned the vicar. "And now I'll look out an old suit of mine, which I'll get Mrs. Fowey to alter. It will want a good deal of cutting down."

"I'll cut it down and alter it myself," said Mipps. "I've a handy huswife in my chest here, and I'll take your advice about steering clear of the women, 'specially that housekeeper of yours."

"Very well then. Open the chest. I'd like to have that harpoon head you spoke about. But first of all, just for the sake of old times, which we'll remember to forget, we'll finish the bottle, eh, old friend?"

And had Mrs. Fowey seen them thus cronying over the bottle of brandy, she would certainly have wondered what strange link it was that bound these two men so different in look, character and station, so extremely ill-assorted, thus fast together.

"To our settling down, Vicar," toasted Mipps.

"To our remembering to forget," toasted Dr. Syn.

CHAPTER XX. The Death of the Riding Officer

Dr. Syn accepted the coming of Mipps as fate, for he was struck by the fact that Death had opened a position for the little sea-dog in Dymchurch as it had done for him by Parson Bolden's tragedy, because only a few days previously the old sexton had died.The squire put no difficulty in the way of the appointment, saying: "If you know of a likely man for the post, appoint him, my good Vicar. Give it to whom you please, so far as I'm concerned, since you'll see more of the fellow than I shall."

Thus Mr. Mipps became sexton and undertaker of Dymchurch, as well as general factotum to the vicar. On Sundays, after tolling the bell, when the ringers had finished, he sat at the lower desk of the three-decker pulpit and fervently cried 'Amen' to the vicar's tune.

During the first week or two of his appointment the vicar took occasion to repeat his injunctions upon the sexton, that were forbidding any reference whatsoever to their association abroad; insisting that he should keep sober and respectable in the eyes of the parish; to do nothing that would bring disrepute upon the church, and, above all, to have no sort of dealing with the smugglers.

All these injunctions Mr. Mipps followed for a time after his own fashion.

Naturally garrulous, he could not keep his tongue from wagging about his own adventures abroad, but with the exception of mentioning hearing Dr. Syn preach that one sermon at New Bedford (a sermon entirely of his own imagination) and telling of the doctor's fame as a missioner, he certainly kept mum about his own association with him. Finding, however, that tales of the pirates made him very popular in the bar-parlours, he owned to having met the notorious Clegg. But it was not the tall, thin, elegant Clegg of reality, but the 'barrel of a man' that he described. In this he felt that he was doing his old master a great service, as indeed he was, for who would connect Dr. Syn with the Clegg that he described so accurately? He found no difficulty at all about keeping sober, for he could stand a great deal more liquor than the most generous of his hearers could afford to 'stand' him.

The dignity of the church he also maintained, for he found that its dignity reflected itself upon him and made him the more looked up to.

But it was the last injunction that he found the most difficult.

Although he had heard the squire and Dr. Syn denying in public that smuggling went on in Dymchurch, he felt pretty certain that both gentlemen knew of the vast quantities of contraband that found its way across the Marsh, and he gathered that they could both name some of their worthiest parishioners as aiders and abettors of the process.

Mipps quite understood why they winked at it. Smuggled goods naturally were expensive commodities to buy in the open market, and since it paid the smugglers to be generous, it was pleasant to find expensive kegs and luxurious cases left on one's doorstep by a kind, if anonymous, donor.

Naturally, it did not suit Dr. Syn to have his own sexton running risks that might bring him within reach of the law. Mipps appreciated that, for lawyers have a way of making people talk and raking up the past, and both Mipps and Dr. Syn had decided to 'remember to forget'.

So for some time even this last injunction the sexton fulfilled faithfully, and he purposely affected a blind eye to many things he saw, a deaf ear to many things he heard, and his tongue would lead the conversation into safer channels when he considered it becoming dangerous. Although he realised that he was losing a lot of profitable excitement by not being drawn into the vortex of what he soon realised was the real if secret life of the community, he found plenty of scope for activity outside this risky circle. In addition to making coffins, he opened a little store where, amongst the coffin planks, you could buy anything from fishing-nets to pickled onions.

Old Tree Cottage, the sexton's residence, which had been furnished at the vicar's expense from the Upton's Curiosity and Antique Shop, became as well as the coffin shop next door a rendezvous for the villagers, old and young. He became popular. His wide experience of foreign lands gave him a superiority over his fellows which inspired a certain amount of awe. This he encouraged, for he liked being feared. If he made a toy for a child, he could not resist accompanying the gift with some fearsome tale of witches or the like. Most children and all grown-ups have a hankering for the weird, and while the villagers shuddered at his stories, they enjoyed their frightening quality. Mipps became generally admired and in the process learned many things that were so profitable that his conscience was quietened with argument. For instance, if the squire and the vicar could accept presents of tobacco, tea and spirits on which they must have guessed no taxation had been paid, well then, he could lend a secret hand in the supplying of such luxuries.

Although at first intending only to disobey the vicar for just a little flutter now and again, the excitement got hold of him, and before he knew where he was, he found himself a leader, and involved in the smuggling business up to the neck. He had been caught in the toils from his first adventuring, which was usually the way with people who came to live on the Marsh. The old families of the district had for generations depended upon smuggling both for sport and a means of income. Descended from the Owlers who smuggled wool from the Marsh to the Continent as far back as Edward I (the thirteenth century), the game was in their blood, and they considered it their right. They saw no disloyalty to the King in cheating his Government officials and they enjoyed the risks of discovery. Not that there was much danger of penalty, for the squire of Dymchurch was head magistrate of the Marsh, and no jury at the Court House Sessions was going to condemn a local man for bringing free luxuries to their back door. That is, all was safe enough so long as the affair was run secretly and without violence.

On this point Mipps was adamant. No firearms were to be carried by his smugglers, only bats or stout poles which, in the hands of well-mounted men, were formidable enough. Even these weapons he discouraged, preferring to push a hateful excise-man into a dyke, saying that whereas a cold in the head was no proof against them, a gashed head might well become so. But with all his caution, disaster came, and from an outside source.

A riding officer from Sandgate was brutally murdered on the hills above the Marsh.

The news burst like a bombshell amongst the secret community of Dymchurch, and the barbarous act not only spread indignation, but also a haunting dread as to what the murderer might say when he was brought to trial, for the man was brutal physically and mean-spirited, so that the general hope was that he would not allow himself to be taken alive. Once in court, there was no doubt but that he would do his utmost to make many others share his fate.

His name was Grinsley and he ran a farm up at Aldington, but his chief source of income, for many years had been derived from 'receiving' smuggled goods from the Marsh and passing them along towards London. His callous brutality to man and beast had gained him the worst reputation, but since his farmhouse was set in the midst of the wild common known locally as Aldington Fright, it was a safe house to use for the delivery of the goods, screened as it was on three sides by a thick spinney, and with its large dark roof at the back honeycombed with apple lofts and its spacious cellars concealed beneath the flagged floors. In addition to these advantages, Grinsley paid cash for what he received, which satisfied the Marsh smugglers, who had no idea of the enormous profits Grinsley made for himself.

Apparently resenting some harsh treatment at his hands, one of his labourers sought revenge by reporting him as a 'receiver' to the Excise Office at Sandgate, and the riding officer on duty had been sent out armed with a warrant to search the premises.

Grinsley, knowing that his lofts and cellars would betray him, refused the officer admittance and threatened to blow off his head if he tried force.

The officer rode off to get an armed guard, which threw Grinsley into an uncontrollable rage. Rushing to his stables, he mounted his fierce black horse and galloped after the officer, who, according to the testimony of an eye-witness, drew rein and waited for him to come up.

"Thought better of it, eh, Mr. Grinsley?" he asked, smiling. "Well, it will save me the long ride to Sandgate."

"But not the short ride to Hell," cried Grinsley, discharging a blunderbuss full in his face.

To the horror of the eye-witness, an old woman who was gathering sticks and who in self-preservation had hidden from Grinsley behind a bush, the officer fell dead from his horse, and the murderer rode off.

When the news was carried to Hythe, a troop of Dragoons was ordered to arrest the murderer. But although they searched his farm at Aldington, watched the high road, and beat up the adjacent woods, Grinsley could not be found. Murderer and horse had disappeared.

CHAPTER XXI. Grinsley Posted for Murder

It did not take long for the hue and cry to reach Dymchurch. Neither did it take certain 'gentlemen' long to realise that Grinsley's death was the best thing that could happen for their own safety, and in an effort to prevent him being taken alive for trial, they seized weapons and with a show of great indignation they hurried to the hill behind the Marsh. They carried firearms in self-defence they said, as Grinsley was the sort to sell his life dearly. It was a rational excuse. Dr. Syn watched the angry mob rush off upon the trail, and thinking it to be as well that someone in authority should be on the spot to restrain them, he followed the hue and cry, riding up towards Aldington on his white pony.

On the way he met Charlotte Cobtree riding towards him.

"I rode out with my father behind the Dragoons," she said, drawing rein. "But when I saw all the people looking so grim, I had to come away. The man Grinsley is a scoundrel, but there are so many against him."

"They have not caught him?" asked the doctor.

"No, but in time they must," she answered. "I heard them planning to burn him out. They think they have missed him beating the Fright. But to burn a man out—why, one wouldn't do that to a fox."

"I'm afraid this man has little reason to earn your sympathy, my dear Charlotte," said Dr. Syn. "A fight is a fight, but what chance did he give that unfortunate riding-officer, who was but fulfilling his unpleasant duty?"

"I know, I know," nodded Charlotte. "But he's a fugitive—and—oh, I know it's all wrong—it must be, but I always want to shield a fugitive."

"That is your beautiful nature, Charlotte," Dr. Syn smiled sadly. "Surely, every crime committed should be traced back to its first cause and every criminal that is condemned should be allowed credit or discredit for his past life. In Grinsley's case, I fear it would not help him, though. He has been a bad man. No, my dear, he has been mean and cruel, dishonest."

"And yet he was once a little boy—" said Charlotte. "And I should think of him like that if I were to see him caught by all those angry people."

"My dear Charlotte, it would be worth being a fugitive from the law if one could take shelter with you. And yet were I in such a pass, I should not take that haven for fear of disappointing you."

"Oh, you," she laughed, and then, growing serious, added: "But if you were a fugitive and turned away from me, I should then have real cause for disappointment. Oh yes, I should, and I can repeat your sentence that was so complimentary. It would be worth it to me, did I know you were not the saint you are; yes, it would be worth that anxiety to know that I could perhaps stand before you and shield you."

"Thank you, Charlotte. I sometimes believe that whatever I had done or were to do, that you would still treat me with the same sweet kindness."

"Will you remember that you have said that, please?" she asked.

"Why do you say that?" asked the doctor.

"Because I want you to remember it, of course, just as I shall. Do you know that when I think of that Mr. Bone, the highwayman, who is sometimes as hard-pressed as this Grinsley, I rather envy the many women and girls who take a hand in watching over his safety. Can't you take the highroad to please me, Doctor?"

"If I did," chuckled the doctor, "I very believe I should lead the authorities a dance."

"I am quite sure you would," she laughed. "Well, you may lead me a dance now. I will ride with you to the hills. I think your presence there will make all different. There is a justice, a fairness written on your face that will shame the awful bloodlust that I saw in all those searching eyes. If they take him while you are there, they will take him at least mercifully."

And so they rode together up to the hills.

It was easy enough to discover the whereabouts of the manhunt by the angry shouts of the mob. As Dr. Syn and Charlotte rode over a hillock that gave them a clear view of the commonland known as Aldington Fright, it was obvious that the hundreds of hunters were afraid of their quarry, for they hunted in strong parties that were scattered all over the Fright. Where the scrub grew thinly, they trampled, beating and prodding, but when they reached one of the innumerable clumps of thick bush they seemed afraid of putting themselves at a disadvantage, and so surrounded it at a safe distance, while two or three set light to the hiding-place. As the flames leapt angrily they watched for the leaping figure. But they watched in vain. When the fire had burnt low they would dash in with their clubs, scattering the smouldering sticks and prodding the ground in search of a charred body.

And watching from various places of vantage on the higher ground, but seeming to take no hand in the game, sat parties of Dragoons, the sun shining on their brass helmets and breastplates, and their scarlet coats showing a vivid red upon the hillocks.

All this Dr. Syn and Charlotte watched from far off.

"The soldiers seem to be leaving it all to others," said Charlotte.

"They are ready for action though," replied the doctor. "There's not one of them dismounted. Should Grinsley appear, you would see that the whole regiment would charge to his rescue. They know well enough that the Marsh men would sooner Grinsley was taken dead."

"Would their vengeance go so far as to kill him without trial?" asked Charlotte.

"They are thinking more of their own safety than any vengeance," answered the doctor. "I think none of them wish to confront Grinsley in the dock. They are telling themselves that since Grinsley deserves legal death, it is as well to give it him before he talks to the authorities."

"You mean—they're afraid this Grinsley man will implicate them as smugglers?"

Dr. Syn nodded.

"Do you believe that any of our own Dymchurch people are in that business?"

Dr. Syn looked at Charlotte. "I would not say so for worlds to any but you or the squire, but I have every reason to fear that the majority of Dymchurch is in it up to the neck."

"If that is so, and since you say it, I believe it, then one can only hope that this Grinsley will not be taken alive. One should not wish the worst man the further crime of suicide, but if he has taken his own life already, it will save a lot of unhappiness and disgrace amongst our poor folk."

Now although Charlotte had already accompanied her father to the hills and had then turned her horse's head back to the Marsh in horror at what she saw, for no tender-hearted woman can endure to watch a man-hunt, yet in company with Dr. Syn she rode on round the edge of the Fright towards the first party of Dragoons. She was not only conscious of this strange perversity, but imagined, quite rightly, that her companion was too.

Charlotte had the reputation of being honestly outspoken. She was so now.

"You'll be wondering why, when I had turned from this horrible scene, I should ride back to it with you, Doctor," she said. "I've been wondering the same thing myself, and I've just given myself the answer. It's because I have such confidence in your fairness. My father is always held to be a fair magistrate, but he is never, I think, entirely unprejudiced."

"My dear Charlotte, what human being could claim otherwise?" objected Dr. Syn.

"I think you are the only one I ever met who could," she answered. "I am sure that no consideration for yourself would ever lead you to deal unfairly with others. That is why I turned my horse's head. If that wretched man is caught, you will see that he is treated at least with justice."

As they talked they had allowed their horses to walk gently on, but this conversation was interrupted by the captain of the Dragoons, who trotted away from his troop to meet them.

"So you have not yet unearthed the fox," said Dr. Syn, as the captain drew rein and saluted.

"Not yet, sir," replied the officer.

"But are you sure he has run to earth?" asked the doctor.

"We are sure of nothing at all, sir," answered the captain. "The rascal may be heading for London Town this minute, and being a man of means and vast connection with rogues and thieves, he will no doubt get very effectually into some hole into which the authorities will have small chance of penetrating."

"The last time I witnessed such a man-hunt was many years ago in Kentucky," said Dr. Syn. "The fugitive was a renegade Indian, and the whole tribe was out after him. They were beating up just such a piece of country as the Aldington Fright."

"I warrant these men are tame in comparison," remarked the captain.

Dr. Syn shook his head. "On the contrary, these men are a great deal noisier. Those Indians went silently to work. They were not boisterous. They did not trample down the bushes like those fellows. They crept on silently, reading the tell-tale ground. Everything, every square foot of grass, became an informer against the miscreant. One of the braves was my good friend, and he showed me how to read the course their quarry had taken. But with these fellows crashing here and there and breaking the undergrowth with their cudgels, his skill would have been of no avail."

"I wish we had him here nevertheless," replied the captain.

"Perhaps his task would not have been so hopeless," went on the doctor. "They seem to have concentrated on the thick undergrowth. Now, I should say my Indian would first take pains to read the signs along that hedge. You see, it runs from Grinsey's farm right down to the high road. If there is anything to read—yes—I should say it would be there."

Mechanically, he touched up his pony and trotted off towards the hedge in question. Mechanically, Charlotte and the captain followed.

"Sir Antony, who has ridden into the woods there with a party of my men, told me that you had turned home in horror, Miss Cobtree," said the captain.

"I did not want to see a man torn to pieces," answered Charlotte.

"Yet you came back?"

Charlotte felt herself blushing. Did this Dragoon guess that she had enjoyed riding with the vicar.

"I changed my mind for a good reason, sir," she explained, laughing. "I realised that the wild fury of these men would be restrained in the presence of Dr. Syn. He has a way of enforcing his wishes. Also, I had not realised that you would be here to keep order with such a strong force."

"From what some of my men have overheard," went on the Dragoon, looking sideways at his fair companion, "it seems that your Dymchurch men have given oath that Grinsley shall not be taken alive."

"He committed a cold-blooded murder, didn't he?" returned Charlotte. "The sort of useless crime that enrages honest men."

"Do you think that is the motive driving all these men to give up their day's work, Miss Cobtree?" asked the Dragoon. "I wish I could think so, but it occurs to me that they are not so disinterested. Look at the way they are beating through that clump of thicket. If Grinsley is there, he would be bound to kill one of them before being taken, and yet they court that risk. Why? Isn't it because they fear more to see Grinsley in the dock? Isn't it that they are mightily afraid of Grinsley putting them into the dock beside him?"

"You think they are implicated in the smuggling business, Captain Faunce?" she asked.

"Miss Cobtree, please believe me when I tell you that assisting the Custom Officers to catch smugglers is not only a distasteful duty to me, but to my men. It is one thing to charge an enemy in the field, for that is why we join the Colours, but quite another to assist in putting halters round the necks of our fellow-country-men. Perhaps I fail in my duty by trying not to notice things, but really the people about here are so misguided that it is difficult even to pretend that one is blind to what is so obviously going on."

"I should hate to think that any of the Dymchurch men were implicated," said Charlotte. "The villagers are like a family to us Cobtrees. If the men-folk are guilty, I shudder to think of the misery it will bring on their women and children."

"But, my dear Miss Cobtree," went on Captain Faunce, "by what I have tried not to notice and even endeavoured to forget, I assure you it is not the men who are alone to blame. Not only by encouragement, but by actual help and in some cases initiative, the women and children are in it too."

This conversation was becoming painful to Charlotte. She genuinely loved the people of her village. From the well-to-do farmers to the humblest fisher-folk she was known, loved and respected, and there were few houses indeed upon the Marsh into which she was not welcomed. What she would have said to this statement of the captain she did not know, for as she was trying to find the right answer for the good of the community, Dr. Syn, who was riding some little way ahead, suddenly put up his hand and drew the pony's rein.

"Our good parson has found something," said the Dragoon, checking his charger. Charlotte drew rein beside him. "He's dismounting."

Dr. Syn with the rein over his arm peered down at the roots of the thick-grown hedge. He then dropped the rein and walked on slowly, looking up and down the hedge. The pony left to his own resources nibbled at the grass and stepped into the circle of the hanging reins, which after a little became a dangerous entanglement. Charlotte slipped from her horse, handed the reins to the captain and ran towards the pony. She soothed the fat little white beast and lifted his forelegs in turn. Dr. Syn turned and looked at her as she freed the pony.

"Thank you, my dear," he said. "It was careless of me to leave the reins dangling. But I have found what I was looking for."

"And what is that?" asked the Dragoon who had ridden slowly towards them, leading Charlotte's horse.

"Just a bundle of clothes—that's all," replied the doctor. He plunged both his hands into the thickness of the hedge and after a deal of tugging brought out a green riding coat tied around with a white cravat. This he laid down on the grass and untied. The coat, a good one with brass buttons, was wrapped around a red waistcoat and a hunting cap.

"The clothes that Grinsley was wearing when he committed the crime," ejaculated the Dragoon.

"Exactly," replied the doctor.

"But why did you expect to find them hidden in the hedge?" asked the captain.

"I thought it most probable that Grinsley would get rid of such tell-tale garments, when I read your posted description," said Dr. Syn. "But I did not expect to find them here till I rode along this hedge and looked into Grinsley's turnip patch. You can see over the hedge yourself, Captain, from your exalted position. Take a look, and you'll own that I should have been dense indeed had I not picked up the clue."

The Dragoon rose in his stirrups and looked across the turnip field in question, but instead of showing any enlightenment from what he saw, he merely shook his head.

"Well then, sir, unless your clue has moved away, I confess to my denseness," he said.

"It certainly could not have moved away," replied the vicar, "and it is certainly conspicuous enough. But what would be denseness in me, is not so with you, for you are not of these parts and therefore the landmarks are not so familiar."

"Let me see if I can guess it," said Charlotte, going to her horse to mount. Dr. Syn helped her to the saddle and she looked across the turnip field.

"Why someone has taken the scarecrow's clothes," she said. "Look, Captain, those sticks in the centre of the field with the black gloves hanging."

"Exactly," laughed Dr. Syn. "There was an old long black coat and waistcoat and a black three-cornered hat. That was all Grinsley required. He hides his conspicuous clothes in the nearest spot, which is obviously the hedge and puts on the scarecrow's over his own riding breeches and boots. Isn't that convincing, Captain?"

"Convincing enough to alter his description on the murder posters," replied the captain. "I'll ride over with this news to the Custom's officer. He's on the other side of the common. Thank you, sir. Thank you, Miss Cobtree," and he galloped away across the rough ground behind the beaters.

By this time one or two fires had been started, to burn down the thickest of the scrub and at the sight of it Charlotte Cobtree cried out in horror.

"Don't alarm yourself," said Dr. Syn, "I would wager a good deal that Grinsley is not above ground at all, so that these fires will not burn him out."

"Do you think he's dead?" asked Charlotte.

Dr. Syn shook his head. "No, but I think he is a clever scoundrel. I put myself in his place and ask myself what I should do under the circumstances."

"And what would you do?" asked Charlotte with a smile.

"I should say to myself: Here is a squadron of Dragoons. Here are some two hundred men hunting me with them. Amongst these men are very many who want to catch me before the Dragoons lay hands on me and hand me over to civil law. These people will kill me out of hand just as mercilessly as I killed the riding-officer. They will kill me to prevent my informing against them. Therefore, if I hide in one of our many and famous 'hides' and if they search for me there—places utterly impossible to discover unless one holds the secret, to unearth me there is going to be as dangerous to them as though I were speaking in the dock. I should guess that the Dragoons wished me to be taken alive, and I should therefore conjecture, quite rightly as we have seen for ourselves, that each posse of men should be watched by a small party of soldiers. That is why, Charlotte, I believe Grinsley is abiding his time to escape from one of the smugglers' 'hides' up in these hills."

And this seemed likely enough to be the truth of the case, for after burning scrub, and surrounding it, and then beating through it, after closing in through the spinney near the farm, searching the woods for some miles, the only clue as to Grinsley's activities was the bundle of clothes discovered by Dr. Syn.

Indeed, as he and Charlotte rode back into Dymchurch they saw Mr. Mipps reading an addition to the murder poster that was stuck to the gibbet post by the Court House. They reined in their mounts and read over his shoulder:

"Believed to be wearing a ragged black suit taken from a scarecrow. Riding a black horse without saddle."

CHAPTER XXII. The Secret of the Figure-Head

On the same evening Dr. Syn, happening to dine at the Court House in company with several gentlemen of influence upon the Marsh, encountered the captain of Dragoons who had ridden down to consult the squire as to the possibility of the murderer having taken hiding in Dymchurch. This notion Sir Antony most vehemently pooh-poohed. Since he felt quite assured that smuggling did not go on in Dymchurch while he was the magistrate, he asked why should his good tenants have any truck with an unpopular 'receiver' in the hills. If Grinsley had dealings with the coast, he maintained it was with the Sussex gangs. Dr. Syn supported him in agreeing that it was no use seeking for the murderer in Dymchurch.

The Dragoon, thinking otherwise, said nothing more on the subject, but no sooner had the ladies left the table than Sennacharib Pepper, under the influence of the squire's good wine, reopened the discussion by affirming that Dymchurch, for all its outward tranquility, was not all it seemed, as on his many night visits across the Marsh to relieve the sick, he had met suspicious processions of men, horses and pack ponies and had recognised several Dymchurch men. "But my calling is sacred. Like the parson I have to keep my mouth shut. I am horrified at what I have seen naturally, but my duty in no way urges me to be an assistant hangman."

Dr. Syn quietly remarked that his spiritual duties also entailed a good deal of crossing the Marsh at night in order to minister to the dying, but he stoutly affirmed that he had never seen anything of a suspicious nature.

"Well, I hope most sincerely that I have the spiritual doctor's luck," laughed the Dragoon. "I don't want to arrest your Dymchurch parishioners. Indeed, for my own part I am quite in sympathy with poor men getting good drink from France for nothing."

"Not quite the sentiments for a gentleman holding His Majesty's commission I venture to suggest, sir," snapped Dr. Pepper.

"Damme, sir," laughed the Dragoon, "a soldier may hold as many erroneous sentiments as he pleases so long as they do not react against his orders. If I were to meet a cavalcade such as you describe, I should use my command to send them to the Assizes, but I could still hold my private opinion of the lawyers who forward them on to the scaffold. I have no desire to send fellow countrymen to their death."

"You'd feel happier fighting the French, sir?" suggested Dr. Syn.

"I' faith, that's so," nodded the Dragoon. "Or this Grinsley rascal. You see that I have laid my pistols over yonder"—and he indicated the ledge of the great chimney-piece. "They are both primed. I never leave them on my saddle for fear they might be tampered with. No, sir, I obey orders and keep 'em in sight, and I shall have no compunction in letting that murderer have both barrels. But I should not care to shoot down a poor Dymchurch lad because he happened to carry a keg of contraband."

"No need to shoot him, sir," said Dr. Pepper. "Send him to trial. He breaks the law and must be tried by the law. Thank God the laws of England are fair enough. It is the only way to stop this 'happening to carry a keg'."

"And how about that excellent brandy you gave me the other day, Sennacharib?" laughed the squire.

"It was a gift, sir, from a patient," returned the physician.

"So you told me, but how did he get it, do you suppose? Leaving his stable door open?" The squire gave the captain of Dragoons a wink.

"I did not inquire where he purchased it," said Pepper. "It was a gift to me. My conscience was quite clear."

When the company broke up, Dr. Syn remained in the library as the squire had something to say to him in private.

"The mail brought down a letter to-night from Lloyd's about the wreck of the City of London," he said. "At last they are in touch with the cargo owners in America and ask for the ship's papers which you had from the captain. If you will let me have them to-morrow, I will see that they are posted by the Hythe mail. By the way, I wish we could cure Sennacharib of riding his hobby-horse in front of strangers. Of course smuggling goes on, but I will always shut my eyes to the fact that any of our people are implicated. I tell you his remarks have made that Dragoon officer suspicious. No doubt he suspects the lot of us."

"Well, Tony, we've heard the captain's sentiments, so I don't think he'll be getting any of our lads into trouble, and he would hardly come here and drink your wine if he intended to arrest you."

"Does Mr. Mipps ever talk to you about smugglers?" asked the squire. "If anything goes on I should say he would ferret it out."

"I think so too, did he consider it his business," replied Dr. Syn. "But no, Mr. Mipps has come to anchor in a haven after his own heart. He is a sensible fellow, and very loyal to both of us who have helped him to his anchorage."

"Well I'll take your word for it," laughed the squire. "But when I look at him I cannot help feeling that there's a mischievous devil laughing underneath that look of injured innocence."

"It amuses him to create such an impression, I verily believe," replied Dr. Syn, joining in the laughter.

On his return to the vicarage, Dr. Syn found Mipps awaiting him for orders. A funeral had to be arranged, and as Mipps put it: "That's not all the trouble, 'cos it's never death but it's birth, and there's a christening." When these matters were settled satisfactorily, Mipps asked whether any news of Grinsley's whereabouts had been delivered at the Court House.

Dr. Syn told him 'no', but that the Dragoon had thought him to be hiding in Dymchurch.

"That's the sort of silly thing a Dragoon would say," replied Mipps. "Dymchurch? Why there ain't a Dymchurch lad who wouldn't cut his throat for that cold-blooded murder. My opinion is that he's done himself in and cheated the undertaker. We'll find his bones one day up in the woods."

"A man takes his life as a last resort, and Grinsley is not cornered yet," replied the doctor. "He knows the roads to London are watched, and he has many a safe hiding-place around Aldington in which to lie snug. He can get to his own house at night for food and drink and no one the wiser, and in the meanwhile he'll try to get across the Channel. The Dragoon officer now agrees with me. He has ridden back to the hills post his men. After to-day's drive which ended so unsatisfactorily, Grinsley may become over confident and betray himself."

"Then the Dragoon's gone back to the hills and given up his Dymchurch search?" asked Mipps.

Dr. Syn nodded, and as he nodded it seemed to him that his sexton looked relieved.

Mipps picked up his old three-cornered hat, and proceeded to light his lantern.

"Where are you going? The 'Ship Inn' to-night, 'The City of London' or the 'Ocean'?" asked the vicar.

"Well I thought I might have just one at each," replied the sexton. "I likes to see that the boys are all behaving themselves."

"Quite right," returned Syn, with a smile. "Well, don't forget to behave yourself and remember to take just one."

"Just one?" repeated Mipps, sadly depressed.

"At each. That makes three—" explained the vicar. "Before now I have drawn a tun barrel of inspiration from three drinks."

"Ah, but they probably was drinks," argued Mipps. "There was drinks out there."

"There were," corrected Syn. "And they are none so bad hereabouts, my friend. So be careful."

"Three it shall be, Vicar," replied the sexton.

"But you might make it more if you care to linger a little at 'The City of London'," went on the vicar. "I have reason to believe that Mr. Merry has broken his parole. In fact that he has taken to visiting Meg's bar at night. Just learn from Mrs. Clouder whether this is so, and if it is find out whether he has behaved himself. I will not have that nice young woman plagued by that fellow."

"Perhaps I'd better wait there a bit and see if he sneaks in eh?" suggested Mipps. "Then he'll blame me for telling you, and not Meg Clouder."

Syn smiled. "You had better seek him out and send him here before he goes to bed. I am not altogether satisfied with one or two things I have heard about friend Merry."

So the sexton departed in search of Merry and many drinks, since he now had the excuse, and Dr. Syn unlocked a cabinet and took from it the ship's papers which the squire had asked for.

In the past, Dr. Syn had had a good deal to do with ship's papers. He had never had the truth of them called in question, although he had often gone to the pains of re-writing them to suit his turn. But that was in the days when he was following his enemy on the high seas, and incidentally amassing a fortune at other ships' expense. All that was behind him. All that must be forgotten, and yet sometimes the thrill of those years glowed again in his veins. He thought of his ship—his Imogene. He once more passed the quarter-deck with the wind whistling through the rigging, all sails unfurled in a half gale, everything carrying on to the last rope yarn. He would draw in his breath till his lungs were full and would laugh at a half-dozen well-remembered typhoons now lashed in one, with the good ship racing through it as though the devil himself were at her helm. The devil? Yes, the devil of the seas. Captain Clegg himself, tall and elegant, holding his wild crew by the magic of his own daring. Impossible to forget it all the time, for he was still in his prime and hungered for adventure.

It was perhaps this old love of the sea and ships that made him turn to his fireplace with the brig's log-book in his hand. He filled a pipe of tobacco, poured himself out a generous allowance of brandy and seated in his high-backed chair, he began to read through the doings of the ill-fated ship. As he read, the captain seemed to stand before him. An honest fellow, that captain. Dr. Syn had taken a great respect for the man, and he regretted his ghastly end. That the man had helped him to save his sea-chest and had, like himself, endured that ghastly swim and unconscious battering upon the sea-wall only to be assassinated by that cowardly vulture, Merry, gave the vicar a loathing for that deed, and he had vowed over and over again that the captain's death would be well avenged by the time he had finished with the rogue.

The plain straight-forwardness of the log-book entries brought the captain very near to him, and in affection the vicar read on till the last entry. 'And now the after hold is blazing fiercely. We must abandon ship, and with very little hope. My ship's company have all done their duty, but none more so than our one passenger, Parson Syn, who was indeed, first aloft to clear the rigging. He worked like a sailor born and a parson. We escaped Dungeness by his knowledge of the coast. Driving now into a bay towards a sea-wall. It is certain disaster to the ship, and may God have mercy on our souls."

Mechanically Dr. Syn turned over the pages—blank pages now that might have been filled with entries of good sailing and profitable returns. It was well that he did so, for on the last page of all was another entry of the dead captain, and it was his Last Will and Testament. Dr. Syn read with astonishment:

'This is the Last Will and Testament of me, Mervin Ransom, Master and Owner of the brig, City of London, trading between New England and Port of London, who having no kith and kin to my knowledge, bequeath what I possess to be divided equally amongst all and sundry persons, with no respect of rank or class, who may be voyaging upon the said brig at the time of my decease. The brig shall be broken up be it that she survive me, and her materials sold, the money divided as stated. I will not risk my brig having another master. She has known only one, the man Mervin Ransom who built her. The figure alone shall not be broken up, but let it be taken to some worthy shipyard or boat-builder's and be left there for a memorial. But before carrying this into effect let my beneficiaries take care for themselves to remove the let-in block between the shoulder-blades. It is caulked in securely and hidden by the folds of the cloak worn by old Gog the London Giant. In the cavity thus revealed will be found a string of pearls. As a young man I collected them myself, matching them carefully. They were plentiful enough in those days if a man cared to fare far and adventure a little. These I would not sell, but collected them for her who I hoped would marry me on my return. My return was postponed a long time, but when at last I made home she was dead. I kept my gift in the body of the figure-head—a gift to my ship. Perhaps in years to come these stones will adorn the neck of a beautiful woman. I pray God that her mind be beautiful too, for she for whom they were meant was perfect in beauty. But let the brig be broken up. That is the solemn adjuration of Mervin Ransom. Signed in the presence of my 1st and 2nd mates, who herewith affix their marks.'

Dr. Syn read the names and date. He was the sole survivor of the brig. The captain and crew were all dead. The pearls were his. The first thing to do was to discover in they were still there.

As he read the extraordinary document through again there came a knocking at his door. Dr. Syn glanced at the clock. It was half-past ten; Mrs. Fowey would have gone to bed. He got up, went across the hall and opened the door, admitting Mr. Merry.

"Mipps said you wanted me," he growled sullenly.

"You met him in 'The City of London', eh?" asked the vicar.

"No, I didn't then," replied Merry hotly. "I met him at the 'Ship'. I was talking to Mrs. Waggetts."

"But you have been to 'The City of London' lately?" asked Syn.

"Well, I had to meet a man there one night last week. It was not my fault."

"You should have come to me for permission first," said Syn sternly. "Avoid it in future, Mr. Merry, and we shall be the better friends. And for your punishment—"

"Punishment?" flashed out Merry. "For just going in to find a man—"

"Which was a breach of discipline, my friend, and that does not suit me. For punishment, you will accompany me to Wraight's yard with a dark lantern. Where is Mipps?"

"He left the 'Ship' on his way to Meg Clouder's tavern."

"Go and fetch him."

"But you said I was not to go there."

"Not without permission, which I now give you. Was Josiah Wraight with Mipps?"

"He left the 'Ship' before Mipps. He was going home to bed."

"All the better. Very much more convenient for what we have to do. We will give him half-an-hour to get to bed. You may go to 'The City of London' and call Mr. Mipps from the door. You will say I want to see him in half-an-hour, and you will wait outside for him. When he joins you, you will tell him that I want him to bring his bag of tools."

"It is raining. It is blowing half a gale," grumbled Merry.

"It was blowing a full gale when you murdered the captain of the brig," replied Syn.

"Will you never stop reminding me of that?"

"Not while you are disobedient. Go. And remember. No drinking at Meg's tavern. And don't forget the bag of tools."

Merry slouched off into the night.

In less than half-an-hour he was back again with Mr. Mipps. They found Dr. Syn waiting for them in his heavy black riding coat, his face muffled in a scarf and his three-cornered hat pulled low on to his forehead.

"I brought the bag o' tools, sir," said Mipps, "but what's the game, sir?"

"A little adventuring, Mr. Sexton. Just we three. Mr. Merry will watch for us and warn us if anyone wakes at Josiah Wraight's, while you and I climb up on to the roof of his shed."

"And what are we going to do that for?" asked Mipps.

"We are going to pay our respects to old Gog, the figure-head of the City of London."

So the three adventurers braved the weather towards the avenue of trees outside Wraight's yard. There was little fear of disturbing old Josiah, who slept on the other side of the house adjoining his yard, but Dr. Syn took the precaution of placing Merry on that side, while he and Mipps took one of the many ladders from the shed and mounted it alongside the figure-head which had been fixed upon the corner of the roof.

When they stood behind it, Syn took the dark lantern and opened the shutter.

"There you are now, Master Carpenter," whispered Dr. Syn, with a grim smile. "You see that line. It is as neat a piece of caulking as ever I saw, and it seems a pity to unpick it. It's got to be done, though, and quickly. The trees are creaking loud enough to drown any sound, but do it as quietly as possible. Get busy, Master Carpenter."

"Right, Vicar," grinned the mystified Mipps.

Syn held the light while Mipps, selecting a sharp tool suitable for the purpose began uncaulking the tight seam of oakum. He had almost completed the circle when he put his spare hand over the lantern.

"What is it?" whispered Syn.

"Why, that skunk Merry. He's left his post. He's watchin' us," whispered Mipps.

"I rather hoped he would. That's why I brought him along. I assure you, the results of this night's work on the roof here will plague him past all bearing. Get on with it."

"Oh, then that's all right," answered Mipps. "So long as it annoys him and not you, enough said. There, sir, it's uncorked."

"Drive in a gimlet and pull," said Syn.

Mipps found a gimlet, screwed it into the loosened block, and then pulled it out. Syn put his hand into the cavity.

"Look out it ain't a snake or something," cautioned Mipps.

""Keep easy in your mind. I've got it, and it's what I expected. Look!" By the lantern light Syn drew out of the cavity a string of pearls. Both men knew something of stones, and it was obvious to both that the pearls were exquisitely matched and highly priced.

"And how in the name of Captain Clegg did you know they was here?" whispered Mipps. "Was our captain of the brig one of the Jolly Brethren?"

Dr. Syn shook his head. He was still holding the pearl string against the lantern's light.

"Listen," cautioned Mipps. "I heard a man gasp for breath. It's Merry watching. He knows what you have found."

"I intended he should. Let us take him back with us to the vicarage and give him the drink I refused him at 'The City of London'."

Dr. Syn dropped the string of pearls into his side pocket and descended the ladder, followed by Mipps who, after putting the ladder back in the shed, went in search of Merry, who had quickly hurried back to his post.

CHAPTER XXIII. The Open Stable Doors

"You will accompany us to the vicarage, Mr. Merry, said Dr. Syn, as they turned for the builder's yard on to the high road and set their faces towards the village. "After your wait you will no doubt be glad of a drink, besides, there is the question of a punishment, if you remember."

"There is also the question of my having something to say which you will not relish," replied Merry, with a note of cunning triumph.

"Oh, I am convinced that anything you say will be charming," said Dr. Syn.

"To me, but not to you," growled Merry.

"Well, you shall say it over my brandy, Mr. Merry."

Dr. Syn led them round to the back of the vicarage. He always went to the stable to bid good night to his fat little pony.

"I have noticed, Mr. Mipps, he said, that periodically my stable door is unlocked."

"Really?" asked Mipps. "Well, there's always a remedy to that, sir."

"You mean, lock it up again?"

"Right, sir. First shot, sir," laughed Mipps.

"Unfortunately, the key seems to unlock the door and then disappear, and strangely enough, every time it has happened I see a chalked cross upon the lintel of the stable. Let us see if it is there now, shall we?"

He led the way in, and approached the stall in which the fat pony was munching contentedly.

"There you are," he said, taking the lantern from Merry. "A white cross. And if it happens as it has happened before on several occasions, to-morrow morning that chalk mark will have gone from the wood. What do you make of it?"

"What ever could one make of it, sir?" asked Mipps. "I'm sure I make nothing. Door that opens and loses its key and lets in a chalk mark? Does the key come back?"

"It has never failed yet," answered the vicar.

"Very strange. Door opens. Key goes. Chalky cross comes. Chalky cross goes, key comes back and door's locked. No, I make nothing of that, sir."

"I make a good deal," growled Merry. "And so will a number of others before very long. Open stable door, eh? You'll find every stable door open to-night, not only here, not only on the Marsh, but far and away over farms and manors as far away as Tenterden. And most of 'em ain't the luck of the chalky cross neither."

"Oh, it's lucky then, is it, that cross?" asked Dr. Syn.

"Aye. It means the party what owns that pony or that horse or that donkey or mule is favoured."

"Favoured?" repeated Dr. Syn. "By whom?"

"By shadows. It ain't healthy to say what them shadows are, is it, Mr. Mipps?"

Mipps looked at Merry as though that gentleman was mad. "I never went to school, Mr. Merry," he said, "'cos I run away to sea and never learnt no gibberish. Can't you speak King's English before the vicar?"

"I'll speak plain enough one of these days," snarled Merry.

"You say that every stable door is open, eh?" asked the vicar. "It would be illuminating to verify that statement. Let us take a look at the squire's stables."

When they reached the long grey stone building in which the squire's magnificent horses lived, they found the door unfastened, and in going in they found every stall empty, except a loose box on which they saw a white chalked cross.

Dr. Syn held the lantern over the loose-box door, and recognised Sirius, Charlotte Cobtree's favourite, on which she had ridden to the hills that very day.

"Another favoured person—Miss Charlotte," sneered Merry. "You see all the other cattle have been taken, ladies' mounts and all. No doubt, the grooms had orders to put this one in the loose-box."

"Orders?" queried the vicar. "From whom, pray?"

"I think Mr. Merry is hinting at smugglers," suggested Mipps.

"I said nothing," growled Merry.

"I said 'hint' not 'said'," replied Mipps.

"But look at these empty stalls. Every animal gone, from Maria's pony to the six coach horses. The squire's favourite hunter, too." Dr. Syn was angry.

"Oh, they'll pay compensation, and a hard run does a horse no harm. It's good to exercise cattle. The squire won't be the loser." Merry grinned.

"You scoundrel, what are you hinting at?" demanded the vicar fiercely. "Who will compensate whom? Speak plainly."

"The 'shadows' who took the horses out will pay, and either the squire or his grooms will be well paid."

"Are you calling the honour of Sir Antony Cobtree in question, you villain?" asked Syn.

"Oh, no," replied Merry. "Honour is a question of law, therefore how can a magistrate lose his honour? He'd never be blamed. No more would his grooms. Did you notice that the yard is a mass of new straw? Them cattle was taken out silently enough, you may depend—after the grooms were gone to bed. No, there's no blame coming to them."

"But the key—my stable key too? How did they manage that?"

"Stable keys ain't the most difficult keys to steal," replied Merry.

"The squire must be informed of this," exclaimed Dr. Syn. "Though it's no use locking the stable doors till the horses return. But he must be warned for the future."

"Do you know what would happen if this door had not been unfastened?" demanded Merry. "Well, the Squire of Bilsington could answer that. He locked his stables five years back and slept with the key under his pillow, and he awoke to the smell of roast horseflesh."

"Do you mean to say that these scoundrels burnt his stables?" exclaimed Syn, horrified. "They dared?"

"I mean to say that they'll dare anything," replied Merry. "There's some in this traffic who mean business, and not in it just for the fun of it, like many."

"I think I'll go round and have a look at some other stables," said Mipps.

"Not yet," replied Dr. Syn. "I want you both in my study for a few minutes."

"Oh well, certainly, sir, but I don't like to think all this going on, any more than you do, sir. We don't want to see any of our parishioners feedin' the churchyard rooks."

"Don't worry on that score. It won't happen yet," replied Merry. "The squire will look after the good name of his Marsh men. How long he'll be able to do it, though, depends on various circumstances that it's no business of mine to talk about."

"And yet you said that you wished to make a statement," remarked Dr. Syn.

"Yes, over a drink which I can well do with," replied Merry.

"Come along, then, both of you." And the doctor led the way to the vicarage.

From a corner cupboard in his study the vicar produced glasses and a bottle.

"Draw up a chair, Mr. Merry, and dry yourself by the fire," he said cheerily. "Oh, and please take off your heavy coat."

"I'll keep it on," replied Merry.

"No. No, indeed, you shall do nothing of the sort. It is wet."

Having poured out three glasses of neat brandy, Dr. Syn, who had thrown off his own top-coat, crossed to Merry and politely but firmly drew off his sullen guest's wrap-rascal.

"There, this can be drying while you drink," he said, placing it over the back of a high chair close to the fire. "Pick up your glasses and drink."

Both men did not need a second invitation, for they were wet to the bone. Mipps, with a 'best respects' swallowed his cheerfully at a draught, while Merry, with a grunt, drank his slowly.

His drink, however, was doomed to be interrupted, for suddenly seeing that Dr. Syn's hand was deep in the pocket of the drying coat, Merry slammed his glass down on the table, and with an oath took a step towards the vicar.

His threatening attitude was arrested by the vicar whipping from the pocket he was searching an ugly sharp knife.

"A very formidable weapon, Mr. Merry, as I live," remarked the vicar. "Mr. Mipps, I take it that a carpenter can always find service for a good blade. Put this amongst your tools."

"You leave it where it is," exploded Merry. "I bought it. What right have you to rob me of it?"

"The right of a good citizen in defending the next wreck on Dymchurch Wall, my friend," replied Dr. Syn. "You were told distinctly enough that you were not to provide yourself with a weapon when I robbed you of the knife that committed murder. Oh, you need not start like that. I'll be honest with you. Mr. Mipps knows all about Captain Ransom's death. You see, he is my confidential servant is Mr. Mipps—"

"That's right," nodded the gratified Mipps, as Syn filled his glass.

"And," continued the vicar, replenishing Merry's glass, "I thought it best that in case of any accident happening to me, that you should not be free to laugh at your deliverance from the murder charge. Now, what is it you have to say?"

"Why," replied Merry firmly, as the brandy gave him courage, "I have broken three of your high-handed orders. First, I have approached Meg Clouder—yes, and with an offer of marriage. What though she refuses, she won't always. She's lonely, and a woman only has to be besieged long enough. Secondly, I have carried that knife for my own protection, and I tell you there's reasons enough for me being on my guard against a good number of these Dymchurch hypocrites, and lastly, I've disobeyed you again to-night. Do you guess how?"

"Of course I do," said Syn with a tolerant smile. "You left your post at Josiah Wraight's, as I knew you would, and you saw me take these from the figure-head, and put them in my pocket. I wanted you to see me do it. That's why I took you along."

"Why did you want me to see?" asked Merry. "I can bring an unpleasant charge against you if I have any more of your high-handed nonsense."

This threat the vicar ignored and contented himself with answering the question. "I told you that you deserved a punishment. Do you know anything about pearls? I suppose not." He took the string of pearls from his coat pocket. "Well, let me assure you that these are so god that they could be sold in London for several thousands of pounds. I wanted you to realise that had you murdered me as well as the captain you would have got away with these as well as my sea-chest full of gold, not to mention the little matter of the captain's money belt. You managed the business very badly that night."

"I wouldn't have known that there was pearls inside that figure-head," argued Merry.

"Oh yes, you would, for their hiding place was revealed in the captain's log-book which you threw aside as useless."

"Very well then, I am no longer your slave to be ordered about just as pleases you," returned Merry. "Accuse me of murder, if you like, and you'll not be a very creditable witness. They'll want to know why you kept your mouth shut so long about it, and when I tell them about the pearls, there will be your motive, especially when I say that I saw you kill the captain, and have kept my mouth shut out of charity. Mind you, I'm not above coming to terms. Every man for himself in this world. Give me the pearls and we'll say no more about it."

"Give you the captain's pearls?" repeated the doctor in amazement. "Now, why ever should I do that?"

"Because I want them," replied Merry promptly. "I don't know so much as a practised thief like yourself about pearls, but I can see they're good, and I'll take your word for it as to their worth. I want Meg Clouder, and it seems to me that any woman would marry the devil himself if he dangled a gift like that in his wooing. So hand 'em over, Mister Parson Thief."

"I take it you can read, Mr. Merry?" asked the vicar pleasantly.

"Oh, I can read and write too, as you'll find if you force me to send a statement to the authorities," said Merry.

"Very well then. Read this. No. I cannot allow you to touch it. The documentary evidence is too valuable to be destroyed and I must show it to the squire before I present these pearls to his daughter. It is her twenty-first birthday to-morrow, Mr. Merry, and I am quite sure that the captain you murdered would approve of my bestowing his legacy to me in that direction. Perhaps I will read it for you."

And removing the book from the table on which he had placed it, Dr. Syn read to Merry and the delighted Mipps every word of Mervin Ransom's pathetic testament.

"And now, Mr. Merry, that you can see I am no thief except perhaps in the matter of robbing you of your knife, which I should advise you to keep to yourself, I further recommend one more glass of brandy and then home to bed." Saying which, he refilled all glasses and pronounced the toast: "To our mutual understanding in the future."

Whereupon Merry was handed his coat and dismissed, while the favoured sexton was detained to drink another glass.

"You have clipped a vulture's wings to-night, Vicar," chuckled Mipps.

"I believe so," replied Dr. Syn, "but there is one thing that worries me, and I venture to suspect that the unmitigated rogue who has just left us will do what he can to increase that worry."

"What is the worry, sir?"

"I am worried about many good people for whom I have a great affection," replied the vicar, "and I worry because they are living in a neighbourhood in which stable doors are, upon occasion, left open at nights. Keep your eyes open, Mr. Mipps, and let me know what is going on. Perhaps you know something already. Come, sit down here before the fire, light that old pipe of yours and let us hear."

Mr. Mipps looked exceedingly down in the mouth at this suggestion, which was strange, for as a rule there was nothing he enjoyed more than sitting up late with the vicar and, in his company, chuckling about old times. Besides, Dr. Syn's liquor was very choice.

"You hesitate, my good fellow," exclaimed the vicar. "Is it possible that you have no wish to discuss the question of smuggling with your old friend?"

Mipps put on a quizzical look and scratched his head. "You see, sir, we can discuss it any of these nights and perhaps get no further. But to-night now, we have seen the stable doors open, and perhaps that means that something of the kind is actually afoot. Let me get out and about then without any more delay, and to-morrow, no doubt, I'll have a good deal of information to tell you."

Dr. Syn seemed to think this a happy notion and dismissed his sexton with one more drink.

Mr. Mipps repaired as fast as his legs would carry him to the parlour of the 'Ship Inn', where he was welcomed by Mrs. Waggetts and the company.

Seeing that Merry was drinking by himself in a far corner, Mipps approached him and in a tone low enough to ensure not being overheard said: "The vicar told me to find you out. He says: 'You tell Merry from me,' he says, 'to forget about them stable doors.' And if ever a Dymchurch lad gets put in the dock for assisting with a keg or two through information laid by you, he says: 'You tell him from me that he'll be put in the dock at the next Assizes,' he says, 'for bloody murder. Aye, bloody murder,' he says, so don't forget it, and I'll send you over a brandy to help you to remember."

All of which, though not the truth, seemed to Mipps to meet the case when leading with a scoundrel like Merry, for since the Dragoons were known to be up in the hills scouring after Grinsley, the ingenious little sexton had seen a wonderful opportunity for a safe 'run' upon the

Marsh, and as the usual signals had been passed a fully-loaded lugger was already lying outside the bay waiting for the final signal to put in for a landing.

But Mipps, having laid all his plans, saw that not a whisper went round the 'Ship' parlour of the intended 'run', for the Preventive man might have set Merry to get information. So he went from group to group, keeping the conversation to the topic of the murder. Where was Grinsley? What had become of his horse?

"I'll lay a guinea he's still on Aldington Fright," he said. "For all the burning and the beating they give it, he knows that wild common and the soldiers don't. Besides, ain't he well mounted? Well, it don't take a man like him much navigation to steer clear of a few lumbering Dragoons. I'd like to see him caught though, for getting the district a bad name."

When he had finished with the 'Ship', he repaired to 'The City of London', following the same policy of discussing the Grinsley affair, and he then repeated the same at the 'Ocean Inn', for outside this tavern on the bank of the great sluice the rendezvous had been fixed.

For some minutes after Mipps had left the vicarage, Dr. Syn thought of the open stable doors and was worried. It would be a lamentable thing, he told himself, were any of the Dymchurch men to be involved in smuggling with the Dragoons in the neighbourhood. Suppose the offence were too flagrant for the squire in his capacity as magistrate to hush up? Well, Mipps would gain information, no doubt. Suppose Mipps were implicated himself? It would be quite in his nature to dabble in such adventures. A leopard cannot change his spots. Yes, the vicar was worried about those stable doors. Who were these smugglers? No doubt, he knew a number of them personally. Of course he did, and his heart warmed towards them at the thought of those white crosses. They had more affection for him than for the squire. The little white pony had been excused. And yet the little fellow would have been useful. It was perfectly fit, and could carry tubs with the best. Its white colour would not matter to the smugglers, for one morning Sennacharib Pepper's light grey mare had been found in his stable bedaubed with black paint to make her the more invisible. No, he was favoured by the smugglers, whoever they were, and they had shown their respect by leaving the white pony, when they were not above borrowing the physician's only mount.

But what made his heart warm towards them even more, was the fact that they had left Charlotte Cobtree's magnificent animal when they had swept the rest from the squire's stables. Thus he fell to thinking of Charlotte. The next day was her twenty-first birthday, and he would give her Captain Ransom's legacy. There was every excuse for such a gift. Was he not her godfather? Was she not the very woman to fulfil Captain Ransom's wish? And the pearls were worthy to be given to a queen.

Dr. Syn found pleasure in thinking out how he would present them. He went to his sea-chest and drew out the scarlet velvet coat that he had discarded for ever. With his scissors he cut off the two gold-embroidered pocket flaps, and these he sewed together with needle and thread from his old sea days housewife. He then removed enough gold braid from the coat to form the letters 'C.C.' and when he had dropped the pearls into their velvet pocket and locked them for the night in his sea-chest, he felt he had spent a good hour, before going up to bed.

His labour of affection had banished all worry about the smugglers.

Worry was the last thing that entered Mr. Mipps' head as he saw the kegs being carried ashore from the lugger. He was safe. He had two men watching the Preventive man's lodgings, who would stop any informer reaching him, and if he were to issue forth on his own initiative, they were to play informers themselves and lead him in the other direction towards Hythe, while the landing was in reality taking place on Knockholt beach.

But one man did worry. Captain Faunce went from patrol to patrol up in the region of Aldington. Not a sign of Grinsley. On reaching the last patrol at Bonnington and receiving the same dispiriting report, he bade the Bonnington party fall in behind the visiting patrol and then re-visiting every picket and patrol he had posted, he once more reached Aldington Fright, and further swelling his force with the troopers he had left there, he took the whole regiment behind him, and as though he had some definite plan in his head, which he afterwards confessed he had not, he trotted off towards the Knole. Dismounting, he climbed the hill with only a sergeant attending him.

Beneath them was stretched out the whole map of the Marsh. It was difficult at first to see just where marsh joined beach and beach the sea, for clouds of mist drove along beneath them. For some minutes, they watched the white vapours rushing along over the flat surface. Mist clouds that seemed to rise from the white ribbons of dyke water and joining others in their mad and windy stampede. In the distance they could hear the grinding of the waves and now and then the sea would show through a blown rift of these ground clouds.

It was during one of these wild whirlings of the mist that the sergeant broke the silence with: "See that, sir?"

"What?" asked Captain Faunce.

"Why, a ship, a boat. There again, sir. See over there."

Faunce nodded. "No doubt it's the Sandgate Revenue cutter."

"Or a smuggling lugger from France," suggested the sergeant.

"From France, eh? And near in shore. See, there's a boat putting off. Damn this mist. It's covered again. Sergeant, what if our man is in hiding on the Marsh after all, in spite of the Dymchurch squire's incredulity? What better way of escape would the rascal get, eh? He's no doubt got many friends across the water with whom he has traded. It's worth trying, anyway, and it will do the village of Dymchurch no harm to hear our horses ride through their street. We'll gallop down through Newchurch and have a look at the boat, if she hasn't gone when we get there."

"If it's Grinsley," said the sergeant, "you may be sure we'll be in time, for he'd let the boat wait for him rather than him wait for the boat."

"Yes, there's something in that, Sergeant. Come along and let's get to horse."

And thus it was that the full regiment of Dragoons rode hell for leather across the Marsh upon this misty, windy night.

In the meantime, Mr. Mipps, now knee-deep in the waves, encouraging the unloading of the kegs, now up on the windswept beach superintending the loading of the horses, saw his dreams of yet another run being successfully terminated.

And back in the vicarage Dr. Syn slept peacefully, dreaming of Charlotte Cobtree and pearls.

Now Dr. Syn always slept with his four-poster curtains drawn back and the lead-rimmed casement set wide open, for he liked to hear the sea grinding up the beach and slapping against the sea-wall. He was a light sleeper, though, when it came to other sounds than the waves to which he was so used.

On this particular night he awoke hearing a noise of someone clambering up the old ivy roots beneath his window.

He raised himself on one elbow and from beneath the bolster he drew out a loaded pistol.

Mr. Mipps climbed the ivy easily and leaned across the window-sill into the bedroom. From this point of vantage he intended to awake and arrest the vicar's attention without alarm. But the vicar was awake, and perceiving only a shadow silhouetted against the driving white clouds, was determined to keep his visitor at that point of disadvantage and to arrest either his escape or advance, for at the moment he afforded him a very sure target.

"If you move, I'll fire," whispered Dr. Syn. "I have you covered."

"Don't shoot, Captain," whispered the intruder in answer. "No, for the love of heaven, don't shoot, 'cos there'll be death enough on the Marsh this night without it."

"Ah, Mipps, is it?" said Dr. Syn. "Now what are you doing here? Why do you talk of death on the Marsh? And why do you call me 'captain'?"

"May I come in and tell you for at the moment my back view is an excellent target for any fool's blunderbuss."

"You may come in," replied Dr. Syn.

"Right, sir, then I'll tell you all about it. An 'orrible affair is takin' place."

"I can guess it, sir," hissed Syn, as Mipps clambered over the sill and slid into the room.

"Oh, then that'll save time," he answered in a tone of relief.

"You've disobeyed orders, eh? Is it smuggling you've been trafficking with?"

"Someone had to look after the fools," pleaded Mipps, "and you know, Captain, you likes a drop o' brandy yourself just as I likes a bit of excitement. Well, we was landing kegs on the beach as calm as you please, when down gallops them damned Dragoons looking for Grinsley and collars the lot of us."

"You too?" demanded the vicar angrily.

"Yes, but I had my face muffled, slipped my cables in no time, slithered off in a passing puff of mist and come 'ere for 'elp. Now, Vicar,

I take it, you ain't never goin' to stand by and see the pick o' the parish strung up like mutineers, I knows. Mind you, it wouldn't have 'appened if you'd been a-leadin' of us. You 'as a way with you, you 'as. You'd soon outdo them Dragoons, even now. If there's one man what can still save the parish necks, it's you, Captain Clegg."

The answer to this flattery came from the dark, and in such tones of finality that the sexton did not relish. "Master Carpenter, you are now sexton. In other words, Mipps, the past is past. I made that very clear to you. Leave me."

Desperately the sexton replied, "Then the pick o' the parish goes to the scaffold, and to think it's my old commander that is sending 'em."

"What do you mean?" demanded the vicar savagely.

"Well, since you could save 'em, and won't, stands to reason, don't it?" argued Mipps.

"How could I save 'em?"

Mipps realised that Dr. Syn was already searching his mind for a possible way out.

"Blest if I knows," he answered honestly, "but you knows or will if you thinks. Fancy being hung for a bit of a game like a cargo run. Makes one lose faith in a Divine Providence. But God be praised, you're the head of the parish. The captured men belongs to your flock, and God's blessed you with brains. The sheep are bleating for the shepherd, and you ain't the one to fail 'em, I knows that."

There was a long pause, during which the vicar, still grasping the pistol, drew his knees up to his chin and clasped them with both hands. As he cudgelled his brain, he allowed the weapon to slide down the tented coverlet beyond his drawn-up toes. He then drew off his nightcap and twisted it convulsively in his fingers.

Mipps, whose eyes were now turned to the darkness of the room, could see quite plainly his master's face lighted up by the window, and he knew, by the deep concentration which he read from that white mask, that although greatly agitated, as indeed he must have been, Dr. Syn was marshalling all his faculties to think of a way out for his unfortunate parishioners and thinking, as he had been accustomed to do in days gone by, of the very longest chances which after careful weighing might promise a possible success.

So the sexton wisely held his peace.

At the time it seemed ages before anything happened, although later Mipps realised that the vicar must have reached his decision in a few minutes. But while standing there like a sentinel waiting for orders, Mipps lived through the many adventures he had taken part in with his old captain. The sinking of this ship and that. The taking of prisoners. The destruction of harbours and towns. The wild feasts and drinkings. The quelling of mutinies. The marooning of a dangerous mulatto upon a coral reef. And, above all, the relentless, unsuccessful search for this man's enemy, who used the seven seas as his hunting ground. And through all these wild doings Dr. Syn coldly and silently thinking out the best means of success as he devoutly hoped he was doing, as he sat so still upon the bed, with the loaded pistol lying just beyond his toes. The only movement, the convulsive twisting of the nightcap in those long, sensitive fingers. Mipps continued to live again in old times. Things happened quickly enough then. Captain Clegg did not take long to make up his mind in a crisis. Had that quick brain lost its cunning? How long would he sit there and do nothing? When would something happen?

Then it happened.

Mipps received the vicar's screwed-up nightcap full in his face. The bedclothes were hurled up and away in an enveloping wave, and with an emphatic "Damn you" Dr. Syn leapt across the room, upset a row of calf-bound volumes from their shelf to the floor, and from behind this ambush grasped a bottle of French brandy.

After taking a long pull, he turned on Mipps with the face of a fiend, the more terrible to the sexton since he could see it so plainly in the darkness. It seemed that the long white face attracted all the light from the window. Then it was that the well-remembered and oft-dreaded voice of Clegg spoke sharply:

"From now on, Mister Sexton, your damned-fool sheep shall have a shepherd who will keep his crook about their silly necks, and the excise-man shall dance to the scarecrow's tune."

"The scarecrow?" echoed Mipps.

"That's what I said, you little fool—the scarecrow. He stands in the Tythe field. You can see him from the casement there. Put your head out and look. He won't bite you—but he'll bite soon and he'll bite hard. Saddle my white pony, which you and your smugglers can thank God you left behind. And put the panniers aboard. In the larboard basket pack me up eggs, butter and any other nourishment for the sick you can lay hands on in the larder, and in the starboard you will put the scarecrow's rags—aye, hat and all and tarred tow wig, and lash 'em down under a white napkin. Where are those fools captured?"

"Knockholt Beach. Tied hand and foot. Sitting on our kegs and guarded by half of those damned Dragoons."

"Where's the captain?"

"Waiting for the other half of his men, who've ridden to Sandgate for the Revenue cutter."

"Take this key and unlock a bag of guineas that you'll find in the top right-hand corner of my sea-chest."

Mipps felt vastly relieved. However angry his master might be, he still trusted him, for none knew better than Mipps how many secrets of their past, their mutual past, that sea-chest contained.

The sexton, however, with the key in his hand, hesitated. "You can't never bribe that captain of Dragoons. He's a gentleman."

"Don't argue—obey—" ordered the vicar. "Has Mother Handaway rented her stables to anyone yet?"

The sexton shook his head. "There's no farmer what would take it. It's cut off from the road by four wide dykes, it's devilish lonely and they say she's a witch. They shun the place by day, let alone night. They say creepy things goes on there. Things that don't bear thinkin' on. The devil has queer taste in women if he visits her, which they all say he does."

"Saddle my pony, and get me the guineas."

Dr. Syn dressed hurriedly without lighting a candle, took another tilt of the brandy which seemed to empty the bottle, slipping the pistol in his side pocket and went down the stairs.

The pony was saddled, and with the guineas in his pocket, and the pony's baskets packed as he had directed, the doctor mounted.

Then turning to the sexton, he whispered: "Now I'm in this against my will, but I would sooner help the parish than the outside authorities. You must get as near to the prisoners as you can with safety, and then if I can draw off the Dragoons, you must free them and get those tell-tale kegs into safety. But, remember, if I get through alive, I have had no share in this night's adventure. I am now going to visit old Mother Handaway. She is sick. Remember that, will you? She is sick and has sent for the vicar."

Saying which, he started off the fat white pony along the coast road.

Mipps followed leisurely, and called in at his cottage. When he came out, he had a pair of loaded horse pistols in his great-coat pocket, a brass-barreled blunderbuss under his arm, and the sharp knife which Dr. Syn had taken from Merry in his belt.

CHAPTER XXV. A Deal with Silas Pettigrand

A quarter of an hour later Dr. Syn was challenged by to Dragoons who were watching the road that led to Jesson Farm. He checked his pony.

"But I am Dr. Syn, vicar of Dymchurch," he protested, "and am on my way to visit a dying old woman on the Marsh."

"Sorry, sir," replied one of the soldiers respectfully, "but we've orders to let no one pass. You'll have to ride with us to the beach and report to the captain. Stay here, Tom, while I conduct the reverend gentleman."

There seemed nothing for it but to obey, so Dr. Syn trotted alongside the Dragoon, rode up the sea-wall slope and down a sandslide to the beach.

Here, around a fire of driftwood, the Dragoons mounted guard over their prisoners.

"I'm sorry this has happened, sir," explained Captain Faunce, "We were hunting for Grinsley when we surprised these wretched men unloading a French lugger. I'd rather by far have captured Grinsley, whom we suspected of being the cause of the lugger in the bay, but I must do my duty."

"And where is this lugger?"

The Dragoon smiled. "We could not ride our horses across the Channel, and the Revenue cutter is some miles away."

"And do you think that Grinsley was on board?" asked Dr. Syn.

"Oh, good gracious, no," exclaimed the officer. "These poor fellows have all taken oath against such a thing, and I know they are honest, except in this unfortunate business of the kegs."

"You, too, are an honest man, Captain Faunce," replied Syn. "You show your sympathy and your sentiment without shame, and I thank you. Therefore on the strength of your generosity, if I pledge you my word that this shall never happen again, will you free these unfortunate fellows. Indeed, I urge you to do so. Though admitting their fault against the Government, I assure you that in the event of war, these friends of mine would be the first to carry arms for His Majesty."

The Dragoon shook his head sadly. "I'm sorry, sir. It is too late. I have sent half my men for the Sandgate cutter to arrest them. I sent so many as I feared that the news of my capture would arouse hostility on the way. I would to God I could release these poor fools, but having failed to catch Grinsley, it's as much as my rank is worth to let them go. But if you are, as I understand, sir, visiting a sick woman upon the Marsh, let me not be further blamed for having detained you."

Dr. Syn looked at the prisoners. Needless to say, he recognised them all and was astonished to find so many respectable parishioners amongst them.

"My poor friends," he said sadly, "you have brought this calamity upon yourselves. I can do nothing for you, it seems."

Turning his pony, he rode up the beach with his Dragoon escort, who passed him by the sentry and watched him jogging across the Marsh until he disappeared into the mist.

Now not far from Mother Handaway's isolated cottage was a gipsy encampment. It was towards this that Dr. Syn directed his pony.

Dr. Syn had a shrewd idea that some of the gipsies would be awake on the night of the run, as it was the cheapest means of obtaining liquor, so he was not surprised at being challenged as he rode into the circle of caravans.

It was a gipsy lad of about eighteen who demanded what he wanted.

"I must see your leader, Silas Pettigrand," he replied.

"The chief is asleep and must not be disturbed. You must see him in the morning," said the gipsy lad, with his hand turning the pony's bridle.

Dr. Syn leant from the saddle and whispered a Romany pass-word.

In three minutes, Silas of the Pettigrands stood before him.

"You know my people, it seems," said the gipsy, by way of greeting.

"In Spanish America—yes," replied the doctor. "I wish to purchase the black horse you have tethered behind your caravan. I noticed it yesterday as I rode up to the hills, and it is a horse after my heart, and I have need of him."

"He would be difficult for you to manage after that pony. He is a wild fellow. My own sons can hardly sit him."

"That is my trouble, not yours," replied the vicar, "and it is good in that you will be all the more ready to sell."

"Oh, they will break him in time, when he will be the more valuable," argued Silas.

"But I prefer an animal of my own breaking," replied the parson. "How much?"

"It is an animal of mettle," went on the gipsy. "But since you come here with such a message on your lips as you gave my youngest son, I will not ask more than twenty guineas. I confess though, I took him for ten from a hunting squire in Sussex who was afraid of him and glad to see him go."

"The labourer is worthy of his hire," quoted the parson, "and you are honest with me since your tribe are horse dealers. I will give you thirty guineas. That is twenty for the horse and ten for your Romany oath of silence concerning the transaction."

"You have him then," answered the old man, "and I will include saddle and bridle."

"I shall not need a saddle—but a bridle—yes, and a pair of spurs until the animal and I are better acquainted."

"You are a horseman, evidently," said the gipsy in admiration.

"You will hide my pony till I call for it in the dawn, and I will come to your caravan now and pay you the gold. I must also change my clothes there."

The gipsy led him to his caravan, took the money and the oath of silence, and then left him to change his clothes, while he went out to cover the pony with a cloth.

Accustomed as he was to strange transactions with queer customers, old Silas could scarce believe his own eyes when his visitor reappeared.

The neat parson had given place to the devil in rags.

It was not only the blackened tow-curls which streamed from the battered three-cornered hat that gave such a fiendish look to the face, but rather a cruel, reckless deviltry that flashed from the eyes and smiled through the tight-set lips. This had obliterated a good face with the stamp of hell.

Striding towards the coal-black horse and leaping on to his back with the accustomed ease of a circus rider, the weird figure spoke to the gipsy in an altered—a croaking, raucous voice. "I shall visit you before the dawn, and we will breakfast together. You will find my contribution to the feast in the near-side pannier upon the pony. And, by the way, look after my pony, for I shall return to you on foot and must ride it back to Dymchurch, after I have bestowed this magnificent creature in hiding. All very mysterious, eh, friend Silas of the Pettigrands? But believe me, it is not for myself but many others for whom I go adventuring. I am secure in your silence?"

"To you I can speak when to others I must keep silent," replied the gipsy solemnly. "For many years the safety of James Bones, the highwayman, has been in my care. Let that satisfy you that I trust you as you may trust me. It is a life bargain."

"Then till the dawn—good tenting," cried Dr. Syn.

As though objecting to the bargain of these weird men, and certainly disapproving of yet another human being thinking he could master him, the black horse reared and plunged furiously.

"You see?" said the gipsy, not displeased that the animal was behaving as he had prophesied.

"And you will see," retorted the rider with a laugh, as he dug in the spurs deliberately.

Off went the beast with a scream of rage across the field, leapt the broad dyke on to the road, and the gipsy listened to the ring of the hoofs as he galloped along it.

Meanwhile he saw the weird figure chased, encircled and again uncovered by the sinuous ghostly ribbons of mist.

Fifty yards ahead the road curved to avoid the dyke, but Syn kept his wild steed straight at it, took off from the road, cleared the water easily and thundered on; took the next dyke and the next in full career, and so across four fields till he reared up at the door of Mother Handaway's hovel.

CHAPTER XXVI. A Witch Deals with the Devil

Whatever the old woman's creed was, she not only looked like a witch, but thought herself one. Her appearance, which had gone a long way to establish her reputation as a witch, was exactly what was expected from such a title. Her features were pinched, her sharp curved nose and pointed chin guarded her one-toothed mumbling mouth like a pair of nutcrackers. Her eyes were beady and bright and protected by thick grey eyebrows that matched the straggly beard upon her chin. Her hair hung loose in long rats' tails. Her fingers were long and bony, and for ever clawing something invisible as she mumbled. She was hump-backed and in the worst weather she would not wear shoes or stockings, but would hobble along in a quick running glide upon bare feet.

Needless to say, her reputation as a witch was not only encouraged by her own pride in her power, but by many stories that were spread about her by the Marsh people. Several people took their oath at having heard unearthly shrieks coming from the hovel at night and some went so far to assert that the oily smoke that coiled from her chimney stack took on the most weird shapes of devils and foul beasts as soon as it escaped into the air. The place had a weird fascination for cats, and people said that she summoned them to assist her in her evil practices, and certain it was that the most domesticated hearthside puss that once got her call was never seen again by the owners.

Perhaps this fact could account for the weird shriekings, as the first thing Dr. Syn noticed was a newly-skinned cat's coat nailed to her door.

Mother Handaway had heard the thud of the horse's hoofs getting nearer and nearer and instead of being surprised she seemed to expect that the wild animal was bringing her a visitor, for she flung open the door, covered her face with her skinny claws, and prostrating herself whimpered: "Hail, Master."

Behind her back was an evil-smelling cauldron that bubbled over the fierce fire and Dr. Syn guessed that the old hag had been attempting to raise the devil. Well this time he saw to it that she was not disappointed, for he had every reason to get the woman into his power, so making the horse rear, plunge and scream with rage, he himself let out the most diabolical yowlings of satanic laughter.

"Aye," replied Syn in a truly terrible voice, "I am your Master. Your Master the Devil. But see to it that you tell no one that I favour you by appearing to you in the flesh, for if you do they will seize you for the witch that you are. Take this bag of guineas"—and he flung down the half-filled sack upon the threshold. "Each coin is stamped with King George's head and spade, though it was minted in the furnaces of Hell. With it I buy your stable, in which you will hide and keep my horse. You will feed it as you are directed. But have a great care that no one sees it, for if they should, it will mean death. So long as you keep it truly well and hidden you shall never lack for gold. Is it a bargain?"

"Yes, Master," answered the old woman. "But are you in truth Satan himself that I have raised by my incantations?"

"Aye," replied Syn in a deep voice. "But you must call me 'the Scarecrow,' for as such I come to rule the Marsh. I shall bring my horse to you before the dawn. After that, I shall send my chief messenger to fetch the horse when I have need of him."

"How shall I know him, Master?" asked the old woman.

"I will send him in the guise of a man who can be seen traveling the Marsh without exciting suspicion. Do you know the sexton of Dymchurch?"

"Yes, Master. He is one of the few men who is not afraid to talk to me," replied the witch. "I know him well. He is often here with his jokes, and he will generally bring me a drop of something to keep an old body cheerful. He and his master, Dr. Syn, have often come to cheer me."

"The holy vicar of Dymchurch?" asked Syn scornfully.

"Aye, but he's a good man, for all his sanctity," argued the witch. "I mean, he is a man of wide sympathies. Both he and Miss Charlotte are not ashamed of bringing me nourishing foods. We must take people as we find them, Master."

"Bah!" exclaimed Syn scornfully. "Good people are my enemies, but I own they have their uses, even to me. Encourage them to visit you, for it will be for your own safety and the safety of my horse if people see them visit you. And I have no blame for you liking them. Were Dr. Syn less full of sanctity I would embrace him gladly as my servant. He is too good to tempt. Are they your only visitors?"

"I see very few, Master," went on the old woman. "No one else comes near me, and I never speak to anyone unless I have to buy something at the shops, which is seldom."

"And that suits my purpose well," went on Syn. "Discourage visitors. Frighten them away. I am glad your acquaintances are so scarce."

"There is another man who is good to me. I forgot," added the old woman. "He also is good to all the poor and is loved by them, although he is accounted a wicked man with a price on his head. I speak of Jimmie Bone, the highwayman. When the chase is hot I harbour him."

"Well that, too, is good," continued Syn, "for he is a fellow that I may yet have use for, and this would be a convenient meeting place. See to it, though, that none of these visitors sets eyes on my horse."

"What must I call the horse, Master? Does he answer to a name?"

"He is called Gehenna, and he is wild and fierce. If you so much as lay hands on him, he'll send you to hell before your time."

"But his grooming, Master?"

"He will be groomed very well without your help. You have but to see that his manger is well supplied."

All this time the horse had been standing stock still as though wondering what manner of man this was upon his back, and just how he could succeed in throwing him. The rider had won the first round in that he had brought him to rest at the hovel. Suddenly he plunged and reared, but Dr. Syn swung him round and gave him both spurs. The horse leapt forward and feeling the spurs drive into him relentlessly, galloped away into the rushing mists.

Meanwhile Mother Handaway barred her door and emptying the bag of guineas upon the old table she fell to counting them, and then she tried each coin separately and found that although minted in Hell, they all rang true.

The storm now took a curious turn. The wind increased till it became a gale and before its fury the mist shrouds leapt as though the Marsh were invaded by sheeted giants. Then a stinging sleet shattered down in a torrential burst. The frozen shafts of rain stung the horse into madness, and Dr. Syn used the cruel elements to subdue the vice in the horse. He kept the animal facing the storm till he had mastered his spirit then at last, when he turned his back to the storm, he knew that the animal was his. The spirit was still there, the high fierce mettle, but the viciousness had gone as far as he was concerned. Then Syn drove the spurs in again and rode like the wind and with the wind towards the distant sea-wall. The pursuing sleet gave the horse pace and in company with the whirling shapes of flying mist, the black animal galloped with the weird black figure of the Scarecrow on his back.

And the thrill of it went to Syn's head like wine and he laughed aloud. "Even the elements are on the devil's side to-night. On, Gehenna. On. Faster, you great brute. Faster. The devil in scarecrow's rags rules the Marsh and he rides to Hell on Gehenna. On. On. Faster."

CHAPTER XXVII. The Scarecrow Rider

On the beach the soldiers tried valiantly to keep their fire alight, for it was to serve as a beacon to the cutter. But the wind had arisen, and already the waves in the Bay were dashing up against the shingle. It was doubtful whether the cutter would brave such a storm. Blinded with smoke, the Dragoons kept piling on driftwood, while the rain ran from their brass helmets. Suddenly one of them cried out: "Look!"

At the same moment a piercing laugh echoed from the sand-hill behind them. Even the officer, Captain Faunce, was transfixed with horror at the spectral horseman that had appeared upon the sky-line. It seemed that the storm had opened hell gates to let the devil ride out.

But their superstitious dread was given the lie by the horseman himself, for after his maniacal laugh, which made his black mount rear and scream, in a derisive voice he cried out: "Leave these poor fools alone. I'm the man you want. Grinsley, the murderer. But you won't catch me this side of hell."

Captain Faunce sprang into the saddle, drew his pistols from the holsters, and pulled both triggers. The right one, damped with the rain, misfired, and the left went wide, though Dr. Syn heard the bullet whizz by.

"Mount, and after him, boys," cried the captain. "Granger and Metcalf, stay here mounted and guard the prisoners. Any treachery, use your sabres without mercy."

The other troopers scrambled for their horses, and led by their officer, galloped towards the sand-hill.

Waving his hand in farewell, Syn turned his horse and slid down the bank on to the road, jumped the dyke on the further side of it and led the hunt madly across country for the distant hills.

In the meantime, Mipps had taken advantage of the confusion and profiting by the smoke of the fire which kept blinding the Dragoons, he managed to crawl behind the prisoners and sever their cords with his knife, going from one to the other with a whispered word of caution and concealing himself behind the captured kegs.

By the time Dr. Syn had led away the chase, he had freed all the men and had only the two Dragoons to deal with.

When he considered that the chase had gone clear away, he sprang up, and covering the chests of both troop horses with his pistols, he sang out: "About turn, you two, and follow the hunt. You may take a murderer, but you don't take us."

"What the hell—" cried one of the troopers, but Mipps interrupted.

"You've no chance. The prisoners are all free. Twenty of us against you two. If you move forward or put your hands to your sabres, I fire, and my pistols ain't damp. Have respect for your horses. About turn."

By this time the smugglers were all on their feet, and were grabbing such weapons as they had been deprived of. These were mostly stout cudgels and poles. Some of them ran to where their horses had been tethered, and mounted.

The Dragoons saw that their only chance of re-capturing the men was by getting more help, so as if bowing to the inevitable they turned their chargers and galloped away after their colleagues.

"Quick, lads," cried Mipps. "Stamp out the fire. Load them kegs on the pack ponies, and away with them as arranged before the soldiers get back."

The smugglers, overjoyed at their deliverance, worked feverishly to get away before the possible arrival of the cutter, which they could now see tacking from Sandgate in the teeth of the driving storm.

"Seems to me," laughed one, "that we owe our freedom to this Grinsley."

"That wasn't Grinsley," replied Mipps. "That's our new leader, if we behaves ourselves. If we get clear away this blessed night, he'll lead us, I'll take my oath. And what's more we'll never get laid by the heels if we obeys him. And if we gets him, why he gives the orders and not me."

"Who is it?" they asked.

"Never you mind. No proper names is best as we've found out, but amongst us he's the Scarecrow, that's what he is."

"I know," cried one of them. "I can tell who he is by the way he rides. It's Jimmie Bone the Highwayman. Now isn't it?"

"Maybe," allowed Mipps, "but he's to be called The Scarecrow from now on, and if he takes on the job and don't lead them Revenue men a dance—well—you wait."

* * * * * *

As the dawn broke, Dr. Syn, looking remarkably clean and fresh in his clerical clothes, jogged along the curving Marshland road towards Dymchurch. He presented a marked contrast to the Dragoon officer whom he met at the crossroads, leading a lamed charger.

Captain Faunce's red coat was mud-stained, and he had lost his helmet.

"My faith, Captain," cried the vicar, drawing his pony's rein, "the storm has wrought havoc with you. I just reached the cottage I was bound for when it broke. I was fortunate. My clothes are dry."

"I've been chasing Grinsley all night," explained the captain. "And all to no purpose. They say that the devil looks after his own. Anyway he taught that recruit of his to ride, for I'll swear Grinsley learned his horsemanship in hell. The rascal played with me. Would wait for me to draw level with him, then off he'd go again like lightning. And so it has been all night, for it's but an hour ago that I lost him for good in the woods behind Lympne. With my horse lamed I gave him best."

"And where are your men?" asked the vicar.

"I outride the rascals early in the chase. Not seen them for hours."

"And your prisoners?"

"Safe under lock and key at Sandgate, I hope," replied the captain.

At that moment a trumpet call rang out, and along the sea-wall they saw the Dragoons riding.

"They make a brave picture in the morning light," said Dr. Syn. "The red coats and the helmets."

"Hope they feel better than I do," grumbled the officer. He blew a shrill blast on a whistle. Up went the leader's hand and the troop halted. Then seeing their officer signalling to them, the troop sergeant slid his horse down the steep embankment and galloped towards them.

"We couldn't keep pace with you, sir," he explained, "but we got Grinsley."

"You've got him?" repeated the officer, smiling.

"Yes, sir. As you disappeared into that first wood, he broke cover, on his black horse to your left, and we chased him inland till finally we ran him down in Tenterden."

"How long ago?"

"Must be over two hours, sir. The church clock struck four as his horse fell dead."

"And where is Grinsley?"

"Dead too, sir. Metcalf ran him through the neck as he tried to break past him."

"But I heard a clock strike four when I sighted him again the other side of the wood. In God's name—was he then dead?"

"Makes one believe in the supernatural, that sort of experience," said Dr. Syn quietly.

"And Metcalf killed him, you say?" questioned the astounded officer. "But I left Metcalf to guard the prisoners."

The sergeant then broke the news of the smugglers' escape and how the cutter had arrived to find a deserted beach.

"Ah, well we can get 'em again," laughed the officer. "I dare swear you can identify your own flock, vicar?"

"I purposely did not look at them," answered Dr. Syn. "Though you could hardly expect me to hand over my own parishioners if I had. I am a man of peace. I can promise you, though, Captain, that you will never take them again in the act of cheating the Revenue."

The captain turned to his troop sergeant. "Are you sure it was four o'clock by Tenterden church?" he asked.

"As surely as I saw Grinsley killed, sir."

"Good God!" muttered the captain—and whether it was from cold or fright, Dr. Syn saw the gallant Dragoon shiver.

When Mipps called at the vicarage for orders that morning at the usual hour of nine, he was informed by the housekeeper that the reverend gentleman had breakfasted in his bedroom, as he had been out all night visiting a sick woman, but that Mr. Mipps was to go up.

The sun was streaming through the open casement, but the curtains of the bed were close-drawn.

"That you, Mipps?" asked the voice of Dr. Syn.

"Yes, Vicar," replied the sexton.

"Shut the door."

Mipps did so.

"Find the bottle behind the books. I have replenished it. Help yourself."

While Mipps carried out this excellent command, Dr. Syn pulled back the curtains of the bed and gave him a detailed account of the Scarecrow's ride.

"And there'll be a fearful ghost story told this day by that captain of Dragoons," he chuckled, "for he'll never realise that there were two scarecrows on black horses riding the hills last night. It was a piece of luck that it was I who made Grinsley break cover from that wood. Hardened sinner though he was he had enough religion in him to make him believe in the Devil. I could see by the fright in his eyes that as we met face to face in the glade, he thought I was Satan come for him. I have never seen a strong man so scared. He forgot everything but his endeavor to get away from me, for I rode neck to neck with him up the glade, laughing in his face and clawing the air for him with my hand, till round he swung in a panic, galloped out of the wood, only to find the Dragoons in full cry after him."

Dr. Syn chuckled again. "But, my faith, that Captain Faunce wanted some shaking off. I began to think that, short of using my pistols, I should never change my horse for my pony before the dawn, and for half an hour I had the uncomfortable feeling that I had made a grave mistake in not allowing the captain to gallop after his men and the real Grinsley."

"Why, did you get such a chance?" asked Mipps.

"Aye, that I did," went on Syn, "and at Grinsley's first break away from the woods, for the captain heard his men hallooing and dashed off in the direction. I was then governed entirely by a philanthropic reason—"

"A how much reason, sir?" asked Mipps.

"I thought of others, Mr. Mipps," exclaimed Dr. Syn. "I put the interests of my erring parishioners before my own safety. I knew that, better mounted than his men, the captain would the more speedily overtake the murderer and, thought I, the chase may be ended all too soon, for the rascal Mipps to get his kegs into hiding. I realised that some delay was necessary, so I galloped after the captain, who in his astonishment at finding the murderer, as he thought, pursuing him, struck his helmet against an overhanging branch and lost it, as he turned to fight. But I had turned already and waiting till he was all but at sabre's length I led him a chase away from his men, to whom he shouted in vain. It was a gallant run we had."

"But how were you quit of him at last?" asked Mipps.

"I led him at length to the Warrens, where I found that my newly-acquired beast had a miraculous instinct for avoiding the rabbit holes. My friend's charger was not so blessed, and although his luck held good for a time, down he came at length, and finished as far as a good rider could allow. I tell you I had much ado to keep my face when the captain spoke of it, for all that I was grieved at his horse's laming. And now, my friend, tell me. When is the next run likely? For I think that I had best lend a hand."

Mipps grinned. "No compunction about being a parson now, sir?"

"My good sexton, I am pledged to look after my flock. Well, if they must smuggle, I really must see that they do it properly."

"And a very praiseworthy sentiment, Vicar. Does you credit," said Mipps.

"And to do it properly," continued Syn, "involves a lot more trouble than you have hitherto found necessary. First of all, where you have used one lugger, I will have ten, and the cargo must be hidden with neat contrivances. We'll carry brandy in tanks beneath live or stinking fish. We'll send back wool packs under false planks with a cargo of dung on top. We'll see if these Custom officers have delicate noses. We'll have hollow masts, sunken rafts, tobacco twist ropes put inside hawsers. When we have a great run in commission, we'll sacrifice a few kegs as a sop to the Preventive men. Abandon a boat-load in a panic, my friend, on one beach while we land a fleet's cargo on another. Oh there are ways—many ways, but it wants the brain behind it. And no robbers like Grinsley shall be employed. No extortion monies. We sell at high prices off the Marsh, but here we give what we get and so build up a local popularity. And meantime I must thunder against the smugglers in the pulpit, for that will keep us on the side of the Customs. Let me think. Let me work, and there will be no repetition of last night's business."

"Where would we be without you, sir, now, I trembles to think," exclaimed Mipps.

"Well, don't tremble, but pass the bottle," ordered Syn.

"Having taken a pull, he nodded at the sexton facetiously, which brought the tassel of his night-cap over one eye.

"Like old times," he added. "Here's to the Scarecrow, the Demon Rider of Romney Marsh. Aye, it's like old times, Master Carpenter."

"Yessir," replied the gratified Mipps, "but with this difference. Clegg is dead. Long live the Scarecrow."

"Aye," muttered Syn to the bottle, "Clegg is dead and so is the Master Carpenter."

"Aye, sir, he's dead, too, so it's long live—who?" asked Mipps. "Hellspite is a good name, ain't it? For I'll serve the Scarecrow same as I did Clegg in spite of hell."

"Hellspite then," replied Syn, drinking to the sexton, and as he passed the bottle he began to sing in a soft voice:

"Oh, here's to the feet what have walked the plank—
Yo-ho For the dead man's throttle.
And here's to the corpses afloat in the tank
And the dead man's teeth in the bottle."

CHAPTER XXIX. Charlotte's Birthday

Half an hour later Dr. Syn stepped out into his garden and surveyed with every mark of pleasure the bright spring morning. Not a sign of his night's exertions could be traced as he briskly walked amongst the flowers, picking the best blooms for a birthday bouquet. When he had collected one of quite vast proportions, he approached the kitchen casement and called his housekeeper.

"Mrs. Fowey, I think you ordered me some wig ribbon. Would you give me some for this?"

"And is that for your dear god-daughter's birthday? Oh, moi dear Vicar, it will never do to toi it with black. An ill omen, moi dear."

"Nonsense. The black indicates the old parson, and the flowers Miss Charlotte," laughed Syn.

"But oi can do better, moi dear," went on the housekeeper. "Oi have some whoite here in the drawer. Oi bought it for moi girl, but she wants pink. Let us toi it with whoite. Weddings are more in Miss Charlotte's loin than funerals oi'm thinkin'."

So she tied the bouquet with white ribbon, and Dr. Syn, with Captain Ransom's log-book in his side pocket and the scarlet velvet sachet of pearls in his breast, walked gaily through the back way to the squire's.

This led him past the stables, where to his secret amusement he saw all the Court House grooms busy rubbing down the squire's horses.

The grooms looked sheepishly at the doctor as he watched them.

"It seems by their coats that the squire's cattle have been worked hard," he remarked.

The nearest ostler shook his head. "It's amazin', sir, how some horses will sleep dirty. Now I take my oath that we ain't had most of these animals out since yesterday morning and then we rubbed 'em clean. But to look at 'em you'd think they'd been careerin' the Marsh in last night's storm."

"You would indeed," replied Syn seriously, though he chuckled to think that in some respects the Romney Marsh smugglers were not so ill organised. It was obvious that the squire's grooms were keeping their mouths shut.

"Are all horses as dirty then in their stables? I would never have credited such a thing," said Syn.

"No, sir, they ain't," replied the ostler. "But we seems fair cursed with 'em here. There's only one in these stables what is clean in the stall and that be Miss Charlotte's hunter. As silky a coat as when I locks the stables last night."

"Splendid," thought Syn. "He even pretends that he locked the stables. I see that I shall not have to teach these fellows the virtue of secrecy."

With a pleasant nod he passed on into the squire's garden, and stepping to the open french window greeted the family at breakfast.

"My dear Charlotte, I have picked a few flowers from my garden," he said, "with an old man's blessing on this important birthday."

"Oh I am entirely spoilt," laughed Charlotte, who ran round the table, took the flowers, pressed them to her face and curtseyed. "I accept the lovely gift, but not the description you give with it. An old man's blessing. Why, my dear godfather, I never saw anyone look more sprightly. No, don't go hunching your shoulder up and trying to look old."

"But I want to look old in order to claim an old man's privilege, my dear," he said smiling. "I should like to be the first outside the family to salute you, and also I claim the privilege of a godfather to give you a gift that will be more to your liking than a few Marsh flowers."

"Nothing could be more to my liking, believe me, and please let me kiss you for them," she answered.

So, much to the amusement of her sisters and mother, Charlotte kissed Dr. Syn and then asked him to kiss her.

"Well, here is the gift," he said, laughing, and handed her the red sachet.

"Oh and my initials on it," cried Charlotte. "Oh, Doctor, did you work this? No. It is too neat for a man's sewing."

"Bless you, I'm an old traveller. I had to learn to sew after a fashion. But open it, please." Dr. Syn watched her face as she bent down towards the sachet.

The beauty and obvious value of the pearls set everyone gasping, including the delighted Charlotte.

Cicely chuckled. "You are not going to tell us that you value the Marsh flowers as much now, I hope."

"Flowers and jewels are both beautiful," answered Charlotte, "and I value them both for themselves and for the kind heart that gives them."

When Dr. Syn had confided the history of the pearls and had hung them round Charlotte's neck with his blessing, he handed the log-book to the squire.

"Well, there's no doubt," exclaimed Sir Antony, "that Charlotte lives up to your dead captain's hopes. Let us quote what he says: 'Perhaps in years to come, these stones will once more adorn the neck of a beautiful woman. I pray God that her mind be beautiful too.' Well, I think we agree that, despite her looks, Charlotte's mind is at least beautiful, and that because she has been well brought up." His eyes twinkled. He winked at Dr. Syn who added:

"And standing there I think we can claim perfect beauty of face and figure. Look at her holding those poor but fortunate flowers. Tony, you are a lucky fellow to be the father of such a perfect picture."

"Oh, pooh," laughed the squire. "Flowers and jewels and a pretty frock work wonders in a girl. Besides, her mother is beautiful, and with a beautiful mother and a handsome father, what can you expect? Praise her parents, not her."

"Well, well, we will not quarrel," chuckled Dr. Syn. "Her mind is at least her own, and that, as you say, is beautiful. We will give her the credit for that."

"Her mind can be dashed obstinate at times," added the squire. "But since you are her advocate, we'll allow then that she deserves the pearls. Secondly, there is no doubt that you, Doctor, by virtue of being the sole survivor of the captain's brig, become his lawful heir. Therefore, since this book comes under my jurisdiction and as magistrate I am responsible for returning it to Lloyd's shipping house, I decide on cutting out this last page, which we will keep. It gives you right of ownership and therefore every right to give them to Charlotte if you so wish. Besides, the absence of the page will insure that we are not drawn into legal dispute. Lloyd's ask for the log-book. Well, we send it to them."

"So," thought Dr. Syn, "my worthy Tony is a cautious magistrate where his own people's interests are concerned. He would rather keep things to himself than run the risk of losing. He is as close as his own grooms appear to be under similar circumstances. All of which bodes well for the scheme I have to direct. He might even be induced to come in with us." Dr. Syn looked at the squire and wondered. He watched him fingering the pearls that hung round Charlotte's neck and patting her lovingly on the cheek. And it was then that Dr. Syn ruled out the notion of implicating the squire. "He is her father and Charlotte must be kept out of anything like that."

All that day the village seethed with excitement over Grinsley's death. Perhaps it was natural that the news was received and handed on amidst lively discussions that had in them no trace of sorrow. Indeed, there was no attempt made to disguise the utter relief which the murderer's death caused. So obvious was the general feeling of jubilation that Mipps, who was working with Merry in the church, thought fit to give his views on the subject to Dr. Syn and the squire as they passed by him arm-in-arm.

"Good news, gentlemen, that this rascal is dead, eh?" he remarked.

"Faith, the village seems all agog as though it were on holiday," answered the squire. "They seem mightily glad that the hangman has missed his commission."

"Now that, I dare swear, sir, ain't entered none of their heads," returned Mipps in defence of the villagers, for he felt that their attitude night reasonably be received with suspicion. "Now, my opinion of their opinion's this—I don't think it's so much glorying over Grinsley's death as being joyful that the Sandgate riding-officer is avenged. He was very beloved that there officer was, as they says in the Psalms."

"I never knew a riding-officer beloved yet," was the squire's sharp comment.

"You shouldn't judge Customs people, sir, by our Preventive man," said Mipps reprovingly. "Gloomy, he's called, gloomy he is, and suspicious of innocent men. But that Sandgate late lamented was a pleasant man, fond of his wife and children and very regular attending church. No wonder everyone bears a grudge against Grinsley for giving him that broadside."

"It ain't that at all," growled Merry, "touching his cap to the gentlemen in a grudging manner. "The villagers are glad Grinsley's dead because he's dead without coming to trial. If he'd got in the dock he'd have informed against 'em, and well they know it. But there's only one man besides me as would own it, and that's the Preventive Officer, and you can ask him if you doubt me, 'cos here he comes."

Preceded by the beadle ringing his bell, and followed by a crowd of gaping school children, the Preventive Officer, carrying a very soiled parchment, proceeded to the foot of the gallows tree, which was fortunately barren of fruit, and signing to the beadle to cease ringing his brass bell, himself began intoning and crying "Oyez" in a lugubrious voice.

"Whereas it is a common practice in Romney Marsh to cause wool to be transported to France in exchange for contraband of rum, sundry spirits and silks, for the future be it enacted that all persons so concerned may be held in close custody at His Majesty's pleasure to be tried on a capital charge. God save the King."

To avoid the clanging of the bell and the indignity of being stared at by the school children, the squire had led Dr. Syn through the little iron gate in the wall that shuts off the Court House shrubbery from the main road.

Such other adults who happened to be lounging or passing by the immediate vicinity, for other reasons best known to their own consciences also made themselves scarce, so that the reading of His Majesty's Proclamation was given for the benefit of Mipps, Merry and the children.

The Preventive Officer ignored everyone but Mipps, and while pronouncing blessing upon King George the Third, he looked from his parchment straight at the sexton in a somewhat sinister fashion.

Mipps, however, was not at all perturbed at this, but appeared very interested. He strolled across to the officer and thrust his long nose into the parchment which he read through as though to make sure that the officer had not left anything out or made any mistake.

"Yes. That's what it says, sure enough," he nodded.

"Aye," replied the officer, and under cover of the noise of the bell, which the beadle had once more set ringing, he added: "You've heard and read. Well, my advice to you is to profit by it, or you may find you're measuring yourself for a coffin."

"Don't know no one as could do it better," replied the sexton, "but what exactly might you be drivin' at?"

"A friendly warnin'. You've seen this parchment. Don't it convey something to you?"

"Oh, yes," nodded Mipps with great conviction.

"It means something to you, eh?"

"Certainly it do," replied Mipps with another serious nod.

"What?" barked out the officer, above the clanging of the bell.

"That it's got very dirty. Now, own up. It is dirty, ain't it? They tells me bread crumbs is a very good thing, and also wash your hands now and again."

Mr. Mipps then turned on the beadle. "Here. Enough of that noise. Come and have a drink at the 'Old Ship', but don't go waking up old man Waggetts with that bit of brass, or he'll start telling us how when he was a boy there used to be smugglers in Dymchurch. I'm tired of tales of smugglers, straight, I am. Coming, Gloomy? No? Oh, well, then I'll drink with the beadle."

And while Mipps led the beadle, nothing loath, towards the back door of the "Old Ship Inn,' the Preventive Officer and Merry put their heads together and talked in whispers.

As for the school children, they followed the man with the brass bell, especially as he was talking and walking with their hero, Mr. Mipps.

All through the day little knots of villagers met here and there, in inn parlours, at street corners or leaning upon the sea-wall, and when they spoke of what might have been, had Grinsley been taken alive, many a face looked troubled. And the mysterious appearance of the second scarecrow was openly discussed. Who could it have been? To most of these inquiries came the answer so subtly suggested by Mipps. For who could ride so fearlessly as Jimmie Bone, the highwayman? Certainly, no one on the Romney Marsh, where he was so often in hiding.

Despite Charlotte's important birthday, which was naturally a great event in the Cobtree household, the squire was also troubled. He knew well enough that his stables had been used the night before, and the knowledge irritated him, especially as he was quite certain that he would hold his tongue and appear to his grooms as an easily-deceived owner, for when Dr. Pepper came bursting in with the news that his horse had been requisitioned the night before on illegal business, the squire retorted: "Of course they take your horse, because you won't leave 'em alone. Now, I say there is no smuggling going on. Well, I've never seen a sign of it, and therefore, you see, my horses are no more used than Dr. Syn's pony."

"Well, he's a gull and no mistake, with all respects," remarked a young ostler to the squire's head coachman.

"Maybe he's not so blind as you think, youngster," reproved the coachman. "He's a wise man is the squire, and a wise man don't go stirring up for trouble as that Dr. Pepper does."

CHAPTER XXX. Doctor Syn in Danger

But although the whole village from the squire down seethed with excitement that day, an exception must be made of Dr. Syn. The events of the night before seemed to interest him not at all. He spent the day largely in the pleasant company of Charlotte Cobtree, for, as he put it, "a twenty-first birthday is a very great occasion.' The dinner hour having been postponed till a late hour that day, the early evening found the doctor on his white pony riding beside Charlotte, and although many times upon the ride he had entreated her not to bother about his slow jogging but to enjoy a gallop, she resolutely refused to ride from him.

"You have sacrificed your whole day for my happiness," she said. "You have remembered every minute that it is my day, when even the family have quite unconsciously, bless them, put off further festivities till dinner time. Therefore, if I wanted to gallop away from you, I couldn't, but you see, I do not want to."

"Well, you are twenty-one, Charlotte," replied Dr. Syn. "You have every right to please yourself. Thank you very much."

For some time they rode forward at a gentle walk, and Dr. Syn's thoughts began to concentrate upon the new life of adventure that seemed to have been thrust upon him. A very different proposition this, to tackle, than directing the guns of the old Imogene in the grim game of piracy. Then he had only the ever-present possibility of violent death to face, and certainly no disgrace, for the best of the sea rovers went to death laughing, and did not give a toss of the dice for shame. But to run as he had given his word to run, a great scheme of law-breaking in England, was to court the risk of a disgrace which he was perfectly willing to face, but he must be careful not to involve the beautiful girl at his side in such disaster.

It was she who interrupted his train of thought with: "Oh, Doctor, whatever makes you scowl like that? Have you forgotten it is my birthday?"

"No, Charlotte," he answered, smiling, but without looking at her. "But when you get to middle age the past has a way of obtruding itself, and to men who have lived an adventurous life it is generally the unpleasantnesses of the past that thrust themselves to the front. A young girl like you could not be expected to understand the depressions that come with middle age."

"No?" she queried. "Perhaps I understand these depressions—in you—better than you imagine. Perhaps I understand more than anyone else where you are concerned, and the reason is that I am certain no one loves you more than I do."

"That is very kind of you, my dear," replied the doctor. He did not dare look back at her, but kept his pony just a little ahead. But she watched him closely.

"You see," she went on, "my father is your oldest friend and I am, in many ways, his confidante. Do you suppose then that, both loving you as we do, that we have not been guilty of discussing you? We have, and I know as well as he does of the tragedy that drove you to America."

"That is all finished. It is a closed book," said Syn simply.

"Not quite, is it?" went on Charlotte. "Now that I am grown up, may I claim the privilege of telling you what I think? From what my father has told me, you were influenced to go abroad in a spirit of revenge. It was natural that when your wife betrayed you, all your love for her should be killed. You never blamed her, so my father tells me, but on the man, who had been your friend, you were determined to heap punishment. Unsuccessful in this, at last even that passion died in you, and you return to start life again with us. Why do you not accept the fact that your wife is dead, Doctor?"

"Because it is not right to accept a fact that is only told by a liar and a cheat," he answered.

"And that is the reason you told my father that you could never marry again?" she asked.

"That is one reason," he replied. "If I were to marry again and there was a child, and then my wife was found to be alive after all, what of my child then? What of the woman that had given it to me?"

"It would be but a legal quibble to make it wrong," replied Charlotte. "For my part, I would break any law for the sake of the man I loved."

The tone of her voice was so compelling that Dr. Syn checked his pony and looked at her. She, too, drew rein involuntarily and met his gaze, leaning slightly towards him from the saddle. Her face was above him, for she rode a man's horse and he was crouched on his pony.

For a few long seconds their eyes met, and with a brave glowing hers took hold and clung to his, binding him to her as the hands do in matrimony. Instinctively the doctor was disarmed. He felt the warm blood of youth once more in his veins. Was it possible that this beautiful girl loved him?

As he asked himself the question, she answered it with a slow nod and added: "I would take the risk. I love you."

He felt his back straighten, he knew his eyes glowed as hers did. Subconsciously, he cursed the secrets that compelled him to ape an older man. He longed to change his pony for the fierce black horse he had conquered in the night. He wanted to appear to her the man of adventure that he was. And that very want betrayed him, for he dismounted like a young man and stood beneath her, drinking her in as, leaning forward, she let her curl brush his face.

"Why don't you say what is in your heart?" she urged.

"I can say that," he whispered. "Yes, at least I can say that with all honesty. I love you. But in all honour I can never ask you to marry me. I would to God I could."

"Because your wife may be alive?" she asked. "I have told you, I put you before the law, and so would our children when they understood."

"There are other things," he went on. "Aye, things black and damnable. Did you know the half of them, you would turn from me."

"Let me be the judge of that," she said quietly. "For now in all fairness, I have the right."

"Aye, were the secrets mine, you should share them. But I put others on their oath never to tell those secrets even to their wives."

"They were men then—these sharers of your secrets? I am glad of that, for I began to be jealous. And do they live—these men? Could you not ask them to release you?"

"I believe the most of them are dead. But an oath is an oath from which even death could not release us."

She bowed her head slowly, dismissing all desire to know, since he had sworn to keep silence. The she laid one hand upon his shoulder and added: "Even though you say these things were black and damnable, I do not blame you, for my heart tells me that in all your life you could never have done anything except your honour forced you."

"Thank God, I can say aye to that," he answered. "In the worst moments of my poor life, when my hands were stained with blood, my honour drove me to it. A rough-hewn honour it may have been, for I was then amongst savage men who had no fine perception of what should be. There were no subtle points to that honour as there are among the duelling gentlemen of the coffee houses. It was rock-bottom honour, the foundation of a crude code of law made mostly by unlettered and ignorant scoundrels. And when fate called on me to administer that law in all its rigour, I knew that I was merely administering justice in that particular community. In the Last Day I shall have no fear in answering the Judge's charge on that score, but to tie you to such a man—who cannot share his memories with you—my honour forbids that, my dear."

"But suppose my honour is rough-hewn, too." Her fingers gripped his shoulders tightly. "For I suppose, according to the rules of society, I have dulled the fine points of mine by telling you I love you. Well, suppose I go further. Suppose I confess that were you the worst of criminals standing with a noose about your neck upon the open scaffold, I should still be proud to say 'I love you'."

"Good evening, Vicar. Good evening, Miss Cobtree."

Out of the flatness of the Marsh a third party had appeared. Hidden by the height of Charlotte's horse, and having taken advantage of the cover of a deep dyke that ran all the way from the highroad to Mother Handaway's field-bound cottage, Merry had approached unseen, and quietly walked round the head of Charlotte's horse upon them.

Dr. Syn's first impulse was to turn angrily upon the intruder, but he found himself unable to turn away from Charlotte. The sudden interruption of a conversation so intimate was enough to have thrown any girl into confusion. She had at least been seen leaning towards the man she loved so closely that her kiss curl caressed his face, and it was quite probable that her last words of love which she had spoken with all the conviction of her brave nature had been overheard. Yet no blush of shame was apparent on her cheeks as she very slowly raised her eyes, dancing with smiles, towards the intruder. It seemed to Dr. Syn that she was as proud of being surprised in her present attitude as she had boasted she would be beneath his scaffold.

"Good evening, Mr. Merry," she said, in a voice clear of any embarrassment. The love that had shown from her eyes during her confession still danced in them. She had not troubled to alter her expression. Mr. Merry might have been her dearest confidant for all the trouble she took to disguise her feelings.

With the doctor it was different. Automatically, imperceptibly and yet rapidly he changed. When he turned towards Merry he was the kindly, elderly parson with something of a stoop that was so familiar a figure to all on Romney Marsh. He looked at Merry's sea-boots, wet with dyke water, and his kindly eyes took on an expression of reproof.

"You ought to know better, my man, than to spring out of a hiding-place without warning when a sensitive animal like Miss Charlotte's horse is standing near. It was foolish. I thought you had horse sense."

Without waiting for his reply he turned to Charlotte's horse and ran his hand beneath the girth. "No, it is not too tight, my dear, though perhaps the saddle needs adjusting."

"Help me to dismount then," she said, "and while you fix it, I will just run over the field to speak to poor Mother Handaway. She is standing by the stable door talking to someone, and she will be hurt if I ride away without a word."

Dr. Syn walked round to the near side of Charlotte's horse. As he lifted her from the saddle, he was again aware that Charlotte made no attempt at hiding her love for him in front of Merry, who at a nod from his master had sullenly complied by holding the animal's head.

Although for the last twenty years his adventurous life had subjected him to an iron control of brain and body, he was hard put to it now not to hurl Merry back into the dyke and then take Charlotte in his arms and hold her tightly, but the discipline of those twenty years saved him from doing anything so mischievously delightful. He even frowned at Charlotte, warning her not to be so provocative. But it was her moment, and a multitude of Merry would have made no difference.

"Lift me, please," she pleaded, "for if I jump I may trip in my skirt and roll into Mr. Merry's dyke." She laid her hand on Dr. Syn's shoulder and turned to Merry. "By the way, what were you doing in the dyke? Catching something?"

"Avoiding someone," answered Merry, turning his head toward Mother Handaway's cottage. The he pointed. "Him, to be exact."

"That man on the horse coming towards us? Why?"

"Ah! You don't know who he is. Neither of you know. But I know. I keeps an eye open on Romney Marsh, and there ain't much I don't know. And I knows that I ain't stopping around to be shot at by no jocular highwayman."

"Highwayman?" repeated Charlotte, with no hint of the usual shudder which was customary amongst women as well as many men at the very sound of the word.

"Aye, and it's the famous Jimmie Bone, if you wants to know," whispered Merry. "For a long while I've wished to see him unmasked, and up by the cottage I did. He was arguing with the old witch. Something about a stable that he could no longer use, and he seemed very put out. There's a hundred pound on his head from the authorities, but I ain't waiting to tell him so," and leaving the horse's head, Merry slithered down the dyke bank and plunged into cover of the rushes.

CHAPTER XXXI. Doctor Syn Shows Fight

Jimmie Bone saw the manoeuvre, and checked his horse, while he tucked his three-cornered hat under his arm for the few seconds required in which to adjust a black mask that covered him to the mouth. Then clapping his spurs he put his horse at the intervening dyke, cleared it and galloped to the next, taking it with an ease that showed consummate horsemanship. In a few seconds he was alongside the dyke in which Merry was plunging, and had pulled from his holster a long pistol. Dr. Syn noted that Mr. Bone rode a black horse, not unlike Gehenna, who had apparently forestalled his stable, and remembering Grinsley's black mount, he told himself that black horses were evidently in fashion amongst the local rogues.

"Now then, what's the game? Come out of it, you water rat," cried the highwayman to Merry. "Trying to cheat an honest gentleman of the road from his lawful dues, is it? Come on, it's your money or your life, so fork out and sharp's the word."

"Come now, Mr. Bone, is it likely as though I had money," whined the terrified Merry.

"Likely, I should say it's certain," replied the highwayman, "considering as how you ain't the cove to do something for nothing and you was give a gold spade for carryin' a message from certain gents I knows in Rye—aye, a message to yonder old Mother at the cottage, and considerin' you showed her that same guinea and there ain't no inn between there and here where you could spend it, considerin' all that, I says stump up sharp."

"But look you, Mr. Bone—"

"And not so free with your Mr. Bones," cut in the highwayman. "We've never been interdooced to my knowledge, and I've no wish to know yer better, although I'll be obliged to be better acquainted with that there guinea. Toss her up."

"I'm a poor man—" began Merry, reluctantly holding out the guinea piece.

"And I'll be the richer by a guinea," laughed the highwayman, stretching his hand down and taking the coin reluctantly held out to him. "And now, you stop over this side of the dyke while I deals with these others. Why, sakes alive, if it ain't a parson. Now, why the devil couldn't you have been anything but that, and an old 'un, too." For while the highwayman had been attending to Merry, Dr. Syn had taken the opportunity of putting on his reading spectacles. "Oh sakes, had you but been a justice of the peace, a well fed lawyer, or even some portly merchant from London city, why then I'd have robbed you willingly. Why, I never yet have robbed a parson. A selfish virtue, sir, but if I did it 'ud be the ruin of all good luck that seems to stand as faithful by me as the horse I ride. Now, the lady is different. I'll relieve you, Miss, of the pretty pearl string about your neck, which I see you have taken pains to hide as far as possible beneath your kerchief. I'll come over for it."

Jimmie Bone turned his horse and rode in a circle back towards the dyke, which he leapt in style. He was now separated from Merry by the water, but upon the same meadow as the others.

He now rode towards them with his horse pistol presented.

Now although the last thing Charlotte wanted was to lose her precious pearls, it was not fear for their safety that now clutched at her heart, but for the danger towards which Dr. Syn was walking. He certainly looked old and very forlorn, as he limped slowly across the rough grass to meet the highwayman, who reined in his horse and waited.

"No nearer, reverend sir," warned Mr. Bone. "I should be loath to break my vow against a churchman. Besides, I've no wish to shoot an unarmed man, parson or no."

Dr. Syn stopped and blinked through his glasses at the black mask. "I have always heard it said of you, Mr. Bone," he replied in a quavering voice, "that as robbers go, you have at least something honourable about you. I do not exactly agree with your mode of life. Naturally, my profession forbids me to go so far, but I have always been pleased to hear you praised for a certain sporting dare-deviltry which every Englishman admires. And just as you have an aversion to rob or ill-treat me because of my black cloth, so have I an aversion to killing you sitting there so magnificently on that fine animal. Whether you get Miss Cobtree's pearls remains to be seen, but it is quite certain that you will have to fight me first."

Mr. Bone laughed. "Do you mean a duel, reverend sir? Is it possible that you carry a piece of artillery in one of those long pockets?"

Dr. Syn shook his head, blinked through his spectacles and continued nervously. "No, no. I do not carry a pistol. Though, strange as it may seem to you, I know a good deal about them, and was at one time accounted a reasonable performer. I take it now, Mr. Bone, that the pistol you are presenting at my head at the moment is made more to intimidate than to give an exhibition of accurate shooting."

"It shoots straight enough, though," replied Mr. Bone, "as you might find to your cost did you attempt to cross me too far."

"Might find, eh?" repeated Dr. Syn. "So you allow that there is room for doubt. I take it that you would not feel too secure in using such a weapon for a duel?"

"Since you are so insistent—well, no. I should use one of these in that case." And Mr. Bone drew from his sash a very fine duelling pistol.

"Ah, that's a weapon," exclaimed Dr. Syn. "That only demands a sense of direction and a steady squeeze on the trigger. Are you an infallible shot, Mr. Bone?"

"What do you mean?" he demanded. "I can hit a mark nine times out of ten."

"A mark may be large or small," replied the vicar, shaking his head in disbelief.

"Make it large enough to see and I'll hit it," said the highwayman.

"I will," answered Dr. Syn. "Now, it is a virtue of mine, and of my capacious coat pockets, that I never stir abroad without a good piece of chalk, a length of pack thread and a good sharp knife. Whenever I see a good stick or a pliable twig, I think of my young rascals in the parish who are for ever crying out for whips, cudgels or fishing rods. My knife"—he fumbled in his side pocket and produced it—"is, as you see, a good one. It is strong, it is sharp, and what is so important, it is admirably balanced. It is a knife to throw, Mr. Bone, and like your pistol, shall I boast of it that nine times out of ten it hits the mark. I am beholden to a dreadful rascal for the instruction, a Chinaman Mr. Bone, and it has amused me to keep in practice a hobby that has on several occasions saved my life. Now, before we begin to settle this business concerning Miss Cobtree's pearls, I will lay you a guinea against the one you have appropriated from poor Merry there, that I will throw more accurately than you can shoot. Don't be alarmed, I beg. The crack of a pistol will excite no comment on Romney Marsh. A rabbit, or a water-rat—why the boys will shoot at them, you know. Besides, look around you. As far as the eye can see there is not a human being stirring but ourselves. You would have ample time on that delightful horse to make good your escape. Here's the chalk. I make a mark on this old gate post. So. Now, Mr. Bone, make good your boast."

Mr. Bone chuckled beneath his mask. "You're a queer cove, ain't you? Well, I'll win your guinea and then take the lady's pearls."

He thrust the cumbersome horse pistol into the holster and leapt to the ground. "And what distance must we set for this stake, Mr. Parson?"

"You see the chalk mark. It is not large, I admit. Make it whatever you please and take the first shot."

The highwayman looked at the parson suspiciously. But the sight of so much blinking senility disarmed suspicion. Mr. Bone was a big man, tall, broad and athletic. One blow from his great fist would catapult the frail parson across the dyke. He walked back some yards from the post, followed by his black horse, who in turn was followed by the black-garbed parson.

"I think that far would be accounted a good shot, eh?" asked the highwayman.

"Just as you like," replied the parson. "The light is good, with the sun behind us."

The highwayman muttered something to his horse, who obediently knelt down. Mr. Bone also crouched on one knee and steadied his pistol upon the saddle.

"Here you," he called to Merry. "Get on that mound there and keep a sharp look out. I have no mind to be taken through this folly."

Merry walked to the mound in question, but he was more interested in the fate of his guinea, and he looked for danger behind the highwayman's back, so that he could watch the shooting.

After a considerable time taken in shuffling himself into a position of comfort, Jimmie Bone took long and deliberate aim. Slowly he squeezed the trigger. The crack of the shot rang out and he got up from his knees.

"I think I have driven in the very centre of your chalkmark," he chuckled.

"I think you have gone so wide that you have missed the mark entirely," chuckled the parson. "Aye, post and all."

"I tell you I can see a mark in the centre of the cross," exclaimed the marksman.

"I think you'll find that is just a mark in the wood. I fear you've gone wide. You shall have nine more shots to hit it if you wish to make good your word. Nine out of ten, you said."

"I'll find the bullet in the post first, before I waste more powder," snapped Mr. Bone, stepping over the prostrate horse and walking to the post.

However, he found that the parson was right in that the centre of the cross was a piece of faulty wood that had not taken the chalk. He began to run his hand slowly down the post, stopping his finger upon every mark in the hope of discovering the passage of his bullet. It annoyed him to fail in front of this parson and the pretty girl.

Charlotte, meanwhile, was watching Dr. Syn and saw what the highwayman had got his back to. Syn's left hand drew the horse pistol from the holster and with a sudden jerking swing flung the knife with full force.

With an oath the highwayman sprang aside, only to find his movement arrested by his coat, for as his hand had lingered on the thick post, the flying knife was driven right through the stuff buckrammed slack of his broad laced cuff.

"I found your sleeve a more tempting mark, Mr. Bone," said Dr. Syn, advancing to the impaled highwayman with the horse pistol levelled.

"Here's your guinea," cried the baffled highwayman, "or do you mean to try for the hundred guineas the authorities have put upon my capture?" He tossed the guinea towards the parson, who caught it and threw it to Merry.

"Oh dear, no, Mr. Bone. I only wished to point out that when you levelled this inaccurate piece of artillery at my head, I was not taken at such a disadvantage as you thought. Indeed, I should very much dislike you to flatter yourself upon that point."

"That pistol's accurate enough with luck," grumbled Jimmie Bone, "so unless you're out to kill me, keep your finger off the trigger."

"Have no fear, Mr. Bone," replied Dr. Syn. "I am well used to pistols, and really could not have missed that post after such preparations. I congratulate you, though, upon the admirable way you have trained your horse. However, we must now deal with Miss Cobtree's pearls, which as I said, you will have to fight to get. Keep your hand away from that knife, Mr. Bone, for a moment. Come across the water, Mr. Merry. You will act for Mr. Bone, no doubt, while Miss Cobtree will act for me. This shall be all in order, Mr. Bone. A fair fight. And I assure you the pearls are worth the fighting for. Several thousands of pounds they would fetch in the London market. But when I tell you that they were given to Miss Cobtree for her birthday to-day, perhaps your sense of fairness will make you withdraw your threat and ride away in peace."

"Miss Cobtree, eh?" repeated Mr. Bone. "She'd be the daughter of Cobtree the magistrate, and ain't he the cove what has put a hundred guineas round my neck? It seems to me then not unfair for me to take several thousand guineas from his daughter's neck."

"As you please, Mr. Bone, and always supposing you can make good your word, which I am at liberty to doubt after the failure of your former boast. Mr. Merry, you will pluck out my knife there, while I help Miss Cobtree to dismount."

He backed towards the horses, still keeping the highwayman covered with the pistol, while Merry splashed his way across the dyke to get the knife.

Charlotte leaned from her horse with one arm about the vicar's shoulder, and as he lifted her to the ground she whispered: "Why not send him packing? You have the pistol and I the pearls."

"Because I have the wish to show you that you have not given your love to a weakling, my dear."

She was about to speak in answer when Merry, who had pulled out the knife from the post and thereby released Mr. Bone's cuff, suddenly sprang at the highwayman with the knife raised.

With a savage curse Mr. Bone ducked, caught Merry with one arm round the waist and with the other hand twisted the wrist till the knife dropped. He then drew back, and with a sledge-hammer blow knocked Merry backwards into the water.

"That was just, Mr. Bone. He deserved it for his treachery," said Dr. Syn.

"Aye, he was tempted by that hundred pounds alive or dead that old Cobtree has put up. Well, he ain't earned it yet, I think. And now what, Master Parson?"

"You have a good punch, I see, which I shall do well to avoid," chuckled Dr. Syn. "I remember now that you were something of a heavyweight before you took to the road. You knocked out the Camberwell Smasher at Tunbridge Fair, if I recollect."

"That's it, and my advice to you is not to tempt me to deal with you as I dealt with him," laughed Mr. Bone. "I'd rather have them pearls without a fight and ride off peaceful."

"Possibly, but oh no," laughed the doctor. "At least, I shall be very surprised if you do ride off with the pearls. But I'll take off my glasses and my coat. I should suggest you take off your riding coat."

"I'll keep it on," replied the highwayman. "When I have finished with you, and let us hope the damage done will not affect your preaching, I shall take the pearls and ride away before you raise the alarm."

"Oh, but there is to be no alarm, I assure you," corrected the parson. "This is a friendly bout, I hope, and I wish you would not boast so of the pearls." Dr. Syn folded his coat and laid it tidily on the grass. "Well, if you will not remove your coat, at least take off your mask. It gives me so much to aim at."

"Do you really mean that we are to fight with fists?" asked the amazed highwayman, seeing that the parson was calmly rolling up his shirt-sleeves, and opening and shutting his hands as he blinked at them.

"But, my dear Mr. Bone, you see I have got ready. We will fight to a finish. A knock-out and with fists. The usual ten to be counted. Slowly, my dear Charlotte."

"Well, it is not my habit to linger too long in one spot," said the highwayman. "True, there's no one visible at the moment likely to cause me trouble, but away yonder towards Dymchurch, there's a clump of trees behind which one cannot see, and I've been warned that the Dragoons are out. So come along, my gallant game-cock and let us hope your preaching will be better than your fighting."

"Oh, I hope it is," replied Dr. Syn devoutly, taking a few steps forward and then awaiting attack in a somewhat awkward attitude of defence.

"It will be no disgrace to say you've been worsted by Gentleman James," laughed Bone, advancing.

"You are sure you would not prefer to remove your mask?" asked the waiting parson timidly.

"I only removes it amongst relations, and they are all dead. I have no wish to give away a description of my beauty."

"Oh, but your heavy boots and spurs," pleaded Dr. Syn.

"Used to 'em. I notice you keep on your buckled shoes. I likes fighting shod, like you."

Mr. Bone suddenly rushed. Dr. Syn stood his ground, and though Charlotte was terrified at the tornado attack of the great highwayman, she was surprised to see him stagger back with his hand on his jaw. Dr. Syn had apparently parried the sledgehammer blows, and struck once, but the stroke got home. It enraged the highwayman, for he leapt forward again and clinched. Dr. Syn seemed mildly surprised at this form of attack. His arms were tied by the great bulk of his antagonist. He seemed to have no space in which to hit. For the moment it seemed that Mr. Bone had got it all his own way, and wishing to finish the comedy and pay the parson back with interest for the lucky blow on his chin, he tried to hold the parson with his left arm while withdrawing his right for a smash-out blow.

What followed was too quick for Charlotte to understand. But the highwayman missed his blow and Syn was clear of that crushing left arm. His knuckles had managed to inflict a murderous jab into Bone's ribs, and as the highwayman's fist whistled past his side-jerked head, up came the parson's left and reached the same spot on the jaw. Mr. Bone cried out in surprise and pain, and recovering his balance, followed up Dr. Syn, who had leapt clear. But unwilling to submit to another of those grim clinches, the parson played for defence, parrying the mighty blows with apparent coolness, but retreating steadily round and round before the infuriated rushes.

At every attack it seemed that the slim figure of the parson must be overwhelmed, and yet his face remained untouched, and even his wig, which he had not removed, was still sitting tidy and tight upon his head, and as blow after blow was rained at him, the parson's face was ever guarded and the blows turned aside.

From a distance it would have seemed that the highwayman was getting it all his own way, because of the other's persistent retreats. After each attack, he leaped back to avoid another clinch.

Mr. Bone felt the blood trickling down his neck and this infuriated him. He now attacked with lower blows, and at last landed a murderous stroke into the parson's ribs. Dr. Syn leapt back, pressing his hand against the spot and drawing in his breath with an audible hiss. It may have been a sporting instinct on the part of Mr. Bone to let the parson recover himself, or it may have been that he took a few seconds to recover himself for a further effort to drive home that advantage, but it is certain that the big man held back for a few definite seconds, breathing hard. Dr. Syn used the pause first by calmly lifting his wig from his head and throwing it clear away upon the grass. He then appeared to Charlotte and Merry to be using his brain and taking the measure of Bone's fighting qualities. The highwayman was just a strong, straight-forward hitter, depending on his blows to reach their objective, and the doctor realised that should this happen, the fight might well be over, for the blows were bone-smashers. He knew, therefore, that his best policy was to fight as he had been doing, on the defensive and at all costs to keep clear till he had worn down his antagonist's patience and strength.

It so happened, however, that the pause had placed Dr. Syn facing the distant clump of Dymchurch trees, and since the highwayman had his back to them, he did not see what the parson did—for between the trees the setting sun was flashing upon the brass helmets and breast-plates of the Dragoons.

Now Dr. Syn had only to mention this fact to Mr. Bone to terminate the fight. What was more to the point, he could finish the fight as victor and by picking up the pistol which he had laid beneath his coat, he could order Mr. Bone to mount without the pearls and to ride for his life.

Against this was his desire to finish the fight under Charlotte's eyes, and it was this that made him risk Mr. Bone's safety.

Once more he threw himself into an attitude of self-defence. Once more Mr. Bone advanced, preparing to launch himself in a tornado attack. But, instead, he was met in full career by a second tornado. Dr. Syn had sprung into the attack like a mad hurricane, and Mr. Bone got a taste of his own smashing method before he was aware that such a thing existed. Back he was driven with well-landed blows steadily back towards the dyke.

"Mind the water, man," cried Dr. Syn, after sending him reeling to the very bank.

But the highwayman was game. He rushed again, only to be met by the parson's counter rush. Down went Mr. Bone, blinded with blood that soaked down through his silk mask.

Charlotte forgot to count. Dr. Syn had to do it, slowly, with one eye on the giant upon the turf and the other towards the Dragoons.

On the ninth count, however, Mr. Bone once more showed fight. Leaping to his feet, he rushed the parson. A quick sidestep and a lightning left hook to the jaw followed almost instantaneously by a punishing to the ribs with his right, left Dr. Syn standing the victor, for Mr. Bone uttered a sigh of pain, sank on his knees and then collapsed.

CHAPTER XXXII. Charlotte Names Her Three Heroes

"Our highwayman is a game fighter, my dear," said the doctor to Charlotte, who had left the horses to Merry and had come closer, "but he has learned in too easy a school. Strength he has, but no knowledge. Get some water from the dyke in my hat while I raise his head." He sank his voice to a whisper so that Merry should not hear, and added: "We must get him away before that party of Dragoons catch sight of him."

Charlotte took the doctor's hat and kneeling beside the dyke, filled it with water, while the doctor gently removed the blood-stained mask from the unconscious man.

It was then that Merry saw the distant Dragoons and determined to gain the hundred guineas for the taking of Mr. Bone. He leapt on to Charlotte's horse and galloped to the dyke, plunged down into the water and climbed the opposite bank, and before the others had realised his purpose he was away at full speed.

"Quick, Charlotte," ordered the doctor, "the man is none so badly hurt, but that rogue is for putting his neck in a halter. Ah, he's coming round."

Indeed, as soon as the water was splashed on to his face, the highwayman opened his eyes.

"Well, it's hands up, Mr. Parson, and I own when I'm beat." He twisted his lips into a smile. "You saved the lady her pearls, and it serves me right for having threatened to take 'em. But had you got to take off my mask?"

"Your face is safe as far as we are concerned," replied the doctor. "We shall only remember you as a masked man who refused to uncover. And the sooner you get on to your horse the better, for the gentleman you deprived of the guinea has ridden off to put the Dragoons on your trail. He was off before we could stop him."

The highwayman struggled to a sitting position and looked at the distant rider.

"Aye, and the curse of it is, that the old witch who lives yonder will no longer give me stable room," he muttered. "I'll confess that for more than a year I have found her place handy. Well, it will have to be riding then, I reckon, and before those soldiers come out from the trees."

"Wait till that scoundrel disappears, and I will see to it that the old woman gives you safe hiding." Dr. Syn recovered his wig and adjusted it.

"She's mad, sir," answered the highwayman. "Said she could no longer see to me or my horse. Nor could she take my money, because she'd seen the devil himself who had forbidden her any other service."

"If the parson cannot override the devil, he is no use at his job," laughed the doctor. "Look, Merry is already behind the trees. Let me mount your horse, and do you get up behind me, and I will undertake your safety. Charlotte, do you mount the pony and troy over by the bridge, and when the Dragoons ride up, let me do the talking."

He sprang into the saddle, but the highwayman's horse, trained only to obey his master, plunged and reared in indignation, till Mr. Bone quietened him.

"You ride as well, Master Parson, as you fight, and you deserve a better mount than yonder fat pony," he said. "As to your fighting power, my faith, but my head is still spinning. I have never been so punished in my life."

He mounted with difficulty.

"Hold on to me," urged Dr. Syn. "And there's need of haste. Can you stand a gallop?"

"I have ridden so full of Bow Street runners' lead that my horse was lamed with the weight of it," laughed Mr. Bone.

"Then hang on," replied Dr. Syn, and he urged the horse down into the dyke, not caring to risk his legs with such a jump. "We can leap the others, but not this," he said, as they plunged through the water up to their thighs, and climbed the further bank. Then he set the horse to the gallop.

Charlotte watched them as she led the pony along the dyke to the nearest brick bridge, and she realised that Syn was the best rider on the Marsh, and the discovery made her understand many things that had long puzzled her. However, she was to be puzzled a good deal more before she reached home, but once more her love gave her the solving of the riddle, which she found only seemed to make her love him the more.

When she reached Mother Handaway's cottage she was met by the old witch, and was most astonished at her words.

"Oh, Miss Cobtree," whispered the old lady, "never come and visit me more. I say this to repay you for all the kindness you have shown to an old witch whom everybody shuns. But never come here again, and oh, above all, never have dealings with the vicar of Dymchurch. You do not understand, but I tell you he is the devil. What has happened to the real vicar I cannot tell, but the devil is going up and down the Marsh in the likeness of him. He'll know I've told you, dearie, but I'll endure his wrath out of love of you."

"You are talking nonsense, Mother," replied Charlotte, who was amused at the old woman's wild fancy. "Why, I love Dr. Syn. He is my godfather, but for all that, I am going to marry him, when he asks me."

"Aye, he'll ask you. The devil will use any wile to get a soul in his clutch. But shun him, my dear. Keep clear of the church when he is there, for the foul fiend can be honey-tongued to a pretty girl. I know, who am his servant. I practiced the black devilry from a child and I have seen manifestations, and he even promised to visit me in a flesh form, and now I am his stable-woman. I feed his great black beast of a horse and I must call him the Scarecrow, he tells me. But he has provided for me. I may have guineas by the bag that are minted in hell for all that they bear the royal spade and head."

"And where is this fierce black horse of his?" asked Charlotte, resolved to humour her.

"In the hidden stable. It is a pit built of stone behind the cow barn. It was made by the smugglers years ago, and my grandmother showed me the secret. Its roof is covered with growing grass. I once saved Jim Bone, the highwayman, by giving him shelter there, and ever since he has used it when the chase was hot. I told him that now he could not use it again, when suddenly the devil appears as he said he would, in the likeness of Dr. Syn. He has stowed him away there. Oh, there's room enough for ten horses. And there's no one could find the door. Ah, those smugglers, they knew things in those days."

"They still do, so they say," laughed Charlotte.

Dr. Syn agreed that they had been cunning fellows who built the door which he had just fastened behind him. It stood in the steep side of a dry dyke and when closed looked nothing else but a great heap of dried bulrush reeds.

Satisfied that all was well, and that in Jimmie Bone he had now a faithful and useful colleague, he walked along the dyke and climbed up it at the side of the cottage.

"You see, my dear Charlotte," he said, with a smile, "a parson must do what he can for all his flock. Now, these gallant Dragoons that are cantering towards us are not my parishioners, and as to the rascal Merry—why, our masked friend is worth a score of such, and he happens to be in the greater need at the moment. Therefore he has my help. It is the lost sheep that the shepherd seeks."

The Dragoons drew up on the highroad, while Captain Faunce, led by Merry still mounted on Charlotte's horse, and followed by two troopers, came galloping across the fields, jumping the dykes, till they reached the three figures grouped around the white pony.

"You've never let him go, sir?" cried Merry, as he looked in vain for the sight of his capture. "You'll have lost me a hundred guineas."

Dr. Syn smiled. "And what are a hundred guineas compared to the safe keeping of Miss Cobtree's pearls? I confess I was mightily glad to see the last of him. And let me add that if you have lamed Miss Cobtree's horse, there will be trouble for you. Good evening, Captain Faunce. If you wish to reach the Sussex border before this masked gentleman of the road, who may or may not be the famous James Bone, I should recommend a cross-country gallop as quick as possible."

"This man tells me that you gave him a lathering," he replied.

"I learned in a scientific school, that is all, sir," laughed Dr. Syn. "Besides, he had the double disadvantage of not wishing to remove his mask, and of not fighting for what was honest. Miss Cobtree's pearls were in danger, so what else could I do, God forgive me, but fight?"

"I take it then that you can only identify his clothes and figure. You did not see his face?"

"I told you he would not remove his mask, but I should imagine that he will be marked where I drew the blood through it. True, my knuckles are torn, but not seriously."

"Might as well chase highwaymen as smugglers," laughed the captain. "It's all in the day's work, and a gallop will do the horses no harm. Hand over Miss Cobtree's horse—you, and get up behind Trooper Harker. We'll need you to identify his clothes and horse."

The wretched Merry was only too glad to obey. The chances of his hundred guinea reward were not quite spoiled, and he was none too eager to be left with Dr. Syn.

"I'll lay you a guinea you will not catch him this side of the border," said Dr. Syn, shaking his head.

"Perhaps not, since he's well mounted and knows the country," answered the Dragoon. "But I'll lay you a guinea that we do catch him over the border—aye, and bring him back, too, in spite of the Sussex magistrates. At all events, his horse will be commandeered for our regiment, and from what I hear, he rides a noble animal."

"Is that him over there?" said Dr. Syn, shading his eyes. "Surely there is a black speck riding straight into the setting sun."

The others looked in the direction.

"Your eyes are stronger than mine then. The sun blinds mine."

"Oh, but surely—surely," went on the doctor. "It seems impossible, though, that he could have ridden such a distance in the time."

"We'll show him that the Army can ride, too," laughed the captain. "Come along, men. If I lose that horse, I lose a guinea too, for the doctor's offertory."

Rising in his stirrups, he signalled his distant troopers with his arm, who after some sharp incomprehensible orders from a junior officer, started off into a canter along the highroad, while Captain Faunce, followed by the two troopers, one of whom carried Merry as a passenger, galloped across country in the direction supposed to have been taken by the redoubtable Bone.

"Did I not tell you he was the devil in disguise?" whispered Mother Handaway to Charlotte. "Avoid him, my dear, if you value your soul. Oh, don't look at me like that with laughter in your eyes, as though you thought me mad. I tell you, he said so himself when he rode to me in the storm on his wild black horse. 'I am the devil,' he said, 'but you may call me Scarecrow. I come to rule the Marsh,' he says, 'and you will keep my horse.' It is an animal from hell, my dear. 'I shall send you a messenger from time to time. He will appear as the sexton of Dymchurch, for I shall be going up and down myself as Dr. Syn, the preacher.' Tell no one, dear, lest he strike us dead, but you are young and pretty and have been good to me. But I cannot have you visit me any more. Avoid me for your own safety, but, above all, avoid him, the devil."

But Charlotte, looking at Dr. Syn as he jumped on to the pony's back in order to get a better view of the pursuit, thought that if this amazing parson were indeed the devil, she would be very well contented to serve him.

On the ride back she put some of her thoughts into words.

"I am glad our friend, Mr. Bone, is safe. I am glad, too, that you saved him. You had certainly punished him enough."

"For wanting to rob you of your pearls?" he laughed. "Oh no, not half enough. He deserved a good hanging."

"But you forgave him," she answered, "and I think I know the reason, for you and I have much in common. We both respect adventurers."

"Well, there is always something attractive about a man who takes great risks, even though they may be taken against law and order."

"Do you believe that our highwayman played the Scarecrow last night in order to help Grinsley?"

"Oh, where did you get that idea?"

"From your henchman, Mipps, of course. I get all my gossip from him."

"I am very fond of that old fellow, as you know, but I find that he can invent a piece of gossip with as great an ease as he can afterwards believe in it. For instance, he most firmly believes that poor old Mother Handaway, who is quite mad, has dealings with the devil."

"Then you think I should not take Mipps and his wild yarns too seriously?" she laughed.

"Certainly not. He is an old sea-dog. Very superstitious. As for his yarns—well, he loves spinning them. Now why should Mr. Jimmie Bone concern himself with trying to save Grinsley at the risk of his own neck?"

"Because he was the better adventurer," she answered promptly. "Just as you, being a greater adventurer than Mr. Bone, have risked a lot to save his life. I have a feeling that we are to hear more of this Scarecrow whoever he may be. Take it from me that his black horse will ride the Marsh just as the highwayman's will be seen again upon the roads."

"You will be adding another adventurous rascal to your romantic list soon," he laughed.

"You mean Clegg the pirate?"

Dr. Syn smiled and laughed. "He at least seems to have disappeared. My correspondents in America have now ceased to mention him."

"And it is a long time since you have spoken to him, too," she pouted. "You know how his adventures thrilled me when you first spoke of them to my father. Now when I want to talk of him I have to put my head close with Mr. Mipps."

"And what has Mipps to say of Clegg these days, my dear, for you may take it from me that the rascal is dead?"

Charlotte shook her head. "Only to the authorities. And I am glad he is dead to them."

"You are a strange, romantic girl, Charlotte," said Dr. Syn. "I wonder now why I was stupid enough to put Clegg into your birthday thoughts. The fellow is not worthy of such a place, I assure you."

"You know he is," replied Charlotte hotly. "Besides, it was not your remark of him that put him in my thoughts. It was this."

With her gloved hand she drew from the bosom of her riding coat the red velvet sachet.

"Why that?" asked Dr. Syn.

"When you first gave it to me this morning, I wondered where I had seen it before," she replied steadily. "I knew that its colour was familiar. That it reminded me of something—and then I remembered. It was the colour worn by my romantic ghost."

"Ghost?" he repeated.

"On the night of your return, as I went to call Mrs. Lovell to Meg's bedside, I saw the vision of a romantic figure reflected in the pier glass of your room. The door of the powder closet was open, you see."

"That was nothing. It was my farewell to vanity. You see, I was not always a practising parson in America. I went there to seek revenge, God forgive me, and not to carry on God's work. That came later."

"You cut this then from that gay coat?"

"I did. Perhaps, Charlotte, I had better destroy the coat. It is in my sea-chest."

"It would be better," she answered simply. "I know now why you do not talk any more of the pirate Clegg."

Dr. Syn said nothing. She went on: "It was Mipps who talked to me about Clegg the other day. He most loyally described him as a thick-set man, but when I said that did not sound as romantic as one could wish, he cried out: 'Ah, but you should have seen him in battle, calmly stalking the poop deck in his red velvet, and the cannon balls flying round him as thick as the tattooings on his own arms and chest."

Dr. Syn recognised the description as his old enemy, Nick Tappitt, but he only sighed and said: "Ah, so the red velvet reminded you of Clegg, eh?"

"Doctor, when you are ready to tell me all your secrets, then I shall be ready to marry you. I could protect you if I knew everything. And remember, I have added to my heroes the Scarecrow who saved the villagers last night."

"Your heroes?" he repeated.

"There are three of them now—Clegg the pirate, the Scarecrow smuggler, and Dr. Syn the fighting preacher."

"Perhaps some day, Charlotte, I may be weak enough to tell you all."

"I shall wait till you do," she answered.

After that they rode in silence to the village.

CHAPTER XXXIII. The Grievance of Mr. Jimmie Bone

Captain Faunce was piqued. The fact that he had failed to arrest the highwayman was annoying, especially when he became convinced that the notorious Bone was also the mysterious Scarecrow by whose daring his prisoners had escaped from his guards.

From what he gathered of the character of Merry, he at first suspected that this slippery rascal had purposely led him a wild goose chase. Merry, however, stoutly denied that he had ever been in the pay of the highwayman, and described in full detail the manner of Dr. Syn's fight, which made the reverend gentleman the popular hero of the Marsh. That the vicar of Dymchurch should have stood up to and punished a well-known fighter in defence of Miss Cobtree's pearls was an heroic effort that lost nothing in the telling.

True, it somewhat damaged the glamorous reputation of the highwayman, but against this was the rumour being spread on all sides and believed in by the Dragoon captain, that Mr. Bone had at least saved the smugglers necks. Mr. Mipps, who was responsible for the rumour, saw to it that it spread, and spread well.

Amongst others who believed in it was the Preventive Officer. For some time past he had had his suspicions that he could put his hand upon the highwayman, but he did not think it his duty to arrest him, since a gentleman of the road had nothing to do with the Customs. Moreover, he was not the man to earn a hundred guineas on a man's head, when the man had a popular reputation amongst the poor. Mr. Bone spent his money lavishly when he was in funds, and saw to it that the poor benefited by the rich man's loss. Besides, it was widely hinted at in all the taverns of the Marsh that were Jimmie Bone to be arrested on information received, it would be short shift for the informer.

This knowledge frightened Merry, and he told as much to Dr. Syn, who took such a serious view of it that he persuaded Merry to slip over into Sussex till Romney Marsh became safer. This plan suited Dr. Syn, for as he mentioned to Mipps: "There is enough to do regarding a certain business without that rascal hanging about the vicarage with his eyes open."

So Merry departed for Rye, and through a kindly recommendation from the vicar of Dymchurch, he was given odd jobs in the 'Mermaid Tavern'.

There was no one more pleased at his going than Meg Clouder, for as she told Dr. Syn: "Of late he has taken to watching my windows, and to following me if I go across the Marsh. The mere fact of your forbidding him to speak to me, makes his passion for me the more frightening."

"Well, well, you are safe enough from him, I promise you," replied Dr. Syn. "He will trouble this village no more, for his attempt to get that highwayman arrested has put him into some danger with Mr. Bone's friends."

Unlike Merry, however, the Preventive Officer was without fear, and no sooner was he convinced that Jimmie Bone had offended against the Customs than he set to watching for the gentleman, who sometimes spent so lavishly at one or the other of the taverns. But Mr. Bone was taking no chances until the tell-tale cuts inflicted by Dr. Syn's knuckles should have healed. Meanwhile, his friends informed him that the Preventive Officer was on the prowl.

"I can tell you one thing," said Captain Faunce to the Customs officer, "these fellows whoever they are, have won the first round against me, and won it handsomely, I'll admit. But they'll not be so sensible as to lie low for long. There'll soon be a cargo run again, and then we will not be hoodwinked. Success goes to such rascals' heads. Keep your eyes and ears open, Mr. Customs."

As the weeks went by, however, the Preventive man realised that the smugglers were still lying very quiet, and yet his experience told him that all the time secret preparations were going forward. So he waited and watched. Word had already been circulated through the channels known to Mipps that small runs were not worth the risk, and that as soon as their new leader, the Scarecrow, had satisfied himself that all was ready, the cargoes would be more than profitable. Promises of great wealth, with small risk, if all was done according to schedule, heartened those whose love and money was in the game.

Dr. Syn worked hard. Ostensibly at his parochial work. It was generally believed that when the flag was flying outside the little white hut on the sea-wall, that the vicar was preparing his next sermon within, so that no one would disturb him.

True, the top of the locker which served as a seat in this cabin was duly packed with ecclesiastical tomes, whose scholarly value warranted the fine old steel lock which the Upton brothers had fixed to it. But if truth were known, Dr. Syn gave little time to his sermons. Not wishing to appear brilliant, his discourses gave him no trouble, and when he was supposedly penning them, he would in reality be working out some new and ingenious method of fooling the Customs. Every vessel at the smugglers' command was drawn to scale by one of the Wraight men and given to Mipps, who undertook to pass them on to the Scarecrow. Then the plans would be returned with all sorts of contrivances added in the way of 'hides'. If the Scarecrow was really Jimmie Bone, then the highwayman astonished old Josiah Wraight with his expert knowledge of ships and boats. Besides which, the draughtsmanship was so uncommonly neat and accurate, and displayed practical knowledge of what could or could not be done at sea. Every available space was utilised on every available vessel and then most cunningly concealed. The smacks—a whole fleet of them—were provided with temporary casings capable of holding quantities of kegs and fitted two feet below the water line down to the keel. It was impossible for the Customs officers to detect this fraud while the vessels were afloat, since there was no communication between the concealments and the interior in which the Preventive man searched.

The Upton brothers were expert cabinet-makers, and there was no suspicion that everything was not just in the way of business when they were found engaged upon a particularly intricate piece of dove-tailing or lock. Mipps was able to work at many things amongst his coffin planks, and the Wraight's yards and sheds had ever been busy with hammerings and screwings. Carpenters and joiners found plenty of employment during that period when Captain Faunce thought the smugglers were lying 'uncommon quiet'.

And wherever the plans of the knowledgeable Scarecrow were faithfully reproduced from scale, then that vessel for which the trick had been designed, could confidently invite inspection from the Customs without fear of discovery.

Methods of sinking tubs through the ship's bottom, false scuttles, hollowed beams, dove-tailed to the solid ones, ropes that ran through leaden pipes concealed in false stanchions, bowsprits and stays hollowed and lead lined, winged lockers in the prow, or a spare bulkhead between the fore and aft, and a hundred other practical devices suited to the particular requirements of each vessel concerned. All these and more Dr. Syn planned and drafted in the little white hut upon the sea-wall, and when the flag flew from the pole, even Charlotte respected his need for privacy and did not disturb him.

It was after a particularly long day of parochial work carried on from this hut that Dr. Syn was roused from his studies by Mipps, who insisted on swinging a lantern before his master through the dark trees by the Court House, and realising that Dr. Syn had had a very exacting day he was then for taking himself back to the coffin shop. However, the doctor was equally insistent that Mipps should join him in his study for a drink, and it was while they were sitting in the dim candle-light that Mipps suddenly cocked his head towards the ceiling and began to sniff like a terrier.

"What's wrong?" whispered the doctor.

"Someone upstairs," replied Mipps. "I heard a creak. Besides, I can smell a horsey sort of odour about the place. Noticed it when I first come in. Been in here, now up in your bedroom."

"Nonsense, who could be up there? Mrs. Fowey will be abed by now; nine o'clock is her hour and up at five."

Mipps sniffed and then sniffed again.

"It's a man, sir. Mrs. Fowey ain't a horsey flavour, and as you say she's abed now by habit. These old houses gives away people what has no right to be in 'em. There's a creak going on now above deck."

"Very well then, Mipps," whispered Syn, "we will satisfy ourselves. Pistols and upstairs."

They left the room quietly, Dr. Syn going first with a pistol in his hand. Through the hall and up the stairs he went, to his bedroom door, which he pushed open, stepping aside into the dark passage as he did so. Mipps waited on the other side of the door, also with his pistol ready.

"Whoever you are," said Dr. Syn quietly, "will you be good enough to show yourself? I may add that there are two of us here, both armed, but purely in self-defence. We have no quarrel with anyone who is in trouble."

Dr. Syn saw the curtains of his four-poster stir by the open window.

"Who is with you?" demanded a voice.

"My sexton, Mr. Mipps," replied the doctor. "He is a man you may trust as myself. But he shoots as well as I do."

"Very well, then there need be no shooting," the voice answered. "I have come to you for help. Where can we talk?"

"You will follow me downstairs to my study, and Mr. Mipps will follow you. Please come out, and consider yourself quite safe."

The shadow of a big man in a long overcoat crossed the window and came out of the door.

Dr. Syn took a quick look at him and smiled. "Ah, it is my old friend of the boxing ring, Mr. Bone. I trust you will honour us by having some of my excellent brandy." He put his pistol in his pocket, and walked down into the hall, followed by the highwayman. Mr. Mipps followed, but taking no chances, kept the stranger's back covered with his pistol.

In the candle-lighted study, Dr. Syn poured out three glasses of brandy. "You may remove your mask, Mr. Bone. I should like to see whether or no your jaw is recovered."

"And that's the devil of it, sir," replied Mr. Bone. "There's a scar upon it which bides well to keep me a close prisoner for some time, unless you come forward to release me. Work's work and play's play, you see. I work at night in a mask, but how can I pick up information by day, when I am not able to take it off? A man can hardly walk into a tavern and drink in this thing." And Mr. Bone removed his black mask and flung it down on the table in disgust.

Dr. Syn handed his guest a glass of brandy.

"You mean that certain parties are now looking for a gentleman who carries a scar on his jaw bone?"

"Aye, you have hit it, reverend sir, as surely as you hit my jaw," replied the highwayman ruefully. "Mind you, there's not the poorest man on this Marsh who'd betray me for a hundred guineas, except that rascal who rode off for the Dragoons, and he's disappeared to Rye, they tell me."

"Then what is it you fear, Mr. Bone?" asked Dr. Syn. "You can surely walk in to your taverns as before our fight."

"No, that is what I cannot do," replied the highwayman. "The fact is, I have got that Preventive Officer on my track. Where he's been sensible enough to leave me alone to my work on the road, which is no business of his, he's now got it into his stupid head that I am the leader of the smugglers. He's after me because he says I'm the Scarecrow."

"And are you?" asked Mipps, looking very interested.

Mr. Bone favoured the sexton with a withering scowl.

"Yes, are you?" repeated Dr. Syn, as seriously.

"No, I am not," replied the highwayman, banging his fist on the table.

"You mean this mysterious being who seems to be putting his wits against the Customs, eh?" asked Syn.

"Aye, I do. And it's not me," roared the highwayman.

"Keep your voice down, sir," warned Mipps. "There's mice in the panelling here, and it's no use fidgeting 'em."

Mr. Bone scowled again at the facetious sexton and went on: "Why should I be hounded down for something I am not doing? The smugglers are keeping quiet at present, but it's common enough knowledge that this new leader is making great preparations. There's whisperings in many a tankard that goes echoing all over the Marsh, and inland, too, up in the hills. Now, I've come here for help. Maybe I know who this Scarecrow is, and, maybe I don't. If I do, as one adventurer salutes another, neither wild horses nor you two gentlemen could drag that information out of James Bone. I hope I know how to behave like a gentleman."

"A gentleman of the road, eh?" smiled Dr. Syn. "Well, Mr. Bone?"

"Well, Mr. Parson, it comes to this," went on the highwayman tersely. "I take it that there's no one who knows more about the Marsh folk than you. Dr. Syn, vicar of Dymchurch has got the reputation of keeping folks' business to himself."

"My dear sir, that is merely one of the duties of a parson."

"Exactly. They tell me so," replied Bone. "Well now, if I can give a guess as to who this Scarecrow is, no doubt you can give a better, and that being so, what about getting this mysterious gentleman to free me from taking over his responsibilities. For believe me, sir, I have sufficient of my own. In plain words, I'm willing to be hanged as Jimmie Bone, gentleman of the road, if they can catch me; but I'd hate like hell to swing as the Scarecrow when I ain't entitled to that privilege."

"I see your point, sir," replied Dr. Syn. "Whether I can help you or no remains to be seen. Have you any proposition to make?"

"I have. That evening when you set this mark on my face, you also saved my life. In so doing, you showed me a horse, a fierce black beast that I take to belong to my brother outlaw—this Scarecrow. Well, I likes the sound of this Scarecrow. He risked his neck to save them smugglers and he saved 'em just as surely as you saved me. That shows him to be a gentleman of spirit. He is the one man who could free me from this absurd rumour that I am the Scarecrow. He would see, if it were so pointed out, that I can hold up coaches very well in spite of the Bow Street runners, but that I cannot do it with the Customs men on my track as well."

"And what could he do to free you?" asked Dr. Syn.

"Listen. I has my agents as well as the Scarecrow," continued the highwayman, "and some of 'em, lots of 'em, are agents to us both. We have friends in common. Now, there's a rumour whispered that in ten days' time, which is the night of the full moon, there's to be a 'run'. Now, sir, I have a little job of my own upon that night, and did them Dragoons know of it, which they won't, they'd act just the same as I intend to act, for on that night there's a coach journeying from the City of Westminster to this part of the coast, and it's going to be full of golden guineas for shipment to certain agents in France. It's bad enough to know that there's traitors in and around Whitehall who'll smuggle British gold to our old enemies, but what about Englishmen who are willing to arrange this matter and then turn traitors to their other traitors and rob both England and France of the lot?"

"And how do you figure in this transaction, Mr. Bone, may I ask?"

"Why, reverend sir, they gets me to do their dirty work, which they're afraid to do themselves. Mr. Bone, gentleman of the road, is to hold up the coach, and then he's to hand over the bulk of the money to these double traitors."

"And do you intend to carry this out?" asked Dr. Syn.

"All but the last clause, reverend sir. Possession being nine points of the outlaw's law, they can whistle for their money, just as the waiting French lugger can whistle for a wind to get 'em clear of our ships of war in the Channel."

"And how does the Scarecrow come into this shuffled counter-plot?"

"Why, reverend sir, like this," went on Mr. Bone. "I holds up the coach. I gets 'em to unload her. I gives the coach her marching orders, when just then up gallops the Scarecrow himself and on behalf of the

Dymchurch smugglers, he robs Mr. Bone and in sight of the others gives Mr. Bone his marching orders. Some of the Scarecrow's men remove the guineas to a place agreed, and we two then goes shares."

"And the story gets around that poor Mr. Bone has been robbed by the Scarecrow of his lawful, or rather unlawful, dues, eh? I see." Dr. Syn chuckled as he filled up the three glasses. He then glanced across at Mipps and asked him what he thought.

"Well, sir," replied Mipps, "if I weren't a respectable sexton talking to my own respectable vicar, I should be bound to say that Mr. Bone's story strikes me as the neatest, pleasantest, and most amusin' little comedy I have ever heard the likes of."

Dr. Syn rose and took a few turns up and down the room. He then filled a churchwarden and lit it at one of the candles. As he stood watching the two men he drew briskly at the pipe, surrounding his head with clouds of tobacco smoke.

Mr. Bone watched him in silence. Mr. Mipps watched Mr. Bone with much sniffing, as though he were trying to ascertain whether this horsey-odoured gentleman of the road was to be trusted.

At length the doctor broke the silence.

"Mr. Bone, I know a good deal about you, as I know a good deal about most of the people on Romney Marsh, ad although you are—shall we say unruly?—you have the reputation for being a man who can be trusted by his friends. Your double dealing with these double dealers in guineas strikes me as a piece of poetical justice, for it is a symphony in cheating to see the cheaters cheated. I confess that it appeals to my sense of justice as also to my humour. I will see what can be done for you. You will return to your 'hide' at Mother Handaway's, and there I will communicate with you as soon as I can make the necessary connection with this Scarecrow. You may wonder a little that I, as a parson, consent to such an action. Well, maybe I am also caught by the romantic dash of this same Scarecrow. I owe him something at least, for saving the necks of my beloved flock, and I admit to a secret admiration for the Scarecrow. I owe you a good turn, Mr. Bone. I have set a mark upon you which I own is awkward. I admit your grievance, too, against the Scarecrow and—"

Dr. Syn paused, put down his pipe and slowly filled his own glass to the brim from the brandy bottle. He then raised it with the steadiest hand, passed it backwards and forwards beneath his nose with obvious appreciation of its aroma, and then looking first at Mipps and then at Mr. Bone, added:

"And if so be that this Scarecrow refuses to free you from your embarrassment—why, damme man, if I don't dress as the Scarecrow myself and rob you of those guineas." And he tossed off the brandy at a gulp.

"Good God," muttered Mipps, following his vicar's example and draining his own glass.

Mr. Bone held up his glass and said: "That is what I expected from the gallant gentleman who knocked me about and then saved me. But you can take this message to the Scarecrow, reverend sir. You can say that the authorities will never get information out of Mr. James Bone regarding any of his secrets; and you can add that should he ever be in need of a brave lieutenant to serve under him, Mr. Bone would not be found wanting."

He then drained his glass. Mr. Mipps took the liberty of filling them again—all three.

CHAPTER XXXIV. The Red-Bearded Bridegroom

In spite of the dryness of his erudite sermons, Dr. Syn, in his capacity of Dean of the Peculiars, which gave him the privilege of periodically preaching in the magnificent parish church of Rye in the adjacent county of Sussex, had gained a considerable popularity in that town. Whenever he took the short journey across the Kentish ditch into Sussex, he would put up at the 'Mermaid', and amidst the bustle of that great old inn he was ever a welcome guest, taking a lively interest in all, for the very exalted 'mine host' down to the humblest kitchen wench. It was, therefore, not surprising that Merry, in spite of his forbidding personality, found himself readily enough employed upon presenting his credentials from Dr. Syn.

He made himself useful in many odd jobs about the rambling old inn, and he kept his eye open to his own advantage, which with so many visitors speeding this way and that by coach, was considerable. Relieved as he was to turn his back on Dymchurch, since the Marsh men were up in arms against him for attempting to sell Mr. Bone to the Dragoons, he by no means gave up the idea of forcibly abducting Meg Clouder, and to this end he saved the many gratuities given to him by the passing guests. These people, relieved at reaching the safety of the 'Mermaid' without misadventure on the road, were usually in generous mood, and Merry found that, despite the smallness of his wage, he more than made up for it in extras, and it looked as though he would soon be in possession of sufficient money for the purpose of getting Meg into his power.

Amidst the fleeting population of the busy 'Mermaid', he did well, but it was towards two permanent guests that he chiefly focused his attention and willingly gave a thousand little services.

These two men were something of a mystery to the townsfolk of Rye. Magnificently dressed in the modish fashion of London, with a deal of foreign swagger, and a prodigal disregard for money, with which they appeared to be possessed in plenty, they cut a brave figure.

Although adorned with much lace and finery, their faces and figures gave the lie to any accusation of foppery which in other men their dress would have proclaimed. They were both sufficiently independent from the prevalent fashion of exquisites to wear bearded chins. The shorter of the two, who called himself Colonel Delacourt, was obviously the lead. Stockily built and tattooed like a South Sea islander, which showed towards evening when, merry with dice and drink, he would cast aside his gay velvet coat, undo his cravat, flowered waistcoat and silk shirt so that he showed his hairy, bepictured chest, and he would call on his companion to cry the stakes. And the play was high. The two men presented a marked contrast, for Captain Vicosa, whom the colonel addressed as "Captain Vic', was a red-bearded giant—a great leonine-looking fellow with perhaps even more swagger than his black-bearded companion and patron.

To the tactful inquiries of mine host of the 'Mermaid', Colonel Delacourt gave out that he had made a fortune in the Indies, where he maintained he owned much home property in plantations, and he introduced the red-bearded and handsome 'Captain Vic' as his partner and manager, who had come to England with him to transact certain businesses connected with the Crown colonies.

Despite their fineries, the two men were excused from anything appertaining to the coxcomb. Men and women recognised and respected their obvious masculinity.

The reason of their enforced stay at the 'Mermaid' was the fact that Madame Delacourt had given birth to a daughter upon the very night of their arrival, and although the child was doing well enough, the mother was rapidly sinking. The Rye doctor who attended her, although a married man, was not above saying that 'Madame' at the 'Mermaid' was the most beautiful woman he had ever seen. He described her to his friends as a Spanish Madonna, but he owned that he was going to be hard put to it to save her life. She was listless. She showed no affection for the baby girl, and the doctor suspected that she not only feared her husband but hated him.

His manner to her was loud and rude, and her enforced convalescence filled him with ungovernable irritation. And yet, strange to say, he showed great affection to the wee mite that lay smiling in the big drawer beside her bed. He would swing into the room when far advanced in drink, swear that the child was his, and catch it up against the protests of the woman whom the doctor had recommended to attend the baby, and carry it into the adjoining room, where he diced and drank with the red-bearded Captain Vic. He would twine the little fingers around the dice-box and help her to throw the dice against his companion, and cry out with joy at her cleverness when the score was thrown high.

On one such occasion the doctor found him, and let him have his mind on the subject.

"Now, understand me well Colonel Delacourt," he said, in low, threatening tones. "I don't know who you are or what you may or may not be in the Indies, but you are behaving in this inn of ours as no gentleman should behave. Gentleman? I should have said, as no plough-boy would behave. Your wife is dying, and do you realise that it is you who are killing her? I warn you that should she die, there will be an inquiry, and as sure as I want to save her I'll take my oath before the magistrate that you are her murderer. You will leave that child alone, and if you must drink and shout and sing your ribald songs, you'll do it in the common rooms below, where the beadle can deal with you. I take your money for my services, it's true, but I'll not be responsible for your lady's life unless you mend your ways with her. A little sympathy from you, a little consideration, might make all the difference between life and death, for I tell you the scales of her fate are dropping fast towards death."

Colonel Delacourt damned him for an interfering sawbones, but when he saw the doctor stride out of the room in a fury, he repented and sent Merry after him with a purseful of guineas, which the doctor resolutely refused. Merry helped himself to a good half of the contents, and returned with the depleted purse and the message that the doctor had already been paid sufficiently for his services, but could not be bribed to keep his mouth shut; whereupon Colonel Delacourt damned him again in good round oaths and flung the purse at Merry's head. Merry, however, thought fit to pocket the insult as well as the guineas, which he knew from his experience of the colonel, would not be remembered when the fumes of the 'Mermaid' wines had cooled from his head.

Merry's chief duty consisted of persuading both gentlemen to bed in the early hours, and then carrying up more bottles till they fell asleep. Not another member of the 'Mermaid' staff would venture near them, so that the landlord blessed the fact that he had employed the man from Dymchurch. It was Merry who tidied up the sitting-room in the cold light of the dawn. Cards all over the floor, spilled wine and broken glass, and many elusive guineas that had rolled from drunken fingers into dark recesses of the old oak floor. After a more than successful hunt for such gold, Merry would sometimes lay a solitary guinea upon the breakfast-table and say he had found it in a crack of the floor, whereupon both colonel and captain would cry out that at last they had found an honest fellow in this cursed land of England.

One service only Merry resolutely refused to perform for them. They told him to ride to the Romney Marsh and find out and order to attend on them, one Jimmie Bone, a highwayman, for whom they had employment.

Merry excused himself, saying that it was more than his life was worth to undergo such a duty. He told them the story of his attempted betrayal of Mr. Bone, making himself out a most worthy citizen in that he wanted the highroads rid of such an outlaw.

The answer he got from Colonel Delacourt surprised him.

"Well, I am rejoiced that you failed, Mr. Merry. You good citizenship, as you call it, may have lost you a hundred guineas, but I tell you we have need of Mr. Bone that is more valuable than such a paltry sum. So you refuse to be our go-between, eh?"

"I tell you, sir," whined Merry, "that if Mr. Bone meets me he'll pistol me without a tremor."

"That means you'll have to do it, Vic my lad," said the colonel, striding in a rage to the window which looked down upon the cobbled street. "You know enough of my history to be sure that I am not in the mood to ride Dymchurch way. The very sight of the Romney Marsh would drive me into the doldrums with my lady's everlasting regrets dinning in my ears."

All of which, at the moment, was Greek to Mr. Merry.

"I'll go if I must," growled Captain Vic, "but be damned to Merry for a cowardly knave, I say."

"No, no, Merry's a good servant to us, you must admit," went on the colonel, "and we'd never get our drinks so easy without him, seeing that all the chambermaids avoid us like the plague since you started kissin' 'em. Merry can't go—that's flat. Merry, give the captain a glass of brandy, and fill one for me."

Merry did as he was told, and at that moment they heard the rumble of wheels over the cobbles, the crack of postboys' whips and the stirring notes of a coach horn.

"More visitors, by God. Let's hope it's someone to dice with," cried the colonel, taking the glass of brandy from Merry's hand. "Fill a glass for yourself, Merry, and never mind what the captain says—he's drunk. There'll be no need for you to meet this Mr. Bone. We want no murder done any more than you."

As Merry proceeded to fill a glass for himself, the colonel gave a cry which was followed by the noise of a smashed glass.

"What the devil's wrong with you?" growled Captain Vic, looking up at his patron with bleared eyes.

Colonel Delacourt had staggered back into the folds of the window curtain, and his glass of brandy lay shattered and unheeded at his feet.

"Good God," he muttered, and all the drink went out of his face, leaving him stark staring sober. In answer to the captain's repeated question, he but mumbled something unintelligible which brought the red-bearded on to his feet with an oath. He lurched across to the casement and peered out at the bustle of inn servants round the coach.

"There's only two passengers alighting," he said, "and I fail to see why they should upset a man of spirit. A doddering old parson and his shabby servant, I presume. A little cove with a ridiculous brass blunderbuss under his arm."

"Doddering parson be damned," gasped the colonel. "And the little cove too. Well I know them."

"Who are they then?" demanded Captain Vic, but got no reply from his patron, who had rushed to the sitting-room door and shot the bolts on the inside.

"Hell, can't you answer a gentleman?" growled Captain Vic. "Here, you," he ordered Merry. "Know either of these old dodderers?"

"Old dodderers—don't be such a fool," snarled the colonel. " You're drunk, or you'd have jumped to it by now."

"Who are they?" repeated Captain Vic to Merry. "Do you know 'em or don't you, since the colonel's daft?"

Merry had looked down at the little man in black who stood awaiting his master, who was collecting a paper case and some books from the inside of the old vehicle.

"I knows 'em too well," replied Merry. "And I wishes 'em both more ill-luck than I fear will come to 'em. That's Parson Syn of Dymchurch and his sexton, Mipps."

"Here, you don't mean—" began Captain Vic, swinging round on the colonel.

"I do," snapped the colonel. "Parson Syn be damned. It's Clegg, I tell you. Aye, and the little rat with the blunderbuss is his ship's carpenter—two of the bloodiest pirates that ever terrorised the seas and my most mortal enemies."

"What did you say, sir?" asked Merry, hardly able to believe what had been said, and yet hoping there might be truth in it.

Whereupon, Colonel Delacourt, with one eye on the bolted door, recounted something of the terrors of Clegg, and how Clegg had followed him from sea to sea in order to get his revenge.

"And revenge for what?" exploded the colonel. "Why, for robbing him of the burden next door. He's welcome to her now, if he cares to relieve me of her. I mean my wife, Mr. Merry."

"Your wife? But was this parson sweet on her, sir?" he asked.

"Sweet?" repeated Delacourt. "He was married to her, you fool, and I, like a fool, carried her off. She's his wife now in the eyes of the law, not mine. But the child's mine. Illegitimate, but mine."

This news was getting better and better. Here was Dr. Syn's wife in the possession of another man, true, but still Dr. Syn's wife.

"I told him she was dead, but even then he followed me," went on Colonel Delacourt.

So Dr. Syn did not know that his wife was living, and so near. Here was at least a means to strike shame to Charlotte Cobtree, and this pirate talk of Clegg—that would be sufficient weapon against the doctor. There was a bigger price on Clegg's head than on a hundred Jimmie Bones. Clegg had fought the world. All manner of ships he had sunk, ships of all nations. Yes, Clegg was wanted internationally. Here indeed was the most glorious and unexpected revenge on a man he hated. Meg would be his yet, and he would strip those pearls from Charlotte Cobtree's neck to give to her.

"And how long will this damned fellow stay here?" asked the colonel. "I've a mind to slip my cable and leave a letter for him to call for his dying wife."

"You'll do nothing of the sort," growled Captain Vic. "Have you forgotten why we are employing this Mr. Bone?"

"I know I'll do nothing of the sort," replied Delacourt. "But not for that reason. I stay here because the child ain't fit to be taken from its mother yet—that's all."

"Well, praise to God you're crazy about the kid," said Captain Vic. "Otherwise, there's no telling but you'd be off if I gave you the chance."

"How long does he stay—this parson, and what's he here for?" asked the colonel of Merry.

Merry told him that he usually came by this—the Saturday—coach and stayed in the 'Mermaid' till Monday. "He will preach a sermon to-morrow morning and will dine with the rector afterwards. He'll no doubt be supping out to-night as well, but he'll take a drink in the common bar and stand treat to all the fishermen. That's his way to popularity."

"Then we must lie low up here. We'll admit no one but the saw-bones, and that only to avoid him talking of us to Dr. Syn. Merry shall watch and fetch and carry for us. We're prisoners here till the fellow takes coach for Dymchurch on Monday."

Merry told them a good deal. The good brandy made him talkative. Besides, it was good to relieve his spleen against Dr. Syn to two men who shared a common hatred. Both colonel and captain dropped their attitude of masters to a servant. They clapped Merry down at the table, plied him with drink, and vowed they were all friends together, and as gentlemen they would take oath to hound Dr. Syn to his death. Merry, who gave them full details of the doctor's miraculous preservation from the wreck, was in favour of a public accusation against him as Clegg, but to this the colonel would not consent.

"We'll kill him first," he declared, "and accuse him after, so that his tongue cannot wag against me. As Colonel Delacourt I am safe enough, but as Nick Tappitt—well, there are things I have no wish to be made public. A gentleman does not care to do his washing in the High Courts. But we'll kill him, by God, and then see him hung in chains. And you, friend Merry, shall be in it with us."

Flattered by their friendliness, Merry went on to tell them of his passion for Meg Clouder, whom he described in such glowing terms, that although the colonel damned all women but his baby girl as plagues and nuisances, Captain Vic became so enthusiastic on Merry's behalf that he avowed he would win Meg for him.

"You're a morose sort of a devil," he declared, filling up Merry's glass, "and for all that I love you as a sworn brother in arms, I'd take my oath you'd never win a cow-girl, much less this beautiful young hostess you speak of. Now, I have a way with women of all classes and ages, as the colonel will bear me out. Many's the kicking filly, aye, and demure young miss, too, who has rued the day the let Captain Vic get away with her; and I'll tell you what I'll do. I'll marry the wench myself and then abandon her. You can then take her on the rebound if you've the manhood in you that I imagine. How's that?"

After a good deal of argument, for at first Colonel Delacourt did not relish staying in the same inn as his arch-enemy without his henchman, it was decided that Captain Vic should have a post-chaise and set off that very afternoon to Dymchurch. Meanwhile, Merry was to watch Dr. Syn as he came in and out, and the colonel was to lie low in his sitting-room, with as much drink as he needed supplied by the dutiful Merry.

"And you'll not take it unkindly of me, friend Merry," asked Captain Vic, when the post-chaise was at the door, "if I make love to this Meg of yours in good earnest?"

"You can do what you like with her," replied Merry. "There's no soft love about me. I doubt whether there's love at all, for at times I hate her for upsetting me. Break her spirit, my captain, then throw her to me. So that I possess her at last—aye, and her inn, too—you can do your worst to her."

"The worst will be well for you," answered the captain. "For if she comes to hate me, why, she'll love you all the more for giving her protection."

"I wonder," growled Merry. "She hates me like hell, but that's all one, so that I get her."

"You shall have her, Mr. Merry; you can take Captain Vic's word for that."

So the red-bearded one departed, full of glee that he was escaping from the gloom of Madame Delacourt's sick-bed, and with the prospects of a diverting adventure at the end of his journey.

Just as the colonel was figuring that the post-chaise carrying Captain Vic would be nearly Dymchurch, Merry announced the local physician. After an examination of his patient, he returned to the sitting-room, closing the bedroom door behind him. He looked more serious than usual, which was quite enough to enrage the colonel without the following pronouncement:

"Colonel Delacourt," he said, "your wife is sinking, and as far as I am concerned, her decline is unnecessary. Her body is well enough, allowing for her condition, but it is her mind that is wrong. She has not the will to exert her strength, and without that will, I am useless. Now it happens, by the best of good fortune, that there is alighted at this inn a man of such high spirituality, and possessed of such charm of manner that where my poor eloquence has failed, he is one who might succeed. He is beloved by all who know him, and it is his mission in life to attend to the comforts of afflicted souls. I propose to bring this gentleman up to see your wife."

"Oh, you do, do you?" growled the colonel. "And who might the gentleman be that he can claim admittance to my lady's sick-room? A doctor?"

"Yes, a doctor," replied the physician gravely. "A learned doctor of divinity, but the broadest-minded man of his cloth that I have ever encountered. In short, it is Dr. Syn, vicar of a place called Dymchurch across the Kent border. He is below stairs now and will be delighted to take a glass of wine with you, so that you may be the better acquainted before he visits your poor wife. I will bring him up, with your permission."

"Which you will not get, my interfering doctor," growled the colonel.

"Eh?" demanded the amazed physician.

"I utterly forbid you to do any such thing," went on the colonel in an angrier tone.

"But when I tell you that the benefits of his visit may—indeed, will—do untold good. In fact, as your medical adviser in this case, I will go so far as to insist upon your seeing him. My confidence in the man is so sure."

"You are dictating now out of your province," retorted the colonel. "My wife is a foreigner, and her religion has nothing to do with the Church of England, and the last person she would wish to see is this parson friend of yours."

"There, Colonel Delacourt, I must contradict you," said the physician. "I spoke of this good man to your good lady, and as I spoke, I could see that her spirit seemed to burn with a new life. Let us go together to her now and ask if it is not her wish to see this Dr. Syn, since you will not take my word for it."

Colonel Delacourt staggered to his feet with his fists clenched.

"You may be a good physician, sir," he said, "but you must own that I have paid for your services up to date in good money. I trust that you will consider it your duty to continue your professional visits to my wife and daughter, just as I shall consider it my duty to pay your fees handsomely. But I do not desire spiritual advice from you or your friends, and I take it as an impertinence that you should propose introducing a stranger to my wife in her present state. Call to-morrow, sir, with your physicals as usual, but let me have no more of this parson nonsense."

"She is your wife," returned the physician, "and on this point I must not go against your authority."

"I can promise you that," interrupted the colonel.

"But I must tell you that I like you the less for your decision," continued the doctor. "And one word more, and here I speak within my province, and if it offends you—blame yourself. Your friend has ridden off in a post-chaise. For long or short, I do not know and care less. But since you are alone, I command you to abstain from further liquor, and I presume you will not now consider it your duty to keep the night-owl awake with your cursed songs. Good afternoon."

"Oh, go to hell, and come to-morrow for your money," retorted the colonel.

* * * * * *

Below stairs, in the handsomely-appointed sitting-room which was always set aside for Dr. Syn, the physician found the Dymchurch parson receiving some of his many friends in Rye. Leading him aside, he told him of the colonel's objection to parsons, adding his opinion of husbands who can drink, gamble and sing ribald songs at the very threshold of their wives' sick-rooms.

"Add to that, sir, the fact that the wife wished to see you, and said your visit would be a great comfort to her, and yet this bully refuses point-blank. I wish he had gone away with his companion, who they tell me has taken chaise for your Dymchurch."

"I wonder now why he has gone there? I must speak to Merry on the subject, and if necessary we will keep an eye upon this other offensive man."

"You'll not have difficulty in recognising him," replied the physician. "I have never seen so conspicuous a man. His red beard flames like a furnace, and he carries two golden balls from his ear-lobes that put one in mind of a pawnbroker's sign. A flashy, handsome, swaggering braggart if ever there was one."

And in the meantime, the gentleman under discussion had arrived at Dymchurch and entered the cosy bar of 'The City of London' inn. To say that such a magnificent specimen of a man lifted poor Meg off her feet is but to state a literal truth, for, after treating the usual following in the bar with as much drink as they could carry and presenting each villager with a guinea when Meg was not looking, to leave him a clear coast for his wooing, he lifted Meg right over the drinking counter and carried her out like a baby on to the sea-wall, crying in one breath to the pot-boy to mind the custom, and in the next declaring his undying passion for the girl in his arms.

The tide was far out and the setting sun reflecting the golden light of the sands caused the beard of Captain Vic to sparkle red. Meg thought she had never seen such a glorious man, never encountered such colossal strength.

With a cry of joy, Captain Vic raced along the deserted beach laughing at the bewildered face against his shoulder. When he had run far from the village, he sat himself down against a breakwater, with Meg still in his arms who, woman-like, protested that he would soil his fine velvet coat if he leaned against the tarred and seaweed-covered wood.

Captain Vic assured her that he had a score of coats every bit as fine hanging up in his wardrobe at the 'Mermaid' in Rye, and that failing those there were a score of fashionable London tailors who were pestering him to order more. He kept vowing that he loved her, that he had never loved before, and that when he had heard of her beauty that very day, he had known she was the right wife for him and had set off immediately to claim her.

When she heard that it was Merry who had raved about her, she trembled with fear and told her impetuous lover of her dread. He assured her that she need have no fear of any man while he lived to protect her, and he went on in the most gentlemanly fashion to tell her the arrangements he was about to make for their immediate wedding.

"Whether we live on for a time at your inn or take ship to my vast plantations in the Indies, is for you to decide, my Meg," he added. "Naturally, I will not sleep at your inn but will take rooms at the 'Ship', for everything must be above board for the sake of your sweet reputation. But on Monday I will ride into Hythe, take out a special licence from the magistrate and then we will be married quietly and return in the evening as man and wife and confront this village with our happiness."

Meg protested against such a hurry, but she owned that the sudden romance of it appealed to her. Whereupon, Captain Vic kissed her heartily and told her the affair was settled.

When he brought her home and kissed her good night under the darkness of the sea-wall, Meg entered 'The City of London' happier than she had ever been since the night of the wreck, and feeling a great sense of relief that at last she could carry on her business under the security of Captain Vic's protection.

By mutual consent, her new lover not only slept at the 'Ship Inn', but mealed there, though the rest of the day he insisted on sitting in Meg's bar, in which he rapidly gained a popularity, owing not only to his generosity but to his gentlemanly manners, for Captain Vic knew how to play his cards in life for his own advantage, just as he knew how to conceal an ace up his sleeve when playing real cards upon the table.

For one, also, he took the care to keep himself reasonably sober, and the more she saw of him, the more confident did Meg feel that he was the man she could safely choose as her protector.

"And as for that rogue Merry," he laughed, "if he so much as annoys you as to show his face in this good 'City of London', why, I'll break his neck between my finger and thumb." And when Meg saw him tear a pack of cards across the middle, which no other man could accomplish in that bar, she knew that he was not idly boasting of his strength.

Her confidence in Captain Vic increased when they discovered that the licence would take some days to prepare, for although annoyed at the delay and damning old England for a puritanical slow-coach, which was excusable in such an impetuous lover, his behaviour never went beyond the bounds required by the most exacting chaperon. "He is a gentleman to his finger-tips," said Meg, and everyone agreed with her.

On the whole, Meg was not averse to being married quietly in Hythe, for she was afraid of the opinion of the Dymchurch folk who had loved her husband. She was not at all easy in her mind, however, in taking such a serious step without consultation with Dr. Syn, but this was impossible since the reverend gentleman had taken the opportunity of his journey to Rye to pay a number of visits to certain of the clergy in that district, keeping with him the redoubtable Mipps as his body-servant, who also took opportunity at each place to pass word from the Scarecrow concerning the arrangements for the mightiest 'run' ever undertaken by the smugglers.

Meg was anxious to take Charlotte Cobtree into her confidence, but Captain Vic, after some argument persuaded her against this, saying that since Meg was so young a widow it was more seemly not to announce her second marriage till it was an established fact.

"Besides," he added, "it will only seem that you are telling her in order to conjure rich presents out of the squire's family, and since I can give you money to play ducks and drakes with, we will buy all you want ourselves and make you feel the more independent."

Thus it was that Meg and Captain Vic departed one morning by special coach to Hythe without a word to anyone as to their purpose, and returned to 'The City of London' as man and wife.

CHAPTER XXXV. The Beacon on Aldington Knoll

The evening that Dr. Syn returned from his profitable little tour over the Sussex border, he dined with the Cobtrees, in order, as he put it, to learn all the gossip of Dymchurch since he had been absent.

"Well, Doctor, the most extraordinary news is this," said the squire. "This daughter of mine here, this Charlotte, has at last, and in your absence, chosen her twenty-first birthday present from me, and you'll never guess what it is. You see, Doctor, like all the other romantic misses of the neighbourhood, she has thought fit to admire this mysterious Scarecrow, because he saved the necks of a number of Dymchurch lads. Now, although her Sirius is accounted one of the best hunters on the Marsh,—she must now have a black horse too. Why? Oh, because the Scarecrow rode a black horse, if you please. Well, I tell her, so did the murderer Grinsley."

"And so did Mr. Bone the highwayman," added Dr. Syn, laughing across the table at Charlotte.

"Oh, and another thing concerning which I have not yet arrived at the truth. Our Meg Clouder has gone off to Hythe only yesterday and returned married, if you please—married to some captain who lays claim to be a gentleman, but who has returned to take up his married quarters in 'The City of London'. It infuriates me to think of it, and I shall most certainly have something to say to our Meg."

"She must have been very lonely there, you know, Squire—" began Dr. Syn.

But the squire cut him short with: "Oh, you will always find excuses for everyone, Doctor, but why couldn't the jade let us into the secret? Our Charlotte called in yester evening to take her a shawl she had worked for her, and it was: 'Oh, Miss Charlotte, what do you think I have been and done? You will not be cross with me? You will not let squire be angry?' Squire angry, if you please, as though I was a bad-tempered curmudgeon. 'But I've been and got married,' she says, 'and oh, Miss Charlotte, he's a gentleman in fine clothes and rolling in guineas.'"

"Whereupon," added Charlotte, "out there steps the bravest looking gentleman, tall, well dressed and handsome, with the largest red beard you ever saw. I should not have been surprised had he announced that he was Clegg the pirate."

"Instead of Captain Vicosa, known as Captain Vic, eh?" added Dr. Syn. "For I take it that in these clean-shaven days there are not two handsome adventurers with red beards in the neighbourhood, and I heard tell of such a man at the 'Mermaid Inn' last week. I wondered why the rascal set off so briskly for Dymchurch in a hired chaise."

"You say 'adventurer' and 'rascal'," said the squire. "Do you know anything about him then?"

"Nothing at all," replied Dr. Syn, "except that his companion, who appears to be a most undesirable colonel, has adopted that rogue Merry as his particular satellite. No doubt this Captain Vic, as they call him, heard of Meg through that very rogue."

"Well, we will keep an eye on him, whoever he may be," said the squire. "Let us hope for Meg's sake that he is not so bad after all, though I suspect a gentleman who marries out of his class as probably not belonging to the gentry at all."

After telling the squire all he had heard from the Rye physician concerning the visitors at the 'Mermaid', Dr. Syn took it upon himself to visit 'The City of London', where he discovered Meg's husband already far gone in liquor, and brow-beating not only his pretty wife but everyone else in the bar-parlour.

Upon Dr. Syn refusing to accept a drink with such a bully, Captain Vic flew into a rage and damned all parsons in good round terms, which brought tears of shame into poor Meg's eyes. The vicar however stood a round of drinks to the men in the bar and proposed Meg's health and happiness; and when Captain Vic with an oath told him not to be high-handed in his bar, the doctor turned on him, saying calmly but sternly:

"I must point out to you, Captain Vic, if that is what you are pleased to call yourself, that this girl whom you have married so hurriedly, is well beloved by everyone of us here in Dymchurch, and for her sake you will do well to behave with the civility which we have been accustomed to receive in this inn—an inn, let me add, that has been re-built by loving hands who wished to show their appreciation of Meg and her gallant husband, who gave his life that others might live."

"Gave his life for you, you mean," retorted Captain Vic. "I heard that you were the sole survivor."

"Perfectly true," replied Dr. Syn, "but had Abel Clouder had his way, he would have saved the whole ship's company. Being the sole survivor, however, makes it all the more my duty to see that Abel's young widow is happy, and to that end I expect you to help me, or you may find that we can force you to do this duty."

There followed a battle of looks between them, but when Dr. Syn added that he knew something of Captain Vic's reputation in Rye, and also what he had seen of his companion, Colonel Delacourt had not predisposed his favour towards that gentleman, Captain Vic cocked his hat with a flourish and went out to cool his head upon the sea-wall.

The vicar turned to Meg and took her hand. "I am grieved for your sake that this has happened, my poor child," he said kindly. "I hope, however, that the ill-humour of this husband of yours is due but to the drink he has taken, and that in soberer moods he may learn civility, but remember this—however much we may humour this fellow for your sake, woe betide him should the least hint be whispered of any unkindness to you, and the quicker you make him understand that, why so much the better for his health."

And to a chorus of approval from the other men in the bar, Dr. Syn walked briskly back to the vicarage.

Here, to a late hour, he sat with Mipps, a large surveying map of Romney Marsh spread out before them, over which they pored, for all the world like two commanders planning a mighty battle. When the various dispositions of men, horses and pack ponies had been settled, Dr. Syn produced the brandy bottle, and pledged success to the greatest 'run' ever planned in the history of the Marsh smugglers.

"And if your leaders carry out these orders to the letter, I can see no flaw in the campaign, my good Master Carpenter. And now for the greatest surprise of all. We have, as you know, allowed Captain Faunce and his Dragoons to know that these preparations are being made for the night of the full moon."

"Aye, sir," interrupted Mipps, "and I still fail to see why we had to let 'em know. No doubt you have some good reason."

"The very best of reasons, my good Mipps," went on the vicar. "It is essential that the Dragoons, or at least a few of them, should be witnesses of the robbing of that coach. In order to establish the fact that Jimmie Bone is not the Scarecrow, they must see the Scarecrow rob the highwayman."

Mipps nodded and scratched his impertinent-looking nose. "We seem to be doing a good deal for this fellow Bone, don't we, sir?"

"He will have his uses later, believe me," replied Syn. "Your rumours about the Scarecrow put him into an awkward fix, and it pleases me to extricate him, so upon that night nothing must go wrong, and nothing left to chance. That is why, like a wise stage manager of a playhouse, I have called out the men three nights before the 'run' to rehearse in full detail."

"And that strikes me as being one of the maddest things I ever heard tell of," said Mipps. "Of course, you must do as you think, sir, but own up it's a bit crazy like. I mean to say—rehearsals is all right for play actors, but rehearsals for a crime against the Crown—well—oh, I say. Mad."

"Have you forgotten Clegg's madnesses so soon, my good Mipps?" asked the doctor sadly. "It was by his craziness that he succeeded. Besides, that order you sent to the luggers in France, I took good care to amend. A good dress rehearsal is usually attended not only by the actors but by the properties. Those thousands of kegs and barrels which you ordered to be landed empty, I have taken good care shall be full. In that, we shall not be wasting our money or our time. We shall accomplish two 'runs' instead of one, that is all, and the Marsh men's profits will be doubled."

Mipps slapped his thighs with enthusiasm and was guilty of executing one or two steps of the sailor's hornpipe. "Now, that's my old commander talking, blime if it ain't. Two 'runs', oh, my eye."

"You need not hornpipe, Mr. Mipps. I am well aware that you have served in the Royal Navy."

Mipps grinned. "And both nights is to go forward on the same plans, sir?"

"There is only one difference," replied Syn. "On the first night it will be necessary for you and me to command the beach, and when the pack ponies leave the hills, the Upton brothers will fire the great beacon from Aldington Knoll, which will bring the luggers in shore. But on the second night, I shall leave you in command of the beach, and no one but the Scarecrow himself must fire the beacon."

Mr. Mipps pulled a long face. "I must say, sir, that in a big affair like this 'ere, I prefers to ride at your side. Is this alteration absolutely necessary?"

"Of course it is," replied Syn. "However careful these guinea runners may be with their preparations, as Mr. Bone has wisely pointed out, one must allow for delays with post horses, and until that coach arrives and puts on its skids at the top of Quarry Hill, Mr. Bone cannot hold it up, and until Mr. Bone holds it up and gets the sacks of guineas out on to the high bank on the right side of the hill going down, the Scarecrow will be powerless to rob him. Just as soon as this happens and the guineas are safely removed by the Scarecrow's men, why then the Scarecrow will gallop to Aldington hell for leather and fire the beacon. See?"

"I see, sir—but—"

"No 'buts,' Master Carpenter. Orders are orders," snapped Syn.

"Yessir. Orders is orders, and 'ere's my best respec's," replied Mipps, draining his glass.

"And don't forget to keep that red-headed bridegroom of poor Meg's under your spy-glass. Remember, he is one of these double-dealing guinea runners that are employing our friend Bone."

"I'll watch him, sir," replied Mipps. "And at the same time I thinks we might put someone's spy-glass to watch this 'ere Colonel Delacourt at Rye. We want to know that he don't go gallivantin' after girls the same as Red-beard Vic! Suppose his wife dies and then old Waggetts dies, what he looks more like a-doin' any day, and then the colonel goes and marries Mrs. Waggetts. Not very comfortable to have a colonel in one inn and a captain in t'other. I prefers landladies to landlords when it comes to inns. They're more amenable, if you asks me, sir, to bachelors like myself."

"I have thought of setting a watch upon this mysterious colonel already," said Syn. "It strikes me that he'll need it when he finds that the Scarecrow has made off with his guineas, and it seems to me that the proper person to watch him will be our gallant Preventive Officer. He will want another Scarecrow to watch when he realises that he has shinned up the wrong bark after Jimmie Bone."

This so appealed to Mr. Mipps that he executed a few more steps of the hornpipe, which were terminated by the vicar refilling his glass.

"By the way, Mipps, I notice that you are wearing your Sunday suit these days. I am glad to know that you have discarded your old coat, and I shall be glad to provide you with a new suit if you will order it. We must have you smart and ship-shape for your Sunday duty."

"The new suit is ordered and paid for, sir," replied Mipps. "I gets two guineas for that torn old suit of mine. We knows that women has strange notions sometimes, but Miss Charlotte wanting my old black suit what was going green, and being willin' to give two guineas for it fair give me a shock. Told me not to tell no one, but I tells my commander, of course."

"So she wanted your old suit, did she?" asked Syn, thinking seriously.

"And what do you think she wanted it for?" went on the sexton. "Why, to put it in the copper and give it a baking, just as we did aboard the Imogene when we run into that plague of lice. Remember?"

"So she put your old suit into the boiler, did she? That's very interesting."

"I thought it was rather silly," replied Mipps. "It wasn't as dirty as all that. And what she wanted my old suit for and give two guineas for it beats me."

But Dr. Syn was thinking of her new black horse, and the two purchases began to find connection in his mind. For many minutes Mipps watched his master closely, not daring to move in case he interrupted the train of thought.

At last Dr. Syn jerked himself out of his reverie.

"I was thinking, Mipps, I was thinking."

"Never seen you look so serious since the time you marooned that 'orrible mulatto on the coral reef," said Mipps.

"Ah," exclaimed the doctor. "We have seen things. We have seen things."

"That we has," returned Mipps. "The glimpse I got of that red-bearded scoundrel of Meg's put me in mind of something. Remember a night a few years back in Jamaica when you was dining with a rich planter?"

Syn nodded. "We sold him a cargo of goods, and I went to collect the money. He told the authorities who I was, and if you and the lads hadn't fired the house, I might not be here to-day."

"Oh, he hadn't caught you. You've got out of worse traps than that without help."

"Maybe, but you saved me nevertheless," returned Syn. "But what put that in your mind? Meg's husband did you say?"

"Aye, sir. That there planter had red hair, and I never sailed yet with a red-haired man that I've took to. Something unnatural about red hair in a man, I says."

"He was a tall handsome fellow too, was that planter," added Syn.

It was Mipps' turn to nod. "Bit queer if it was the same, only growed a beard, for I tell you, I don't like the sound of this Captain Vic."

"It would be very queer, Mipps," replied Syn thoughtfully. "I am sorry enough for poor Meg as it is, without wishing your idea a fact."

"But if it is a fact, eh? Oh, well, we'd have to kill him, that's all. Couldn't have him strollin' about. But my! How he would bleed. Not that a bit of blood would notice round there now. He's turned Meg's cellar into a slaughter-house. He was cutting a pig's throat in it last night with one of the butcher boys. I heard the screams from my coffin shop, when I was at work on old man Waggetts' coffin."

"But Waggetts is alive. What are you talking of?" demanded the vicar.

"Dr. Pepper told me he couldn't last long, so being matey with 'em, I thought I'd get his box knocked up so as he could see what a treat I'm making for him. Best pine and brass knobs. Mrs. W. said 'Spare no expense.' I think old Waggetts will be delighted."

"I have yet to meet the man who could be delighted at the sight of his own coffin, Mr. Mipps," replied Syn.

"Oh, I think he'll like it," went on Mipps. "He ought to. Well, as I was saying, when I first heard the screams, I jumped, thinking maybe it was Waggetts who had gone and his ghost was 'owling at me. Then I goes out and locates the screams, and thinkin' it was that captain murderin' poor Meg, I creeps to the rescue and sees that red-bearded 'orror sticking a pig in the cellar. Not a pleasant night's recreation for a young bride, I thinks."

"Captain Vic seems to be asking us to remove him. Well, we shall see. And in the meanwhile, keep a close eye on him."

"I'll do a creep that way now and see what he's up to."

"Are you going home then?" asked the vicar.

"I'm going to harness up the donkey and ride to Aldington while it's dark. The boys there are building the beacon to-night, and I want to make sure they will build two."

"Very wise. Very wise," replied Dr. Syn. "You're a good lieutenant, Mipps. Make it clear to the lads of Aldington that the success of both 'runs' depends upon their beacons. They must be able to be picked up five miles at sea, and make it clear that the Uptons fire the first and the Scarecrow himself the second. Where are you meeting them?"

"At the Walnut Tree," said Mipps. "We set out from there to the Knoll."

"Are you armed?" asked Syn.

"Aye, aye, sir. The old blunderbuss there in the corner," replied the sexton. "She throws as good a broadside as a King's frigate."

"Well, I think there is little danger of interruption," said the vicar. "It's a wild, eerie spot is Aldington Knoll."

"And could tell a wild, eerified tale too, if it had a tongue in its head," grinned the sexton.

Leaving the vicarage, Mipps did one of his 'creeps' beneath the sea-wall, and producing a brace and bit from his tool-bag, he proceeded to open up a peep-hole through the cellar door of 'The City of London.' He knew there was little danger of his being overheard while that heavy snoring kept regular in the cellar. When the tool gave place to his eye, the sight which it fell on disgusted him.

The cellar was lighted with a wax dip stuck in a bottle. Hanging in the centre from a hook in the ceiling was the body of a pig, while sprawled out beneath it lay the drunken body of Captain Vic, surrounded with empty bottles.

"A dead pig and a drunk one," muttered Mipps, as he walked away towards the coffin shop, saddled his donkey and with his blunderbuss at the ready jogged away over the winding Marsh roads towards the distant hill of Aldington, where the white chalk shone out in a pale reflection towards the beacon on the mast of the old Varne Lightship in the Channel fairway.

CHAPTER XXXVI. "Death to the Scarecrow"

Neither Captain Faunce nor the Dymchurch Preventive Officer were the men to ignore the information they had gleaned about the Scarecrow's proposed 'run' on the night of the full moon, and three days before, the village looked on with secret misgivings at the arrival of Colonel Troubridge, who had personally led a full squadron of Dragoons from Dover Castle, to augment the little force already commanded by Captain Faunce.

They commandeered the big field that lay between the sea-wall and the 'Ship Inn', and here they set up camp. Although outwardly declaring that their presence was but due to a summer manoeuvring, it was plainly evident to the village that they had deliberately come to war against the mysterious Scarecrow and his men.

Both colonel and captain elected to sleep under canvas and to share camp discomforts with their men, and the tents had hardly been pitched and the horse lines laid down before such of the villagers who were in trade called upon the officers to offer their services and goods.

Of these, Mr. Mipps was the first to come. Followed by a vast crowd of school children who were attracted by so much pageantry of brass and scarlet, he entered the colonel's tent, and after saluting that gentleman in true Royal Naval style, he banged on to the table a broadsheet advertising the goods he had to dispose of from his little shop adjoining Old Tree Cottage.

The colonel glared at the paper and then glared at Mipps.

"Who are you and what's this?" he demanded.

"Bit o' paper and Mr. Mipps," replied the sexton.

Not quite knowing what to say in answer to this, the colonel shouted: "What?"

Mipps took a deep breath and then shouted at the top of his voice:

"Bit o' paper and Mr. Mipps."

"And who the hell is Mr. Mipps?" thundered the colonel.

"Undertaker," answered Mipps sadly, and quickly: "I just called to say that if so be that any of your gallant Dragoons or you yourself should find Dymchurch unhealthy and die of it, why, I can fix you up with a very good coffin and bury you quite pleasant with brass knobs or not, as you desire. I also sells at a reasonable price, as you will observe from that there paper, other things besides coffins. Here, give it me and let me read it to you."

"Get out of here," yelled the colonel.

"Good morning, Colonel," replied Mipps. "And I hopes as how the sea air will do you good after being cooped up so long in that 'orrible

Dover Castle. Don't it remind you of being in prison? It would me, but you see, I've never been in prison myself."

"If you don't get out, you will be," shouted the colonel. "Or in one of your own coffins."

"Now that's an idea, Colonel, that never fails to depress me," said Mipps solemnly. "I don't suppose I shall ever take the trouble to knock up a coffin for myself. Whereas for you now I'd take a lot of trouble."

"Will you get out, sir, or shall I have you thrown out?" cried the colonel.

"I'm a-going, sir," replied Mipps. "And don't forget, if anything should happen to you, come to me to knock you up solid in pine, elm or oak. Good morning, Colonel, and thank you kindly."

And with a grave salute, Mr. Mipps backed out of the presence.

The colonel was speechless with indignation, but on the disappearance of the facetious sexton, he could not resist picking up the paper which that worthy had left behind. And this is what he read:

        'Cats skins and kettles,
        A forge for all metals,
        Yards and ham,
        Pickles and jam,
        Eggs and fishes
        Plates and dishes
        Sweets for the kiddies
        Comforts for widdies,
        Apples and onions
        Plasters for bunions.
        Knock at the door
        And open your lips
        You'll get what you want
        At the shop of old Mipps
        And if so be as you wants a good coffin.
        You'll own it's a box to knock solid a toff in'.

"And did you ever read such a piece of gross impertinence?" asked the colonel, when he was joined by Captain Faunce.

Captain Faunce nodded and permitted himself to smile. "I know this man Mipps. I have had my eye on him for some time, sir. I believe he could tell us who this Scarecrow is, but he never would. I sometimes wish that the fellow had been built bigger."

"Why?" demanded the colonel.

"Because then he might have qualified for a Dragoon, sir," explained the captain. "And believe me, sir, there's something about that little man that makes me covet his loyalty for the regiment. If he serves this Scarecrow, why then, sir, I envy the Scarecrow his lieutenant."

"Ah," said the colonel, "then keep an eye on the little rat."

And while Colonel Troubridge and Captain Faunce were discussing the Scarecrow and Mr. Mipps in the tent, Dr. Syn was inspecting Charlotte Cobtree's new black hunter in the squire's stables.

"And will you tell me, Charlotte, why you have not only bought this glorious animal when I know you were more than satisfied with Sirius, but also why you purchased for two guineas that old suit of poor Mipps? For I believe I see the semblance of a connection between the two purchases."

"And that semblance is?" she asked.

"Why, the Scarecrow," he replied. "The ragged black suit, and the magnificent black horse."

"How clever you are, Doctor," she answered. "Yes, you are quite right, but I trust you will keep my confession and your guess to yourself. If this Scarecrow will not tell me who he is, I am curious enough to take the pains of finding him out. You remember he is one of my heroes. He, and Clegg and yourself. Perhaps I may even have the privilege of helping the smugglers as the Scarecrow did. At all events, I'll satisfy my woman's curiosity. There is, at least, one who can ride safely on the Marsh at night—the Scarecrow. Well, I have the horse and I have the clothes, too. If the Scarecrow cannot trust me and say 'I am the Scarecrow', why, I can ride out as he does until I can say: 'Ah, so you are the Scarecrow.'"

"I beg of you, Charlotte, not to undertake any such mad adventure," said Dr. Syn sternly. You don't realise your danger."

"My dear doctor, when you ask me to marry you, why then I promise you I will mend my ways, but till then I must do as I think best."

"If I could ask you, you know that I would," he answered. "But for you and your future, I can still be unselfish, I pray God."

"Honourable men are so often most selfish in their very unselfishness," she answered.

He might then and there have demanded an explanation. He might even have made the confession that had been in his heart to make to her for some time, but the squire joined them, full of indignation that the Dragoons had been so greatly increased in numbers.

"I'll not brook this interference from the Dover military while I am magistrate upon the Marsh," he cried. "Captain Faunce is a nice enough fellow, I admit. His behaviour has always been most respectful towards me as Lord of the Level, but this colonel is as red in his temper as his face. I could find in my heart to wish that this Scarecrow fellow would give him a good fooling."

"I shouldn't be at all surprised if he does, Father," said Charlotte, with a mischievous glance at Dr. Syn.

"I shouldn't be at all surprised either, my dear," replied the doctor solemnly.

The worthy squire would have been very much surprised had he read what was passing in his vicar's brain. And sure enough, the 'fooling' that the squire wished for took place that very night.

Since there were three nights before the full moon, and the proposed 'run', Colonel Troubridge thought it highly strategic on his part to allow most of the men village leave till eleven o'clock, and they were all instructed to keep their ears open for any information that might be dropped from garrulous villagers in the bars. But Mr. Mipps was equally strategic, and he trotted from bar to bar and back again, the picture of injured innocence in the eyes of the troopers, but seeing to it very ably that the villagers kept their mouths shut.

Certain hints about the full moon 'run' he allowed to get about, but no one gave away the important fact that thousands of barrels were only awaiting the signal from Aldington to be landed on Jesson Beach and carried to the hills for hiding.

The Upton brothers had been instructed to stand by their beacon after 'lanterns out' had been sounded by the Dragoon trumpeters. They then were to wait two hours by Monty Upton's great turnip watch, which could be relied upon, and then the beacon was to be fired.

An hour and a half of this allotted time had gone. The Marsh lay black and ominous; a vast stretch of mystery and dark horror to the Dragoon sentry who stood guard upon the sea-wall. He did not feel comfortable. He recalled a conversation he had had that evening with the queer little sexton of Dymchurch. "The Marsh? It's an 'orrible place, my lad. 'Bout this time of year every dyke flowin' in her seems full of dead men floatin' and waitin' for the moon to rise. And when it does rise, you sort of see it reflected in their starin' eyes." Yes, it had all been very laughable recounted in the crowded bar of the 'Ship Inn', but now that he was alone on the sea-wall, the Marsh did strike him as an "orrible place'. What if the line guards below him in the field were all asleep? What if he were the only one awake in the whole camp? He wished that damned sexton had not told him about those corpses. He wished he were not on foot. He missed the companionship of his horse. The words of the sexton came back to him. "Once on much such a night as this will be when the moon gets up, I was diggin' a grave in the churchyard 'ere. Very still it was. No noise but me old pick and spade a-workin' fit to kill themselves. Suddenly I sort of feels there's someone behind me lookin' down at me. I didn't hear no one, you understand. I just felt someone, and so there was. I turns and sees a thin, tall old man dressed in black and his face was chalky and his eyes was glassy. He beckoned me, he did, and I gets out of the grave and follows him. He glides along to the tythe field and makes straight for the old brick bridge. When he gets there, he sits on the parapet and pats it, meaning me to do ditto. I tells him to move up. He did. There we sits with our legs dangling over the water of the dyke. Then he begins in a sepulchral voice, sayin' 'Eena, deena, dinah'—you know, and pointin' down. He was playin' 'eena deena' with corpses floatin' under our bridge."

"Where did the corpses come from?" the sentry had laughed.

"Churchyard, of course. Very 'orrible it was, too," the sexton had said. "They was all men till he come to the end, you know, where it says 'Out goes he', and blime! it weren't a he. It was the fattest old woman corpse I ever see—floatin' beneath us and starin' up."

The story had been received with howls of laughter. The sentry had laughed himself—but now it was not so funny. The sight of that Marsh seemed to make the yarn ring true.

And then suddenly the Marsh changed. With a suddenness he had not expected, the moon came up over the Channel. It flooded the Marsh with its eerie light. He could see the black shadows of the dyke hollows. Were there corpses there? It was easy to imagine so in that still silence. He did not know that those dykes were filled with crouching waiting men. It spoke well for the Scarecrow's preparation that the sentry thought he had never seen a vast track of land so desolate. So destitute of life. If only he could see just one living man. He did not know that his eyes were travelling over hundreds of hidden heads.

"There's only corpses floatin' in the dykes. Blast that there sexton," he said to himself.

He turned to the sea for comfort. He looked first in the direction of Folkestone and the increasing moonlight showed him a sight that made him gasp. A lugger had been run ashore some two hundred yards away. There were men sitting upon barrels. They had their backs to him, for they were facing the lugger and a man who leaned against the mast with one hand steadying himself in the rigging.

What were the orders for the Regiment? "And any rank meeting with a man dressed as a scarecrow may shoot to kill. Death to the Scarecrow."

The sentry forgot his terror of the sexton's yarn as he dropped down behind the sand-hill that crowned the sea-wall. He was shaking with excitement. The man standing on the lugger was obviously dressed as a scarecrow. He sighted his carbine upon the Scarecrow's chest. He must wait till he could keep his sight steadier. Damn that sexton whose story had made him jumpy.

As he dropped, the sexton whom he had already damned, slithered upon his stomach immediately behind him and wriggled down the slope of the sea-wall. With the silence and skill of a Red Indian from whom he had learned much, Mr. Mipps, a sharp knife in his teeth, crawled towards the horse lines guarded by the two drunken and sleepy Dragoons.

Along the lines he crawled, noiselessly severing the picketing ropes.

The sentry took his time, steadying his aim. 'Death to the Scarecrow.' Well, he must not, would not miss; and behind him crouched two fantastically dressed men with their faces smeared with tar, waiting for him to shoot. But the sentry took his time. It was not pleasant to kill a man in cold blood. And yet orders protected him. The blame would not be his. He wished to kill and yet he wavered, and in the interim he slowly steadied his aim.

Behind him, under the shadow of the sea-wall, Mipps crawled silently and went on with his cutting. To two horses out of every three he gave unconscious freedom.

Suddenly one horse stampeded down the lines.

"'Ware horse," cried an awakened guard.

The noise acted upon the nerves of the sentry's slowly squeezing finger. With a sharp crack his carbine fired.

Immediately there arose pandemonium from the sleeping camp. The sentry heard it for a few seconds only, for a heavy weight seemed to drop upon him from the sky. He was bound round the legs and arms with cord. He was lifted by two strong and dreadful-looking men. They swung him backwards and forwards and then he was flung out from the sea-wall down upon the sand beneath. As he went through the air he remembered that the man who had been his target had fallen forward over the bulwarks of the lugger. He had fired and hit. Had he killed the Scarecrow, and would the smugglers now seek full retribution? Heavy in cuirass and helmet, he fell hard, and for a time remembered no more.

In the awakening camp everything was in wild disorder. The majority of the horses which had been freed by Mipps stampeded past the 'Ship Inn' and out upon the highroad, where they were goaded into a full stretch gallop by a dozen or so of wildly caparisoned horsemen, who, in fantastic costume and waving lighted jack-o'-lanterns above their heads, encouraged the frightened horses to make their escape, with wild yells and howlings.

The remaining horses added even more to the camp's discomfiture, for dragging the damaged lines and pegs behind them they galloped this way and that, became entangled in tent ropes and upset the piled stacks of carbines. Men awoke into a cursing confusion. The colonel, in night attire, shrieked and swore and shouted for Captain Faunce to turn out the guard.

"Stand to your horses, you fools," he roared.

But there were no horses that his men could stand to. They were a struggling mass of entangled rage—those that were left, and already two-thirds of the fine animals were heading in wild stampede towards Hythe.

Swearing, as became a colonel of Dragoons, he pulled on breeches and boots, jammed his brass helmet on the top of his tasseled night-cap and buckled on his sabre over his white flapping shirt.

In this incongruous costume he dashed out of his tent.

The sight which now met his infuriated gaze would have been enough to irritate a saint, much less a roaring Dragoon. Tents were collapsing on all sides, smothering men in a writhing mass. The canvas of his own tent was being ripped by the lashing hoofs of an entangled charger, while such of his men who were in the open were rushing this way and that, some to save their own skins, and others more dutifully trying to catch the maddened animals.

It was then that a strange apparition galloped at full speed through the camp. A snorting black horse on whose back sat the fearsome figure of a man dressed as a scarecrow.

CPSIA information can be obtained
at www.ICGtesting.com
Printed in the USA
BVHW031123260919
559484BV00001B/208/P